The Devil's Necklace

BOOKS BY
JULIETTE BENZONI

One Love Is Enough
Catherine
Belle Catherine
Catherine and Armand
Catherine and a Time for Love
A Snare for Catherine
Marianne
Marianne and the Masked Prince
Marianne and the Privateer
Marianne and the Rebels
Marianne and the Lords of the East
Marianne and the Crown of Fire
The Lure of the Falcon
The Devil's Necklace
The Girl Who Had Everything

THE
DEVIL'S NECKLACE

JULIETTE BENZONI

G. P. Putnam's Sons
New York

First American Edition 1980
Translation © 1980 by William Heinemann Ltd.
First published as *Un Collier pour le Diable*
© 1978 by Opera Mundi, Paris

Library of Congress Cataloging in Publication Data

Benzoni, Juliette.
  The devil's necklace.

  Translation of Un collier pour le diable.
  Sequel to The lure of the falcon.
  I. Title.
PQ2662.E5C613   1980   843'.914   80-21997
ISBN 0-399-12515-9

Printed in the United States of America

Contents

PART THREE
STORM OVER VERSAILLES
1784–5

PROLOGUE

The Falcon's Nest
Autumn 1783

The autumn wind was ripping the clouds to shreds, rolling them up and driving them in whirling gusts to catch among the treetops, only the woods would have none of them. They tossed their great red-gold heads until the birds, shaken from their ruined nests, flew up out of the branches. With a loud squawking and beating of wings, they mounted up into the murky sky, there to sort themselves into neat formations and take wing for the warm south.

Only the starlings continued to make their endless rounds of the ramparts of La Hunaudaye where it reared, silent and dark as a long deserted grave. Yet the old castle of the Tournemines, restored by the Rieux who had succeeded them, was very far from a ruin. Its pentagonal breastworks rose up between the sides of the valley, five formidable towers joined by thick curtain walls, five separate holds, menacing even yet with their unbroken parapets and machicolations underlined with great streaks of gleaming black, the glorious sign manual of the battles fought there of old. All around the castle was a moat of great depth, fed by the nearby lake.

Night was falling. The daylight was fading fast. Yet the three horsemen lingering by the corner of the lake seemed in no hurry to move on. Very straight in the saddle, they sat with the night wind stirring the heavy folds of the cloaks they wore, as unmoving as if they had been carved out of the very granite of the castle itself. As if they were waiting for something ... something that did not come.

They made a curious group, contrasting yet complementary, like the different climes from which they sprang. Gilles de

3

Tournemine, with his great height and lithe, energetic frame, seemed as indestructible as his native Brittany. His tanned face was preserved from the snare of perfect beauty by the arrogance of the nose and the icy blue stare, by the strength of his jaw and the light, ironic smile with its rare glimpse of perfect white teeth.

Beside him Jean de Batz looked small, although he was nothing of the kind. He was a pure southern type, dark hair and eyes, warm olive skin, bright, darting eyes and wiry arms and legs. If his companion could have stepped out of some romance of the Round Table, he was the image, even down to the moustaches, of that famous musketeer of the days of Louis XIII, whose blood did indeed run in his veins, d'Artagnan himself.

The third rider was ugly to look at, but with a barbaric ugliness wholly unexpected under French skies. His face, with its two long incisors, was not unlike a rabbit's, but his ferocious bearing amply preserved him from any mockery on that score. He was an American Indian, an Iroquois of the Onondaga tribe, but apart from his colouring there was nothing in his dress to indicate this to the casual eye. A suit of plain black cloth, white linen and long, supple boots concealed his barrel chest and rather short legs, covering the old ritual scars and the later ones gained in battle, as well as the indelible traces of war paint. Similarly, the club wig and tricorn hat overlaid an egg-shaped skull, clean shaven except for a single long black lock, carefully tended, which adorned his crown and which he was in the habit of wearing coiled into a funny little bun underneath his European headgear.

His name, in the language of his own country, was virtually unpronounceable and meant, in English, 'Beaver who found the Magic Eagle's Feather', but Gilles de Tournemine, who had acquired his devotion by saving his life, had cut through this difficulty by simply calling him Pongo.

Pongo and the master he had chosen to serve had been separated for more than a year when Gilles was sent home at speed, with the Duc de Lauzun, to bring the news of the victory of Yorktown to the King. Reluctantly, he had left Pongo behind, anticipating no more than a brief absence before sailing back to the infant United States to share in the conclu-

4

sion of a campaign which General Washington, assisted by the French expeditionary force under Rochambeau, now had well in hand. The young man had grown to love the vast, splendid land where virgin nature seemed still to have sprung fresh from the hand of God, and where the hearts of men still possessed the freshness, the audacity, the enthusiasm and also the unconscious cruelty of children. That land had reunited him for a brief instant with the father he had never hoped to find and had made of an illegitimate youth named Gilles Goëlo the Chevalier de Tournemine de la Hunaudaye. A man with a healthy sense of values can grow fond of a place from such a cause.

But the King's will had not permitted the new chevalier, now promoted to lieutenant in the Queen's Dragoons, to rejoin his comrades in the skirmishing and fierce ambuscades which had earned him his Indian totem, 'the pitiless Gerfalcon that strikes in the Mist', very soon contracted simply to the Falcon.

When General Rochambeau brought the rest of his force home in the spring of 1783, however, Gilles had been surprised to find Pongo among the baggage brought by his friend Axel de Fersen.

'If I'd not brought him, he'd have been perfectly capable of trying to swim,' the Swede confided after their first affectionate greeting. 'What you have got yourself there, chevalier, is matchless loyalty. The man has been barely living since you left. He simply sat there on the quayside, day and night, until I promised to bring him.'

So Pongo had come back to Gilles as simply and as naturally as a river flowing into the sea. He had resumed his role of body servant and protector with no noticeable alteration in his impassive countenance to mark the changed way of life. And although his presence at the Chevalier's heels aroused a good deal of interest, Pongo himself showed none at all at the sight of the towns, streets, manners and customs which France had to offer. In his own way, he was keeping faith with a race which demanded equal stoicism in the face of joy and suffering alike.

To his youthful master, Pongo's arrival also marked the end of a long penance. When, after the nightmare at Trecesson, he

5

had joined his regiment, then quartered at Pontivy, Gilles had met a situation that was not at all what he had expected. As a supernumerary lieutenant, he had imagined that in reporting to his colonel, the Chevalier de Coigny, he was performing a mere formality. Instead, owing to the fatal consequences of a duel which had taken place between two officers of the regiment immediately prior to his arrival, which had resulted in the prompt despatch of one of the protagonists to the hospital and the other to the local cemetery, he found himself very much on the active list.

'You, sir, are manna from heaven,' de Coigny informed him, surveying the American veteran who had arrived so opportunely with an interested eye. 'For once they haven't sent me a Court popinjay with nothing in his head, but the gloss on his boots and the whiteness of his cuffs. I intend to keep hold of you. Do you play chess?'

'A little, yes,' Gilles said, having gained his initiation into the subtleties of that noble game from early practice with his godfather, the Abbé de Talhouet.

'Excellent! Then we shall pass some tolerable evenings, at least. Apart from that, one is bored to death here. You'll find a lodging at Widow Jan's, in the Place du Martray. That was where your unfortunate predecessor lived.'

The result of which was that Gilles, burning all the time to dash off to Paris and search for some trace of his beloved, to try and find the red-haired Judith de Saint-Mélaine who had vanished in such mysterious circumstances, was obliged to waste the better part of a year in his red and green uniform and leopard-trimmed brass helm, with no better distractions than regimental manoeuvres, rides with his horse, Merlin, along the banks of the Blavet, that river of his childhood out of which, one fine evening, had come Judith to alter his life, occasional letters from Axel de Fersen and Tim Thocker in America and games of chess with his colonel. He was deprived even of this last amusement in the autumn when de Coigny was replaced by the Marquis de Jaucourt, fresh from the bombardment of Geneva and no lover of chess.

Fersen's tempestuous arrival, straight from disembarkation at Brest, dissipated the routine greyness of the Brittany garrison. With him, the Swede brought a letter from General de

Rochambeau expressing a cordial wish to have his former secretary present at Versailles along with the rest of the expeditionary force. So Gilles, in a fever of joy and provided with a formal ticket of leave, got himself on to Merlin's back, not now to trot nostalgically along the Blavet in search of a shade from the past, but to eat up the miles to the capital. But the hopeful sun rising on the skyline ahead of him was not so much the dazzle of a royal court but that of a woman's flaming hair.

Daylight had turned to dusk. The red blaze of the setting sun faded into the shadows of evening that mingled with the mist rising from the lake. Deceived by the stillness of the three riders, a badger ventured incautiously from his earth almost under Merlin's hooves. The horse, sensing it, quivered, whinnied fiercely and began to fidget, shaking his master roughly out of his meditation. He was gentled in a moment.

'Quiet, boy,' the young man said softly, patting the long, silky neck. 'Only one more minute—'

But the spell had been broken. Jean de Batz brought his mount up alongside his friend's.

'It will be dark in a moment,' he said. 'We won't be able to tell the walls from the towers. What are you waiting for?'

Gilles shrugged, his eyes on the massive gatehouse and the double drawbridge leading to it.

'I don't know. A miracle, perhaps. I felt that if I were to come here to the castle something would happen ... that it would know me and open up to me, like a hand held out. Perhaps even offer up its keys to me of its own accord.'

The Gascon's deep laugh woke echoes in the woods and made a teal fly up from the edge of the lake.

'The key – there's only one – you can find it whenever you will, if you'll listen to me. Its name is money. Money opens all doors, even to hearts. Make yourself master of it and this old place will open to you like a woman in love.'

The Chevalier's grey eyes rested on the Gascon baron's face in which the eyes were gleaming with an almost demoniacal brilliance in the gathering dark. But the one-time pupil of St Yves College at Vannes had long lost that superstitious fear of

7

the Evil One which had been so carefully instilled into him in his youth, and although he had more than once discovered in his friend notions that smacked strongly of sulphur, it made no difference at all to the friendship which had grown spontaneously between them some months earlier.

Although Batz, like himself, belonged to the Queen's Dragoons, this friendship had not been born of regimental association, for the very good reason that the Gascon never set foot there. Not for several years at any rate, for he had enlisted as a volunteer – at the age of twelve, and had conducted himself in such a way that by 1776, when he was fifteen, he had become a sub-lieutenant – and to do so had had recourse to a gasconnade since, in order to obtain that rank he had added five years to his age, falsifying his birth certificate without a moment's hesitation. But once the officer's epaulette was securely on his uniform, Batz, as pleased with himself as if he had won a marshal's baton, had completely lost interest in the future of a regiment which persisted in remaining quartered in garrisons as unattractive as Vesoul or Pontivy. Because the place he wanted to be was Paris, that amazing Pandora's box which was close enough to the sun of Versailles for every kind of fortune to be possible, and far enough to let one be forgotten or even die of hunger without anyone caring.

In Paris, the young baron was sure of very quickly succeeding in carving out a path for himself, thanks to the friends he was not slow to make there. Money, in fact, was the key word as far as he was concerned, money which alone could spell power to a lad born, certainly, to a noble station but too far from the great offices of state, money, of which, like many of the provincial nobility, he was always in dire need, money, in short, which with the naïve cynicism of his extreme youth, he declared himself to prize above all else. Nevertheless, much as he longed to be rich, it was not for the pleasure of hoarding but in order to be able to indulge in all the comforts, elegancies and brilliance which fortune could introduce into daily life, and also to have the means now and then to set right some of the crying injustices of Fate. Because this Gascon, with all his greed and rapacity, capable even of coolly stripping a dowager of her diamonds at play or dabbling in speculative colonial enterprise, was equally capable of leaving his last guineas on

8

the rickety table of a broken-legged mason threatened with eviction by a ruthless landlord. Which same landlord would moreover find himself subjected to a severe thrashing a few hours later, in the deep dark of the night.

Cynical, realistic and cheerfully amoral, especially where women were concerned, but recklessly brave and generous to a fault and clever as the very devil, this was the man whom Fate had thrown in Gilles' way one evening for a friend.

This memorable encounter had taken place on the previous 28th of April. That was the night that Paris was to inaugurate the new theatre built for the Comédie Italienne on an extensive site adjoining the Boulevards, which had been donated by the Duc de Choiseul and backed onto his town house. The evening was to be one of more than usual brilliance for the Queen was to be present and had herself selected the programme: a work by Grétry entitled *Les Événements Imprévus* in which the charming Madame Dugazon, star of the Comédie Italienne, was to take the part of Lisette.

People had fought for those places which were not reserved for the Queen and her entourage all the more eagerly since, as not infrequently occurred on such occasions, a group had been formed dedicated to wrecking the evening. The tenants of the Opéra, jealous at seeing the Italians quit the venerable, but extremely shabby, Hotel de Bourgogne for this handsome theatre, had determined to cause as much disruption as possible.

The operation had been well planned. To begin with there had been lengthy criticism of the architecture of the new theatre, and care was taken to get the rest of the theatrical profession against its future occupants. Hadn't the Italians insisted on the building turning its back on the Boulevard so that there should be no danger of its entrance being confused with those of the numerous other small theatres round about? To punish them for their presumption a venomous little verse was current in Paris:

Now the new theatre's built, you can tell with one eye,
That the actors who play there are from Italy,
Instead of its face to the people that pass
It is built back to front, so it shows them its . . .

9

Scurrilous broadsheets had also been circulated concerning the Queen's protection of the Comédie Italienne and laying heavy stress on her persistence in bestowing her favours on those unworthy to receive them.

These effusions were naturally not without effect and, on the opening night, the handsome new auditorium bore some resemblance to a witch's cauldron in which those spectators who had come to applaud to the skies, and those bent on systematically booing, were all seething together.

As cauldrons go it was a brilliant one, for the boxes were filled with ladies dripping with jewels under their extravagantly piled hair, which gave the house the look of a weird landscape of snowy mountains surmounted by a heterogeneous assortment of objects, while the pit was no less brilliant and echoed to the red heels of a crowd of gentlemen.

That Gilles had obtained a place was due to Fersen. Ever since his arrival in Paris, the young Swede had constituted himself both host and mentor to his friend. While awaiting his presentation to the Queen, a task he was not prepared to leave to anyone else, he introduced him into every Parisian salon where he himself was a familiar figure: from the house of the Swedish ambassador, Count Creutz, to that belonging to the ex-minister Necker, and not excluding those of the many members of the powerful family of financiers, the Lecoulteux. The young man was an instant success. His charm and his noble bearing assured him of a flattering welcome from the ladies which was transformed into a lively interest as soon as Fersen, like the good comrade he was, launched into a recital of his exploits.

Passing tactfully over the theft of his horse, the Swede was never tired of describing how Tournemine had saved his life at Yorktown and then, taking two or three pretty girls aside into a corner, he would tell them in whispers the secret of the passionate love story of his friend and a dazzling Indian princess and so, gradually, the young man became something of a hero to the ladies of society. To such an extent that it occasionally irked him.

'You've given me the most astounding reputation,' he said one day. 'You'll have to stop singing my praises like this. My past doesn't deserve such eulogies. Besides, why are you so determined to interest people in me?'

'Not people, the ladies! You want to make your fortune – well, marry! You have plenty to choose from!'

'It's no good. There's only one woman in the world for me. The only one I want is her, with or without a fortune. I'll marry Judith or no one—'

'Who is there can boast of never having once changed his mind?' And so Fersen went on with his tales of heroic gallantry more energetically than before.

But for all his drawing-room successes, this evening at the theatre was for the young Breton his first great Parisian social occasion and he made no secret of his pleasure in it.

Many of those around were in fact his former comrades-in-arms. There was Lauzun, Noailles, the Lameths, Ségur and many more, made fashionable by their recent return from America. Some of the audience, though not yet numbered among his friends, were nevertheless not altogether strangers, such as the trio of delightful and unholy young scapegraces he had met at Creutz's, the youthful Abbé de Périgord, with his charm and his lame leg, an engaging bastard of the late King Louis XIV's Count Louis de Narbonne-Lara and their inseparable companion, the effervescent young diplomat, Count de Choiseul-Gouffier.

The women, of course, were much less familiar to the Chevalier and if his eye seemed to linger on the shimmering garland that ran round the boxes it was less out of curiosity than in the hope of recognizing one face among the many, one special smile among them all. His gaze which could penetrate deep into misty woods or the darkest shadows of the night, studied each feminine countenance, nearly all of which were both young and beautiful. But his heart which so yearned to beat faster was obliged to maintain its steady rhythm, for none of these women was Judith.

'Still nothing?' Fersen asked, for he was well aware of his friend's secret love and had been watching him out of the corner of his eye. 'She is not here?'

'No. Paris is too big, you know. I was mad to think that I might find her in the broad light of such a social gathering. After all that she has been through, she must rather be in

11

hiding, seeking the shadows, for she does not know that I have killed one of her brothers. And it is true the other one is still at large.'

'But there is no reason why he should be in Paris. As for your fair Judith, she is supposed to be dead, remember, no one knows her here and so she has no cause to hide.'

'Maybe. Yet there are times when I lose heart, when I feel as if I shall never find her.'

The Swede smiled.

'Look, Chevalier, you've only been here a short while. Has the Falcon, who could watch the enemy for hours on end, lost the art of patience? We've not yet made any serious attempt to find her. Tomorrow, my friend Creutz shall give you an introduction to the Provost of Paris and then – two more days and I'll take you to Versailles! In two days you shall be in the presence of one who may do anything, whom all obey, who reigns higher even than the king, since she reigns over the king also, who—'

Fersen broke off because at that moment a sudden hush fell on the theatre. Tournemine stared in surprise for his friend seemed smitten into ecstasy. Following his gaze to the royal box he too was struck motionless with admiration. The Queen had entered.

To anyone seeing Marie-Antoinette for the first time, her appearance always came as a slight shock. There were undoubtedly women more beautiful, but none more radiant. She had such grace and brilliance, and so much natural majesty, that one did not even notice the rather heavy lower lip or the fact that her eyes, of a pretty soft blue, were somewhat protuberant.

That night she was wearing a wide dress of China satin in a creamy white, embroidered with delicate gold leaves. Her beautiful fair hair, worn very high and lightly powdered, supported a hat of gold leaves with a cluster of feathers rising from it. She wore very little jewellery: a pearl bracelet or two at her wrists and, between her breasts, a single diamond, sparkling magnificently: the fabulous Sancy. She was accompanied by the Comte d'Artois, who was also dressed entirely in white, and the Duchesse de Polignac.

The pit bowed in unison, presenting an amazing

chequerboard of coloured backs dotted with white wigs while, in the boxes, the snow mountains were lowered all at once to the level of the red velvet parapets as the ladies made their curtsies. The Queen smiled, raised a hand and seated herself to a prolonged applause from the audience which was perhaps a tribute less to the dignity of the Queen than to the beauty of the woman.

It was then that the Chevalier de Tournemine first observed the man on his left, who was displaying a pleasing enthusiasm. Faultlessly dressed in dove grey satin, he was giving vent to resounding cheers in a loud voice, warmed by the accents of Gascony and quite disproportionate in volume to the gentleman's moderate height. The man in dove grey was by himself making more noise than all the rest of the pit put together.

His eagerness was not at all to the liking of his left hand neighbour, a tall exquisite of some thirty summers who carried off his handsome crimson velvet suit with assurance, but whose admirable roman profile was somewhat marred by an air of invincible stupidity.

Tapping the enthusiastic one on the shoulder, the crimson gentleman addressed him:

'I say, little man, less noise, if you please! Here's a pretty racket!'

The other started as though bitten by an adder.

'Racket? What do you mean?'

'What I say! To my mind you're making a deal too much noise about nothing!'

'I'm sorry you don't care for it, but it is intended for the Queen.'

'Just so. Much ado about nothing!'

The dove grey gentleman's warm brown skin took on a curious olive tinge.

'You're either a madman, Sir, or you're the ultimate scoundrel. Choose which! And choose fast!'

'Neither. A Queen who frequents low haunts, who takes lovers—'

He was given no time to finish. Quick as a flash, the Gascon had snatched the hat from under his arm and rammed it so hard down on his head that the crown split and the

13

upper part of the abusive gentleman's face completely disappeared.

The scene had erupted very swiftly, while the applause was still going on, and had attracted very little attention. Everyone was looking at the Queen. Fersen, therefore, who seemed wrapped in adoration, had seen nothing, but Gilles had not missed a thing. And when the crimson gentleman had managed to extricate himself, frothing with rage, from his hat which had scratched his nose in passing, he leaned towards his neighbour.

'If you require a second, Sir, I am at your service.'

The Gascon's bright eyes summed him up.

'Faith, sir, I'll not say no! It's not easy to find one's friends in this crush and the play is about to begin.'

The Queen's detractor seemed to have encountered no difficulty in this respect and the four men left their places just as the rest of the audience was taking its seats and the orchestra embarking on the overture.

'Where are you going?' Fersen asked in surprise.

'I'll be back. This gentleman is in need of some assistance. No, don't get up, it won't take us long.'

Adversaries and seconds foregathered under the theatre colonnade and debated briefly. The large square which stretched before the theatre was brightly lit and filled with a host of carriages, servants, coachmen and link boys awaiting the emergence of those members of the audience who might require their services for their homeward journey. But the two streets linking it to the boulevard on either side of the theatre were empty and fairly dark. By common consent they chose the one later to be named the Rue Favart and made in that direction.

As they went, the gentleman in dove grey inquired his companion's identity.

'This is most kind of you, Sir, but may I know to whom I have the honour of speaking?'

'Chevalier de Tournemine de la Hunaudaye, Lieutenant in the Queen's Dragoons.'

The Gascon gave a shout of laughter.

'You too? A pleasure to meet you. I am Baron Jean de Batz, likewise lieutenant in the Queen's Dragoons. At least – in theory.'

14

Now it was Gilles' turn to laugh.

'Is that who you are? I am delighted to meet you.'

'How's this? You know me?'

'You are very nearly famous in the Dragoons. They call you the Invisible Man.'

'It's true they don't often see me. But I think we shall do here,' he added, turning back to the other two men who were following. Not even stopping to take off his coat, he drew his sword and swished it impatiently.

'Now! Let us make haste. I'd as lief not miss the whole of the first act. Madame Dugazon is excessively charming and I am much enamoured of her voice. And by the by, sir scoundrel, perhaps you would be good enough to furnish me with your name? Despite your manners, you appear to have the accoutrements of a gentleman.'

'I am the Comte d'Antraigues, and most assuredly better born than you, Monsieur de Batz!'

'Ah, so you know me? Decidedly, this is my day. I cannot say the same of you, but since we are not here to compare family trees – *en garde*, Monsieur, and say your prayers. I may not be a count but I am descended from d'Artagnan!'

While the combatants fell to with a fury that spoke volumes for their mutual sentiments, Gilles approached d'Antraigues' second with a proposal that they two should measure swords, as was still frequently done, but the other, an undistinguished fellow of mediocre stature, stared at him with something like horror.

'Are you out of your mind? I am only here to oblige a friend. I heartily disapprove of these encounters, which serve no useful purpose.'

Tournemine leaned down to look the other in the face.

'You are a prudent man, I see,' he said with a sneer.

'I am a sensible man and a magistrate. My name is Jean-Jacques d'Eprémenil, barrister to Parliament.'

'A lawyer!' Gilles exclaimed. 'That explains it.'

And leaving the other to his reflections, he withdrew into the angle of a doorway to watch the swordplay. In his enjoyment of it he very soon forgot all about the cautious little lawyer. Both men were indubitably masters of fence, although their styles were very different. D'Antraigues fought scientifically,

15

like a man who knew what he was doing and meant to see it through, but Batz was like a man inspired. He fought with incredible fire and agility, like a man pressed for time but never letting his haste lead him into error. He darted round his opponent like a wasp, forever shifting his guard and his ground. His blade flickered on the end of a wrist of steel, seeking an opening.

A burst of music floated out from one of the side doors of the theatre, muffled and light as the evening breeze. Then a woman's voice, fresh and limpid as a rivulet in spring.

'There now, Madame Dugazon is singing,' Batz said with a groan. 'This pleasantry has gone on long enough.'

He lunged with such ferocity that his adversary, taken off his guard, tried to disengage too swiftly, lost his balance and stumbled. His curse was followed instantly by a grunt of pain as Batz's blade penetrated the fine crimson velvet coat. He staggered and fell into the arms of d'Eprémenil who had leapt forward to receive him, while Batz, after a brief salute, coolly sheathed his sword.

'Are you dead, Sir?' he inquired pleasantly. 'Or do you desire us to continue?'

'Deeply regret ... no longer possible. But I shall recover, have no fear ... and we shall meet again.'

'Nothing will afford me greater pleasure. I am entirely at your service. In future, however, allow me to advise you to keep a guard on your tongue.'

'Go to the devil!'

'By no means. I should have too much fear of meeting you.' He slipped his arm through Gilles'. 'Come on, Chevalier. If we hurry ourselves we may catch the end of this delicious song.'

The remainder of the evening passed without incident. The Dugazon scored such a triumph that the cabal so carefully got up was extinguished almost before it could make itself heard. As they left the theatre, Jean de Batz thanked Gilles once more for his support and invited him to sup at his house in the Rue Cassette.

The supper, washed down by large quantities of wine, was a merry occasion. The two young men, while doing justice to the cooking of the nearby chop house, furthered their acquaintance and discovered a great many notions in common. Quite delighted with one another, they expressed their feelings in so many toasts that they ended the evening both royally drunk.

It was the start of a firm friendship which grew the more quickly because Fersen, a few days after presenting Tournemine to the Queen, left Paris to rejoin his master, King Gustave IV of Sweden, who was demanding his company on a European journey. In order to spare his new friend the expense of remaining at the York Hotel – a heavy charge for his light purse – Batz proposed that he should come and share his lodging in the Rue Cassette, and the attentions of the pretty lightskirts who frequented it.

Both young men liked women and frequented them with the appetites of their age, without attaching more importance to it than to a good dinner. Gilles' heart, entirely filled with the image of the missing Judith, was secure from ambush, but his vigorous body and passionate temperament were unsuited to long periods of abstinence. Batz was another of the same kind and before long the pair were inseparable.

The towers of La Hunaudaye were no longer more than a black mass faintly outlined against a scarcely lighter sky. Yet the chevalier could not bring himself to move away.

Yet it had to be done, however regretfully and with the feeling that one was tearing away a piece of one's own flesh. Sighing, he swung Merlin round when the creaking of a heavy door was added to the other nocturnal forest sounds.

A lantern, held at arm's length, appeared on the drawbridge, illuminating the lower half of a man dressed in peasant clothes, his heavy clogs half covered with buttoned gaiters.

Gilles stared at the apparition for a moment and then suddenly urged his horse forward.

'Follow me,' he called.

The three horsemen made for the castle, a brief gallop that halted at the planks of the drawbridge. The man raised his lantern in surprise, revealing, below the brim of his hat, a young face shining with health, framed in straight hair the colour of ripe corn.

'Who's there?' he asked, speaking in the old celtic tongue

17

and seeming in no way disconcerted by the sudden appearance of three unknown riders.

'We are travellers who have missed our way,' the chevalier answered in the same language. 'We saw your lantern. Would the master of this castle perhaps give us a lodging for the night?'

The young man smiled and bowed with the natural courtesy of the Breton peasant.

'The master rarely comes here, good Sir. But my grandfather, Joel Gauthier, is caretaker of this castle and he will be proud and happy to offer you hospitality if you will honour his humble house, for the state rooms have not been habitable for a long time.'

'Never mind that! We are soldiers – any truckle bed will do. And thank you for your welcome.'

It was with no little emotion that Tournemine passed through the deep rounded archway, more than six feet wide and embossed with armorial bearings surrounded by a tressure, which opened into the heart of the castle. The first thing the light of the young peasant's lantern fell on was a gigantic ash tree whose knotty branches overspread the courtyard like protecting arms. Yet, huge as it was, it seemed dwarfed by the bulk of the towers and the reflections of the tall crested windows of the great lodging built up against the western walls.

It was a magnificent building, adorned with all the graces of the renaissance and flanked by a noble staircase of straight flights whose fluted pilasters declared it to have been built at the start of the previous century. But the general effect, for all its beauty, was one of unconquerable sadness, of a house built for bustle and light and life and abandoned to solitude and loneliness.

Slowly, his eyes fixed on that granite ghost, Tournemine dismounted, striving to master his suddenly shaking hands. He wanted to run to the crumbling stone stairs, to the door with its worn carvings and the walls which were already showing dangerous cracks. He wanted to embrace it all, to clasp it to him and he felt his heart drawn to this past grandeur of his family, like a dog on a leash.

'It's this way, Sir,' came the easy voice of the peasant youth.

Regretfully, the Chevalier turned away and followed his

guide towards the kitchen quarters built against the curtain wall to the east. A rosy glow came from the small windows. At the sound of the horses, a door had opened and a man's tall figure, wearing a wide black hat and leaning on a stick, stood framed in it, vividly outlined against the yellow light from within.

As they drew nearer, the three riders saw that he was an old man, tall and vigorous, with long white hair falling on either side of a stern face. The wrinkles in his face declared his age, yet there was a flash in his eye which said that he had lost none of his energy. His grandson bowed before him as though to a great lord.

'Father,' he said respectfully, 'here are travellers who have missed their way and seek shelter for the night.'

'Have you told them, Pierre, that this is the shelter of a peasant cot?'

'I have told them, father.'

'Enter, then, Sirs, and take a seat by the fire. Supper will be on the table in an instant. Pierre, see to their horses.'

He stood aside to let them enter. Impressed in spite of themselves by the strange nobility emanating from the man, the two gentlemen bowed as they crossed his threshold, while Pongo, still without a word, gathered up the bridles of their three horses preparatory to leading them to the stables. The room in which they found themselves was low with a ceiling of heavy beams running in the direction of the fireplace which occupied the whole of one end of the room. Two women clothed in black, one elderly, the other hardly more than a child, were busy about the blazing hearth preparing supper.

'These are my daughter-in-law, Anna, and my grand-daughter, Madalen,' old Joel said. 'Be seated, they will serve you in a moment.'

The men sat at the long table of chestnut wood and, after the old man had said grace, the women embarked on the silent ballet of serving the meal. No one spoke. Old Joel and his grandson ate gravely, like men to whom each mouthful of food is sacred, because it is the product of daily toil. The women would not have dared open their mouths without permission from the greybeard, let alone that Pongo, at whom they shot

19

furtive glances, evidently filled with terror by his ferocious appearance. Jean de Batz, uncharacteristically silent, had not opened his lips since crossing the threshold. As for Gilles, he was glutting his eyes and feelings on his austere surroundings, which he so yearned to know more closely, unconscious of the fact that old Joel was watching him attentively from beneath his bushy white brows. In fact his eyes had never left the young man's face for an instant from his first entering the lighted room.

The entire meal, which consisted of cabbage, bacon, and bread and butter, passed without a single word uttered, except once, when the old man whispered a few words into the ear of his daughter-in-law after which, with a scared look, she withdrew, taking her daughter with her, and at the grace which concluded the repast. Gilles was the first to break the silence, thanking his host as they rose from the table for his food and hospitality.

'You have welcomed us as friends to your table, yet you know nothing of us, not even our names.'

For the first time a faint smile touched the old man's stern lips.

'The guest sent by God is always a friend in this house. As for your name—' he added, in an odd voice. He broke off to take a resin torch from a corner of the hearth and plunge it into the flames. The two women returned at that moment and he cast a swift glance at them.

'Is it done?'

'Yes, Father, I have done as you bid.'

'Good.'

The flaming torch grasped firmly in one gnarled hand, he turned towards his guests.

'Follow me, gentlemen. I will take you to your room. You'll not be over-comfortable, but you'll find yourselves at home.'

He led the way, without further explanation, out of the house and across the courtyard, holding the torch aloft in a majestic fashion. He made straight for the great hall through the windows of which the ruddy glow of a fire could now be seen. The worm-eaten door creaked open to his hand, revealing a heavily vaulted chamber with pillars massive enough to sustain a cathedral and a royal hearth with an armorial bearing

20

above, whose simple quarterings made Gilles' heart beat faster. A tree trunk was blazing within.

The room was bare of furniture. There were only three piles of fresh straw covered with white sheepskins, and, in one of the window embrasures, a welcoming bunch of late broom and brilliant holly branches in a great bronze bowl.

Gilles, Batz and Pongo, the latter carrying the saddlebags, moved forward into this hall as slowly and as cautiously as though into a church. Midway, the Chevalier turned to the old man.

'Your grandson spoke of a barn. This is the great hall—'

'It is. Did I not tell you you should find yourself at home? Just now, Sir, you expressed surprise that I had not inquired your name. But I had known that name from the first moment you entered my house. You are, are you not, the last of the great Tournemines? And I, my lord, am your servant – only too happy to see a descendant of the old masters, the true masters, back here at last.'

Slowly, he took off the tall black hat which no Breton peasant is ever without, and, going down on one knee, took Gilles' hand and carried it reverently to his lips.

The young man bent quickly to take the old man by the arms and bring him to his feet and kissed him, tears in his eyes.

'It's true. I am Gilles de Tournemine. But how did you know—?'

'Some twenty years ago a man came here. His name was Pierre de Tournemine and he was about to leave on a long, long voyage from which he hoped to bring back gold enough to buy this castle, for no male Tournemine had lived in it since the sixteenth century. The owner at that time, Baron Louis-François de Rieux, happened to be at the castle, but was too proud to receive this distant and evidently poor relation who had come to his door. It was I, then a humble gamekeeper, who took him into my house in the woods where he wept for shame and anger. Yes, my lord, I saw him weep, a man who was as like to you as a father. Poor man, I saw the last descendant of the formidable Falcon weep before me, and I wept with him. But he recovered himself quickly. "I will return, Joel Gauthier," he said to me. "By the memory of my forbears I swear that I will return and take back these lands which a

21

woman's womb has allowed to pass into the hands of strangers." When I saw you tonight, I knew that he had returned—'

'No,' Gilles sighed. 'He has not returned. He is dead, far from here, on American soil, before a town called Yorktown, like Olivier the Falcon before Mansurah, like Geoffrey before la Roche-Derrien, like Olivier II before Auray, like Jean before Pontorson, like René, the last, before Rouen. He died a hero but he was still as poor. He left nothing but his dream—'

'But you, lord, you are young and strong, you will surely fulfil your father's vow! You will surely take La Hunaudaye back from those who little deserve it and who leave it to perish! Baron Louis-François sold it to a rich nobleman, the Comte de la Moussaye, but distant descendants of your family fell on him like vultures. There was a court case and these people were awarded the estate: one took the castle, its appurtenances and feudal rights, the other took the forest. It was not hard for them, they were both lawyers,' Joel said with contempt. 'You must win back the castle at least, master, so that I may die happy.'

'I wish I could! Yes, I do wish it with all my heart, but I fear I may not succeed. Yet the Queen has promised me that castle, and lands shall be restored to me if the present owners are willing to sell. But the one I saw in Rennes would not listen to any idea of giving up even La Hunaudaye – unless I pay him an exorbitant price, a price I could not possibly ask of Her Majesty, however favourably disposed she is towards me ...'

On the day, in fact, when Axel de Fersen had taken his friend to the Trianon, Marie-Antoinette had treated the young man to a most charming welcome. She had listened with unfeigned interest to the account of his adventures, and especially of the Swede's rescue in the Virginia woods.[1] She had been so pleased with the tale that she had spontaneously extended her royal hand to the Chevalier.

'Sir Falcon, you have preserved the best of my servants for me. I owe you a reward. What would you like?'

Fersen, without giving his friend time to reply, promptly stepped in:

[1] See *The Lure of the Falcon*.

'His Majesty the King was good enough to restore the Chevalier to his name and title. But, since he desires to marry, he would wish to regain the lands and estates of his ancestors which have unfortunately passed into other hands.'

'Never mind! See these others, Chevalier, and then come and tell me how much they want to sell. The Queen, Monsieur de Tournemine, can refuse you nothing.'

The words were royal, the tone one of great sweetness, the Queen was evidently full of goodwill, but after his visit to the Marquis de Talhouet-Boishorand, who was in fact a cousin of his godfather, the rector of Hennebont, Tournemine found the high hopes which had taken him into Brittany evaporating. How could he go back to Versailles and ask the Queen for the fabulous sum which had been demanded?

'Will you tell me how much he asked?'

It was Batz who answered.

'Five hundred thousand livres! A mere nothing, you see. There's no understanding it when you think of the state of the castle and there's practically no land with it, since the forest belongs to someone else.'

Old Joel looked suddenly aged, drained of the amazing vitality which kept him so upright, so proudly lifted up above the level of other men. But it was only for an instant. Almost at once, he said:

'I think I can explain. I can think of only one reason why he should refuse to sell – for to name such a price amounts to a refusal. He is hoping to find the treasure.'

The light of the fire was momentarily transferred to Batz's eyes.

'Treasure?' he murmured. 'What treasure is this?'

'The treasure of Raoul de Tournemine, the one who fought in Italy and was later ambassador to the King of England and Pope Julius II. He was very rich and he loved jewellery and had a great collection, much of it obtained in Italy. He allowed no one but himself to look at it. It was kept in a coffer in the main tower, but when he knew that he was dying he hid it in a place which no one has ever been able to discover. Though it's not for want of searching, all through the centuries.'

'Why did he hide it? Why not leave it to his children?'

'I think because he could not bear the idea of anyone else

23

touching and handling his gems. And because he was afraid of the collection being broken up. Moreover, he did not like his children. The Falcon's blood is a strong blood. It is not easy to carry it without letting it take over your soul.'

'I am not afraid,' Gilles said.

'Then, I beg of you, try to give it back its nest. Myself, I will pray God to leave me on this earth for long enough to witness that return.'

The old man bowed with dignity and then withdrew. The door creaked above his retreating footsteps and then closed. Left alone, the two friends looked at one another for a long moment in silence while Pongo, by the fire, was opening his master's saddlebags. The only sound was the crackling of the fire, for Joel had left behind him dreams enough to fill many nights and those dreams now occupied the minds of the three, very different men who were together in that formidable granite shell, like grains of corn in a closed fist. At daybreak the fist would open and they would be cast to the morrow's winds to germinate and bear fruit.

Gilles went slowly over to Pongo, who was holding out an uncorked bottle which he had taken from one of the bags.

'Rum? You think I need it?'

The Indian nodded.

'Fire water stimulate the mind! You need make big decision.'

'He's right,' Jean broke in. 'There are three roads before you and you have to choose between them. The first is straight, flat and unadventurous. That's the one that lies before you if you renounce your inheritance. You'll go back to the Queen's Dragoons and have an honourable career, not very brilliant, perhaps, except in time of war, but one that will make you a decent living. Of course, I'd be surprised if it got you a marshal's baton . . .'

'You know perfectly well what I'll do. I want La Hunaudaye! I want to build my own nest here. I want it for Judith and me, if God wills that I should ever find her.'

'That's only a question of time. She's alive, she's almost certainly in Paris, and Boulainvilliers, the Provost, has put the affair into the hands of the lieutenant of police, M. Lenoir.

24

He's a capable man, he'll let you know as soon as he has any news, wherever you are. He has given his word for that.'

'We can always hope,' Gilles said with a sigh. 'Let's hear about your other roads.'

'You can stay here, live like a peasant and scrabble and dig and search everywhere, pull down the castle stone by stone to find the treasure – but that could take a long time.'

'And is quite absurd.'

'I think so too, but I saw it as a poetic image – rather in the style of old Rousseau. The third way you know, that's the road to Spain. Do as I am, ask leave to serve the Bourbon there for a while under the Family Pact. You'll set out with the rank of captain and once there I'll warrant to help you to a fortune. There's more gold there than anywhere in Europe.'

'That, too, from your banker friends?'

'Yes. And it's in your interest to make them yours as well. Spain pays well and in their hands even a simple officer's pay can grow attractively. So, what do you think?'

The young man said nothing, unable in fact to make up his mind. He began pacing up and down the hall which, dating from the time of the castle's first foundations, must have seen the gold glinting on the white neck feathers of Taran, the legendary white gyrfalcon. Gilles ran his hands lingeringly over the rough old walls and the sturdy, blackened pillars that upheld the roof. The deep roots of his breeding, fast in this Breton soil, had sent up strong suckers, unyielding as chains, tough as those tropical vines which entrap a man and will not let him go, hardy shoots which had now grown so far into his flesh that he could no longer tear them loose without injury to himself. Here was his house, his roof, his hearth. Here, navigator of storms and rider on the wild winds, he wanted to build his nest with the woman, as wild as himself, whom he had chosen for his wife.

But the domain he felt so intensely was his own belonged to another and, paradoxically, to win it he must go away. The castle, like some pitiless god, was already demanding a cruel sacrifice of him, he must leave France, tear himself once again from his native soil, and go to beg of Spain a fraction of that gold which she was still squeezing with blood and tears out of

25

her Americas, over which her only rights were those of conquest and rediscovery by an eccentric mercenary.

Worse still, this self-exile meant abandoning his personal search for Judith's trail, growing fainter day by day, and entrusting to others, to officials who, however efficient, had no interest in it, that quest for his beloved which, for him, was a matter of such pain and tenderness.

The silence into which he had fallen, staring up with tears in his eyes at the mould-spotted shield of the Tournemines, was broken by Pongo's voice.

'To go from land of one's father.is hard,' he said. 'But in Indian country, Wise Men who seek truth in burning heart of fire, say Happy Valley only open after long, difficult journey of thorns and sharp stones. Often, to know how to choose hard way is to choose victory – and to be proper man!'

'—Because strait is the gate and narrow is the way,' Batz quoted gravely. 'Indian lore has a good deal in common with the Gospel, it would seem. Now, come, my friend, drink a little of this excellent rum to drive away black humours and let us to sleep! Tomorrow you shall decide which road you take, whether to Versailles and Madrid with me – or to Pontivy on your own.'

Gilles took the flask and took a long pull at it, then wiped his mouth and passed the bottle to his friend. His eyes were no longer troubled.

'To Madrid, by heaven! Devil take you!'

Not until then did old Joel, still standing like a rock outside the door, all his attention focused on the conversation within, cross himself fervently and, with a muttered prayer, leaning on his gnarled stick, betake himself to his own house. He was smiling, happier than he had been for many a day, with the hope that one day he would see the young master return. In the meanwhile, with Pierre to help him, he would continue his search for the treasure, asking the ancient stones, the knotty tree trunks and the crumbling cellars, the thing they had always refused to tell. But now he knew for whom he and his grandson were toiling.

PART ONE

Aranjuez

Spring 1784

1

The May Queen

The melody of a song rose into the blue morning air, borne on the merry voices of a group of young girls. It came from the far end of the garden and was growing nearer with every moment. It was as if the river had elected to climb the hill and water the garden, and at the song's approach even the birds fell silent.

All at once, beneath the vine arbour alongside the lawn, there was something like a bouquet of flowers in motion. Red skirts and striped aprons swayed about neat, white-stockinged ankles, criss-crossed by the ribbons of brand new pumps. Shawls fluttered their long fringes in the gentle breeze.

The girls were advancing two by two, those in front bearing a tall arch of lilac blossoms, the rest carrying bunches of the tall blue heath that softens the harshness of the sierra. Last of all came one bearing in her hands, with all the gravity of a bishop with the holy sacrament, a dainty crown of honeysuckle and jasmine.

Gilles, who had spent the night at San Pedro de Caraban-chel, the home of his friends the Cabarrus, was preparing to mount Merlin, just brought round for him by a groom, and return to Aranjuez. He paused in the act of drawing on his gloves, startled by the unexpected vision.

'What's this?'

The man smiled broadly.

'The procession for the Queen of the May, Señor! Today is the third of May and every year on this day the young girls of the village choose the fairest among them to reign over us all for the day. Today they've chosen our young lady.'

'Young as she is, it would be hard to find a prettier, that's true.'

At that moment a whirlwind of white muslin and rose-coloured ribbons erupted from the french window and hurled itself at him impetuously.

'Chevalier! My beautiful Chevalier! You aren't going away already?'

Teresia must have escaped out of the hands of her maid, for her black hair was tumbling in confusion down her back, and in fact the maid was hard on her heels, brush in hand, closely followed by the governess and, behind her again, trotted little Madame Cabarrus. Her papa, the banker François Cabarrus, brought up the rear in a somewhat more dignified fashion. The young man smiled.

'I have to, Teresia. I am on guard at Aranjuez tonight and you know it is the duty of the Bodyguard to be always as near to the royal person as possible.'

The little girl, for she was only eleven years old, even if her height and figure were more those of fifteen, raised magnificent dark eyes, now filled with tears.

'That was true last night. But, see Gilles, today I too am going to be a queen, Queen of the May! You must stay here with me. If you are not here, there will be no point in anything any more!'

She had clasped her hands together and two big tears were already rolling down the warm brown cheeks, so delicately flushed with pink. But she smiled at the same time and at the charm of that smile the young man had to summon up all his strength of character to resist her. The child was a little witch and it was safe to bet that the years would make her a perilous siren. But although, since his arrival in Spain, Gilles had become really fond of her, his heart was too well protected to be in any danger of playing him false in this direction.

'Do you know it is nearly twelve leagues from Carabanchel to Aranjuez? I have to cover them.'

Rather than let the young May Queen's ladies find their sovereign in tears, François Cabarrus intervened.

'A mere nothing for that steel-limbed mount of yours, my friend. Stay at least until after mass – long enough to see our pretty Teresia enthroned.'

30

'No, no!' the girl broke in. 'I want him to stay until the end. I want to dance with him tonight!'

'Now you are asking too much. A soldier is bound by his duty. You wouldn't like our friend to be court-martialled for your whim?'

The threat went home. Even so, Teresia, hanging on Gilles' arm, could not bring herself to let go.

'If he stays until mass is over, then I'll let him go,' she said at last, reluctantly, 'but only on one condition.'

'And what's that?'

'That you'll take me to the Pradero of St Isidore.'

The great festival of St Isidore, patron saint of the city of Madrid, was to take place twelve days later, on the fifteenth of May. On that day, after mass, the citizens of Madrid, regardless of rank or fortune, would flock out to the open ground along the Manzanares to mingle in a joyous throng, dancing and making merry almost until dawn. Young girls did not go except in the company of their parents or affianced husbands.

Gilles laughed.

'Do you really need me? I could name a score of young men dying to take you.'

'It's you I want! And I won't let you go unless you promise.'

The little hand, fragile as a bird's claw, trembled lightly on the young man's arm and he gave it a brotherly pat with his long fingers. It was too cool, almost cold.

'I promise, Teresia – if I'm not on duty! And now, your majesty's subjects are waiting.'

The other girls were approaching the steps where they stood and the maid, uttering a series of indignant squawks, fell upon her mistress and finished dressing her hair with furious energy. In a trice the queen was ready and handed over to her maids of honour who danced round her in a circle, singing. Next the crown of spring flowers was placed on the black curls and the May Queen took her place beneath the arch of flowers and, flanked by her escort of maidens, made her way solemnly to the village church, where the bells were now ringing for all they were worth.

Madame Cabarrus had vanished briefly and reappeared beneath a vast straw hat in the latest Paris style, adorned with a profusion of Nattier blue taffeta ribbons and a long plume of white ostrich feathers, anchored precariously on her piled and powdered hair and giving her the appearance of a mushroom. She was a tiny little woman, as quick and lively as a sparrow. Never still, she had the kind of temperament wearing to a husband and an acid wit which few could boast of escaping. In addition, she was an impossible snob and inexpressibly proud of the title of count which King Charles III had bestowed on her husband, by then one of the greatest financiers in Spain, three years previously, at the same time as his naturalization papers.

The austere Spanish nobles, of course, did not trouble to hide their contempt for 'Count' Cabarrus, manufactured out of the shipowner François Cabarrus from Cap Breton in the Landes and for his countess whose maiden name was merely Antoinette Galabert. But Teresia's parents were perfectly content with their own greatness, they were happy to live a retired life in their luxurious house at Carabanchel with their three children, being well aware that when the time came, their fortune would enable their daughter to choose her own husband from among the high-nosed local nobility, covered in titles and noble names but for the most part nearly penniless.

Countess Antoinette took a firm hold on the arm vacated by her daughter.

'Don't you think we are a well matched pair, Chevalier, you and I? Your uniform is precisely the same blue as my dress.'

For the young man wore the elegant Guards' uniform copied with only a few variations by the first Bourbon king from its Versailles equivalent: blue coat with scarlet facings, braided with silver, buff breeches and waistcoat, thigh boots and cocked hat.

He had to thank his tall stature, his name and his physical appearance for his entry into this crack regiment, while his friend Batz had to be content with the infinitely less prestigious Numantia Dragoons. The Gascon bore it philosophically, putting in no less infrequent appearances than in the Queen's Dragoons. The gaming houses of Madrid, on the other hand, he frequented assiduously, plunging with utter recklessness, and also the houses of certain members of the Indies office through whom he claimed to be about to make a killing on goods imported from the American colonies. He had even persuaded his friend to entrust some of the modest savings acquired in the service of the king of France to invest in such luxuries as cocoa and spices.

The remainder Gilles had, with a wise caution, put into the hands of François Cabarrus whose capabilities had been warmly recommended to him by the ex-minister Necker when he paid him a farewell visit in Paris, for while he had complete faith in his friend's real financial acumen, he feared his passion for the tables. In fact, he was very well satisfied with the arrangement. Every month, as regularly as clockwork, the banker presented him with a statement of his affairs and when the young man came for two or three days' visit to Carabanchel he initiated him, a little at a time, into the exciting business of finance which up to that time had held little interest for him and had, indeed, seemed somewhat beneath his aristocratic breeding.

'You'd be surprised,' he had been told, that first day, 'at the number of Spanish grandees who can not only add up as well as any of my clerks, but could even give points to Shylock. With a good many of them, that haughty bearing is firmly based on piles of solid cash.'

'Teach me, then,' the young man said eagerly. 'The family I'll have one day will be deeply grateful to you – and at least I'll stop looking like a fool when Batz starts lecturing me on stock jobbing, bank rates and all the rest of it, which is all Greek to me.'

Held on a firm leash by little Madame Cabarrus, Gilles attended mass in the village, then escorted the May Queen to the flowered throne prepared for her beside the church porch. But before he was permitted to kiss the little hand which Teresia was clearly bursting to offer him he had to pay the customary toll in response to the delighted demands of her train. So he contributed his mite and, dropping to one knee before Teresia, deposited a light kiss on the slim fingers which gripped his with unexpected strength.

'You'll come for me on the fifteenth? You promise?' the little girl entreated.

'I'll be there, if it is in my power. I promise. And I can certainly promise not to go to the Pradera with anyone else—'

'*Vaya con Dios, Señor!* I'll be waiting for you.'

33

More 'loyal subjects' were approaching, brought forward by the maidens who impressed them shamelessly as long as they looked attractive or well dressed; Gilles moved away to where a groom was waiting in the shade of the plane trees with his horse.

All at once he had lost his haste to return to the stifling atmosphere of a royal palace, even one as exquisite as Aranjuez. The weather was superb. High above the young leaves on the trees, the sun shed its warm glory from a lapis lazuli sky and, in the church square, the fair was getting under way. Open-air cafés had sprung up, offering peppers, garlic sausages, tomatoes, melons, almond cakes and heavy aromatic wine to drink. Mountebanks were spreading out their cloths on the ground, ready to show off the tricks of their trained goats and performing monkeys. Water sellers and peddlers of sunshades moved among the ever-increasing crowd that thronged about the queen's throne: hidalgos, their arrogance in opposite proportion to their worldly wealth, coxcombs prinking and crowing in silks copied from the fashions of Versailles, brilliant *majos*, strutting like fighting cocks in delicately tinted silk stockings, all brought together for an instant by their common admiration for Teresia and vying with one another in their occasionally outrageous praises of her beauty.

'A blessing on the womb that fashioned such loveliness!'

'The man who shares your bed will be equal to the gods!'

There were women also, a great many of them, peasants in striped gowns with shawls over their heads, impudent majas, teasing eyes under lacy mantillas, supple waists in unboned bodices and slender legs beneath their full, flounced skirts. All of them were pretty.

The music of guitars thrummed in the air, bringing fresh life to the picture. Light feet shod in beribboned slippers were flying below swinging skirts in the rhythm of fandango or seguedilla. The dust rose in a gentle cloud from imperiously stamping heels. Gilles spared it all a regretful sigh, feeling reluctant to leave the scene.

'There's a sad face for a fair day, Señor Capitano!' A cheerful voice was hailing him from beneath the trees. 'The sky is clear, the wine is cool and the girls are beautiful! And the Queen is loveliest of all! What more could a man want?'

Narrowing his eyes against the sun, the young man searched the shadows until he could make out the sturdy figure of a man, his back propped against a plane tree, sketching idly with a cigar between his teeth. His face brightened instantly.

'Paco! Lord, man, it's an age since I've seen you!'

'Then the splendours of court life have blurred your eyes, my friend. It wasn't I who left for Aranjuez at Easter. I only know the *manolas* in the Taverna de Los Reyes are weeping their eyes out because you don't return.'

Black eyes under jutting brows were gleaming in a pale olive face. The face itself was heavy-featured, framed in long square-cut black whiskers. A peasant's face, not beautiful but interesting, inhabited by an inner light. The splendid *majo* costume moulded the lean, powerful body: a short, crimson velvet jacket, adorned with massive black braided epaulettes, worn open over an embroidered shirt of fine lawn and revealing a broad black satin waistband, tight trousers of straw-coloured silk with silver buttons and stockings to match, buckled shoes and the long hair confined at the nape with a heavy black silk snood. A full black cape hung waiting over a branch of a tree.

This exotic personage was Don Francisco de Goya y Lucientes. He was thirty-seven years old and had been painter to the king for four years.

Gilles de Tournemine had met him not long after his arrival in Madrid, in the Plaza Mayor, during the last corrida, to which he had gone because he had been told it was a spectacle he should not miss. But he had very quickly regretted his curiosity and had not in fact stayed to witness the end. The sight of the arena strewn with the bodies of horses disembowelled by the bull's horns had roused him to anger and disgust.

Unwilling to watch longer and unused to hiding his feelings, he had made his attitude known to those around him much too loudly and clearly. His protests produced a minor riot among the enthusiasts round about. In a moment, he was facing a howling mob, bent on teaching him the beauties of bullfighting by tearing him limb from limb.

Too angry to appreciate his peril, Tournemine drew his

35

sword and made a few passes in the air, keeping the crowd of outraged aficionados at bay for a space. But the long knives were out in several hands and the young man would infallibly have succumbed at last to the sheer weight of numbers if the man he now hailed amicably as Paco had not fought his way through to him.

'You insult the honour of Spain, for the sake of a few worthless pieces of carrion? You must be mad, señor!'

'I have never looked on horses as worthless carrion! To my mind the word belongs rather to the human race. The horse, Sir, is the noblest animal God ever made! It was not fashioned for senseless slaughter.'

'What is a horse, when a man's life is at stake? You should see the corrida through to the end before you judge!'

'I have seen enough – unless you can promise me the satisfaction of seeing the bull avenge the horses!'

A howl of rage greeted this remark. Gilles raised his sword in ironical salute.

'At your service, gentlemen. I too can play the bull's part.'

'Oh no,' the stranger broke in swiftly. 'You are going to fight me first.'

'With pleasure – only you have no sword.'

'Don't think I don't know how to use one. Merely, I do not have it with me. But my fists I have,' he added, thrusting a pair like small hams under the Frenchman's nose. 'We'll fight my way, if you will. Of course, no gentleman should be expected to fight with his fists—'

'You think not? Try me, then!'

A wide circle formed, the two men engaged and soon both were on the ground. The stranger was immensely strong but shorter and slower than Gilles who, with Pongo's help, had brought to perfection the art of Indian fighting learned in the forests of Virginia. The fight was long, hard and inconclusive. After neither of them knew how long, the two men found themselves sitting on the ground regarding one another breathlessly and completely alone except for one ragged urchin, staring at them over the slice of watermelon he was eating. Their audience had tired and returned to the more exciting spectacle in the arena. The Spaniard burst out laughing.

'I think we can leave it there! At least you are no longer in danger of being murdered—'

'In other words, you only fought to save me? I must confess I can't see why – unless you are not Spanish.'

'I am from Aragon, and so more Spanish than all Spain. But I'm a painter and I'd like to paint you – when you're a better colour, at least! Let's go and drink a bottle of amontillado to recover. The Taverna de Los Reyes is nearby – and I'll explain the corrida to you. I know all about it, I'm still able to *matar al toro* – to kill the bull, that is.'

Two hours later, still just as dirty and now magnificently drunk, the two adversaries were snoring loudly either side of a tavern table, but by this time they were sworn friends.

Gilles leaned over to see what his friend was drawing. It was the May Queen's throne with her maidens and her worshippers all around it.

'Another sketch for a tapestry for the Academy of San Fernando?'

'*Naturalmente!* That's the only painting including secular portraits my wife will let me do,' Paco retorted, with a touch of scorn that was not without bitterness. Gilles knew already that his marriage to Josefa Bayou, prudish, austere and wholly dedicated to the academic in art, was not a success. 'It won't last for ever,' the painter went on, stuffing his sketchbook abruptly into his pocket. 'But that's enough for today! Let's go and drink a glass of wine and eat some garlic sausage and after that we'll dance—'

The Chevalier shook his head.

'Paco, I can't! I'm on guard at the palace tonight. I must get back. There's your reason why I'm not looking very cheerful.'

'I see. Only tell me, *amigo*, what kind of guard will you be mounting at the palace?'

'What kind – what do you mean? You're the king's painter, you should know all about the duties of the Bodyguard.'

'Precisely. It's just a matter of which body is in question. Is it our old king – or the Princess of Asturia?'

Gilles relaxed suddenly and gave a shout of laughter.

'Paco, my friend, you spend too much time listening to the blind beggars at the Puerta del Sol, they're a regular gazette, crying every bit of gossip from the court, true or false.'

37

'The blind sometimes speak truth. Or did I dream that one of your fellow guards has just been discreetly sent packing for giving her highness nocturnal lessons on the guitar?'

'People say a lot of things,' Gilles said evasively, unwilling to discuss an affair which, it seemed to him, was none of his business.

Goya extracted a long cigar from his waistcoat pocket and lit it carefully, watching his friend out of the corner of his eye. He drew on it luxuriously for a few moments before remarking:

'You're discreet. That's good. *Esprit de corps*, I suppose? All the same, everyone in Madrid knows the Princess Maria-Luisa is a lusty piece, that her boor of a husband cannot satisfy her and that she has an eye to the Guards. If it hasn't already, your turn will come. Only have a care!'

'To what?'

'To three people. The Duchess of Sotomayor, first of all. She's the Camerera Mayor and has spying in her blood. The King's Confessor next, the enigmatic Joaquin d'Eleta. He's so thin he could slip through a crack in the shutters. And finally, Florida Blanca, the minister who usually gets the job of tidying up the royal couple's affairs. He was the one who got rid of the guitar merchant so neatly. But he came of a great Castilian family. You are a foreigner and might be got rid of rather more drastically. Which, since I've not yet finished your portrait, would be a source of grief to me.'

'Don't worry. You'll have plenty of time to finish it. The princess no more thinks of me than I of her. Between you and me, your guitar merchant was a brave fellow and for my part I much prefer the pretty dancers at Los Reyes! Adios, Francisco. I'll come and ask you to supper one day this week.'

'Adios, Francès. I'll hold you to that, but at my studio at El Rastro. Josefa would give you lenten fare!'

The two friends embraced and Paco returned to his drawing while Gilles made his way to his horse at last and, climbing into the saddle, prepared to leave Carabanchel. He was just about to ride over to Teresia, whose eyes had been watching him eagerly in hope of a last farewell, when his attention was caught by a vehicle which was approaching with a great tinkling of bells.

It was a small cabriolet with gleaming brasswork, drawn by a frisky Andalusian and known to all Madrid to belong to the most celebrated matador of the day, the great Pedro Romero, and it was he who was driving it.

Shouts and cheers greeted the idol's appearance, sumptuously dressed in canary yellow velvet, gold-trimmed, and smiling with a flash of white teeth. Gilles, however, accorded him no more than a cursory glance for, seated on the red-cushioned bench beside Romero, he had recognized the one woman who had succeeded in arousing a real interest in him since his coming to Spain. A splendid maja, the fire in her eyes had made his blood race suddenly with a burning remembrance of Sitapanoki, the Indian princess whose image still came sometimes to haunt his waking nights.

The Spaniard was not as beautiful as the Indian but every inch of her radiated an almost demonic vitality. A mass of dark curling hair, barely confined by a snood trimmed with multicoloured ribbons, cascaded halfway down her back, framing a pale face, all eyes and a mouth which alone could have roused a nonagenarian hermit to desire. Her black bodice, shouldered with layers of coloured braid, was slit down to the wide scarlet belt with two dark red roses in it, showing a long triangle of luminous flesh between the two flaunting breasts. A slim coral necklace encircled her pretty neck. A patch at the corner of one eye, a narrow black ribbon binding another rose to her slender wrist and a large black lace fan added the final touches to the costume of the torero's mistress, for from his complacent bearing the lovely maja could be nothing else.

To Gilles, this discovery was unpleasing. It was his second encounter with the girl. The first had been on the last night of the Madrid carnival, in the plaza de la Cebada. She had burst out of a dark alleyway and seized the young man's hands, dragging him into the grinning, shrieking farandole that was surging by in a glare of smoky torches. Gilles had taken her for a ghost at first, for she was dressed all in white and the mask she was wearing under her lace mantilla bore the face of Death. She had laughed at his instinctive movement of recoil.

'You a soldier, *hombre*, and afraid of Death?'

'I have never been afraid. May my death be as lovely – for I can tell you are!'

She only laughed and for a while the pair abandoned

39

themselves to the long chain of dancers. Then, all at once, the girl broke free, drawing Gilles with her, as suddenly as she had entered it. They found themselves standing in a church porch, looking through the open doors at the lighted chancel. The girl let go of Gilles' hand and turned as if to enter, but he caught her back.

'Show me your face, pretty Death, and let me see if I can dream of you.'

She had hesitated briefly. Gilles could see her bosom rising and falling beneath the lace of her bodice. She was panting a little. He drew her, unresisting, into his arms.

'You really want me to?' she whispered.

'I do.'

She pulled off the grinning mask and sent it spinning away and for a long moment they gazed at one another without speaking. Then, in the same instant, both moved spontaneously. Gilles tightened his hold and bent his head while the girl raised her face to his.

It seemed to him that he had plunged into a fire. The girl's lips burned, her kiss was a work of art and her whole body, like an incense burner, gave off a bewitching scent of amber. But just as he would have pursued the acquaintance, the girl slipped from his arms and fled with a ripple of laughter.

Seeing his companion of a moment once more, in the broad light of day, Gilles thought her lovelier than ever. She was smiling and the sun shone on her red lips and little sharp, white teeth. The young man found the torero's air of complacent ownership intolerable. He thrust his way towards the little carriage with such force that Romero was obliged to pull up to avoid a collision. But Merlin, held by his master's iron hand, was already back on his haunches. His forelegs pawed the air close enough to the bullfighter's head to make him blench and curse, while Gilles snatched off his cocked hat and flourished it in salute to his companion.

She had not been afraid. By her smile and the provocative glance she threw him, Gilles knew that she had recognized him. Romero, for his part, had merely recognized the uniform of the Guards and, despite the pride habitual to his calling, the words of abuse died on his lips to a vague mutter, but his eyes on the officer were murderous.

In his pleasure at seeing his phantom of the carnival once more, Gilles did not even notice.

'Whenever and wherever you please, my fair one,' he cried, when he had Merlin in hand again. 'One word, one look and I am yours! My name is Gilles de Tournemine!'

Equally indifferent to her escort's obvious annoyance, the maja smiled more charmingly than ever. The black fan fluttered a little faster as her hand went to the roses at her belt and she took one and tossed it to the young man, who caught it deftly. He breathed in the scent of it before tucking it, still warm from the touch of her breast, inside his coat. Then, bowing low, as if to a queen: '*Adios señorita*,' he cried. 'We shall meet again.'

Without looking back, he set Merlin at a canter on the southward road, but the lovely maja's black eyes followed his figure until the dust hid it.

Meanwhile, outside the church, something was happening. No one in Carabanchel understood why, at the height of the festivities, when her throne was besieged with admirers, the prettiest May Queen ever suddenly jumped up from her seat and ran, with tears in her eyes, back to her father's house.

The palace of Aranjuez, built originally by the gloomy Philip II but rebuilt, after its destruction by fire, by the first Bourbon king of Spain, was admittedly not the grandest or most splendid of the royal dwellings, especially since the construction in recent times of the monumental palace of Madrid, but it was certainly the pleasantest.

A jewel of sunrise pink, noble without rigidity, set amid the verdure of a luxuriant *vega* created by the Tagus out of the brown plain, Aranjuez extended its graceful rose-coloured battlements among the sweet softness of gardens whose tossing greenery vied with its springing fountains. All this was fitted into the curves of the river whose willow-shaded banks served as harbour for the royal gondolas upholstered in yellow silk and fringed with gold.

It was a place of privilege, made for rest, relaxation and the pleasures of the senses, and if the gardens no longer formed a background for the gazelles, ostriches and camels of Philip II's time, the thousands of flowers that filled it were none the worse.

Unfortunately, as ill luck would have it, this charming palace, in common with the other royal residences, suffered the curse of boredom. It might be jollier than the stern Escurial, more graceful than the Royal Palace, more comfortable than the mountain resort of La Granja, between which the Court divided its time, but that did not preserve it from the leaden weight of Spanish etiquette or the dreary solemnity spread about himself by its master, King Charles III.

Yet he was a good king, the best, beyond doubt, of all the Bourbon dynasty of Spain: a great builder, a fine statesman, bred up to philosophy, a great reformer and an able judge of his servants, only, widowed after twenty-four years of marriage to Maria Amelia of Saxe, who had given him thirteen children, he remained stubbornly faithful to her memory. A widower and celibate, the king cracked down mercilessly on irregular liaisons among his courtiers, confined his own pleasures to the chase, never changed his clothes and cherished a hearty dislike of everything smacking of frivolity. At his court there were no balls, no concerts, no banquets. The only entertainment was the 'hand-kissing', an unexciting ceremony in which, on a set day, the king sat on his throne while his entire court and the high officers of his realm filed past him in their robes of state. Each in turn made his bow, kissed the royal fingers resting on the arm of the throne, rose and made way for the next. After which, everybody went home. The princes and princesses were also entitled to take part in this somewhat relative diversion, although they rarely availed themselves of it.

By the time Gilles perceived the baroque façade of the palace before him, dusk was falling. Merlin had cast a shoe on the road and this had delayed him, but he knew that this excuse would not satisfy the captain of the Royal Guard, the Duke of Almodovar, who had his own strict ideas of discipline and time-keeping.

Luck, however, was on his side. He was urging his mount to a faster pace, his mind dwelling anxiously on what lay before him, when he realized that his arrival at least would probably go unnoticed since, happily for him, the king was at that moment returning from the hunt. The palace courtyard, bright with lantern light, was filled with a dense crowd of people and, towering above the rest on his tall horse, the latecomer recognized his own captain at the king's side.

Without pausing to feast his eyes on the royal person, clothed as usual in a cloak of coarse grey Segovia cloth and buff boots, Gilles dismounted lightly and, leading his horse, made his way to the Guards' quarters which lay close to the palace in the Casas de Officios y Caballeros. The shadows of the portico outside the billets swallowed him up.

There he was surprised to find Pongo, his Indian stoicism for once forgotten, pacing the floor, biting his nails. He literally flung himself at Gilles.

'Master forget time—'

'No, but Merlin cast a shoe. You'd better take a look at it because I don't trust the smith who dealt with it. But what's bothering you? Has anyone been asking for me? Who? The Duke?'

Pongo nodded and elaborated:

'He angry. By good luck, King back from hunting earlier than usual. He go see. Not back yet. I ask Great Spirit bring you quick!'

'It seems the Great Spirit can refuse you nothing since you left Virginia,' Gilles said, laughing. 'With a bit of luck I may even have time to make myself look presentable before he comes back.'

Tossing his bridle to the servant, he made a dash for the stairs leading to his rooms, for, all being of commissioned rank, the men of His Most Catholic Majesty's Bodyguard were each allotted their own lodgings in all the royal residences outside Madrid. On these occasions, only one or two brigades would be involved, serving in rotation, the rest of the regiment remaining in its luxurious barracks in the capital. As a second lieutenant, Gilles was entitled to a suite of two rooms.

Sprinting down the passage leading to them, he cannoned into a fellow guardsman, young Don Rafael de Mollina, coming the other way. They collided sharply but the Spaniard took it with equanimity.

'Ah, Tournemine,' he said, rubbing his shoulder. 'Just the man I wanted! My dear fellow, do you know they're looking for you everywhere?'

'You as well? Why the devil am I so much in demand all of a sudden? My company is on duty this evening and I am a trifle late, but I don't see—'

'Well, you're going to see now! You may as well be warned before you see the captain. Your company is a man short.'

'Why? Is someone sick?'

'Sick indeed – cashiered! Ordered to leave the palace within two hours!'

'In two hours! What the devil for?'

Young Mollina looked mysterious.

'That, my friend, is something I'm not authorized to divulge. His Excellency will do that himself. I may add that, with you and the Marquis de Peñaflor both away and our brigadier nursing an old wound, His Excellency has been obliged to do his own dirty work, which has not put him in the best of humours. Dukes of Almodovar were not created to sweep floors!'

'Real soldiers can do much more than that,' Gilles retorted roundly. 'You'd be surprised at the things I've seen General Washington do, though he's one of the greatest men of our age. Not that I'd dream of comparing His Excellency to the general,' he added, as an insolent afterthought.

At the sudden mention of the American's name, the young Spaniard gave a kind of horrified gasp and crossed himself hurriedly, as if his companion had mentioned Antichrist.

'That general is not a great nobleman. Everyone knows the Americans are savages and—'

Gilles had no desire to embark on an argument with Mollina. King Charles III might be an enlightened despot but he was the only one of his court with any hint of liberalism. Only men like Paco could look with any kind of sympathy on the new American republic.

'Very well,' he broke in quickly. 'Who is it who is dismissed?'

'Don Luis Godoy.'

'Oh. Well, thanks for telling me.'

As he hurried through a rapid toilet and changed his travel-worn boots for a fresh, immaculate pair, Tournemine tried to imagine what it was that Mollina had not told him. It needed no effort of memory to recall Luis Godoy, a young hidalgo of a

44

good Estremaduran family whose fair skin and grey eyes contrasted strikingly with the appearance of most of the Bodyguard, in which olive skins largely predominated. He was, besides, a likeable youth, with a ready smile and a boyish appetite for life and its pleasures. Well-mannered and invariably good-humoured, carrying out his duties with exemplary correctness, what could Don Luis have done to get himself dismissed like an insolent servant?

Gilles knew the answer fifteen minutes later, confronting the six feet of splendid arrogance that was his commanding officer. Not that the first Duke of Almodovar condescended to explanations which were, in his view, in no way due to officers of foreign extraction. After treating the young man to a dressing down for what he called his 'quite unjustifiable absence' and refusing to listen to his somewhat heated excuses, he merely informed him:

'You, Sir, will personally undertake the guard duty at the door of the Princess of Asturia's apartments. Your orders are to permit no one to enter, no one, do you hear! Except, of course, the King or his highness the heir to the throne.'

So that was it. First Montijo, then San Fernando and now it was the turn of Luis Godoy. Goya's warning came back to his mind.

'The princess has an eye to the Guards. If it hasn't already, your turn will come. Only have a care!'

But his own independent mind, coupled with the ideas of liberty imbibed in America, drove Tournemine to press, not altogether humbly, for the explanations which were denied him.

'May I be told, my lord, to what I owe this flattering distinction? It cannot be to my lateness on duty.'

Don Alfonso's somewhat bulging eyes annihilated him.

'To the simple fact, Sir, that you are not a Spaniard, and that consequently nothing of what passes in this palace concerns you – any more than you are of the smallest concern to anyone here. You may thank the same cause for preserving you from the disciplinary effects of such a question.'

Because he was a foreigner – or because they needed him? For the thing was becoming clearer now: he was being set to guard the inflammable princess because, in the blinkered eyes of the royal circle, the young Princess of Asturia could not so much as glance at a barbarian from the north, let alone allow her heart to dwell on him.

The formulation of this somewhat simplistic theory reminded him of a story which had been current among the Guard. At the time of the Montijo affair, when the King was angrily drawing his son's attention to his marital responsibilities and misfortunes, Prince Charles had merely laughed, declaring that it was all a pack of idle gossip and that for his part he was perfectly easy in his mind since for a princess of the blood royal to cherish affections for a commoner was patently impossible. King Charles had been so stunned by this complacency in the husband that he could only gasp: 'What a fool you are, Charles! You ought to know they're all the same, whores every one of them!'

The worthy prince had obstinately refused to follow his father into realms which threatened to disturb his comfort, but he was by no means the only person at court to hold to such ideas. Maria Luisa might take half the Bodyguard for her lovers, the whole regiment even, there would still be those found to insist, straightfaced, that the thing was impossible and so could not be – and how much less with a creature so inferior as a Frenchman! It would never have occurred to the noble duke that the Princess of Asturia, born Bourbon-Parma and a granddaughter of Louis XV, could find pleasure in the company of a compatriot of her charming grandfather.

Having no desire to plumb further the murky depths of a Spanish grandee's mind, Tournemine shrugged inwardly and went off to collect his men and proceed to relieve the bodyguard on duty at the palace.

Standing, rigid as a statue, beside the door, he was present while the princess supped, which she always did alone, seeing nothing but the silently moving backs of the priests and women who filled the room. Not that he paid much attention. In the hierarchy of the court he was, he knew, no more than a piece of furniture, equivalent to the heavy gilt bronze candelabra placed about the floor to light the room but this did not trouble him. The room was hushed in an almost religious silence, scarcely broken by the chink of cutlery and serving dishes, and he could let his mind wander freely after

46

the scented figure of the lovely maja he had seen again at Carabanchel. The princess's extra-marital adventures were forgotten.

With his mind full of agreeable plans to do with dining with Goya and with keeping a close eye on Pedro Romero's favourite haunts in Madrid, Gilles was unaware of the progress of the interminable ceremony of the meal. He did not come back to earth until the stern figure of the Camerera Mayor sailed towards him, all black lace like a funeral galley, driving before her in a reverential flock the spectators of the event, who were now withdrawing to permit her Highness to retire for the night.

'Your post will be in the first antechamber,' this aristocratic person informed Gilles. 'Close all the doors. His Highness the Crown Prince is suffering from a slight indisposition and will remain in his own apartments tonight. You are to ensure that the soldiers of the Walloon Guard are at their posts in the gallery.'

This last instruction drew a faint grin from the officer as he thought of Almodovar's reaction if he could have heard the autocratic Duchess of Sotomayor thus invading his territory. But, anxious to be rid of the woman whose beady eye was observing him with a kind of polite disdain, he merely bowed and departed in obedience to her instructions.

Gradually, the palace slept. The noises died away one by one, the murmur of evening prayers last of all. Soon there was no sound but the regular crunch of footsteps from the sentry on the gravel outside. Even the song of the fountains had ceased.

Alone in his small antechamber, Gilles gazed out for a while at the marvellous picture of the river silvered by moonlight, then dragged himself away and took his place on a stool of no comfort whatever to sit out the remainder of an unenjoyable night. Little by little, he lost all notion of time.

All the same, it must have been very late, so late that he had almost begun to doze off, when a faint, a very faint sound brought him instantly to his feet, listening. It came from the princess's apartment.

It did not take him long to realize that someone, on the other side of the door it was his stern duty to guard, was turning a

47

key in the lock so securely fastened earlier by the Camerera Mayor.

More cautiously still, the door opened a crack, letting a thin ribbon of light fall across the floor. It widened, until there was room enough for the passage of a feminine head in a beribboned cap.

'Lieutenant,' a voice whispered carefully. 'Are you there, lieutenant?'

'Yes, I am here.'

'Come with me, only for pity's sake don't make a sound! Her Highness wishes to speak to you.'

2

Maria Luisa

Once on the other side of the door, the head revealed itself as belonging to a young waiting woman, looking singularly wide awake for this late hour. In one hand this engaging person held a candle while the other was pressing a finger to her lips, enjoining the officer to silence.

Not that the warning was necessary. The room through which he was led on tiptoe was serving as a dormitory where four women of varying ages lay sleeping soundly, the cadences of their breathing ranging from the light sigh of girlhood to a duenna's majestic snores.

Fast asleep though they were, the sight of this slumbering company filled the young officer with justifiable anxiety. If one of them were to wake, he would be in a fine pickle! But, as if she guessed his thoughts, the girl turned and smiled.

'Don't be afraid,' she whispered. 'I made sure they would sleep well. All the same, it's best to be careful.'

The room into which Gilles was ushered was magnificent in the extreme. The gold silk hangings emphasized the richness of the heavy renaissance furniture and the splendid austerity of several El Greco canvases ranged discouragingly on either side of the great pillared bed. Casting a sideways glance at the long olive-skinned faces, Tournemine could not help thinking that amorous indiscretion must be slightly heavy going under the disapproving eyes of those painted figures. But he was not there to look at the pictures.

Seated by a window, a woman was waiting, her white nightgown billowing beneath a red robe of faintly ecclesiastical cut,

49

stiff with silver embroidery. She was evidently in a state of some excitement, her hands clasping and unclasping continuously while her head moved from side to side like a nervous sparrow's, unable to focus in any one direction.

As the young man came in and bowed with all the deference due to a crown princess, Maria Luisa jumped up like a jack-in-a-box.

'Come in, Sir,' she cried in French. 'Come in! I have to talk to you.'

'At your Royal Highness' service.' Gilles spoke formally.

She made a gesture of irritation.

'I said talk. Converse, if you prefer! Not hold forth to a blue brick wall. Leave your military manners outside, my friend, and come and sit down by me,' she went on, pointing to a stool placed next to her chair. Fiametta! Keep watch in the next room and see that none of those old crows wakes up!'

As she spoke, Gilles was studying the princess whom he had not seen before at close quarters. Maria Louisa of Parma, now Maria Luisa de las Asturias, was thirty-three years old and had already borne her husband eight children, including a pair of twins born in the September of the previous year, and Court rumour had it that she was once again pregnant. Even so, she was still youthful-looking, with pretty arms, fine hands and a deep bosom in no way impaired by regular childbearing, as the low cut of her nightdress made abundantly clear. But this and the over-brilliance of her eyes was all that remained of once great beauty, all sparkling life and gaiety, before the stifling and inhuman etiquette of Spanish palaces extinguished all that and turned it into mere restlessness. Her face, already showing signs of broken veins at cheeks and nostrils, had something inescapably owlish about it, something emanating from the roundness of the eyes, the thin, aquiline nose which, in time, would probably come to meet the slightly jutting chin, the thin-lipped mouth, a straight, red line beneath the droop of the nose. Black hair, too elaborately curled, framed a face which, if not beautiful, was not without character.

The sound of the door shutting cut short Gille's examination. Feeling the princess's eyes return to him, he dropped his gaze to the silver slippers peeping from below a frill of lace.

There was a silence, occupied, on the princess's side, by a reciprocal study of her bodyguard.

'They tell me you are French and hold the rank of second lieutenant?'

Gilles looked up at the question. His steel blue eyes met those of Maria Luisa's.

'Yes, Your Highness. I am French – and Breton.'

'You are fortunate. I did so wish they would have married me to a French prince. But young girls are not often asked for their opinion, princesses least of all. We are simply thrown to the winds.'

The frail voice, accentuating her birdlike quality, was so bitter and the twist at the corner of the thin lips so pathetic that compassion woke in the young man. Among the bodyguards, Maria Luisa had a reputation not far short of Messalina and only her royal birth saved her from the coarser adjectives applied to a camp follower. It would not have occurred to anyone that the woman could be simply unhappy.

'Your Highness is sad,' he said gently, in the tone of voice he might have used to a sick animal. 'Are you perhaps – unhappy?'

Maria Luisa shrugged.

'Unhappy? How could I be? A future Queen of Spain is a highly placed corpse. Corpses do not feel.'

Then, without a pause, as though unable to contain the words that burned on her lips: 'What has happened to Don Luis Godoy?'

Gilles felt the ground under his feet becoming dangerously steep and slippery. He could not see himself in intimate conversation with this unstable woman who seemed on the verge of hysteria. He fenced cautiously.

'I have been absent all day, madame. I returned from Carabanchel only late this evening, just in time to come on duty. So I have only just heard that Don Luis has gone. Gone somewhat – er – abruptly, as I heard.'

'Shockingly so!' the princess exclaimed, with force. 'Every rule of the army, every law of this land has been violated! It is a crying shame, a flagrant injustice! Poor boy! With practically no fortune, to be dismissed like a dishonest servant! Where can he have gone to, in God's name?'

51

She was flushed with anger. Gilles sought to calm her.

'Why – home, surely, Your Highness. To Estremadura, where I believe his father has some property. There are sisters, a younger brother—'

The grief vanished from Maria Luisa's face as though by magic.

'Why yes. Don Luis spoke of them. A brother, not much younger than himself. A year or two, I think? A younger brother, very handsome, I believe. Don Manuel, is it not?'

'I do not know, Madame, I was not on intimate terms with Don Luis. It is not quite seven months since I entered the service of Spain—'

But the princess was clearly not listening. She seemed lost in some private reverie.

'Yes ... I'm sure it was Manuel,' she repeated, as if to herself. 'We'll see if we can get him here next year. It would be only fair. A bodyguard's pay is a consideration, especially for a family of no great wealth ...'

Tournemine suppressed a smile. Were the future queen's charitable intentions directed more to the family of no great wealth, or to her own empty bed, he wondered. But she gave him no time to consider the matter. A fear had revived in her which she was not slow to voice.

'Are you quite sure Don Luis has gone away? Really gone?'

'I do not understand what Your Highness means.'

'Surely it's clear enough,' she flashed angrily, but the anger left her almost at once. 'Of course, you are French and so it is less obvious than it seems. I mean that there are – various ways in which a king may cause someone to – go away.'

'I see. Your Highness feels that Don Luis may have gone, not to Estremadura but to a better world. Have no fear. Several of my fellow officers saw him mount and ride away from the palace, alone. And I know that he was carrying a letter from Count Florida Blanca to his father. Under the circumstances, I don't think there is much fear even of an accident on the road.'

'Oh! You have done me so much good,' Maria Luisa sighed, sinking back in her cushioned chair. 'I feel as if a great weight had been lifted from me, a great fear! Ever since this morning, I have been in such anxiety for the poor boy, but now it is better.

I will send someone to his home to make sure he has reached it safely.'

Gilles rose, thinking his audience at an end.

'Have I Your Highness' permission to return to my post?'

For the first time, Maria Luisa smiled, a smile of pure mischief, unexpected in that restless face. She looked suddenly ten years younger.

'There's no hurry. You must be very uncomfortable in that antechamber of yours and I can't think that anyone would be so odd as to look in to see that you are there.'

'Nor I, but I have my orders—'

'And I am giving you another. Stay a little longer. It amuses me to talk to you. Aren't we almost fellow countrymen? I know! Open the window. It is stifling in here – and the night is so lovely.' The princess sighed, and made a faint cooing sound in her throat which warned the young man. He took his time opening the window. It was indeed a lovely night, brilliant with stars that silvered its blue depths. The scents of the gardens came up to him, along with a danker smell from the nearby river. But he could feel the princess's eyes like pinpricks on his back and shoulders.

'Tell me your name again,' she murmured, so close that he shivered. She must have risen and moved up behind him without his knowledge. A carnation scent, rich and spicy, was mingling with the fragrance of the garden.

It needed courage to turn and face those brilliant eyes, the moist lips and vague, cloudy form. Her Highness, feeling the heat, had removed her outer robe.

The ground was becoming slipperier than ever, although in a somewhat different way. Struggling to preserve some semblance of normality, Gilles recited: 'Chevalier de Tournemine de la Hunaudaye, so please Your—'

'Not that one ... the other ... The name that women call you by ...'

'My mother christened me Gilles, Madame,' he said, surprising himself. Things must be serious indeed for him to seek refuge behind the unyielding figure of Marie-Jeanne Goëlo, who had so unwillingly brought him into the world. But Maria Luisa had no idea what this handsome boy's mother might have been like.

'That's a nice name,' she said caressingly. 'Your mother must be a woman of taste, Chevalier. But you, surely you too must be feeling much too hot – those uniforms are impossibly thick! Take off your coat for a while. You will feel a great deal better ...'

It was, however unlikely, quite definitely an order, with another implied which might never be uttered in so many words. As he obeyed, it occurred to Gilles that, for his own and his country's honour, he was about to be called upon to perform an unusual feat, that of making love to a woman he did not desire. Yet after all, her body seemed agreeable enough, so that desire might come. He had never needed all that much encouragement.

Before Maria Luisa could say another word, he had swept her off the ground and carried her to the bed, dumped her there, none too gently, and, with both hands, ripped the nightgown from neck to hem, regardless of its precious Malines lace. Flinging himself down beside her, he let his hands rove over her naked body, but Maria Luisa was shaken by a passion which needed no arousal. She twined herself about him like bindweed and pressed her mouth to his with such force that their teeth clashed.

Gilles felt as if a leech were sucking out his breath, but the Princess's lips were cunning and his own body responded suddenly. He tried to free himself for a moment to remove the rest of his own clothing but she clung to him with a passionate strength that amazed him and whispered hoarsely against his mouth.

'Keep your boots on ... I've always dreamed of being raped by the soldiery in the sack of a city.'

Before all thought was annihilated by physical passion, Gilles found himself reflecting, to his own surprise, that sometimes princesses seemed to have the oddest dreams.

The sack continued unabated for a good three hours. The three most exhausting hours the Breton had ever experienced. It was his first encounter with a nymphomaniac and he was obliged to realize that Maria Luisa, once aroused, was quite insatiable.

Nevertheless the honour of France emerged unscathed, and even enhanced, and when at last the Princess's new lover was permitted to return to his antechamber Maria Luisa was both radiant and satisfied.

Stretching like a cat in the ravaged bed, she murmured: 'Since you are not on guard tomorrow night, wait for me in the pavilion in the garden of La Isla at midnight. I will come to you.'

'At midnight? It's impossible! How will you get out? Your door is locked. Besides, the Prince your husband might decide to visit you. And the pavilion is a long way from the palace—'

Maria Luisa laughed.

'That's why I chose it. As for your other objections, listen. First of all, I sleep alone when I like. Secondly, my duennas are the soundest sleepers in Spain, thanks to Fiametta, who takes good care of that. She is devoted to me, body and soul, for she came with me from Parma where her father is an apothecary. Go quickly now, and, above all, pay no attention to Court rumours. Tonight I shall be indisposed – and the following nights as well. My husband fears illness as he fears fire!'

He was turning to go when she sprang out of bed and, flinging her arms round his neck, clung to him in a last, greedy embrace.

'Don't forget! Tonight, at midnight! Not a second after. Already the time seems so unbearably long!'

Gilles left the overheated room like a man hunted. He returned to Fiametta and to his antechamber with a feeling of relief. It was quiet and peaceful, deliciously so with the growls of the raging lioness Maria Luisa still ringing in his ears. His only regret was that he was unable to light his pipe, smoking being strictly forbidden to Guards on duty. Instead, he made himself as comfortable as possible for the remainder of a night which, all in all, had passed more pleasantly than he could have foreseen.

But for the young Bodyguard the days that followed took on, more and more, the colours of a nightmare. Whereas Maria Luisa, safe in her bed, surrounded by her physicians, priests and elderly duchesses, was playing the invalid and spending as much of her time as possible sleeping, to recruit her strength for her nights, Gilles' days acquired a grinding pattern.

When he was not on duty, he stayed shut in his rooms with Pongo for company or else roamed the immense grounds, unable to get away from Aranjuez even for so much as a day. Terrified at the thought that he might not return in time to meet her, the Princess of Asturia had expressly forbidden it. He must, she told him romantically, spend his days looking forward to the pleasures of the night.

Then, night by night, in the little pavilion beside the Tagus, where he had to wait in darkness, the same scene took place: the well-oiled door would open without a sound, admitting the dark form of a woman dressed like a maidservant. As it closed, a voice would whisper cautiously: 'Are you there?'

'Yes.'

There would be a soft rustle of fabric and the next moment Maria Luisa, already panting and stark naked, would be in his arms, drawing him into an incredible storm of passion from which he emerged each morning a little wearier, in spirit at least, for in the physical sense his sound constitution and unbounded virility made him a partner after his royal mistress's own heart.

Yet he was growing increasingly to loathe her for her insatiable desire for him. The compassion of that first evening had died before the selfishness of a woman who, regardless of the demands his life might make upon him, could bring to the satisfaction of her own physical needs a sensual expertise a gipsy prostitute might have envied. There was an element of the praying mantis in Maria Luisa. In her company, Gilles descended into a kind of hell from which it sometimes seemed to him he would never again emerge into the light. Gradually their encounters became a battle, fought fiercely and without quarter, in which each seemed to be striving to extinguish the other's passions once and for all. Gilles could only wonder grimly how it would all end.

One morning he came back to his lodging after a parade held by their colonel, the duke, and was handed a letter by Pongo.

'Come from Madrid,' he said simply. Then, as the young man tossed it on to the table without even opening it, he added: 'Pongo think you should read. May be important.'

'Surely it can wait. I daresay it's from Jean de Batz, telling me he's had a win at cards – or lost – and I've a shocking headache.'

'Headache will go,' Pongo said, obliging his master to be

seated and beginning to massage his skull with both hands. 'Writing not that of your friend.'

Gilles picked up the letter again. The Indian was right. It was not from Batz. It was from Goya and consisted of no more than a few words.

'Amigo, where is your caution? For two days past the blind beggars in the Plaza Mayor have been talking of a certain lady's new lover. Take care. Death is a snake that can lie hidden among flowers. Have you forgotten you were going to ask me to supper?'

The painter's warning was serious. Gilles decided to heed it.

'What day is it?' he asked Pongo.

'The thirteenth.'

'Already? You did well to make me read this letter. It is important – very.'

While Pongo finished his massage, Gilles reflected that the day after tomorrow was the Pradera de San Isidro, to which he had promised Teresia he would take her. The little girl would be bitterly disappointed if he failed her, and besides, he wanted very much to go to the festival. For one thing, he liked Teresia and she was too sweet to be disappointed. For another, the lovely maja, whose image had been haunting his memory more than usual recently, could not decently fail to put in an appearance at the year's biggest event.

His first thought was to leave Maria Luisa to wait at their nightly meeting place in vain. Then, knowing her unpredictable nature, he thought better of it. She was quite capable of doing something stupid which would ruin them both. Then he reflected that surely her passion for him could not last much longer. Straw burned brightly but the flames did not endure. What was more, the Princess could not go on pretending to be ill for ever, to keep Prince Charles from her bed. The best thing might be to have it out with her. After all, there was no reason why she should deny him a short visit to Madrid, if only so that he could see for himself the precise extent and accuracy of the rumours being echoed by the blind beggars.

Having it out with the excitable princess was not, in the event, the easiest thing in the world. Almost before Gilles had opened his mouth on the subject nearest his heart she flew into a violent passion, declaring at the top of her voice, regardless of who might hear her, that he only wanted to go and enjoy the Pradera and that all this talk of rumours was a mere pretence.

'Who could possibly know of our meeting here at night? Fiametta is the only person in the secret and she would die before she betrayed me.'

'We can't go on much longer like this, in any case. I suppose you don't mean to spend the rest of your life in bed?'

'I'll stay there as long as I like. I don't see who is to stop me.'

'The King, perhaps. He might think it odd for an invalid to look as well as you do.'

'I'm pregnant. I deserve some consideration.'

'I'm glad you reminded me. In your condition, Madame, you would be wise to shun violent exercise.'

By the light of the candle which she had lighted because she seemed to find it difficult to argue in pitch darkness, he suddenly saw the tears in her eyes and knew that he had hurt her.

'Should you be the one to blame me for the excesses of our passion?' she murmured plaintively. 'I thought you took as much joy in them as I?'

To comfort her, he smiled and drew her close and dropped a kiss on her dishevelled hair.

'No question. Only, you must realize that you are not like any other woman. You are the future Queen of Spain and the King is not blind.'

'That intolerable old bigot, thinking himself damned if he doesn't remain pointlessly faithful to a wife dead these twenty years?' Maria Luisa burst out. 'If he'd stop denying himself the pleasures he's dying to have, he might be more indulgent to the weaknesses of others! He wouldn't harry them into their very thoughts! He gets his own back by being hard on us!'

'I dare say. But if the blind beggars are beginning to talk about us, then you are in danger. You must be careful, not just for yourself but for the child you are carrying. And the first thing is that you must resume your usual occupations – at the religious celebrations of the feast of St Isidore, for example. You'll never be forgiven if you are not present.'

'I know. But what is to become of us, of our delicious meetings?'

'We shall find a way,' Gilles said, without much conviction. 'We must—'

But already she had ceased to think of it and was clinging to him, purring like a she-cat in heat in search of fresh caresses. He tried to wriggle out of it.

'It's late. We must go.'

'No, not yet! I shall be so miserable. Love me again – just once. Oh, and look, I've brought you a present. With all this, I nearly forgot it.'

She ran barefoot to the little heap of clothes abandoned by the door, rummaged for a moment and then returned to cast herself into his arms, clutching something which she slid into Gilles' reluctant palm.

'But I don't want anything,' he protested, 'especially not a thing as valuable as this!' The feeble glimmer of the candle struck fire from a magnificent emerald ring.

'Why shouldn't I give you a valuable present? What you give me is beyond price.'

'Just because I give it. This ring makes it seem as if I were being paid!'

'Don't be so stupid, *mio amor*! The emerald is a talisman. It is green, for hope, green for the spring, and an old wise man once told me that the ancient Egyptians looked on it as the lovers' stone. You came to Spain to make your fortune, well, let me begin it. And don't offend me any more by refusing.'

He had to take it. Moreover Gilles was conscious of a new, nobler emotion. He had thought that he meant nothing to the Princess but a means of satisfying her own desires, regardless of how he felt. The jewel showed him a kind of tenderness, a warmth of heart which, if it was not perhaps love, at least bore some resemblance to it. Tenderly, he kissed the hand which had bestowed this royal gift upon him.

'My Queen, I shall not forget this.'

The kiss that followed was warmed by his gratitude and when, half an hour later, Maria Luisa at last tore herself from his arms to return to the palace, he did not feel the same relief as on other mornings. His first impression, when she had summoned him to her room on that first evening had been right: the future Queen of Spain was a woman desperately seeking happiness. And God alone knew the power a clever man might

59

wield through her once she wore the crown, for one did not have to be long at Court to realize Prince Charles was a mere simpleton, mild and credulous to the point of idiocy, living in permanent awestruck admiration of his wife. The real ruler would be Maria Luisa, but who would be the ruler of Maria Luisa?

'God help Spain,' Gilles murmured to himself as he wrapped the ring in his handkerchief before slipping it into his belt with the pleasant sensation that what he was pressing to his side was one of the old stones of La Hunaudaye.

His heart felt content, his mind at ease. The affair which had begun to irk him was about to end of its own accord, through force of circumstances, without hurt or recriminations, he was sure of that, and when, later, he looked back on it, it would not leave the bitter taste that he had feared.

A clock somewhere struck three. It was high time he went and got some rest. Softly, Gilles let himself out of the pavilion, closed the door behind him and began to stroll along the river, filling his lungs with the cool night air. It was deliciously sweet, the whole garden filled with fragrance.

An owl hooted close beside him. Almost in the same instant, a number of masked men sprang out of the bushes and fell on the young man. Before he could so much as draw his sword, he was bound and gagged with the efficiency of long practice.

When he was totally helpless, one of his attackers, a great dark giant of a fellow, hoisted him on to his back and they set off along the river to a tiny clearing planted with umbrella pines, where three paths met and a short flight of steps ran down to the Tagus.

From his uncomfortable perch, the prisoner was able to make out the figure of a man standing in the middle of this space, apparently waiting. The outline was vaguely familiar. A commanding voice, making no effort to speak softly, called out: 'Is it done?'

'Yes, Sire. We have him here,' someone answered.

'Very well. Put him down.'

Gilles' bearer deposited him roughly, a fact which at that moment was the least of his worries. If the King had taken the trouble to arrange this trap himself, then the rash Maria Luisa's lover was lost indeed.

Lying stretched out on the cold marble of the little landing stage, Gilles watched the King approach with his odd, bow-legged horseman's stride. His stomach cramped with sudden terror. If his hands had been free, he would have used them instinctively to make the sign of the cross, for never had a man looked so like the devil. With his drooping nose, grinning mouth, dead eyes and stooping shoulders, Charles III's ugliness was at once repulsive and satanic. Behind him suddenly showed the black robe of a monk.

The King stared down for a moment at the bundle laid at his feet. Then he nodded.

'Take off the gag for a minute so that Father Joaquin can hear his confession. Then put it back and do as I ordered you.'

He was already moving away but, on an afterthought, turned back and addressed the prisoner.

'I am sorry to have to do this to you, my boy. Unless I execute you as an example, every man in the Bodyguard will soon be familiar with my daughter-in-law's charms.'

Temporarily released from his gag, Gilles used the opportunity to protest.

'But this is not an execution, Sire! It's murder! Executions are carried out in daylight, where everyone can see. How else can it be an example? Put me to death, if you will, but let it be before the world.'

'An execution is as I decide. Moreover, you will agree that if you were to mount the scaffold, you would take with you your mistress's reputation – not to mention that of her husband. What matters is to frighten the woman so that she behaves. And when your body is found, she will be frightened. She's not a fool and she'll know how it happened.'

Death was too near for Tournemine not to strain every nerve to keep it at bay.

'I am a Frenchman, Sire, and an officer of King Louis the Sixteenth! I am not yours to dispose of. You have no right—'

'I have every right! You yourself acknowledged that the day you signed yourself into my service. You knew quite well that in return for my gold I had the right to ask for your blood, to the last drop. It is, I concede, more glorious to die in battle, rather than drowned like a rat in a river, even a royal one. But you should have thought of that before you cuckolded a Prince

61

of Asturia. And you may console yourself with the thought that, in a way, your death will be serving the Spanish crown. Farewell, Sir. God have mercy on you. Father, do your office.'

He strode off. Gilles writhed furiously in his bonds.

'If you wanted to keep this a secret, you should have killed me yourself. Your murderers may talk, repeat what you've said about your son and your daughter-in-law.'

Charles III turned briefly. His shoulders lifted.

'They are mutes, and I have taken care they never learned to write. Die in peace, young man.'

In another moment, the shadows had swallowed him. The monk, who was Father Joaquin d'Eleta, the King's confessor, signed to the mutes to move away and knelt beside the condemned man.

'It is time for you to confess your sins, my son.'

The monk's oily voice, sugary with false sympathy, was the last straw to Gilles' flaring anger.

'Go to the devil! I don't need a murderer's help to face my God! Kill me, since that's what you're here for, only leave me alone.'

'You are not willing to make confession?' Gilles almost laughed at the incredulous horror in the other's voice.

'Not to you, at all events. So that you may go and tell your master everything I've said.'

'The secrets of the confessional are sacred, you should know that.'

'That depends on the confessor.'

Father Joaquin stood up, towering over the man on the ground. He crossed himself deliberately.

'God have mercy on your soul. I forgot that you come from a land where godlessness is spreading like the wind. Die, then, in sin, if that is your desire.'

He made a sign to the mutes and moved away. The men approached, refastened the gag and lifted Gilles from the ground. One holding him by the feet, another by the shoulders, they carried him down the steps of the landing stage. One quick swing and the bound figure curved briefly through the air and fell with a resounding splash into the Tagus. Gilles filled his lungs in one despairing breath before he hit the water.

His mind fumbled for a prayer but all that came into it was the bizarre thought that now the emerald hidden in his belt would never help to save La Hunaudaye, and old Joel Gauthier would wait in vain.

His eyes were open and he seemed to be sinking into an inky abyss. The water was cool, but that was the last pleasant thing he was conscious of. His boots, filling with water, dragged him inexorably downwards. Soon he felt as if his lungs would burst. The blood thundered in his temples. The air in his chest was bursting to come out.

He did his best to breathe out through his nose, for his gagged mouth was no help to him now, but the water only rushed into his dilated nostrils while images of his short life chased one another through his brain. He was choking. Death was almost upon him, death by water which had always been his friend. His body jerked in a last spasm and then, mercifully, he lost consciousness.

When he came to, it was to a belief that he was in hell. It was still just as dark and some kind of watery demon was tearing at his chest as though trying to extract his ribs.

With an agonized groan, he vomited a stream of water, which produced a grunt of satisfaction from his torturer.

'Better,' said Pongo, and turned his master over on to his stomach to help him to get rid of the water he had swallowed.

Gilles discovered that he was lying on the grass of the river bank, not far from the little landing stage, and still very much alive. Someone had removed his tunic and his boots. In the cool, pre-dawn air he was shivering.

'Pongo!' he gasped, through chattering teeth. 'H-how did you d-do it? What m-miracle b-brought you here?'

'Pongo disobey master. Pongo follow every night. Great Spirit warn of danger. Woman bring bad mischief.'

Gilles lay back for a moment on the soft grass, slowly getting his breath back and feeling his heartbeats return to normal. Mentally, he was thanking God for saving him. Death had never seemed so near. Pulling Pongo out of the flooded Delaware had evidently been the best day's work of his life.

'I can't think straight,' he said weakly when at last he was able to sit up without the earth turning upside down. 'What do you suggest we do now?'

'Run. Run quick, before daylight. They think you dead. You know place to go?'

'That's not what's worrying me. Francisco de Goya could certainly hide me, or the Baron de Batz, if I can find him. Or even the Cabarrus, perhaps. Luckily, I've plenty of friends. But I don't want to leave without Merlin. He's still in the stables and I won't leave my horse for these swine!'

'Pongo think. Pongo go fetch. But you go now. See!' He waved his hand towards the other side of the river. 'Over there, by road to city. Plenty trees and bushes. You hide there and wait.'

On the far side of the Tagus ran the main road to Madrid. No railings or guard posts lay between, the width of the river was considered protection enough for the royal park it enclosed.

'Better you swim,' the Indian went on. 'You have strength?'

Gilles began to laugh.

'If I told you I was dying for a swim, you wouldn't believe me I dare say, but don't worry. I'll manage. Thanks to you, I'm not merely alive but as well as ever. I won't forget what you've done, my friend,' he added feelingly and, laying his hand on the Indian's shoulder, gripped it with reassuring firmness. The long rabbit's teeth gleamed happily in the darkness.

'You save Pongo once in River Delaware. Now Pongo save you in Spanish river. Very good. All right. Pongo happy.'

Left alone, Gilles stretched carefully, testing the elasticity of his muscles. Then, making a bundle of his sodden uniform coat and the boots which had nearly been his death, he weighted them with a large stone or two and, since he had no means of getting them to the other side, consigned them to the river again. As well leave as few traces as possible.

It was then he remembered Maria Luisa's gift and, feeling in his belt, discovered to his joy that the emerald was still there. He said a mental thank you to her, thinking she might spare a tear for him before replacing him with someone else. This was going to be a serious check in his fortunes, but at least he wouldn't have lost everything. Then, bracing himself, he slid into the black water and swam vigorously to the other side, where he was able to haul himself out without much difficulty. He rested there for a moment to get his breath back. The place

64

was deserted and the silence complete until it was broken by the sound of a cock crowing. Dawn was not far off now. Getting to his feet, Gilles made his way towards the clump of trees Pongo had pointed out to him. He was not even conscious of the stones underfoot. One of the gifts of his stay in America was the hardening of the soles of his feet which enabled him, at need, to go, like the Indians, without shoes.

Soon afterwards, just as the sky in the east was starting to pale, a sound of galloping hooves was heard and Pongo appeared, mounted on his own charger and leading Merlin by the bridle. Gilles caught sight of his valise strapped to the crupper and breathed another prayer of thanks. The invaluable Pongo had managed somehow to get into his master's rooms and lay hands on his weapons and the greater part of his belongings. Gilles could have hugged him.

'You really are my guardian angel, Pongo! I don't know what I'd do without you. To horse, now. I can dress later. It's nearly daylight.'

With Merlin under him, a wave of unfamiliar happiness swept over Gilles. It was a long time since he had felt so glad to be alive. He was glad, too, to be on the road again. In Spain he was dead, his business now was to return to France where he might come to life again at his leisure.

One thing was certain, he would feel no regrets for this scorching land, wilder even than his native Brittany. The affair with Maria Luisa had become a burden and, in his heart, he still cherished a longing for France and the twofold service he had left behind him, to good King Louis, whom he was glad to call master, and to Judith, whose bittersweet memory he found lodged ever more deeply in his heart after each new encounter with another woman; Judith, of whom he had heard no news at all since his arrival in Spain. Had the Provost of Paris and the Lieutenant of Police really been searching for her, or had they nothing but fine words to offer? Deep down, Gilles knew himself well enough to be sure that he could never have borne this silence, this lack of any information for years, or even months on end. Not even if he had been able to satisfy his fancy for the fair unknown maja.

You'll never taste her kisses now, my lad, he told himself as Merlin's hooves thudded lightly over the dusty yellow road. A night or two at Paco's, long enough to warn Jean so that he won't believe me dead and appropriate my possessions prematurely, and then it's the high road for sweet France for us. Back to where people are civilized!

They rode for an hour, by which time Gilles' chilled muscles had warmed up, then halted by a half-ruined barn not far from the road where he was able to dress himself in a more orthodox fashion. The sun, the wind of the ride and the warmth of his body had more or less dried shirt and breeches, so he did no more than put on a coat of plain grey cloth and a pair of soft leather boots of the same colour and run a comb through his thick fair hair. This done he grinned broadly at Pongo.

'I'm dying of hunger. I know I'm supposed to be dead already, but I could still eat a horse. Haven't you anything in your saddlebags?'

'Not a thing. Time too short to visit kitchens.'

'Then we'll have to find an inn. There is one by the Jajama bridge. I don't expect it's any better than the rest, but we're sure to find bread and onions and a jug of wine. The great advantage of being dead is that no one is likely to pursue me.'

Despite this fine conviction, Gilles and Pongo, crossing the narrow Roman bridge whose pointed arch spanned the Jajama, moved with the instinctive caution of men on the wrong side of the law. Once in sight of the inn, they saw a vehicle already drawn up before it.

Nor was it just any vehicle, such as frequented the rutted lane which, in Spain, went by the dignified name of Camino Real. It was not one of the heavy leather aproned stage coaches, packed with dispirited travellers, or even one of the *coche de colleras*, great creaking coaches with room for no more than six passengers, not was it the swift cabriolet belonging to some young man of fashion. It was an equipage so splendid that it could only belong to some noble grandee of Spain, a fact indeed proclaimed by the armorial complexities painted on the panels.

Pongo shot out one hand to grasp his master's arm while with the other he pointed to the carriage, its black lacquer and gleaming brasswork brilliant in the sunshine, under only the lightest powdering of dust. But Gilles had already decided on his course.

'My *execution* took place in secret,' he said with a shrug, 'and I've not lived long enough in Spain to know or be known by many people. Anyway, what the devil! I'm hungry.'

Under the interested gaze of the platoon of servants and outriders in red and gold livery grouped round the carriage, he hitched his mount to one of the wooden posts outside the inn and made for the doorway. But he stopped short on the threshold, catching his breath. A woman was standing there, and she was none other than the lovely maja whose image had so haunted his thoughts. The lovely maja, his one regret at leaving Spain.

It was she, and yet not altogether she. The clothes she wore were not those usually associated with women of her sort. She had on a dress like a riding habit made in smooth, heavy silk of the same deep red as her lips, moulded gracefully to her slender waist. Fine lace foamed at her wrists and throat and, perched at a jaunty angle on the dark mass of her hair which was dressed in the latest Paris style, was a wide red hat, trimmed with a saucy white feather. The white gloved hand holding up the long skirts of her habit was adorned with a single magnificent ring, as magnificent as the ruby, trembling on a thin gold chain, which lay like blood on her breast.

Their eyes met and locked fast. Gilles had forgotten his hunger, his weariness, even his haste to reach Madrid. This woman's beauty blotted out the whole world, the landscape of scorched earth with its few trees stunted by the winds of the Castilian winter, and the wizened figures of the occasional ragged peasant in dusty sandals.

The lovely painted lips parted in a sudden smile which, travelling upwards, illumined the black eyes.

'What chance brings you here, Sir?' the lady said softly, in impeccable French with the faintest musical hint of accent.

Conscious that this woman was something quite other than he had supposed at first, Gilles stepped back to let her pass and bowed deeply.

'A fortunate chance, Madame, since it has brought me, what I had despaired of, another glimpse of you.'

She acknowledged his bow with a glint of amusement, tapping her skirts with the light riding cane she carried.

'How very punctilious you are today, Chevalier. I seem to

67

recall that on the occasion of our last meeting at Carabanchel you called me your fair one?'

'Majas in general like to be spoken to in their own language. At Carabanchel, that is what you were . . .'

'And today, what am I, if you please?'

'I do not know. A noblewoman, I imagine. That carriage fits too well with your dress not to be yours, although I have not seen you at Court. Which does not alter the fact that you are still, to my eyes, the loveliest woman in all Spain.'

The smile deepened.

'The woman who cannot accept a compliment, even one a trifle crudely phrased, is either a fool or a hypocrite. But why do you say you despaired of seeing me again?'

'Because, Madame, I am leaving Spain, with no hope of ever returning.'

The beautiful black eyebrows lifted delicately above the great dark eyes.

'You are leaving Spain? Just when, it is said, you are most high in favour? That is strange.'

'The heights are full of pitfalls. And favours can be dangerous. I must return to France, Madame. The sooner the better. I am more sorry than you can think—'

But she had ceased to listen to him. For the past few seconds her eyes had been, not on him, but on some point in the distance, an expression of anxiety in them. Gilles turned in surprise to follow the direction of her look and saw two horsemen sweeping, as though shot from a gun, down the stony slope beyond the bridge down which he had come a few minutes before. He had no need to look closely to know that they were alguazils.

They thundered across the bridge and drew rein by a big dead tree not far from the inn. Dismounting, one took a scroll of paper from his saddle and unrolled it. The young woman's gloved hand came to rest uneasily on Gilles' arm.

'Back into the inn,' she said sharply. 'There is no one there at present.'

'That is precisely what I meant to do. I'm very hungry. But—'

'Don't argue, Chevalier. Do as I tell you. If you're hungry, tell Pedro, the innkeeper, to get you something. He has a decent ham. Only don't, whatever you do, come outside. Hurry. And take your servant with you. Wait for me in there.'

Gilles obeyed without further argument and plunged into the half-darkness of the interior. He had time to hear one of the alguazils rounding up the bystanders with the aid of a small drum while the other was evidently preparing to read the paper aloud.

Inside, it was impossible to hear anything at all. An old woman, crouched in the ashes of the hearth at one end of the smoky room, was cleaning saucepans with a noise like a drum-roll, while in the opposite corner a boy was chopping kindling for the fire. An ill-favoured man, dressed in dirty linen, with a large knife stuck in the red woollen waistband stretched across his stomach, emerged almost under Gilles' feet from a hole in the ground which was presumably the cellar.

'What do you want, *hombre*?' he asked roughly.

'Food. Drink.'

'I've none here. On your way.'

Tournemine had little to learn about Spanish inns. He had long discovered that if you wanted to find any comforts there, you must provide them yourself. All the same, it was generally possible to obtain bread and onions, and now and then tomatoes with which to make a salad, seasoned with the oil used in the lamps.

'For an innkeeper, that's not very welcoming,' Gilles said, his hand playing with the hilt of his sword. 'The lady who just went out mentioned a ham ...'

'The lady— Oh, well, in that case, señor, be pleased to sit. You shall be served in an instant.'

Transformed, suddenly, into all eager obsequiousness, the man flicked a cloth over a rickety table and, as if by magic, conjured up a huge ham, barely started, some flat bread, not too hard, the traditional salad of tomatoes and onions mixed in lamp oil and a jug of wine, less vinegary than usual. But Gilles was too hungry to waste time wondering over his host's sudden change of heart. He seated himself opposite Pongo and set about recruiting his strength.

Nor was it long before the lovely unknown returned, looking so obviously anxious that Gilles put down his mug and rose. Waving the innkeeper away with a brusque flick of her gloved hand, the lady came towards him.

'Finish your meal quickly, Chevalier. I'm taking you with me. In any case, I have no business at Aranjuez now.'

'You are taking me with you? Forgive me, madame, but I don't understand.'

'There's no time to explain now. You can tell me all about it in Madrid. But you must know that they are searching for you. There is a price on your head and the alguazils you saw arrive are going to proclaim it along every road in Spain.'

'But that's impossible! How can they be searching for me? They threw me into the Tagus, on the King's orders, and before his very eyes. Everyone thinks I'm dead.'

'"Anyone encountering the Frenchman by name Gilles de Tournemine de la Hunaudaye, lieutenant in the Bodyguard of his Most Catholic Majesty King Charles III, condemned to death by royal command and now in hiding, is hereby authorised to apprehend and deliver him to the proper authorities,"' she said, quoting, and added: 'There follows a fairly accurate description of yourself, your servant and the sum to be paid for your capture. Five thousand reals. There must have been a witness to your rescue. The palace is stuffed with spies. Well, will you come with me? I may say that my people are at this moment putting my saddlecloths on your horses. Two of my servants will change clothes with you, so that you may reach Madrid unmolested. In my palace you will be safe. Will you come?'

Gilles stared at her for a moment. At once imperious and beseeching, she possessed an indefinable charm which was not easy to resist. Nevertheless, he did his best.

'We have never been introduced,' he said, 'and yet you are prepared to upset all your plans to help me. It's not right. You said you were going to Aranjuez? Well, you must go.'

'No. I told you also that I had no more business there. If you must know, the reason I was going was to warn you. The rumours in the Plaza Mayor made it clear to me that if you were not already in danger, you soon would be. I had no wish to hear of your death, nor have I now.'

'I am deeply touched. But I have no right to let you run such risks. I am nothing to you and there is no reason why you should put yourself in danger.'

The young woman laughed, a low, musical laugh, and stepped closer to Gilles, until they were almost touching.

'I have a thousand reasons,' she said, looking up at him so boldly that he thought for a moment she was offering him her lips. 'The soundest of them is that I loathe and despise Maria Luisa. She is a fool, a sick woman and a monster of selfishness. I love to serve her an ill turn. As for the risk to me, it is minimal, in fact non-existent. Do not let it give you ideas. I am not in love with you. I like you, as I like everything handsome. That is all.'

'Then I thank you. But I find it hard to believe you are not running into danger.'

'Not in the least. In fact I am probably the one woman in Spain who can flout both King and Court with impunity. Anyone is safe in my house for neither Charles nor his ministers, nor even the Holy Inquisition would dare to lift a finger against me. There is not woman in all Spain greater than I.'

'Then you are—'

'I had hoped you might have known me, at least from my shocking reputation, and from my many portraits. Yes, Chevalier, I am the Duchess of Alba. Now will you wear my livery for a while? To get you into Madrid, at least?'

In answer, Gilles bowed deeply, hand on heart, in the best Castilian manner.

'Your grace has only to command, and I obey.'

71

3

Hunted

So that was who she was! Maria Pilar Cayetana de Silva Alvarez de Toledo, thirteenth Duchess of Alba, possessor of eight ducal coronets, fifteen marquisates, twenty counties and any number of other titles. The greatest lady in all Spain, as she herself had so sweepingly declared, although without the slightest suggestion of conceit. For her it was the simple truth, no more, no less.

The greatest, but also the strangest and most fantastic. Court and city both re-echoed daily to the rumours of her freakish whims, and the incessant war she waged against the two other most prominent women in society, the Princess of Asturia and the Duchess of Benavente.

With the first of these, her quarrel existed on a somewhat abstract plane. Shut up in her palaces under the suspicious eye of her father-in-law, Maria Luisa took little part in the life of Madrid. Cayetana d'Alba dealt with her in pinpricks, in little insolences of dress on the days of handkissing, at which she would generally appear dressed in morning dress, her fabulous jewels borne behind her by servants.

These jewels were, in fact, the one ground over which the two women were openly at loggerheads. Both shared the same passion for fine stones, a passion which the jewellers were at pains to exploit, although the problems of diplomacy involved were now and then acute. For although the duchess might be richer than the princess, still, it might prove unwise always to give her the preference.

With Doña Josefa, Duchess of Benavente and Ossuna,

things were altogether different. These two were in blatant competition for the leadership of Spanish society.

Ten years older than Cayetana, Doña Josefa had seen her title as reigning queen of fashion filched from her by the younger woman. Moreover, since the two were equally addicted to building, one could no sooner put up a palace than the other hastened to do the same, even more luxuriously, and they divided the artists between them.

Bosom friends on the surface, sworn enemies underneath, they could agree on nothing except their common loathing of the Princess of Asturia, who seemed to have the doubtful privilege of putting both their backs up.

Curbing his restless mount level with the duchess's carriage door, Gilles, in the outrider's livery, glanced now and then at the charming profile visible within. Cayetana was even lovelier than he remembered. The luxury with which she was surrounded suited her, emphasizing her imperious sweetness. All the same, he was a little disappointed, a little sorry to lose his provocative maja, her eyes heavy with promise and her whole being alive with sensuality. This was a simpler, more straightforward woman, and love with her would be an adventure, exciting but short-lived. She was too great a lady. She lived on a pinnacle so lofty that it was hard to forget it, even if it pleased her now and then to descend to a less rarefied atmosphere.

Goya, who was on excellent terms with the Duchess of Benavente, of whom he had already painted one most beautiful portrait, had a good deal to say about her young rival, but it seemed probable that some of it was inspired by pique, since he had not been summoned to the Alba palace to immortalize Doña Cayetana's lovely face on canvas, as he might have expected after completing a portrait of Josefa. And in fact it was unusual, given the enthusiasm with which one was in the habit of lifting friends from the other. So unusual that the painter came near to regarding it as an insult to his skill.

'She seems positively to delight in shocking people,' Paco would say. 'She'd be more likely to exaggerate the numbers of lovers they credit her with. Women detest her and she, far from minding, revels in the almost universal loathing, as though nothing could touch her, she is so far above them. She's like a witch!'

However that might be, her magic was not, at that moment, working on Tournemine. The affair with Maria Luisa had rid him of any desire to become the plaything of a great lady again, however beautiful. He did not like having his life arranged for him, even for the purpose of saving it, and while God knew how ardently he had desired the lovely maja, he was far from inclined to become the lover of the autocratic Cayetana.

Madrid parted like the sea beneath the prow of a ship before the Duchess of Alba's foaming horses. It was the hour of vespers. The city was full of life, despite the heat, which was still intense. The narrow, crooked streets, humpy with ill-laid cobbles, staggering from hill to hill between the sealed white cubes of low houses, with their slim, barred windows and heavy dark wooden doors, were thick with people. Here and there, the brilliant green of a garden softened the still feudal bulk of an ancient palace, its time-smoothed walls rising sharply as a drawing in pen and ink above the endless white of the peasants' dwellings.

The coach hurtled on without a second's pause, spreading panic among the chickens, geese, dogs and cats cluttering the thoroughfare almost as much as the human traffic, until it came to the less congested eastern district. It passed through a gateway, climbed the slope to a noble façade of new stone, and stopped before a vast door which opened, as if by magic, to reveal the dark figure of a majordomo, an army of lackeys and the fine curves of a great staircase. Already, the duchess had opened the door with her own hand and, springing out, hastened towards the stairs, making a sign to Gilles to follow.

He had barely time to toss his bridle to Pongo and go after her. She was already halfway up the stairs, throwing an order to her majordomo as she went. He bowed and loftily waved away the host of waiting women making towards her.

The duchess moved swiftly and lightly down a long gallery where some excellent Flemish pictures alternated with French tapestries on the walls. A door opened to her hand, giving on to a small room done in gold rococo and sea-green silk to which the sun, filtering through the lowered blinds, gave the watery hues of an underwater cavern.

Inside, Cayetana, pulling out hatpins, shook out the curling

74

mass of her hair, then, going to a side table, poured out two glasses and offered one to her guest. That done, she dropped heavily into a dainty armchair and sighed.

'You are safe now, Chevalier. So, while a room is being prepared for you, let us talk. Sit down. Either you are too tall or this room is too small, but you are filling it.'

Gilles drained his glass. The journey had seemed endless. He was thirsty and the Alicante wine was excellent. Then he said abruptly:

'Is it really necessary to have a room made ready for me? You have enabled me to enter Madrid without falling into the hands of the alguazils and for that, your grace, I am most deeply grateful. But I have no intention of troubling you further.'

'Then where will you go? Have I not told you that in my house you have nothing to fear?'

'I do not doubt that for a moment. But I am a soldier, madame, and a soldier's life is not spent in the avoidance of fear. Since I am now a hunted man, my wish is to return immediately to France, from which I have no more than leave of absence, and resume my duties there.'

'What are you in France?'

'A lieutenant in the Queen's Dragoons. I should have stayed there for, to tell the truth, there is nothing to match the service of one's rightful king.'

'If you believe that, why are you here? What did you come to Spain to find?'

Gilles laughed.

'My answer will probably damn me in your eyes, madame. I came for money.'

As he had expected, Cayetana's lip curled in light, urbane contempt.

'Money? What for?'

The naïvety of the question amused Gilles. For centuries, the treasures of Flanders, Spain and the Americas had poured into the coffers of the Dukes of Alba and their latest heir was so accustomed to the filthy lucre that she really could not see why others should seek it. A man suffering from indigestion would always be sickened by the appetite of a famished one.

'To buy back my lands and the home of my ancestors. The price is very high.'

75

'How high?'

'Five hundred thousand livres. An enormous sum.'

'Not a great deal. But I suppose your royal mistress must have been delighted to make you a gift of this – bagatelle, to judge by your haste to return to France. Indeed—'

Before she could finish, the young man was on his feet. In his eyes was the hard gleam of cold steel. He bowed icily.

'I am at your feet, duchess, but one thing I must say. When a woman, queen or no, bestows her favours on a gentleman, that gentleman, were he as poor as Job, would be betraying his honour if he permitted her one glimpse of his financial embarrassments.'

'Yet you told me?'

'You asked me a question and I answered it. Nor, I believe, have I the honour to be your lover.'

The insolence of his tone did not seem to displease Cayetana. She smiled, letting her eyelids droop and gazing up at him through her lashes with consummate art.

'Why should you not be?' she shot at him boldly. 'Have I not said I like you?'

'Yes, but I am not such a coxcomb as to take you at your word. Besides, that is not enough.'

'It is enough for me. Is my memory at fault or did you not say to me, not so long ago: "Whenever and wherever you please"?'

Gilles bowed with a respect so exaggerated that it was an insult.

'I did say so – but not to the Duchess of Alba. I said it to someone else, a stranger, the queen of the Manolas who make the streets of Madrid a garden of wild flowers. I was drawn to her bold beauty, I confess it. She was simple, free, full of joy – and I know now that she was no more than a dream.'

He bowed, turned on his heel and walked to the door. Cayetana's foot stamped furiously on the gleaming floor.

'Now where are you going? Are you mad?'

'By no means. I have told you once. I am going back to France. In the meanwhile, I am going to seek shelter for a day or two with a friend I trust.'

'Will you not stay here?'

Her voice was all at once soft and winsome, like a little girl deprived of her favourite toy.

'No. I thank you. I should be too much afraid of playing an equivocal role in this house. You are married, I believe, madame, and the Duke of Alba—'

'There is no Duke of Alba! My husband bears that title for no other reason than because he is my husband. You may forget him, as you forgot the Prince of Asturia. That poor fool Carlos matters no more to his wife than my husband, the Marquis de Villafranca, does to me.'

'Which is no reason to offend him under his own roof. And I know that, living close to you, I could not help my thoughts being a continual offence. Farewell, duchess. You have saved my life and for that my life is yours, always at your service.'

'But your nights are not?' she said, smiling faintly.

'You may say so. Oh, I almost forgot.' As he spoke he was stripping off the outrider's coat which had been given him at the inn and he tossed it onto a chair.

'Will you be good enough to restore my own clothes, my servant and our horses?'

'You're mad, you're mad, I tell you. You'll be sought for in Madrid more busily than anywhere. And like that you'll stand out as clearly as the Escurial in the middle of the Sierra. Even that Red Indian servant of yours is as well known as the White Wolf in Madrid. Besides, where are you going? Who is this friend you trust?'

'A painter. Don Francisco de Goya y Lucientes. He has a studio in the Rastro district – a studio he keeps a secret from his wife and where he goes to paint – to paint in his own way.'

The woman's face flushed with anger.

'Goya! The Benavente's friend and favourite painter. And it is to him that you are going?'

'Yes. He is my friend, madame. He is a true, an honest and a courageous man. I know you do not like him. Yet you should try to win him to you because he is a great artist, the greatest painter Spain has produced for a long time.'

Cayetana made a face. 'His work has not seemed to me so wonderful,' she said. 'But I agree he is a brave man – and a fine matador. I saw him fight once and I thought that he and the bull were much alike. Very well, go to him if you insist. But, take my advice, wear the livery and keep the saddlecloth with my arms on your horse. It may safeguard you a little. Tomorrow, I will send your servant and the other horse, disguised. It will be wiser. *Au revoir*, Chevalier.'

He came back then and, dropping to one knee, kissed the hand she held out to him.

'Farewell, your grace. I shall carry away the memory of your kindness – and a great sorrow that things have not been other than they are.'

In a charming gesture, she carried the hand he had just kissed to her cheek.

'I said *au revoir*, Chevalier, not farewell. We shall meet again.'

'If it please God.'

'It pleases me, and must therefore please Him also.'

After the splendours of the Alba palace, it was with something of relief that Gilles plunged into the maze of mean streets, the *barrios bajos* of Madrid. The scents of orange trees in flower and French perfumes gave place to odours of frying onions, coarse wine and unwashed bodies, but the crowds, girls with carnations in their oiled and gleaming hair, cheeky, ragged urchins, old women draped in black shawls, marbled with the dust, and lean, shifty-eyed gipsies, all thrust Aranjuez, its luxuries and the scented peril of its gardens, back into the limbo of time. Moreover, the Alba livery was a good passport. The whimsical duchess was both loved and respected and the dense stream moving towards the banks of the Manzanares good-naturedly made room for him when they took him for a servant of hers.

It was therefore without incident that Gilles gained the tiny square, beflagged with washing lines, off which lay the house the painter had selected as his secret retreat. All he had to hope now was that Goya would be there, but the nearness of the Pradera, which would see the whole neighbourhood given over to rejoicing by the morning, gave him grounds for hope

A small boy, a beggar who might have stepped straight out of one of Murillo's canvases, was sitting in the doorway, stroking a little cat and humming the tonadilla being played by an invisible guitarist inside the nearby tavern.

'*Es el señor Goya aquí?*' Gilles asked, slipping a coin into the child's hand.

'*Si, caballero.*'

He had to knock three times. The painter was there all right but he must have been working because it was a long time before the door opened on his swarthy face and dubious eye.

'It's me, Paco,' Gilles said softly. 'Open quickly. I mustn't stand out here.'

But already the door had been flung wide and the painter's hand was drawing man and horse vigorously inside. Still holding the bridle, he led them into the little sunlit inner courtyard where a fat ginger cat lay snoozing on a wall.

'What's this you're wearing?' Goya said suddenly, startled eyes on his friend. 'Have you entered Alba service now?'

'Give me a glass of wine and I'll tell you. Can you keep me here for a day or two?'

'Aha! It's come to that, has it?'

'You're the one with his ear to the blind beggar's gossip. Don't you know?'

Goya gestured to the fresh paint spattering his smock and breeches. There was paint even in his hair.

'I've been shut up here painting for the past two days and nights. I wasn't going out until tomorrow, for the Pradera. But of course you can stay, as long as you like. My house is yours. We'll have a drink and celebrate.'

'I'm afraid there may not be much celebration in it,' Gilles said with a laugh. 'I must leave Spain as fast as possible if I want to stay alive. Besides, I don't want to make trouble for you. They're after me.'

'I'm not surprised. But how are you planning to get out of the country?'

'I think I have an idea. But it would help if you could warn my friend Jean de Batz. He must be wondering what's up, in any case, because he's probably the first person they went to to look for me.'

Goya slipped his arm through his friend's.

'Let's not stay here. It's never wise to talk in the open in

Madrid, even between walls. You can never be sure the Holy Office isn't listening at the door. It's nowhere near as virulent as it was, but it still exists, alas. We'll be better indoors. And Micaela might wonder ...'

'Micaela?'

'Come in and you'll see. You are my friend. You've a right to know all about me.'

The painter's studio was a rather large room to which a long north light covered with an awning gave a cooler light than would have seemed possible from the bright sunshine outside. The only furniture, apart from a large painted wooden stature of Our Lady of Atocha, for which Goya had a real reverence, was a large easel, a number of scattered canvases, pots of paint, dirty palettes and a low divan covered with a jumble of shawls and cushions. But once inside the room, Gilles noticed none of this. He simply opened his eyes wide and stared. In front of him, on a low dais, was a beautiful girl, holding up the dark mass of her hair as though about to enter her bath. It was not her presence, though, which startled him but the fact that she was perfectly naked and, as one glance was enough to show him, ravishingly lovely.

'This is Micaela,' the painter said in French. 'Pretty, isn't she? Her body, I mean. Unfortunately, her face doesn't match up to it.'

'Very,' Gilles agreed. His eyes suddenly met those of the young woman and he saw in them a quick flicker of mischievous laughter, as though she were enjoying his evident embarrassment. He glanced away, at the unfinished canvas, and added: 'But I didn't know the kind of work you were doing here. It's not a bit like—'

'Like my tapestry sketches and my rustic gatherings and all the charming stuff a court painter can't avoid? I hope not! I wasn't made for the graces, *amigo mio*. I'm for the fullness of life, for digging my teeth into it until it splits and spurts like a tomato, I'm for painting everything that moves and flames and crawls in the bottom of men's souls, the nightmares as well as the ecstasies, the filth as well as the purest light.'

Thoughtfully, Gilles contemplated the portrait of Micaela. He was not a judge of painting but he had liked his friend's work instinctively, sensing, with the same sureness and certainty as he believed in God, that here was a great painter. But this was something outside his experience. Coming into the studio, he had seen only a pretty girl with no clothes on but, on the canvas, Micaela was transformed into a bold bacchante whose every inch of flesh, passionately delineated, was a sensual invitation. Goya had no need to say how fiercely he desired this girl: his picture cried it loud enough to raise the roof.

The painter's voice reached Gilles as though through a mist.

'You understand why I chose this poverty-stricken district? Why I go to ground here? To paint what I want to paint, I have to hide, like a thief. No one would understand ... and they would never forgive me. Josefa especially ... and the Holy Inquisition.'

The mention of Goya's wife drew a smile from Gilles. Doña Josefa, with her downcast eyes and unbending manner, was like a nun masquerading as a well-to-do bourgeoise. She did not care for her husband's painting. Only the conventional portraits done by her brother, the painter Bayou, found favour in her eyes. That, according to her, was the only respectable kind of painting, and she would have fainted with shock if she had been able to enter this studio which also contained a good many sketches of a dramatic, not to say horrifying kind: an all too realistic old beggar, a horse, its guts spilling into the sand of the arena, a man dying by the garrotte.

As for the Holy Inquisition, it would surely have despatched the audacious artist to its deepest dungeon without a second's hesitation, at the same time making a bonfire of his pictures in the Plaza Mayor.

Gilles returned from the canvas to his friend and looked at him curiously.

'What are you really like deep down, Paco?'

The painter showed him his most boyishly disarming smile, then turned its echo on the girl.

'A great deal of friendship for my fellow beings – and rather more than that for you, *hombre*. Get dressed, Micaela. I've done for today. I have to talk to my friend now.'

The model having resumed her dress and with it her character of an unremarkable servant girl, the two men were soon seated before the meal she brought them.

81

When Gilles had finished eating and telling his story, Goya fetched a large red pottery jar from a corner and offered him a long cigar from it.

'Speaking as a man, you were quite right to give Cayetana d'Alba the brush off,' he said. 'But, as a fugitive, it was a mistake. She could almost certainly have got you out of the country without trouble. How do you hope to manage it now?'

'Perhaps with some help from François Cabarrus, the banker. He owns ships and warehouses and has a great many connections. It shouldn't be difficult for him to get hold of a false passport. With that and a good disguise and God's help, I dare say I can get myself out of Spain without too much difficulty. It can't be any harder than escaping from a tribe of Indians in a forest.'

'Except that Señor Carbarrus lives at Carabanchel and to get there you've got to pass through the gates. I don't see how you'll manage that. There's usually a strong guard on them. I, on the other hand, can do it easily.'

'You would do that for me?'

Goya shrugged.

'Anyone would think it was a deed of daring! Just a nice little trip to Carabanchel. No one suspects me. Which reminds me, does your Gascon friend know what's happened?'

'No. I risked getting picked up if I went near him. They're bound to look for me there. 'Though I'd have liked to ask him for some money. I haven't a bean.'

'I'll go there too. Don't worry.'

'But Paco, what about your work?'

The painter was not listening. He was already pulling his paint-stained smock over his head. Only when his dark locks were emerging from the snowy folds of a freshly laundered shirt did he say calmly:

'My work can wait. And Micaela too. While I'm away she'll have enough to do catching up with the washing up and taking care of the house, which you will please look on as your own. Eat, drink and sleep. Make yourself at home. You'll probably need all your strength before much longer.'

It was late when Goya came back. The sound of the door closing woke Gilles, who was asleep on the divan, with a start.

82

In the yellow light of the candle he carried, Goya's face looked creased with worry, more troubled than ever.

'Well?' Gilles demanded.

The painter shrugged off the big black cloak he was wearing, and his sombrero with it. The heat had gone with the daylight and outside, with the wind sweeping down from the sierra, the night was cold.

'I've been everywhere but I've not managed to find your friend,' he said at last. 'I looked in the taverns and gaming houses, and even at the Benavente's, where he has been seen a good deal just recently. There was no one at his lodging, but his landlady, coming back from church, told me that the Numancia Dragoons left yesterday for Salamanca where there are student riots.'

Gilles made a face.

'My chances seem to be getting slimmer.'

'More so than you guess. I thought of going to your Cabarrus friends but tonight it's impossible. There are guards on the gates and the district is teeming with alguazils.'

'This district? But why? Have I been recognized? Followed?'

'I don't think so, but when a man wants to hide and doesn't know many people, it's in the poorest quarters that he stands the most chance. It's simply—' He broke off as Micaela came hurrying from the kitchen, looking distraught.

'There are people at the door! I'm wondering who it can be at this time of night.'

The two friends looked at one another in silence, each a prey to the same fear. If it was the police they would both end the night in prison and the week, perhaps, in the next world.

'I'm wondering too,' Goya said quietly. He was hurriedly turning his sketches to the wall and throwing a cloth over the shameless portrait of his maid. Outside, the brass knocker went on banging.

'I'm coming!' the painter yelled. Under his breath, he added: 'Go into the kitchen with Micaela. You'll be able to hear everything we say. If it looks bad, get up on to the roof and stay there until I come for you.'

'I'd better leave, Paco. That's the best way not to drag you into it.'

83

'The best way to get yourself caught. I told you, there are police spies all over the district. Do as I tell you. Believe me, this is no time for heroics.'

In silence, Gilles followed the maidservant out into the small kitchen, cluttered with cooking utensils and strings of onions in a wild confusion which said little for Micaela's domestic skills. There was, however, a small window through which it was possible to see what was going on in the courtyard. See and hear.

Paco's powerful voice floated up to them.

'Who's there?' he was asking roughly. 'What do you want?'

Not even Gilles' keen ear could catch the answer, muffled by the thickness of the wall, but he saw Goya open the door, then raise his lantern. The next moment he was bowing deeply.

A woman wrapped in a long black shawl appeared in the circle of light. Gilles did not have to look twice: peeping from the dark folds was the pale face of Cayetana d'Alba. His fears had fled and he turned to hurry back with something like joy in his heart. Why should the proud duchess have come to this squalid *barrio* except to see him?

He was in time to see her enter the studio, followed by the painter who was still evidently suffering somewhat from the surprise of this unexpected visitor. But, face to face with her, Gilles could find nothing more brilliant to say than: 'You!'

Her clear laugh cut across the doomladen air of the house.

'Of course. I wished to see for myself that you were in a safe place and not busy committing fresh idiocies.'

She cast off her shawl, revealing that she was dressed in the maja's costume Gilles had seen her in with Romero at the May Queen's crowning, and, leaving it where it fell, moved forward into the room, her bright eyes taking in everything.

'I hope you will forgive me for invading your – secret garden, like this, Señor Goya. You are not, I think, one of my admirers, or so I hear from Doña Josefa's many friends – of whom you are one.'

The artist bowed, one hand on his heart.

'Doña Josefa's many friends, who would rather die than number a mere painter among their elegant ranks, do not always know what they are talking about, your grace. How can one love or hate that which one does not know? Nor has the Duchess of Alba ever seemed aware of my humble existence.'

'*Touché*,' Cayetana cried merrily. 'I deserved that, señor – and I think I shall be aware of you in future.'

As she spoke, she swung round on the dainty feet, shod in black satin slippers, which showed to the ankle under her short skirt, and walking over to the easel twitched off the cloth with a decisive air.

Gilles, who was watching her, saw a sudden flush spread over her face and neck and an odd glint in her eyes. She was standing quite still, her hands clasped about her waist in the maja's favourite attitude, and he could see the whitening of her knuckles and the slim fingers tightening on the silk of her bodice. But when she turned back to the painter, her face was as unreadable as before.

'I do not think, Señor Goya,' she said slowly, 'that I shall be able to forget you in future. Your French friend told me you were a very great painter. He was right... Now, may I ask you to set the seal on your friendship by leaving me alone with him? I have much to say to him and time is short.'

The painter bowed without a word and, moving backwards to the door, closed it carefully behind him.

'Now that we are alone,' Cayetana said. 'It was extremely foolish of you to go to ground here, and even more foolish of me to come in search of you, but I could not leave you in the mess you'd got yourself into. May I know how far your plans have progressed and will you at least trust me so far as to tell me how you mean to get out of Madrid? The gates are shut fast, the alguazils are patrolling the streets—'

'Are you sure it's me they're after? After all, the King wanted me out of the way as discreetly as possible. And I don't see how he could have known so quickly that I didn't stay in the Tagus as long as he'd have liked.'

'In the simplest way in the world. There was a gardener hiding in his kitchen garden to guard his apricots from pilfering small boys. He saw the whole thing. He saw and heard everything, the sentence passed, your rejection of the last rites and finally your rescue by a demon with a red face and your flight. It was, of course, this last brilliant feat which convinced him you were in league with the devil. Once he got over his first fright, he made so much noise about it that it was no longer possible to keep the matter quiet, which is why you are now being hunted, not only by the King's people, but also by the Holy Inquisition, as a blasphemer and a sorcerer. In other words, if you are caught, what awaits you is the stake. So you see all this fuss being made about you is not without cause.'

For all his courage, Tournemine's face was white. The stake, that medieval horror, for a crime which amounted to nothing more than one additional pair of horns upon the august brow of a royal prince who already bore any number of them? It was enough to make the bravest blench. Yet he would not betray his revulsion and his voice, as he answered, was perfectly calm.

'If that is so, why did Goya not tell me the whole? By seeking refuge with him I have put him into far worse danger than I ever imagined.'

The duchess's beautiful, passionate face was suddenly grave.

'Far worse, for if you are taken here, the police will find this – and this – and this,' she said, pointing first to Micaela's portrait and then to other canvases as she turned them quickly. 'They will burn along with you. But this only goes to prove that Señor Goya possesses a greater spirit than I knew and that the word friendship has a strong meaning for him. Now, what are your plans?'

Gilles shook his head.

'I have none now. My friend Jean de Batz has gone with his regiment to Salamanca and as things are, I cannot possibly call on other friends.'

'Of whom were you thinking?'

'Cabarrus, the banker. I meant to ask him for a way to get to France in secret, either on one of his ships or by way of one of his frontier trading posts. But that is now out of the question. He has a family.'

'And financiers are not generally known for their chivalry. Well,' Cayetana concluded with a sigh, 'I fear you have no choice. I am all you have left.'

Gilles started.

'Madame, you have done all too much already, but that does not give you the right to insult me. Do you think I could allow a woman, even a duchess as powerful as a queen, to run the deadly risk that my friend Paco is doing? You must have a poor idea of me, if that is so.'

Hands still on hips and hips swaying as she walked, Cayetana came towards him, lifting up her face to look him in the eye. She laughed lightly.

'If that were my idea of you, my friend, I should not be here, for I hate cowards and especially those who try to hide behind other people's affections. All the same you know – or have you forgotten? – that I am a duchess like no other. As to the woman, you know already what her feelings are. But, I repeat, you have no choice. Accept my offer.'

'No, no! A thousand times no! I will not accept! You can hardly drag me away by force, I imagine?'

'Can't I?'

'No. In less than an hour, I shall have left this house.'

'Indeed? Then let us see how we may spend this hour, for I've no mind to leave you sooner. May I tell you a secret? I'm dying of hunger and thirst. Won't you go to the kitchen and see if you can find me something to eat? You, too, are going to need all your strength. Escaping is strenuous exercise.'

Gilles stared at her in perplexity, unable to work out what was going on behind that obstinate little forehead. Cayetana was strangely elusive. She could move from gravity to the most lighthearted flippancy, from tragedy to farce with staggering ease. Hard as steel at one moment, she could be flexible as a foil the next, yet without losing any of her strength. She was as changeable, and as formidable, as the Breton seas. But the ascendancy she had gained already over Gilles was unquestionable and it did not even occur to him to dispute it. So he bowed, not ill-pleased in his heart that this whim of hers would give him the pleasure of her company for a little longer and, with it, the sensual beauty which had reawakened the desire born of that carnival night and which only his pride had enabled him to reject.

'I'll go and see what I can find for you,' he said, moving towards the kitchen.

The little room, smelling of garlic and cooking oil, was empty. Goya and Micaela must have found their own means of occupying the time left on their hands. Gilles soon managed to assemble a jug of wine, some sweet peppers, a bit of ham and a

87

few sesame cakes. He put it all on a tray, added two wine glasses, plates and some cutlery and turned back to the studio, pushing the door open with his foot. The sight that met his eyes almost made him drop the lot on the tiled floor.

The little dais facing the unveiled portrait of the maid was no longer empty. Strewn in front of it were islands of black silk and white lace and standing in the exact attitude of the model, one hand holding up the black mass of her hair and emphasizing the hard swell of her breasts, was a naked woman, but this woman was not Micaela.

The eyes observing his reaction through the thick dark tresses mantling half her face were as black as the maid's but much more brilliant. The mouth, deep red, was parted in a teasing smile over perfect little teeth and the unclothed limbs had a sheen like pearl.

Gulping privately, Gilles showed nothing of it. Not an eyelid flickered as, without haste, he merely set the tray down on a stool then turned, like a lion-tamer facing a perilous beast, and caught and held the woman's eyes. Then, still standing a yard or two away from her, he undressed without speaking, revealing, with a shamelessness that matched her own, the strength of his desire. He saw her eyes widen and heard her breath quicken.

Not until then did he step swiftly on to the dais and take her with a rush that lifted her off the ground and gave her no chance to escape him, crushing her lips beneath his own.

Thrust off her balance, she squealed and dug her nails into his back, twisting like a snake in sudden pain, but already he had her on the divan.

Never before had he made love with such violence. It was foreign to his nature and he did not even try to analyse it. He was beside himself with a complexity of primitive emotions which included resentment of the casual, shameless way this woman had challenged him, anger at himself for having failed to resist her and also despair, because there seemed a strong likelihood that this silky form would be the last that he would ever embrace. The trap was set and his chances of leaving Madrid were slim. But he very quickly saw that his roughness had done him no disservice. Her body tensed, her eyes and cheeks wet with tears, she was gasping for breath but clung to him fiercely to a climax which all but threw them off the divan in its violence.

Soon after that, while he was still lying spreadeagled across her, his heart thudding against hers, her hand moved gently, caressing his back, with an odd timidity, as though she feared to reawaken the sleeping demon within him. Then, her mouth pressed very softly against his: 'Brute,' she whispered, the cooing tone belying the word. 'You hurt me, you know. Is that the way to treat a great lady?'

He recoiled from her as if she had burned him. In the cold eyes staring into hers there was no trace of the eager lover.

'Was that the great lady?' he said lightly. 'I saw no one but an alley cat in heat, a manola following her instincts. And since it was a creature I had long desired—'

She smiled at the insult, her supple hands running slyly over his skin.

'You *had*? I don't like your choice of tense. The hour is not yet done, my friend, although it seems you are.'

The lie to that came instantly. The hour was long gone, and a second and a third, punctuated by the watchman's musical cry and his heavy footsteps echoing in the street. And when at last she lay exhausted on her lover's breast, the murmuring voice was very humble:

'And now – will you listen, will you come with me?'

He kissed her delicately on her eyes, her lips, her breasts.

'No, my sweet – now less than ever. Thanks to you I shall now be strong enough to laugh at all the Holy Office can do.'

At that, she flew into a rage.

'Mule! Stubborn mule! You won't laugh at the stake! Do you think I could bear now to see you got up in a *sanbenito*, tied to a stake and writhing in the flames? And all because of that slut Maria Luisa? Did you or did you not say yesterday that your life was mine?'

'I did, but—'

'No buts. Then it seems to me I have the right to order that life as I see fit and in consequence I order you, yes, order, do you hear, I order you to wait here until I come for you tomorrow morning. No, no protests. You must not refuse. You have no right to because, you see, I think I have found an excellent way of getting you out of Madrid – and almost without risk.'

'*Almost!* You know—'

'Don't be silly. One can never be quite sure. But I love danger, it is the very spice of life to me, and I do not get it often enough. What we are going to do together will be great fun for me and I shan't forgive you if you take it away from me. What is more, if you must know, I need you in France. You can do me a great service there – a service I could not ask of anyone else. So you see, we are quits.'

'Is this true? I don't believe it! Tell me, then, what can I do?'

'No. Tomorrow. Tomorrow even the devil himself will be on my side. He'll have nothing else to do because of the festival. And don't worry. I'll not forget your Indian servant. Now it is time for me to go. No,' she added, seeing Gilles about to protest, 'I run no risks in the streets of Madrid at night, have no fear. The people know and love me. Enough at least for the blind beggars – to whom I give alms in secret – to say nothing of my visit to this unsavoury district. They keep to my encounters with the Benavente, where I usually get the last word. Trust me and wait! In any case, I'm going to tell Señor Goya to keep you under lock and key. You'll have to knock the house down to get out.'

She kissed him and was gone as suddenly and much more quietly than she had come. All that remained was her warm amber scent, recalling her presence as softly as a last caress. The house and the streets outside were silent once more. Only the melancholy watchman's call rang in the distance.

'Twelve o'clock and all Christians sleep!'

Hope stirring once more, Gilles gave himself up to God's will. God's and Cayetana's, who was quite capable of deflecting the purposes of the Almighty himself, being one of these women who are irresistible because the possibility of resistance simply never occurs to them.

This soothing silence was shattered just before daybreak by the clamour of bells from countless churches, the strains of guitars and clash of tambourines, by girlish laughter and boys shouting: Madrid was waking noisily beneath a mauve dawn sky to celebrate the festival of its patron Saint Isidore.

Paco's entrance, superbly dressed in a magnificent *majo*

costume of gold satin and black embroidery, brought the festival right into the studio. He gave off an atmosphere almost as sensual as the duchess's and seemed in high good humour, not at all as though the Frenchman's presence under his roof meant that any night he was in danger of incineration.

'If I don't want to attract attention, I have to accompany my wife to the mass of St Isidore. But you, my friend, what have you decided? Or rather, what has the fine lady who condescended to visit this poor house to find you decided?'

'She's coming for me this morning. She claims to have found some miraculous means of getting me out of Madrid. I'm afraid she's deceiving herself.'

'What about? Her power? That woman would confront the devil himself and win. I envy you your friends.'

'Why shouldn't you be one also? Remember, she said she would not forget you.'

A sudden, unexpected flame of joy transfigured the painter's harsh face and it came to Gilles then that the duchess, whom he had not met before at such close quarters, had left her image imprinted on his friend's eyes, and perhaps also in his heart.

'You think so?' he murmured in a pensive voice that told the Frenchman he had guessed aright. 'I'd like to work for her – to paint her again and again, because she is always the same and yet always different, an idol, a woman, a girl of Madrid, a queen ...'

'Let's just call her Woman,' Gilles said with a grin. 'And now, Paco, let me embrace you and say farewell. I don't suppose I shall be here when you get back and I cannot tell whether we will ever meet again. But I want to tell you I shall never forget, in my heart, what you have risked, and still risk, for my sake.'

'You have become a brother to me, Frenchman, and one owes everything to a brother. I know, too, that we will meet again some day. Go with God. I'll pray to St Isidore and to Our Lady of Atocha for you.'

The two men embraced, tears in their eyes. Then, with a last reminder to Micaela not to open the door to anyone without good reason, Goya left the studio abruptly, like a man concealing an emotion beyond his control.

Before he could have had time to reach the church, the street

91

outside filled with a royal commotion. It was the Duchess of Alba and her train, involving nothing less than a complete household on the move: one massive travelling carriage followed by two or three lesser vehicles for her staff, all drawn by plumed horses with bells on their harness. A number of postilions rode ahead to clear the way for the impressive coachmen resplendent, despite the heat, in driving coats with triple capes. Footmen clung on behind the travelling berline and the whole procession concluded with a company of mounted outriders and a long line of mules, tintinnabulating more even than the horses and laden with leather trunks and bundles, all the paraphernalia of a great lady about to take a journey.

The whole cavalcade came to a halt outside Goya's house and someone banged the knocker vigorously. The next moment, Micaela was curtsying down to the ground with the deepest humility before the Duchess of Alba. Dressed in an elegant travelling costume and a hat so plumed that it was a challenge in itself, she swept into the room in her own inimitable fashion followed, a good deal more quietly, by a tall, thin duenna muffled in heavy black veils.

For the benefit of the small crowd which had gathered around her carriage, the duchess announced in a loud voice that, being on her way to her villa of San Lucar de Barrameda, she had called to collect the picture she had purchased from Señor Goya the previous evening, which was intended to hang in that same villa. She went on to say that she would be grateful if Señor Goya could also lend her a horse, one of hers having cast a shoe and time being too short to allow of a return to her palace to change horses.

The outcome of this was that, while she went in to the house, her servants were busy changing one of the trace horses, Merlin himself being put in its place.

Another moment and, ignoring the presence of her duenna, Cayetana had flung herself into Gilles' arms and was kissing him quickly and fiercely.

'We've not much time,' she murmured, her lips brushing his. 'Quickly, get your clothes off!'

He stared at her, his jaw dropping.

'Get my— Are you out of your mind? *Now?*'

She gave a ripple of delighted laughter, clear as a fountain. 'Not for that, stupid! This is my most loyal servant, Doña Concepcion. She has been with me from a child and I trust her completely. You are going to wear her clothes, and sit beside me in my coach. Luckily, she is tall and, even if you do look a bit strange, no one will think of looking for you in the person of a respectable duenna. Especially as it's not known that we've ever met. Hurry. The guard on the gates has been relaxed a little because of the excitement of the Pradera. We'll have no trouble getting out and by this evening you'll be far away.'

That Cayetana's scheme was a good one was beyond a doubt. Unprotesting, Gilles began to strip off his clothes while Doña Concepcion did the same behind a screen, without losing one scrap of her dignity. The screen was, in any case, superfluous since, under her own, she was already wearing another set of garments, those of an ordinary peasant woman.

'Once it is dark,' the duchess explained, 'Concepcion will be able to get back into the palace without attracting attention.'

Helped by the two women,. Gilles donned the long, wide-skirted black dress, the jet necklaces, the lace cap which fell over his face and the full, hooded cloak which went over all. For extra safety, Cayetana darkened his eyebrows and placed a dab of rouge on each cheek to give him the same dutch doll appearance as Concepcion. Then she stood back to view the effect.

'Not bad at all,' she said with satisfaction. 'The cap is wonderful and does a lot to hide your face. Now for the picture.'

'My servant,' Gilles said. 'What has become of him?'

Her attention on the pictures propped against the wall, the duchess answered without looking round.

'He's in the provision basket in my coach. We'll get him out when we've gone far enough. I think this one will do,' she went on, holding up a street scene showing some beggars round a church door. 'Here,' she said to Micaela, tossing her a well-filled purse. 'Make my apologies to your master and give him this. I hope he'll think it's enough. And now, let's be off.'

Followed by Gilles, doing his best not to trip over his skirts, and Micaela carrying the picture to hand to the servants, the Duchess of Alba returned to her coach. That sunlit passage through the crowd was, for Gilles, a formidable ordeal and it was with a sigh of relief that he entered the shade of the coach and sank into the deep velvet cushions.

Through the window, he could see a frieze of curious faces, gazing avidly, ragged urchins, women in mantillas, not new and not overclean but mantillas none-the-less, worn for mass on this feast day. A blaze of fierce colours against the blinding walls and bright blue sky and brilliant sunlight. And beyond, under the cool shade of an awning, the black robe of a monk, while farther off Gilles caught the ominous shapes of two watching alguazils: the Inquisition and the police, living proof of the threat hanging over the fugitive. The monk's face, inside his hood, might have been designed for his role, thin and pale with two slits for eyes, the narrow eyes of the fanatic. As for the others, they looked what they were, a pair of brainless louts inflated with the consciousness of power.

The Duchess of Alba's sumptuous train seemed to have given them some food for thought, unlikely as that seemed. Gilles, watching uneasily, saw them begin to stroll heavily, like Fate, towards the coach, parting the crowd roughly with the flat of their sheathed swords. They might simply have been going to pay their respects but Cayetana, too, had seen them. A brief order to her coachman and he bent at once, pulled a heavy bag from under his box and, opening it, plunged in a hand like a ham. When it came out it held a fistful of gold coins which he scattered wide among the crowd who greeted it with an animal roar.

'Her Grace the Duchess of Alba invites you all to celebrate San Isidore with her. She is sorry to be obliged to leave Madrid on this blessed day and asks you all to pray for her and her house. God and St Isidore be with you!' the coachman bellowed.

He was answered by another roar from the crowd as, like the sea pounding on the shore, the people fell on the gold as it rolled on the ground. More handfuls followed, tossed judiciously to either side of the coach so as to leave, as far as possible, a clear space ahead, until the bag was empty. The policemen, too, had joined in the scramble and even the monk's eyes left their heavenly contemplation long enough to see and trap adroitly under one sandal two coins which rolled close by his foot. Everyone was far too busy to remember the coach as it moved off gently and rumbled away down the steep street.

Without relaxing the stiff, remote posture she had held all through the scattering of the golden rain, Cayetana slid a mocking, sideways smile towards her supposed duenna.

'It's always wise to take some precautions,' she said softly. 'Something told me we were up against a pair of fools, over-zealous in their duty. Gold is the best cure for that kind of stupidity.'

'I think your precautions are wonderful. You've just thrown a small fortune to the winds.'

She shrugged easily.

'What is gold? The ancient Aztecs used to call it the excrement of the gods. Those wretched people never see it, and I have far too much. Besides, I have a reputation for eccentricity to support.'

Gently, Gilles took hold of the white-gloved hand that lay beside him on the mulberry-coloured cloth of her dress and, sliding off the glove, pressed his lips to the skin with a kind of grateful adoration. The duchess turned to look at him, her eyes sparkling with mischief.

'When I travel,' she said, 'Doña Concepcion is accustomed to share my chamber. She will, of course, do so tonight – and other nights. I must say, I never expected to be so excited at the thought of making love to my duenna.'

Gilles made no answer but he lowered the window a trifle. All at once he was feeling unusually warm.

They passed through the gates not merely without trouble but with full military honours. The Alba coat-of-arms was almost as widely known and respected as the King's own. The sentries presented arms and were thanked for their courtesy by a radiant smile from the duchess. The duenna, on the other hand, was seized with a fit of coughing which forced her to keep her handkerchief pressed to her face.

The coughing lasted while they crossed slowly over the Toledo bridge, crowded with people flocking in from the country to take part in the Pradera. From the shelter of his handkerchief, Gilles could see the banks of the Manzanares transformed for the occasion. The green fields on either side of the river exhibited an astonishing collection of temporary

95

shacks which had sprung up during the night: taverns, cake shops already swarming with flies, peddlars of pins and images of the saint and medicinal herbs, gipsies ready to seize a palm and read it, their hips rolling in their full skirts and their eyes alert for the glimpse of a monastic robe, lithe-limbed dancers circling round a man with a guitar to a rhythmic click of castanets: an amazing combination of holiday and religious festival swirling between the white tents that looked like out-sized washing spread to dry by the stream. In a little while, when mass was over, would come the carriages overflowing with pretty dresses, with scintillating majas, gentlemen and society ladies. And, once over the bridge, Gilles watched, from his side, the road to Carabanchel go by. For the first time, he was going to break his promise to Teresia who, at that moment, must be cursing him roundly, unless the rumour had already reached her. Would he, he wondered, ever see her again, the Cabarrus' charming daughter who had presented him with so much schoolgirl devotion?

'Are you so sorry to be leaving Madrid?' Cayetana asked, hearing him sigh. 'Or is it that we shall both miss the festival?'

'Both, perhaps. My stay in Spain, which I had hoped would be longer, has ended in failure. No man likes to lose—'

'No woman, either. But do not despair. You will come back. The King will not live for ever. One day, your friend Maria Luisa will be queen and – and I think,' she added, bending forward to raise the lid of the food hamper placed opposite her, 'we may now release your servant for a while.' Pongo, scarlet with heat, had been awaiting the moment with truly Indian stoicism.

The horses had now broken into a canter along the road to Toledo from which they would shortly branch off towards Talavera and from there turn north again, swinging wide of the capital. Madrid, white under its pealing bells, lay shrouded in the golden mist of a fine spring day.

Resigned to his fate, Gilles arranged his veils as best he could and leaned back as though to sleep, if only to avoid Pongo's bulging eyes. Faced suddenly with this amazing transforma-tion on the part of his master, the Iroquois, who could endure torture without batting an eyelid, was obviously having a mighty struggle not to laugh.

4

The Inn at Fontarabia

It was a strange journey, a journey the Chevalier de Tournemine was to recall with a mixture of nostalgia and irritation.
He loathed the old woman's garments he had been put into
although they were his protection. He longed to throw them
off, but even when they were traversing the most arid plateaux
of old Castile, Cayetana opposed him with such energy that he
began to suspect her of enjoying the masquerade.

Every night, moreover, when they halted, the nightmare
changed into a seductive reality. For as the duchess had foretold, the bowing innkeepers saw nothing unusual in the great
lady's refusal to be parted from her duenna.

And so, once enclosed with the woman who was now
doubly his mistress, Gilles, freed of his petticoats, resumed
with joy the prestige and privileges of a man in the fair
duchess's bed. Each night was more intoxicating, madder than
the last. More exhausting, also. So much so that at last he
discovered a simple and quite natural answer to his distasteful
daytime role: no sooner were they back in the coach again than
he would settle himself in his corner and, with a beaming smile
for Cayetana, fall straight into the sleep of the just.

As for Pongo who, once out of Madrid, had little to fear on
his own account, they had provided him with a livery, some
skilful make-up and a patch over one eye which sufficiently
disguised an appearance exotic even for Spain, and he travelled
placidly astride Merlin, whom they had been obliged to liber-
ate from harness a mile or two out of the capital. His part,
which he accepted philosophically, was that of a dumb servant,

and he understood enough Spanish now to acquit himself adequately.

They travelled slowly, almost lazily, as befitted a great lady, so as to arouse no curiosity.

Segovia, where they were late arriving on account of a loose wheel, brought an abrupt change in the monotonous rhythm of their journey. A glorious sunset was flushing the delicate flesh colours of the city and setting fire to the cathedral, gilded like an apricot beneath the strange pointed domes, like those of a Burmese temple. The air was soft and scented with the golden lichens of the hillsides, warmed all day in the sun. The prospect of one of the best inns in Spain added to the travellers' pleasure in reaching their night's destination.

But when the caravan emerged into the cornmarket square and came in sight of the inn called Los Picos, Cayetana uttered an exclamation of annoyance. An entire regiment was bivouacked in the square and under the arches of the old Roman aqueduct, and it was evident that the officers had taken over the inn.

'*Madre de Dios!* What is this?' she said, sighing.

'It looks obvious enough,' Gilles muttered gloomily. 'A regiment of troops. The Numantia Dragoons, to be precise.'

'But what are they doing here?' the duchess cried impatiently.

'They're on their way back from Salamanca where they've been putting down some uprising at the university.'

She threw him a glance of mingled anxiety and respect.

'Do the Bodyguard usually know so much about the whereabouts of other regiments?'

'If you mean have I been engaged in spying, my dear, do not alarm yourself. It's merely that my friend Jean de Batz, a Frenchman like myself, is serving with this regiment.'

'Good God! Suppose he recognizes you?'

'It would be little enough risk to you. As I said, he is a friend. But if he once sets eyes on me in this ridiculous get-up, I'm in danger of becoming a laughing stock for life. Whatever happens,' he went on with a shrug, 'we have to run the risk. We can't draw back now.'

This was true. The duchess's cavalcade was producing its usual effect. The soldiers stepped back respectfully to let it pass and a number of officers were gathering at the inn door. One of these came forward as the footman was letting down the steps and, with the white plumes of his cocked hat sweeping the dust, bade the lady welcome on behalf of the staff.

'Count Ignacio de San Esteban, at your grace's service,' he introduced himself, bowing again.

He stepped up and offered his gloved hand with ceremony to assist the Duchess of Alba to descend. At the same time three of his officers fell to arguing over who should have the honour of giving up his room to the beautiful lady.

She accepted the hand and descended with her customary grace, smiling a little distantly, while Gilles, sticking to his character, pulled his cap desperately over his face and made a great to-do about his descent from the coach. He was torn between satisfaction that fate had granted him this opportunity of seeing his friend and the fear of hearing him laugh aloud. As luck would have it, a quick glance around showed him that Batz was not among those present.

Somewhat reassured, he followed Cayetana, her skirts rippling snakelike across the cobbles, through the braided group of officers and into the inn doorway. He was about to enter the common room when someone coming out at speed ran into him and trod heavily on his foot.

'Clumsy oaf!' he exclaimed aloud and realized too late that he had spoken French.

The other turned quickly. It was Jean de Batz. His eyes, quite blank at first, took in the supposed duenna and widened suddenly, with an arrested expression. Gilles, with a grin and a wink, picked up his skirts and whisked himself into the room in the duchess's wake, although not fast enough to miss a strangled sound from Jean's throat as he went. But the worst was over and at least he knew his friend's wits were sharp enough not to fail him now. He would certainly be imagining some amorous intrigue with the tempestuous duchess and would be discreet.

In the room which was being hastily cleared for her, Cayetana waited for her own servants to take possession and exchanged some final courtesies with San Esteban, who was clearly angling for an invitation to supper. He had to be content, however, with the lady's gracious thanks.

'I am so grateful to you, Don Ignacio! I do not know how I should have managed but for your courtesy. You must know, I am on my way to Luchon for my health but I am finding the journey dreadfully fatiguing. But for you—'

The gentleman bowed again, flushed with gratification.

'We could not, for our honour, have failed to ensure the comfort of the Duchess of Alba. This poor hostelry is quite unworthy of her.'

Cayetana lowered her eyes, the picture of sweet piety.

'It is right to mortify the flesh when one is seeking heaven's blessing on its cure. I wish you a good night, Don Ignacio.'

Another bow and the officer was walking steadily to the door, with all the air of a man hoping against hope that he will be recalled. He was, but not quite as he hoped.

'Don Ignacio!'

'Your grace?'

'Is there not a Frenchman in your regiment? A Gascon, as I believe. A certain Baron de Batz?'

'Yes indeed. But—'

'My husband is acquainted with him and it seems he is familiar with the wild Pyrenean region to which I am going to take the waters. Since chance has thrown him in my way, would you be good enough to ask him to spare me a few moments of his time?'

It was clear that Don Ignacio was less than pleased.

'A great honour for the gentleman, I am sure. But—'

'My friends,' Cayetana's voice had taken on a dangerous softness, 'never argue with my wishes, Don Ignacio. In general, they vie with one another to comply with them.'

Don Ignacio withdrew, defeated.

'That was what you wanted?' Cayetana said, as soon as the door had shut behind him.

'You are the most amazing woman in the world,' Gilles told her. He was hurriedly divesting himself of the duenna's costume, having no wish to let his friend behold him in it a second time.

A few moments later, neat in his canary yellow uniform, the forage cap with its leather cockade over one ear, Jean de Batz entered the room and bowed to the Duchess of Alba as though to a queen. But his quick black eyes had no sooner offered the homage of admiration to a pretty woman natural to any Frenchman worthy of the name, than they were peering unobtrusively into every corner of the room, and especially among the curtains of the big bed, seeking something. Cayetana did not leave him long in doubt.

'There is someone here who wishes to see you, Baron,' she said smiling. She, too, was moving towards the bed. 'You may talk quite safely.'

Batz bowed again, more deeply still, but straightened abruptly as Gilles stepped out from the shelter of the bed curtains. The Gascon gave a shout of laughter.

'So it was you? *Sacrebleu*, my friend, I all but doubted my senses, but I knew I'd not drunk more than two cups of poor wine since this morning, or I'd have thought I was seeing things.'

'Well you weren't. Nor, I may say, is there anything to laugh at. But for that damned costume and the duchess's protection, at this moment I'd be rotting in the dungeons of the Inquisition, expecting any minute to be burned publicly in the Plaza Mayor, to the tune of the *Dies Irae*.'

Batz' face altered at that.

'The Inquisition? But what have you done?'

'To the Inquisition, nothing.' And Gilles gave a brief account of what had happened at Aranjuez and in Madrid. At the end of his recital, he took from his waistband the emerald ring given him by Maria Luisa.

'Look. This is all I have now to add to my Spanish fortune. As a fugitive from justice, I can hardly go and ask the regimental paymaster for my back pay. Will you give it to Cabarrus?'

Batz held the jewel to the light with the air of one who knew, then tucked it away in his waistcoat pocket with a grin.

'I know exactly what to turn it into,' he said. 'Our affairs, as it happens, are in very good trim. I've been making some promising investments, through the San Carlos bank and your friend Cabarrus in fact, including several shares in a merchantman bound for the Gold Coast.'

'The Gold Coast? What for?'

'Well ... various things. Coffee, cocoa ...'

'You're sure?'

101

'Look, now you're the one playing Inquisitor! I don't understand what you mean, much less your tone of voice.'

'I'm sorry. Only, you see, I'd hate to find out we were trying to make our fortunes out of what they call "black ivory". It's a dreadful trade. I've seen slaves in America. Some are well treated, even happy, I agree, but they are still the dregs of humanity – yet they have souls like you and me.'

Batz shrugged with what, to an informed observer, might have seemed a rather forced casualness.

'There are times when I wonder if you aren't still cherishing a hankering after the priesthood. What a bishop you'd have made! No, don't worry. So far there's been no mention of anything but foodstuffs. Trust me, for heaven's sake! I'm sorry you're going, of course, but you can be sure your business affairs won't suffer. One thing, though. If I understood you, this ring is all you possess? What will you live on until you can rejoin the regiment and lay hands on your back pay?'

Gilles laughed. 'Didn't you show me the way in the happy days of our first meeting? I'll do like you – run up debts.'

Batz lifted his eyes to heaven.

'My God! He's all virtuous indignation when it comes to trafficking in slaves, yet he can face the prospect of living off the honest tradesmen of Paris without a qualm.'

'Running up debts doesn't mean you don't intend to pay them.'

'Whatever it means, you're not going to do it.'

Cayetana cut into the conversation with the absolute assurance of a person knowing she could eavesdrop with impunity. Gilles rounded on her, frowning, already on the defensive.

'What's that you say?'

'Merely that when we left Madrid I told you I needed you in France to perform a confidential service for me. I think the time has come to tell you the nature of that service. Your friend, who seems to have a keen eye for business, may, I think, be able to help us.'

'We are both at your service, but—'

'No buts! It's a word I dislike intensely.'

She sank gracefully into the only armchair in the room, inviting them, with a wave of her hand, to seat themselves, one on a stool, the other on a travelling trunk.

'You cannot,' she said, a hint of mischief in her voice, 'be unaware of the warm friendship existing between myself and the Princess of Asturia. In the matter of our mutual delight in jewels, this friendship reaches extraordinary heights. Now, just before we left Madrid, I learned, from a reliable source, that Maria Luisa had entrusted Spain's consul general in France, the Chevalier d'Ocariz, with a mission as important as it was confidential: to buy, from the French Queen's jewellers, a certain diamond necklace. This necklace is, it seems, unique, but the price is so high that Marie-Antoinette, much as she wanted it, could not afford to buy it.'

'You mean,' Batz said, his eyes suddenly widening, 'the famous necklace made by Boehmer and Bassange, the necklace with six hundred and forty-seven diamonds?'

'The very same. They say it is a miracle, a river of fire which would have suited the noble neck of the Queen of France to perfection. It seems to me that it would be quite unsuited to the countenance of the future Queen of Spain.'

Though not in general much interested in feminine trinkets, Tournemine, too, had heard the story of the fabulous necklace ordered some years earlier by King Louis XV for the Countess Du Barry. The Queen's jewellers had taken a long time scouring the world's markets for stones perfect enough to match the King's demanding taste. Unfortunately for them, the King died at about the same time as the last jewels arrived in Paris, depriving the two men, now over their ears in debt, of a virtually irreplaceable client. Gilles could hear again the contempt in Fersen's voice as he told the story.

'If King Louis XV had only lived a few months longer, a strumpet would have been decked out in a treasure beyond the reach of a queen.'

'As far as her Majesty is concerned,' he broke in, a trifle sharply, 'your grace has been misinformed. She could easily have had the necklace. Everyone in France knows that the King tried to give it to her in 1778, at the birth of their first child, Princess Marie-Thérèse. The Queen refused it, horrified by the price, which was the equivalent of that of a ship of the line. It

103

may be in no small measure due to her that we now have the best navy in the world.'

The Duchess of Alba gave a tinkling laugh which did not ring quite true.

'That may be so. But I have no call to present my lord with battleships. He would have no use for them. Nor would Spain be in the least grateful. So I have decided that the necklace shall belong to me. You, my dear, will therefore be good enough to negotiate the purchase for me. The price, you understand, is immaterial. What matters is to beat Maria Luisa to it. When this is done, you will bring it as far as the Spanish border yourself and your friend here can come and fetch it, since, under the present regime, it will scarcely be possible for you to set foot on Spanish soil.'

Batz spoke. 'To buy it at any price – and I seem to recall the jewellers are asking something in the region of a million and a half – implies an ability on the part of the purchaser to lay hands on a very large sum of money.'

'That has been taken care of, Baron. Señor Cabarrus is to lodge two million with the Cadiz office of the Parisian bankers Lecoulteux.'

Batz and Tournemine exchanged glances.

'We know the Lecoulteux very well,' the latter said.

'So much the better. It will simplify the matter of letters of introduction and tells me once again that I have chosen my messenger well,' Cayetana said, with a smile. 'As to your own concerns, Diego will hand over to you at the border, along with all the bank papers, a sum in gold and a bill of exchange to cover your expenses. No,' she added, cutting with authority through the young man's protest, 'you must accept that. The man who represents the Dukes of Alba to Messrs Boehmer and Bassange must not look shabby, nor have I ever heard that an ambassador, were he a prince, ever demurred at receiving a just reward for his trouble. Moreover, Chevalier, make no mistake, the matter will not prove as simple as it may look from here. If I know Maria Luisa, her envoy will do everything in his power – and I mean everything – to bring her back the jewels she craves. You will have to be very careful and look to yourself, because you will quite simply be risking your life.'

'Well, I'm glad to hear it,' Gilles said, with a note of relief that drew a smile from Batz. 'A little danger will make the business much more amusing.'

'That is not the only danger. You may also have some trouble with your minister for foreign affairs. As soon as Ocariz, who, let me remind you, is consul general, knows that you have entered the lists, he will fight you tooth and nail. You may also be risking your career – or the Bastille!'

'I will take those risks also. If the world stands, you shall have your necklace.'

'I do not doubt it for a moment. Well, since we are agreed, we had better part. Both of you, you may be sure, have my gratitude.'

Batz bowed with barely suppressed delight. It was clear that he was thrilled to be on these terms with the Duchess of Alba. He gripped his friend's hand eagerly.

'One thing more,' Gilles said for his ear alone. 'You have heard nothing from Count Boulainvilliers, or from the Lieutenant of Police?'

'Nothing. But there's nothing in that. Short of a miracle, these things take time. Goodbye, for the present, and God go with you.'

In order to avoid Don Ignacio, whose anxiety to further his acquaintance with the Duchess had led him to offer her an escort of his regiment, led by himself, Cayetana determined to leave Segovia before daylight and to travel with greater speed than before. Speed became haste when, after they had passed Aranda de Duera, which they did with celerity so that the duchess was not obliged to stop at the castle, which belonged to her, they were overtaken on the main highway, the Camino Real, by another vehicle travelling with even greater urgency. It was none other than the consul general returning to Paris in fine style. After that, there was no more dawdling. They kept up the fastest pace possible without tiring the horses. They passed through Burgos, where Ocariz had halted for the night, and themselves slept far from any town. Four days after leaving Segovia, they came in sight of the Bidassoa, the little coastal river whose waters marked the boundary between France and Spain.

Gilles himself was all for speed. He was longing with all his heart to find himself a man again among men. He was sick to death of the masquerade. Safe it might be, but it irked him all the more because he suspected Cayetana of a perverse pleasure in it. Struggling into his petticoats again each morning, he felt as if he were climbing back into the pillory.

Moreover, his first violent passion for the lovely maja was beginning to fade. Insensibly, his nightly role was becoming like that of a galley slave to love, chained to the whims of a woman for ever seeking fresh sensual experiences, experiences she would pursue, disguised as a *manola* even among the common bullfighters and Don Juans of the streets. Any new man, as long as he had a spark in his eye, an active body and the power to awaken her curiosity, could rouse her most primitive instincts.

Very frequently, for instance, in those long days spent driving through the dust and heat, the duchess's thoughts and conversation had turned to Goya. Clearly, the painter's directness of speech, his powerful physique and lust for life had interested Cayetana and she demanded to be told more about the private life of the man she, like Gilles himself, now regarded as one of the artistic giants of the future.

If I ever come back to Spain, Gilles thought, half uneasy, half amused, I'll be willing to bet she will have made him her lover. He asks nothing better. It was in his eyes the other day, when she was flitting round his studio. What Paco would get out of such an affair remains to be seen. A more burning inspiration? Or a disaster?

For himself, his eyes devoured the road stretching ahead, to France, with a kind of hunger. Now and then, they would turn to Pongo, riding Merlin quietly beside the coach, and he would feel a choking urge to fling off his ridiculous black petticoats and, with the warmth of powerful energy of his beloved horse between his knees, gallop away to the horizon to find his own life again, a fiery dream which had too long been damped in cloud.

The sight of the ancient walls of Fontarabia, reflected in the greenish waters of the Bidassoa, tore from him an exclamation he could not control. Cayetana's beautiful eyebrows drew together, frowning.

'Are you in such haste to leave me?' she murmured.

106

He smiled at her with affection and a trace of compunction.

'I'm in haste to be myself again, Cayetana, and to begin the adventure you have offered me. God made me, I think, more for trouble and fighting than to sit and spin under a woman's eyes, be they the most beautiful eyes in the world,' he added, planting a kiss on his mistress's finger tips. But, as he made to lay her hand back in her lap, the fingers twisted in his and clutched his nervously.

'Look! What is it?'

They had come in sight of Behobia and the old bridge, built by the Romans, whose stout arches had for centuries borne the weight of hosts of pilgrims journeying to Compostella in Galicia. But now the ancient causeway was deserted. On a level with the stone cross bearing the symbols of St James, the space between the parapets was filled with a line of soldiers. The bridge was closed.

The coach stopped and Diego, with the assurance natural to the servant of a great house, pushed his horse right up to the breasts of the soldiers.

'Make way!' he cried. 'Make way for the carriage of her grace the Duchess of Alba!'

The officer, leaning idly against the cross, removed his hat. 'The way shall be cleared for her grace as soon as we have seen her pass,' he said coolly.

Diego pulled a bundle of papers from his pocket.

'Here are the passports of her grace and her grace's retinue. We are travelling to the baths at Luchon where Dr de Barrié is awaiting her grace.'

The officer shook his head.

'I said pass, my friend, not passport. For the past week no one has been allowed to cross the frontier into France without a special pass, signed by the King himself or by the Marquis de Florida Blanca. Until further notice.'

'But surely this cannot apply to the greatest lady in all Spain!'

'It applies to everyone – even the members of the royal family if they should take it into their heads to come here.'

Cayetana's face had gone a little pale as she heard this but she was used to taking the bold course. Letting down the window, she put out her head.

107

'Lieutenant! Come here. Come and tell me at least the reason for these extraordinary orders.'

The officer walked back to the coach door and bowed politely.

'There is a criminal on the run, your grace. A man sought both by the law and by the Holy Inquisition. And since the man is a Frenchman, all ways into his country must of course be blocked. We have his description. Here it is. Your grace may be sure we shall not let him slip through.'

'I am quite sure of that, lieutenant. My congratulations. But will you tell me how I am going to reach Luchon in these circumstances? I have never been accustomed to seek permission from anyone in this world, not even from the King! Moreover, I am sick. I need care. You would not, I hope, have me return to Aranjuez and beg an audience with Florida Blanca? Come now, lieutenant. No one will blame you for opening the frontier for the Duchess of Alba. The Inquisition is not seeking me, or any of my people. I can promise you that.'

The officer was obviously in torment. He would probably have preferred the *strappado* a thousand times rather than suffer the anger of a woman whose power he knew, who could break his career with a snap of her finger if the fancy took her.

'Your grace! Your grace, I implore you, pardon me. I know that I am nothing to your grace. All I have is my honour as a soldier. But if you were the Princess Royal herself, without a pass, I could not let you through.'

'Not the most felicitous comparison,' Cayetana muttered angrily. 'But I imagine you have a superior officer? There is a colonel or a general somewhere? Then kindly fetch him.'

'I would, but it is impossible. Our colonel, Don Garcia Morales, was called to Burgos this morning by the governor. There, there is a decent inn in Fontarabia, though. Opposite the old castle. I directed two ladies there not long ago who were in the same situation. Your grace might put up there for a few days, while a messenger can be sent to Madrid for a pass – or to Burgos, to fetch Don Garcia.'

Hidden in the folds of his full skirts, Gilles' hand sought Cayetana's and gripped it hard.

'Don't make a fuss,' he whispered. 'We'll have to give in. Let's go to this inn and think what we can do.'

The duchess sighed wearily.

'Ah well! I see I have no choice. I will do as you advise, lieutenant. And do not be anxious,' she added, seeing him looking at her uneasily. 'I do not blame you. You are doing your duty and doing it well. It does you credit. Good day to you. Pedro!' This to her coachman. 'To Fontarabia!'

The heavy vehicle backed and turned in a cloud of dust and at that moment another carriage came full tilt round the corner behind them. It was an elegant *calesa*, a two-wheeled cabriolet with a leather curtain in front, drawn by two smoking horses and driven by a small black, bustling coachman. The occupants of the ducal berline recognized it with sinking hearts.

Stiff with indignation, Cayetana watched as after a brief exchange of words and the production of a piece of paper, the line of soldiers stepped aside and the Chevalier d'Ocariz crossed quietly over the Bidassoa and, picking up speed, went racing, without let or hindrance, along the road to Paris.

'He, it appears, possesses one of these famous passes! That is another score I have to settle with Maria Luisa!'

Gilles, recovering from his disappointment, had swiftly made up his mind to a new course of action. Now he broke into laughter.

'Come, my dear. Don't look so tragic! All is not lost. Your Ocariz has a slight advantage over me, but I don't despair of catching him up, and even overtaking him.'

'Really? How do you think you'll catch him if we must spend two days kicking our heels inside Fontarabia. Its walls once gave my ancestor, the Duke of Berwick, trouble enough.'

'I'll see.'

A moment later, the berline with its escort of horsemen and mules was entering the ancient fifteenth-century ramparts by way of the Santa-Maria gate, blazoned with angels worshipping the image of Our Lady of Guadaloupe. The *Fonda de los Reyes Catholicos* was found without difficulty. Two carriages, of very different kinds, stood before it. One was the heavy, comfortable travelling carriage of a gentleman, its door panels too thickly coated with dust to allow the coat-of-arms to be deciphered, the other a thing like a large stage coach, horseless, its shafts in the air and its leather curtains hooked up to reveal the squalid, empty interior. On the box, however, filthy and splendid in sheepskin trousers, short embroidered jacket and a red scarf tied round his head, the *mayoral* or coachman was majestically smoking a long black cigar and gazing round him, like an emperor, at the confusion in the square.

A great many people were jostling about an open-air theatre which was being erected in front of the old palace of the Catholic Kings. The work was proceeding to music, three guitarists were strumming on their instruments while a crowd of men and women in brightly coloured costumes were merrily engaged in setting up the stage.

'I don't for a moment intend to stay here more than a few hours. Before daylight tomorrow, Doña Cayetana, I will be in France. I give you my word on that.'

'How will you do it?'

Tournemine pointed to the Bidassoa. The water ran blue and swift between its reedy banks, framing the little Pheasant Island and then widening into a broad estuary where, in the distance, there was a glimpse of waves forming a light fringe of spray along the bar.

'It's only water,' he said simply. 'And I'm a Breton, which means first cousin to a fish. Pongo swims like the beaver which is his totem, and my horse, Merlin, is perfectly at home in water.'

'Are you mad? It's nearly a mile from Fontarabia point across to the French side.'

'In my own country, in this same sea, I've often swum six miles. I'll do it easily, believe me. But it may not be so easy to get out of this town if the gates are shut at night.'

'Don't worry about that. The walls are old and they suffered a good deal in the siege of 1719 and no one has ever thought of repairing them. Nor is there any need for a guard. There is the Family Treaty between France and Spain, so Fontarabia no longer has any enemies. On the other hand, there may be patrols along the river.'

Cayetana sighed and changed the subject abruptly, as was her way.

'Travelling players! That's all we needed!'

'You should be thankful,' Gilles told her. 'I can cross the river undisturbed while the show is on. The whole town will be in the square.'

110

The innkeeper had arrived on the scene by this time, thrown into a state of distressful agitation by the appearance of the duchess's train. Dripping with obsequious respect, he explained that his hostelry was packed to the roof with these wretched actors but that he was prepared to throw the lot of them out, to sleep in the barn, or go to the devil for that matter, they and everyone else in the inn, to make room for the Duchess of Alba.

'I hope you don't mean to put us out also?' The plaintive voice spoke from above their heads. 'With every respect to her grace the duchess, we implore her to tolerate our presence, at least, remembering that we are not merely women, but women also of good family.'

There were, in fact, two ladies standing on the wooden balcony which ran the whole length of the inn's frontage and Gilles, looking up, barely repressed an oath, for the two were none other than Señora Cabarrus and Teresia.

'We are coming down,' Antoinette called out then. 'If your grace would be good enough to just wait there!'

'Gentle Jesus!' Cayetana breathed. 'Who is that creature?'

'Your banker's wife, my dear. The Countess de Cabarrus and her daughter. Good friends of mine but just at this moment I'd prefer them not to see me. I'll stay in the coach. I wonder what they're doing here?'

Concealed behind the lowered blinds, he was able to watch the meeting of the three women. Cayetana, now he had told her whom she was dealing with, was amiable. Antoinette Cabarrus, as talkative as ever, overwhelmed her with effusive friendliness and assurances of her delight in making the acquaintance of 'the greatest lady in all Spain', and implored her to spare 'just one teeny little chamber' for herself and her poor daughter. Her two sons, François and Dominique, with their clerical tutor, Don Bartholomeo, would of course be perfectly happy in the barn or even the hen house...

Gilles' view through the curtains, though restricted, did afford him a glimpse of Teresia. The girl had not spoken. She had curtsyed to the Duchess of Alba, like a well-brought-up child and had then withdrawn a little from the conversation. She seemed oddly indifferent to all that was going on around her.

111

In a month, the little May Queen had changed. Her exquisite face was set like a mask. It was as though a melancholy fog had blurred its colours and veiled the brilliance of eyes now marked with the blue shadows of sleepless nights. What had brought her and her family to this small frontier town? Why this sudden journey to France when, at the time of that rustic coronation, there had been no suggestion of it in the Cabarrus household? Gilles' real fondness for the child made him think of a hundred answers to the questions raised by Teresia's sadness. To be unhappy, as she undoubtedly was, did not suit her at all.

She moved a little farther away from the two older women, as though bored by their talk. Everything about her spoke of a lack of interest and at the same time of the longing to escape characteristic of a child too closely watched. Her movement took her out of Gilles' field of vision and he did not see her turn to look at the actors and then drift back to the coach, the door of which had been left open, revealing the rich velvet lining.

Then, unexpectedly, she leaned forward and poked her head inside. Her face appeared a few inches from the knee of the supposed duenna who had not been expecting it and had no time to draw back. For an instant they were face to face, the fugitive and the child, but nothing happened.

'Teresia?' Antoinette called, apparently in the mood to assert her maternal authority. 'What are you thinking of? Such impertinent curiosity! Your grace will pardon her, she is just a child.'

'A most charming child, I believe. Come here, my dear! Come and let me see your face,' Cayetana said.

Teresia's head disappeared, leaving Gilles with a near-certitude of having been recognized. He felt no alarm, however. Teresia was not the girl to betray him, whatever crime she thought he had committed. He was her friend.

The two women, meanwhile, had agreed to share the fonda between them. The actors, generously recompensed by the duchess who further promised to watch their performance from the balcony, were quite willing to sleep in the barn. Both parties moved in. 'Doña Concepcion', declared by her mistress to be suffering from the vapours, hastened, muffled in shawls, to the small chamber next door to the duchess's which had been vacated for her by Antoinette's maid.

'If she is unwell, she will prefer to be alone. And in this hot weather the odour of a sick person can be disagreeable to a woman of refinement such as yourself,' Antoinette had said, insisting.

Gilles could have kissed her for the tart phrase. The thought of being alone, even in a cupboard, even for the few hours that had still to pass before his nocturnal plans could be put into operation, was pure joy to him. Living day by day in close proximity even with a woman as ravishing as Cayetana had finally become an intolerable ordeal to him.

Luxuriously, he pulled off his shoes and climbed out of the hateful petticoats, determined in his own mind never to wear them again. Then, wrapped in his cloak, he threw himself down on the narrow bed with its dubious sheets and slept like a man who could ask for nothing better.

When he woke up, darkness was falling and someone was knocking with gentle insistence on his door.

'Who's there?' he called, striving to make his voice, still hoarse with sleep, rise to the right feminine pitch.

'Me! Teresia! Open the door, please. I must talk to you.'

He lifted the latch at once and the girl, her white dress hidden under a dark cloak, slipped inside and promptly threw both arms round his neck and kissed him firmly on both cheeks. He returned the greeting automatically, then put her gently from him.

'Teresia!' he said reprovingly. 'This is very unwise. Suppose you were seen or heard?'

'No fear of that. My mother and the Duchess of Alba – the Duchess of Alba and my mother, I should say, my mother absolutely bursting with pride, are having supper together downstairs. I said I had a headache, and wasn't hungry. Oh Gilles! Is that lady your mistress?'

'What kind of a question is that from a well-brought-up little girl? Is that why you came? To ask me?'

'Of course not. But for one thing I'm not a little girl any more and for another, if she's hiding you, it must be because she's in love with you. She's awfully pretty, too. Although I don't really like her much. She looks too much as though she thought the world was made up of her and God and a few minor bits and bobs.'

'Teresia!' the young man said sharply. 'Once again—'

'What have I come for? To help you. Oh, my dear friend, I was so happy just now when I recognized you! People have been saying such dreadful things. And I didn't even know if you were alive.'

The child's simplicity was refreshing and Gilles relented.

'If I understand you correctly, you don't believe these dreadful things?'

She considered him with the look of affronted pity common to the young when adults say something idiotic.

'Have you lost your senses? I know you and I am a good judge of people, too,' she added with a comical dignity. 'And my parents didn't believe it, either. We're all very fond of you. Papa said it was a lot of nonsense and something to do with the Princess of Asturia. Women play a big part in your life, don't they?'

Gilles looked at her and laughed.

'They play a big part in all men's lives, Teresia. You'll play a big part yourself one day – in many men's lives, perhaps.'

She dropped to sit on the edge of the bed and heaved a world-weary sigh.

'I know that. I've begun already.'

'Have you, indeed?'

'Oh yes. You haven't asked what we're doing here, on the way to France, as though all Spain were on fire. It's because of me.'

'Because of you?'

'Yes, me! And Uncle Maximilian. He fell in love with me and asked my papa for my hand. It caused a frightful scandal.'

Gilles stared at her in blank amazement. Yet she seemed to be perfectly sane.

'Your uncle? Your mother's brother?'

'Yes, my Galabert uncle, that is. You know him. I shouldn't have disliked it, either. He's charming.'

Gilles had in fact met Uncle Maximilian at the Cabarrus' house on more than one occasion. He had come from Bayonne early in the year on family business. Nor was it in the least surprising that Teresia should have found him charming. Thirty years old, elegant and distinguished with a bright eye, a sensual mouth and a strong, athletic body clad in tasteful, beautifully-cut clothes. In addition to that, he possessed a lively wit and an inclination for gallantry. Enough to turn more than one feminine head including, it seemed, that of a niece somewhat precocious for her age. But as to wanting to marry her...

'Do you mean to say that such a marriage would have appealed to you? Good Lord, anyone would think you were sorry!'

'Well I am. I'm very fond of Uncle Maximilian. He says such pretty things.'

'But, God in heaven, he's your uncle! Your mother's brother!'

'He's a man, and a man is a man. As far as I'm concerned there are only two kinds, those who are attractive and those who aren't. You are – but so is Uncle Max. Besides, I needed comforting. You had deserted me. You forgot all about me because your head was full of other things – like your duchess, for instance! I saw that on the day I was crowned May Queen. If you—'

'Teresia, Teresia, we are getting away from the point. To go back to your parents. They were very much against the idea, were they?'

'Worse than that. Mama fainted. Papa flew into the worst rage I've ever seen and then, after he'd done stamping and roaring up and down his room, he made up his mind that we were to go straight to France, Mama and my brothers and I, because in Spain we wouldn't help but all grow up into savages. He's sending us to one of his correspondents in Paris, a Monsieur de Boisgeloup who is a judge in the high court and will make us welcome in his house on the Ile St Louis until we can find a house of our own. And that's the whole story.'

'Only,' Gilles said, 'your father was in such a hurry he did not have time to find out that a pass was needed to cross the frontier?'

'Of course he did,' Teresia said with a sigh. 'Papa never overlooks anything. But you know Mama. She has windmills in her head. She left the wretched pass on her dressing table. All the same, we shall be crossing into France tomorrow morning. That's why I said I've come to help you.'

'How?'

'I woke you up, didn't I? You were fast asleep? You didn't hear a horseman arrive?'

'Good God, no. I was sleeping too soundly.'

'It was one of my father's servants who has ridden after us from Madrid, bringing the pass. So tomorrow we'll take you across the frontier with us. And that's more than your lady friend could do, Duchess of Alba or no!'

'Just like that? But how will you get me through?'

Teresia got up, went to the door and put her ear to it. 'Here they are, I think,' she said with satisfaction, 'so we'll tell you.'

Before Gilles could protest she had opened the door just enough to allow her two elder brothers, fourteen-year-old François and thirteen-year-old Dominique, to tiptoe into the room with a conspiratorial air.

'Well?' Teresia demanded imperiously. 'How did it go?'

François, a good-looking dark boy much like his sister, fumbled in the skirts of his coat and produced a small packet wrapped in grimy cloth.

'I've got what we need. There's an apothecary's near the church. The watchman at the castle pointed it out to me. I said I had a horse so highly strung it couldn't sleep and he gave me this.'

'He said it's wonderful,' put in young Dominique, who was fair and had inherited his mother's tongue and her inquisitive eyes. 'Give him a third of an ounce and he'll sleep like the dead for twenty-four hours.'

Gilles had been regarding this invasion of his privacy with folded arms and a sparkling eye.

'Suppose you explain, gentlemen, just what it is you have in mind to do? I don't doubt the purity of your intentions, but your proceedings alarm me. Do I gather you're planning to put someone to sleep?'

Dominique lifted a pair of perfectly angelic blue eyes to his face.

'Our tutor, Don Bartholomeo. He's very fond of wine. Tonight, we're going to give him a big jug of the best, to stop him being ill, and we'll put the powder in it.'

'Then, once he's asleep,' François continued, 'we'll put him to bed comfortably and take away his clothes. And of course

116

we'll give the innkeeper some money to take care of him after we've gone.'

'And you,' Teresia finished triumphantly, 'can wear his clothes and take his place in our carriage. Our pass mentions a tutor, so you'll be able to cross into France quite safely. Isn't that a good scheme?'

Watched admiringly by the two boys, Gilles seized Teresia round the waist and swung her off the ground as easily as if she had been a child of five, and kissed her on both round, downy cheeks.

'Marvellous!' he cried laughing. 'You are all true friends – and excellent conspirators. Only—'

'Oh no!' Teresia wailed, on the verge of tears. 'You aren't going to refuse?'

'Of course I'm going to refuse. I thank you with all my heart, but I must refuse all the same.'

'But why?' all three children cried at once.

'Several reasons. The first is that it would be wrong to put your mother into danger. She might very well be uneasy at crossing the frontier like that.'

François frowned. 'You mean she might do something silly? With Mother, of course, that's always possible, but if we explain it to her properly—'

'It's not just that. Your tutor, too, might well be very much annoyed. What will he do after you've gone? He'll go back to Madrid and, because he is in holy orders, he may well go and complain to the Inquisition, which is looking for me. Can you imagine what trouble that might mean for your father, for all his influence with the King?'

He paused for a moment to let the implications of his words sink into the young heads before him. Then, as they gazed at the floor in obvious discomfort, he added, more gently, 'Not only that, but your plan has room only for me, and I will not go without my Indian servant. Pongo's description has been circulated as well as mine and I don't see what disguise you could find for him, unless you took your servants into your confidence.'

'The Duchess of Alba's must know all about you being the duenna?' Teresia said bitterly.

'Yes. But she has only brought people she trusts, who have

117

been with her all their lives and would die for her. Could you say the same of yours? There, you see. Now, after all that, I am going to tell you the best reason of all. By tomorrow morning I shall be in France and I'll wait for you on the road to Bayonne. I'm going to swim over the river, with Pongo and our horses, while the actors are playing. It won't be all that difficult.'

'But the river is terribly wide. Won't you drown?' Dominique said.

'I hope not. Run along now. Supper must be nearly over and they will be looking for you. And I'll remember what you tried to do for me. Perhaps one day, I'll be able to repay you. We'll meet tomorrow – in France!'

He shook hands, English fashion, with both boys, kissed Teresia, whose face was already brightening, and pushed them out of the door.

It was dark now and the actors out in the square were beginning to beat their tambourines, summoning the people of Fontarabia to the play. Torches were blazing everywhere and on the stage a man in a parti-coloured red and blue costume was busy with a tinder box, lighting the candles. This, his last night in Spain, was perhaps the loveliest of any the Frenchman had seen. The blue of the sky had never been so warm and deep, the stars had never shone so brightly and the massive outline of the old palace took on a delicate, dreamlike quality in the unreal light. The green twilight had given way to flickering shadows.

Counterpointing the open-air music came bursts of laughter from the gathering crowd. For this one night, the travelling players were waking the old fortress town from its long sleep beside the ocean and on this night, for the man who was leaving her, Spain was coloured with the soft hues of regret.

And so when Cayetana thrust open his chamber door in a rustle of scented silks, he took her in his arms with a tenderness he had not before shown in their encounters. In that moment, he was nearer to loving her than he had ever been.

'We have one hour left,' he murmured into her warm throat, 'and no one shall take it from us.'

When he joined Pongo, who was waiting for him with the horses in the deep shadow of the ancient walls, he carried with him the image of a woman in a red silk dress standing on a balcony, a fan in her hand, watching with tears shining in her eyes, the players dancing below.

It was perfectly quiet. The watch, if there was one, must be trusting to the sea to do their work for them.

The tide was out. The estuary, so broad a little while before, showed sandbanks, dark against the silver ribbons of the waves, outlined against the rising moon. The ships in the little harbour slept below the leaning spires of their masts. Standing by a clump of marram grass at the edge of the sand, Pongo stared distrustfully at the sea.

'What are you thinking?' Gilles asked, swinging himself on to Merlin's back with the heartfelt joy of a man rediscovering a long lost friend.

The Indian made a face. 'Sand! Not good! Perhaps deadly.'

'Are you afraid of quicksands? Look over there. There are sea birds on that bank. We'll have nothing to fear there, except perhaps the current may be a trifle fast. But those little lights opposite are France. Home. We've lived with women long enough, don't you think?'

The Indian's long front teeth gleamed in the moonlight.

'Women like sand. Dangerous.'

With a shout of laughter, Gilles urged his mount down towards the water.

PART TWO

The Sorcerer

1784

5

The King's Gerfalcon

Ten days after that, Gilles, Pongo and Merlin, riding as escort behind the coach bearing the Cabarrus ladies, came in sight of Paris. It was towards the end of a fine spring morning, with a touch of summer already in the air, that they came to the Ile St Louis, where the travellers were to take up residence in the house of the obliging M. de Boisgeloup.

There, a disappointment awaited them, the obliging M. de Boisgeloup having departed this life a few days previously. He was no more than two days buried and his widow, inconsolable, in the words of her majordomo, in her grief, received them in such funereal weeds and with a face so disfigured with tears, that Antoinette could hardly dream of imposing herself on such a house of mourning. She stayed long enough to condole suitably with Madame de Boisgeloup, assured her of her sincerest sympathy and in response to that lady's somewhat limp renewal of her invitation, begged her rather to recommend her to some furnished house worthy of the wife and children of Spain's most prominent banker.

Madame de Boisgeloup, whose mind was clearly not on such things as rented accommodation, pulled herself together sufficiently to mention one, in the St Eustache *quartier*, which she had heard was very clean. Armed with which information, Antoinette thanked her gracefully, promised to pay for a *trentin* of masses for the soul of her husband's departed friend, mounted again into her mud-splashed coach and departed, bearing her family and servants with her, to the extreme disappointment of her younger son, Dominique, who had been much attracted to the trees and the sunny waters of the Seine flowing past the house.

'That lady asked us to stay, so why do we have to go somewhere else? Look at Teresia. She can hardly keep her eyes open.'

'Maybe so,' the girl retorted. 'But I don't want to wake up in a funeral parlour. Mother was quite right. We haven't come to Paris to be miserable. Do you know this place we're going to, Señor Gilles?'

'No,' said that young man smiling. 'But it can't help but be more cheerful than this.'

In fact the house, which was owned by another and much jollier widow, was charming, the rooms agreeably furnished, and there was a pretty garden. So Gilles did not hesitate to leave his friends to settle in while he went to deal with his own affairs. These, if any complaint about him from Madrid had reached Versailles, might well prove awkward.

He hurried back across the Seine to the Rue du Colombier to deposit his baggage at the York Hotel, to which Fersen had taken him on his arrival from Brittany, hoping there would be room there, since it was incontrovertibly one of the best hotels in the capital. Once the town house of the family of Rosambo, it numbered among its clients persons of distinction such as the English ambassador, Sir David Hartley, who had come the previous summer to sign with Benjamin Franklin the peace treaty at Versailles, recognizing the independence of the United States.

Luck was with him. The hotel was full but the proprietor, Nicholas Carton, recognized the young man at a glance and welcomed him as an old friend.

'I have been expecting to see you, Sir, ever since Monsieur the Count arrived on the seventh,' he said, preceding him up the broad stone staircase.

'Monsieur the Count? Which one?'

'Why – Count Fersen. You did not know, then, Sir, that my house is filled with Swedes?'

'So many? Have we been invaded?'

'Aha, you still like your little joke, Sir, I see. It is the suite of His Majesty King Gustave III, Monsieur the Count of Haga, I should say, visiting our country on his way home from Italy.

124

Monsieur de Fersen is with them. He is putting up here, along with the Baron Stedingk.'

'Oh?' Gilles said, delighted at the news. 'So he is here?'

'Not at this moment, sir. The gentlemen are all at Versailles for the day. They are extremely popular – being made most welcome. Your old room is just free, but it is not yet prepared for you.'

'Never mind. I don't want to go to bed at noon. All I need is a wash and something to eat for myself and my man – and one horse. Mine is in need of rest and I must have a fresh mount. I have a number of urgent calls to make.'

An hour later, washed, shaved and dressed in his old Dragoon uniform, Tournemine mounted horse and set off at a brisk trot in the direction of the Hotel de Rochambeau, leaving Pongo free to pursue his acquaintance with the plump, dark-haired chambermaid called Louise who, on the Indian's first visit to Paris, had fallen victim to the exotic charms of his buck teeth and shaven crown.

It was no great distance to the Rochambeau's house in the Rue de Charche-Midi, not far from the convent of the Filles du Bon Pasteur, but Gilles passed the whole way offering prayers to God, the Virgin and every saint in the calendar that his own particular good shepherd was not away at the ends of the earth, or even on his estates in Touraine.

Luck had not deserted him. The general was not only in Paris but at home and a mention of his own name and rank was enough to open the door to him. Inside, however, he was met by all the bustle of what appeared to be imminent removal: soldiers coming and going in the hall and stairway with arms full of papers and servants carrying travelling trunks and portmanteaux.

'Is the general about to leave for a campaign?' Gilles asked, carried back several years to a house in Brest and preparations for the American expedition. The youthful cornet in the Touraine regiment was passing, a large ledger under his arm, recognizing an officer, paused and saluted.

'Not a campaign, Sir. For Calais. The King has appointed General Rochambeau to succeed Marshal de Croy as commander of the northern military division, the most important.'

'The devil! Is he leaving soon?'

'At the end of the month. If you would excuse me, I have to—'

Well, well, Gilles told himself, his eyes on the young man who was so like what he himself had once been, I have just arrived in time.

Rochambeau welcomed his former secretary like a long lost son, kissed him on both cheeks, jabbed him cordially in the ribs, congratulated him on his appearance and then thrust him into a big armchair, calling loudly for servants to bring them champagne on the instant.

'By God, Chevalier, you can't think how glad I am to see you!' he exclaimed, after the younger man had congratulated him on his new appointment. 'You bring a breath of the Atlantic with you, and of old times and our glorious days in America, which leave the most brilliant appointments standing. Oh but I'm glad of this! Not that I'm surprised, mind. I'd have sworn Spain wouldn't suit you for long. That stuffy, narrow-minded Court, all boredom and ceremony. That wouldn't do for you, not after the forests of Virginia.'

'I rather think I was the one who did not suit, Sir. If I may say so, I think you should wait to hear the tale of my adventures before you start opening the champagne.'

'Wait? What for? Champagne is like a pretty woman, it must never be kept waiting or it's no good for anything.'

'Because you may not feel like sharing it with a man on the run from a sentence of death. Both the king's police and the Inquisition are after me.'

The scarred visage of the hero of the War of Independence registered no greater surprise than a slight raising of the eyebrows. By way of an answer, he leaned over and fished a dark bottle out of the wine cooler, opened it and, filling two tall translucent glasses, handed one to his visitor.

'When did you get here?'

'Two or three hours ago.'

'Then have a drink. It'll give you heart to tell me your story. Lord, if you had anything discreditable on your conscience, you'd have taken care not to come to me with it. If you're here, it's Spain that's in the wrong. As for that Inquisition of theirs, a barbarous institution hiding its blood-thirsty instincts under the mantle of Christ, I'd rather not tell you what I think of that. Drink and then talk.'

Thus encouraged, Gilles gave as strict and honest an account of his adventures as if he had been speaking to his confessor. He trusted the man before him implicitly and had a respect for him not far short of idolatry. Whatever Rochambeau's verdict might be, Gilles would accept it without question.

Rochambeau heard him out in absolute silence, his face expressionless, except that on two occasions Gilles thought he caught the shadow of a smile round the other man's mouth. When it was over he said nothing either but rose and, treading over to the fireplace, pulled the silken bell-pull that hung beside it.

'The carriage and horses,' Rochambeau said to the servant who answered it. 'We are going to Versailles.'

Then, as Gilles gazed at him, uncomprehending, he added: 'Yes, you too. I'm taking you to the King. There's just time for one more glass while they're bringing the horses round.'

'To the King!' Gilles stammered in amazement. 'But General—'

'Of course to the King! He's the only one who can sort this out. You're in serious trouble, no use mincing words. Bedding the future Queen of Spain must be *lèse-majesté* at least. And I don't mean to give His Most Catholic Majesty's busy ambassador, Count D'Aranda, time to come asking for one of my men's heads in the name of the Family Treaty.'

As he spoke he filled the Chevalier's glass once more and Gilles drank it off at a draught, like a man in need of a restorative.

'So,' he said hesitantly, 'so you mean to tell his Majesty the whole story?'

'Everything! The King is not himself an amorous man. His habits are abstemious and his sense of family honour is strong but he has, what is rarer in a King, a heart, and his heart is good and just and generous. What is more, he likes frankness. Finally, you may be guilty of *lèse-majesté* but I'll wager it was, if you'll forgive the expression, over your dead body! Are you ready?'

Gilles bowed with respect and something else a good deal warmer.

'I made up my mind long ago, general, that I would follow where you led, even to hell itself.'

'I'll not ask you to go as far as that. And if the King will not listen, I can always take you to Calais in my baggage.'

His gaze, roaming the room in search of his stick, which finally came to light on top of a side table, paused abruptly on a small secretaire made of precious woods and balanced on fragile legs. Then it swung back critically to the young man.

'There's something you ought to have,' he said slowly, almost to himself, 'something that's slipped my mind ...'

He strode over to·the little desk, opened it and took out a dark blue leather case. He held it in his hands for a moment, without lifting the lid.

'A year ago,' he said, a touch of gravity in his voice, 'in May 1783, the officers of the American army formed a society of friends which should endure for as long as they themselves lived, or their eldest male heirs or, failing those, whichever member of a collateral branch should be deemed worthy of membership. Because they were civilians, returning to civilian life, they chose to represent them the name of the illustrious Roman, Lucius Quintus Cincinnatus, the farmer who returned to his plough after saving Rome, and they call themselves the Society of the·Cincinnati.

'Next, wishing to pay tribute to their French companions-in-arms, they decided to admit to membership of the society, not only our ministers plenipotentiary, but also our admirals, ships' captains, generals and colonels.

'The King gave his gracious assent, last January, to the formation of a French branch and the first meeting took place in this very house, presided over by Admiral d'Estaing.'

'Why d'Estaing?' Gilles broke in, shocked. 'You surely did far more for the American cause than he did.'

'That is not a matter for you, or for me. Don't interrupt me, if you please, we've not much time. As I was saying, you, of course, were not present at that meeting and, since you have not attained the rank of colonel, you are not, in theory, eligible for membership of the Cincinnati. But there was no doubt in any of our minds, or in General Washington's either, when he wrote to us, that the Gerfalcon well deserved to wear the golden eagle.'

128

His face suddenly very pale, Gilles watched Rochambeau open the case, revealing the strange decoration. It was the American bald eagle made in solid gold with a blue ribbon. He lifted it and pinned it quickly to the younger man's uniform coat which seemed suddenly tight across his chest.

'By special permission of the President General of the Society of the Cincinnati, General George Washington, and of His Majesty King Louis the Sixteenth of that name, by the Grace of God, King of France and of Navarre, you the Chevalier de Tournemine de la Hunaudaye, are henceforth a member of the Society of the Cincinnati, you and your son after you and your son's sons after him. I trust that they, too, will prove worthy of the honour.'

Rochambeau shook hands warmly, in the American fashion, with his one-time secretary who was aware of tears pricking at his eyelids. Then, turning away abruptly to conceal his feelings, the general roared: 'Hey there, Poitevin! My hat and gloves! I'm going out!'

Two hours after that, bowed forward by a gentleman usher, Gilles followed his general's broad back into the King's library on the first floor of the palace of Versailles and made his bow to the man, barely thirty, whom he called master.

The King was in an excellent humour. He was just returned from hunting at Marly and the day had been a good one, as it generally was for he was a dedicated huntsman. Which was to say, since the King hunted every day, that he was in his customary humour.

He was still booted and dressed in a coat of plain steel grey with no other ornament than the dazzling whiteness of the lace at his throat and wrists which went some way to disguise his already pronounced corpulence. The room in which he stood was huge, with pale woodwork and long windows and had once been the card room of his predecessor Louis XV. This King, as befitted a scholar and a friend to learning, had converted it into an impressive library filled with works of scholarship. Beside him, a large plan of Paris was spread out on a table, flanked by a number of model buildings.

'Ah! Rochambeau!' the King cried, cutting through his visitor's apologies for this unceremonious arrival. 'Come in,

129

come in! And no apologies, please. I am always delighted to see you.'

'And yet I very much fear we are disturbing you, Sire. Your Majesty was working—'

'Not at all. I was looking at the results of some other people's work and finding it most interesting. Ever since last year, when I set up my commission to look into projected plans for improving the convenience, healthfulness and beauty of Paris, my architects have been throwing themselves into it wholeheartedly and I must say they have produced some very interesting ideas. See here, Monsieur Soufflot, who is controller of buildings in Paris, suggests cutting a broad thoroughfare running east-west beside the Louvre and the Tuileries. And Monsieur Patte wants to take Les Halles out of Paris, pull down the Hôtel Dieu as a hotbed of infection, clear the Ile de la Cité and cut another great road, north-south this time, parallel to the Rue St Jacques. And what do you say to my own idea? This model made from my designs has just been brought to me.'

Moving with unexpected lightness for a man of his build, Louis crossed the library and lifted a large model of a handsome open space planted with ornamental trees and with a magnificent fountain at its centre from a side table.

'It's a fine square,' Rochambeau said with a smile, 'and a handsome fountain, but where does your Majesty mean to erect these marvels?'

'You'll never guess, unless I tell you. I hardly dare say it. My idea is so revolutionary. This square will come into being when I have demolished the Bastille.'

'The Bastille? Your Majesty does not mean—'

'Why yes! I mean it quite seriously. That blackened old fortress offends my eyes whenever I'm in Paris. It's ugly and outdated. I am no medieval monarch, dammit! What's more, it blocks most of the Rue St Antoine, and it serves no useful purpose, or none to speak of. There are plenty of other prisons for the malefactors of Paris. And I have a horror of *lettres de cachet*. Well, what do you say?'

Rochambeau bowed. 'That your Majesty is a father to your people, which I never doubted, and that I have here a young man for whom the demolition of a state prison must certainly be a matter for rejoicing.'

130

The smile faded from the King's face. He laid down the model with an appearance of regret and then, his hands lightly clasped behind his back, walked over to his desk but did not sit. When he turned Gilles saw, with a sudden unease, that he was a changed man. Gone was the pleasant-tempered gentleman, the man of science. What faced him now was the King, instinct with a majesty which, whatever his detractors might say, Louis XVI knew very well how to put on at need.

'What am I to understand from that?' he asked. 'What has this young man done to risk the Bastille? He is one of your people I gather, from the decoration he is wearing. What is your name, Sir?'

Gilles made haste to correct this impression.

'Chevalier de Tournemine de la Hunaudaye, Sire. Lieutenant unattached in the Queen's Dragoons.'

'Unattached for what reason?'

'May it please your Majesty, I was given leave of absence to serve in Spain. I was, until recently, a junior officer in his Most Catholic Majesty's Bodyguard.'

'It pleases me not at all. I do not care to have my troops take service under foreign flags. In God's name, Sir, have you itchy feet? First America and now Spain? Is France not good enough for you? Now I come to look at you, I've seen you before, I think?'

'I had the honour to be presented to your Majesty by his grace the Duc de Lauzun after the victory of Yorktown. We were sent home with the despatches.'

The King's face cleared a fraction.

'Now I have it! You are the Indian scout who fought with the Marquis de la Fayette. You were given the name of some bird, I seem to recall?'

'The Gerfalcon, Sire.'

'That's it. I said I wanted to see you again so that you could teach me to hunt like the Iroquois, but you did not come.'

'I dared not, Sire.'

'You were mistaken. You were even more mistaken in going to my cousin of Spain. Very well, Sir. Since we are already acquainted, I am more inclined to hear you. Tell me your story and we'll see what you've been doing to deserve the Bastille.'

131

Gilles gulped and cast a helpless glance at Rochambeau who had followed the irascible start to the conversation with some disquiet. It seemed to him that it was now time for him to intervene. He coughed slightly.

'Sire.' His voice came as near to a gentle murmur as it was possible for him to achieve. 'If your Majesty permits—'

'What is it?'

'I will put your Majesty in possession of the facts. It is a serious business – delicate, certainly – in fact highly delicate, and I fear that in your Majesty's presence the Chevalier may not—'

The King's fist smashed down among the papers on his desk, making them jump.

'What the devil are you on about, Rochambeau? Are you trying to tell me I can terrify a young fellow who isn't frightened of savages, or of the English, who can be worse than savages when they put their minds to it? You stay out of this. If he's got himself into trouble, then he can tell me so himself, I hope. What is he accused of?'

'Of – of *lèse majesté*, Sire.'

'What?'

Louis's face had flushed brick red with anger. Rochambeau continued hurriedly.

'Towards her Royal Highness, the Princess of Asturia, Sire. It was, I dare assure your Majesty, of a quite involuntary kind. He really had no alternative.'

'Oho!'

There followed a pause, heavy with doubt. Then the King threw himself into his chair with a sigh.

'Very well, Chevalier. Tell me about your misdemeanours.'

This time Gilles did not hesitate. He sensed a slight relaxation of the atmosphere and he made the most of it. He gave a restrained, but perfectly honest, account of the whole affair and, when he had done, dropped on one knee before the King, his head held high.

'I should not like your Majesty to think that I am seeking to protect myself by hiding behind a woman. I have been guilty to the simple extent that I took pleasure in what occurred. Should Spain require my head, your Majesty will not hesitate to give it, only, I entreat you, spare my honour. I am a Breton, Sire, and I hold by my faith. Loyal to my God, as to my King, I will not be condemned for sorcery and blasphemy. If I must die, let it be by the axe, Sire, as befits a gentleman, and not, like a devil worshipper, by the fire!'

Louis did not answer. He gazed at the young man for a long time, then sat with his chin sunk in his chest, apparently lost in thought. The silence in the big room, broken only by the almost inaudible tick of the large Boule clock on the mantelshelf, was weighed down with unspoken thoughts. Gilles, frozen in his reverential attitude, hardly dared to breathe and behind him the general too was holding his breath, waiting for the words which would fall from the royal lips.

Louis XVI sighed again and lifted his head.

'You may rise, Sir,' he said quietly, 'and listen to me.'

Before he could say more, the gentleman who had ushered them in reappeared with the news that the Comte de Vergennes, minister for foreign affairs, requested an audience. The count followed hard on his heels, like a man assured of his right to see the King at any time, and one whose business would not wait.

'Sire,' he said, his level, diplomatist's voice retaining the faintest hint of a Burgundian accent, 'I must beg your Majesty's attention on a most urgent matter—'

Catching sight of Rochambeau, whom he knew well, he broke off and bowed, his eyes travelling meditatively from the general to the Lieutenant of Dragoons. They rested briefly on the decoration, blazing brand new on the younger man's chest, and after a moment he smiled, the rare smile which, for that very reason, lit his face with such charm. De Vergennes was not a man who studied to please. A great statesman and a diplomat whose quiet competence would only be appreciated by others of his exacting trade, he was both farsighted and dedicated to the service of his country, but his contempt for the courtier's arts made him few friends in high places. Choiseul had not liked him and neither did the Queen. It was further held against him that, while ambassador in Constantinople he had married, for love, a Madame Testa, a woman of no birth. It had all but finished his career and he had been compelled to retire for two years to his estates at Toulongeon, in Burgundy.

But Louis liked him and recognized his worth. Since his

appointment to the post of foreign minister, Vergennes had had the distinction of negotiating the treaties recognizing the independence of the American States, for which he had worked so hard. He was also expert at holding the balance in a Europe rocked by the ambitions of Frederick of Prussia, Joseph of Austria and Catherine of Russia, although the general public remained quite oblivious of his prowess.

'In a hundred years, they'll do me justice,' he would say. 'To be fair to themselves, it's the least the French can do.'

For the present he was, at sixty-five, a man of a good height with a high forehead, and a pair of direct eyes in a fine-boned face with a thin, uncommunicative mouth. A mouth which, whatever his detractors said, was perfectly capable of laughter.

'I assume, Sire, that this officer is the Chevalier de Tournemine?'

'You assume correctly, my dear Vergennes. Though how the devil you knew—'

'The devil had little to do with it, Sire. I have Count Aranda in my office clamouring for this young man's extradition, in order, as I understand, that he may be handed over to the Holy Office for all sorts of crimes perfectly incomprehensible to a modern mind.'

Louis XVI did not often lose his temper but now he did so with a vengeance.

'Extradition!' The Holy Office! Which means the stake, of course! And all because the boy made a cuckold of that ape Don Carlos? Tomfoolery!'

Vergennes was laughing. 'Your Majesty is a mathematician and possesses the secret of synthesis. I should say that the ambassador, who is a man of sense, appears more than a trifle embarrassed at his message, but he can hardly fail to carry it. The Chevalier d'Ocariz arrived yesterday, bearing urgent letters about the matter.'

'Can't you sort things out on your own, minister?'

'It concerns the royal family, your Majesty, and I know the king has strong feelings on the subject, and also regarding his and his family's honour.'

'My family, yes, but my brother of Spain has never seemed to me to be among my closest connections. He is welcome to watch over the Infanta's honour, though he'll have his work cut out to defend the invisible. But let him not ask me to share his vigil.'

'Nevertheless, it is my duty to keep your Majesty informed. What is your pleasure?'

The King said nothing but went to his desk and, opening a drawer, took out a sheet of paper, impressively sealed and already covered with large black letters. He scribbled a few words on it, apparently filling in the blank spaces. He sanded it, tossed down his pen and melted a little red wax on it, into which he pressed the heavy ring he wore on his finger.

'There is your answer, Vergennes. Tell the ambassador that Monsieur de Tournemine was not at that time within the jurisdiction either of his King or of the Holy Office. He is a French citizen and no longer in the service of Spain for, as this commission witnesses, he had already been recalled to France to take up a post as second lieutenant in the First Company of our Guard.'

Vergennes' smile broadened widely.

'The Scottish Company, the most highly privileged of all? Perfect, Sire. I shall go instantly and acquaint the ambassador most faithfully with your Majesty's words.'

'Upon my word, one would say it gave you pleasure? A moment ago you looked as though you'd like to have the heads of an entire regiment.'

'I could not help sympathizing somewhat with Count Aranda's troubles, Sire, but I was prepared – if he had not already found a far better advocate than I could ever be – to rise to the young man's defence, for if we had delivered him up to Spain we should have forfeited the esteem of our American allies. Neither General Washington, nor General La Fayette would ever have forgiven us. They would have accused us of being feudal and outdated.'

When his foreign minister had gone Louis handed the commission to Gilles, who went down on his knee again to receive it. Too moved to speak, he seized the King's hand and pressed his lips to it respectfully.

'Well, Sir?' Louis XVI said, kindly. 'Are you satisfied with your King?'

Miraculously, Gilles' vocal chords began to function once again.

135

'Sire,' he said, 'this is the second time your Majesty has granted me my life. The first was when you condescended to ratify my father's will. Now you have shielded me with this royal generosity. I have always been your servant but now that I am to have the honour of guarding your own person, your Majesty may be sure that I am wholly yours, you may command my loyalty in all things. If Gerfalcon there be, I shall from henceforth be the King's, to fly at any time against any foe, in peace or war, in darkness or in light.'

A shadow of emotion passed over Louis's heavy face as he looked down at the passionate one uplifted to his, a passion at strange variance with the blue ice of the eyes which gave this young officer so formidable an air.

'Very well, sir. The King accepts your fealty and will not forget your promise. You will be a sure weapon in his hand and one which, rest assured, we shall use only in a cause which is just. From this day forth, you are the King's Gerfalcon, although that is between the three of us, myself and you and Monsieur de Rochambeau here, who witnesses your appointment.'

'And can bear witness here and now that your Majesty will never have a better servant than this young man. He is one of those who in times past might have sat with honour at the Round Table. May I offer your Majesty my thanks.'

By way of an answer Louis shook hands with both men and they took their leave, joyfully. Gilles was still too shaken with his experience to realize what had happened. He had gone to Rochambeau like a drowning man grasping for the only branch within reach and Rochambeau had not concealed from him the gravity of his case. Had the King chosen to honour the Family Compact, the culprit would have been sent, if not to the stake, at least to the Bastille and thence to the scaffold, with all convenient speed. But clearly Louis XVI cared more for his subjects than for any printed treaty. He was a good judge of men and far from dismissing the man pursued by his cousin to outer darkness, he was keeping him close at hand and even trusting his person to him.

As they left the palace, where everything was preparing for that most important moment of the day when the King supped, Gilles could not restrain a quiver of happiness as they passed through doors at which stood the men who, in a day or two, would be his fellows. The Guard was the principle corps of the King's Household. None might enter it without the quarterings of nobility and of those only the tall and good-looking. Tomorrow, he would don with pride the uniform coat of dark blue and silver with its broad red facings, white breeches and long, glossy boots and cocked hat with white feathers, while Merlin would receive the blue and silver saddlecloth and the saucy blue ribbon for his long, silky tail. He was going to belong to the Scottish Company founded in the fifteenth century by the Constable John Stewart of Buchan, the parent not only of the King's gendarmerie but of all the other regiments of the Household. Tomorrow, he would have an interview with the regiment's commander, Marshal de Castries ...

'You've taken on a heavy burden, my friend,' Rochambeau said pensively, as they climbed into the coach. 'A watchdog, that's what you'll be – and henchman, as you demanded. And of all our kings, this, for all his kindness, learning and humanity, or perhaps because of it, he will probably be the one to suffer most from his contemporaries.'

'While there is breath in my body, general, I will serve and defend the King. Woe to any man who touches him, for, while I live, if I cannot save him, I shall surely avenge him. And if I can do neither, for all I fear God, I shall take my own life, for to me the oath I have just taken binds me as surely as any religious vows. A hawk knows only one master.'

'Well then, my boy, let me give you three pieces of advice, for you are yet ignorant of the Court and its dangers. If you want to guard your master effectively, get yourself made a member of one of these masonic lodges that are popping up all over Paris these days, the strongest you can find. Once you're in, keep your eyes and ears open, but learn to hold your tongue.'

'I'll take that advice. What of the others?'

'Two named, both of them highly dangerous to the King. The first is his cousin, the Duke of Chartres, the Duke of Orleans' eldest son. A hothead, with no real vice in him and no evil intent but suffering from an ulcerating resentment ever since the battle of Ushant, when the Queen's circle got him branded, quite unjustly, as a coward. Philip of Chartres may

137

be mad and rather too much of a demagogue, but a coward he has never been.'

'And – the other?'

'The King's own brother.'

'Which one? The King has two, has he not?'

'Oh, I'm not talking about Monseigneur d'Artois, the younger. He's a jovial, agreeable prince, devoted to all forms of pleasure. He's nothing but a butterfly, a Prince Charming in the true tradition of old man Perrault's fairy tales, with a brain like a pea. He likes everyone – his brother, his sister-in-law especially, for he amuses her and shares the same pleasures, men and women, except perhaps his own wife for whom he feels nothing but an amiable and politely concealed boredom. No, I'm talking about the one really political brain in the family, the prince of darkness and silence, the man who is furbishing up his weapons in secret, the man who for a long time, while Louis failed to get his wife with child, thought of himself as his brother's sole heir and future king of France, until his hopes faded with the birth of the princess royal and vanished pretty well altogether when the Dauphin came along, for the Queen may not have said her last word yet. I am talking about the man who is capable of anything – and will do it too, believe me – to supplant his brother and don the crown of France, which he has always thought would suit his own head better than Louis's. I am talking about Monseigneur the Count of Provence. I am talking about Monsieur!'[2]

Impressed by the expression on his chief's battle-scarred face and by the vehemence of his tone, Gilles asked quietly: 'That is a grave accusation, Sir. Are you quite sure of what you are saying? Are the Bourbons indeed like the House of Atreus?'

Rochambeau shrugged and leaned forward to rub a clear space on the window glass, for with the darkness had come the rain, the soft, gentle rain of the Ile de France that relieves the dryness of the parched earth as tears relieve a heart whose feelings have been too long pent up. He opened a silver box set into one wall of the coach and selected a cigar, a habit he had picked up in America. He offered one to his young companion, extracted a tinder box and lit both pale brown cylinders so

[2] Only the brother next in age to the King had the right to the title of Monsieur, unadorned. His wife was Madame.

that the air in the confined space was filled almost at once with their scented smoke.

'The resemblance has cropped up,' he said, 'more than once in history. Brotherhood does not mean much when there is a crown in prospect. Remember Gaston d'Orléans and his endless conspiracies against his brother, Louis XIII. How many heads rolled in the course of his stubborn pursuit of a throne to which he had no right! The prince would desert his friends, win forgiveness, and then do it again. Remember François d'Alençon plotting against Henri III. Kings' worst enemies are often their own brothers. Monsieur is no exception to the rule, only he hides it better. He is, it must be admitted, formidably intelligent. Much more so than our good king. And, unhappily, he knows it.'

'How does he hope to gain power now that the King has given the country an heir? By fostering revolution?'

'I told you he was intelligent. Suppose Louis were to be obliged to abdicate, through illness for instance, or were to die. Monsieur would become Regent during his nephew's minority.'

'Why him? Why not the Queen?'

'She has made too many enemies among the nobility, and she is becoming unpopular, too. No, it would be Monsieur. It takes a long time to bring up a king. Nor is it always easy.'

'You surely don't think—'

'With Monsieur, anything is possible. His body is clumsy, but his mind is subtle, active and cunning. As for his heart, if he has one, which I doubt, it is so well hidden that he himself must have forgotten where it is.

'You see, Monsieur is weaving his web in darkness with the tacit connivance of all the great nobles in the kingdom. They've been dreaming feudal dreams ever since the days of Louis XIV, and are pinning their hopes on him. Each time any misadventure comes to trouble the King, you can be sure that Monsieur is not far to seek. He's a combination of vulture and snake . . .'

'But he is a man also, I imagine, and no man can be so black that there isn't a speck of blue sky somewhere.'

'You're so young! And this is where you're wrong. Monseigneur de Provence isn't a man in the way you mean, because he is more or less impotent. So much so that his wife, Princess

Marie-Josephine, has been obliged to resort to the discreet charms of Lesbos with her lady-in-waiting, Madame de Gourbillon. He's a brain.'

'But I thought I heard he had a mistress?'

'That's so. But I don't think it's more than a meeting of minds. Young Countess Balbi has the devil's own wit and she knows how to use it. Monsieur is enchanted by her jibes and repartee. What's more, she's not bad to look at, which Madame is not. All of which enables her to queen it at the Luxembourg and dream now and then of queening it at Versailles.'

Rochambeau's hand found the younger man's shoulder, gripped and shook it, as though the general sought to impress his convictions by main force.

'Serve the King, my friend. Defend him, love him. You won't find yourself in a very large company. His gentlemen are disgusted by his bourgeois tastes, his love of knowledge and of manual work – and his inability to make up his mind on occasion. The real power lies with the Queen. Her husband can refuse her nothing. As for the members of the Queen's circle, they mock the King almost openly.'

'And the Queen permits it?'

'Mostly she is unaware. But she is a prisoner of her own brainless set of fools and flatterers, Polignac, Vaudreuil, the Besenvals, with whom she leads a life of endless frivolities which cut her off both from the Court, which comes no nearer than the gates of the Trianon, and from the people, who are paying for the enormous pensions bestowed on all these creatures and are beginning to object. You'll see what I mean if you are ever privileged to behold her majesty playing at shepherdesses in her own domain.'

'Is it so difficult to gain admission to the Trianon?'

Rochambeau laughed harshly, with a note of bitterness. 'The notice boards on its bounds bearing the Queen's name are harder to cross than any frontier for anyone excluded from the Queen's circle. You'll find that out. Hey, Martin! Drive faster! We'll not be in Paris before morning at this rate. I don't want to eat my supper by the roadside!'

6

The Trianon, Nocturne...

Despite the general's gloomy predictions, seven days later, on
the twenty-first of June 1784, Gilles de Tournemine passed
those same notice boards on the occasion of what was to be the
last great festivity of the Ancien Régime, given in the gardens
of the Trianon, that most intimate of royal pleasure grounds.

The play ended with a transformation scene. As if by magic,
the Queen's little blue and gold theatre blazed with light and
gigantic bouquets of flowers blossomed at the front of the stage
and soared like rockets up to the flies, while the artistes of the
Comédie Italienne and the dancers from the Opéra made their
bows, over and over again, sinking like flowers beneath the
storm of applause.

Marmontel's *Sleeper Awaked*, to music by Grétry, was
enthusiastically received by its noble audience. The youthful
Hassan, becoming caliph while asleep, had finally made his
choice and settled on the love of the slave girl, to the accompani-
ment of thunderous applause, from none more than the evening's guest of honour, King Gustavus III of Sweden, visiting
France incognito, under the transparent pseudonym of Count
Haga, on his way home from his Italian tour.

Standing with folded arms, his back against one of the pillars
of a small box rather over-full of the visitor's aides, Taube,
Stedingk and Armfelt, all of them former comrades from
America, Gilles had heard little of the piece. His attention had
been riveted on the fascinating spectacle of the audience.

Marie-Antoinette had arranged this pretty entertainment to
honour her nordic guest and everything, by her command, was

141

to recall the colour of his Swedish snows. Satins, laces, muslins, velvets and feathers were all of a dazzling whiteness with, over all, the glitter of myriads of diamonds. It was as though the little theatre, the flowers and the rich greenery of the Trianon had all at once been overlaid with a covering of snow.

Yet, looking at King Gustavus, a short, fair, active man of thirty-eight, with a high, intelligent brow and blue-grey eyes, Gilles could not suppress the thought, which had marred his pleasure in the evening from the first, that he was not the real hero of the hour. That belonged to the man who stood behind him, magnificent in white velvet frosted with silver, on whom the Queen's eyes were so often bent, his friend Axel de Fersen.

The quality of that look made Gilles more uneasy every time he saw it, until he wondered whether the night's enchantment was not interfering with his judgement and making him imagine things that were not so. For surely it was inconceivable that a Queen of France should look thus at a young foreigner while all the time there stood at her side the good, plain, quiet man who shared her bed and her crown. Could it be that Marie-Antoinette had come to return the love which, Gilles knew all too well, filled Fersen's heart and life?

Even at that very moment, as she rose from her chair, her paniers of pearly satin embroidered with great silver lilies sewn with pearls swaying gracefully, and accepted the arm Count Hago offered to lead her in to supper, her blue eyes were still turning with a soft, sideways look to Fersen and in them was that slightly strained expression of one who loves and fears at any moment to see the beloved vanish in a puff of smoke. And it was to him that the Queen's beautiful plumed head on its long, graceful neck inclined almost imperceptibly, inviting him to follow.

Marie-Antoinette was royally beautiful tonight and, more than that, she radiated happiness. To the young Chevalier towards whom she had always shown such kindness, she looked happier than he had ever seen her, happier even than in the hour of her triumph when she had just given France an heir. Hers was a queenly beauty, certainly, enhanced by her gown, her jewels and the unreal atmosphere surrounding her, but it

142

was womanly also, and womanly in that most touching way, being the full blossoming beauty of a woman who knows her love is returned.

Gilles, brooding gloomily, could not decide whether to rejoice at his friend's dizzy but perilous good fortune, or to fear for the hurt that the Queen's love for Fersen might do to his King.

Louis's feelings towards his wife were a secret from no one. It was an undemonstrative, perhaps even an unromantic love, but deep and genuine and containing an element of humility due to the seventeen years in which a physical impediment had made their union incomplete, and it had come to a late flowering since his exquisite princess, now truly his wife, had borne him children. He had become so devoted to her that he could refuse her nothing, not even, unfortunately, a deal of unconsidered meddling in affairs of state.

As self-imposed guardian of the King's life, honour and greatness, Gilles could not but feel it hard that the first foe he came up against should be his greatest friend.

Trying to put his fears down to his over-active Breton imagination, Gilles did his best to shake off his uneasiness and followed the elegant crowd of spectators out into the brightly-lit gardens. His duties on this particular evening were of the lightest for, although present in his capacity of one of the Queen's bodyguard, the occasion was so far informal that, as an officer, Gilles' status was more that of a guest than a watchdog.

When Ferson passed him, literally at Count Haga's coat tails, Gilles tried to detain him for a moment, but got from his friend no more than a vague smile and the faintly hallucinated expression of a man awakened from sleep before he plunged off again in the wake of the white gown with its long train sweeping softly over the marble pavement.

'Later,' he said in a murmur. 'I'll see you later.'

Gilles shrugged irritably. Axel, certainly, was by no means himself. That was something he had observed on the very day after his arrival, when he had called on his friend in his room at the York Hotel. Fersen had welcomed him joyfully, of course, and his joy was undoubtedly real, but there had been a hint of abstraction in it which was unlike him. It was as though, caught up in his own life, Fersen had no interest to spare for others.

Dressing himself with extraordinary care, the Swede had also given Gilles the impression that he could not breathe outside the rarefied air of Versailles. Only the news that his friend had been posted to the Guard penetrated his self-absorption.

'Wonderful!' he exclaimed. 'You lucky dog! Lieutenant in the Guard! You'll spend all your time in the presence of the – of the royal family, that is. You will belong to Versailles. When I come back, we shall be able to meet often.'

'When you come back? Are you going away?'

Fersen hunched his shoulders without enthusiasm.

'I have to. I can't abandon Count Haga in the middle of his tour. I have to see him home to Sweden. It will give me the chance to visit my father, at least. Last time I left you I went no farther than Germany, and there joined the King on his way to Italy. It will also enable me to sort out some family business – or so I hope.'

Gilles did not take him up on this since he already knew, from Rochambeau, what the business was. Fersen, in his passion for France, longed to buy himself into the Royal-Swedish regiment, but he did not possess the means himself and his father, Count Frederick Axel, was needing some persuasion to disburse a large sum of money which the family could ill-afford for an appointment which would keep his son away from home for years. Instead, he asked simply: 'When are you going?'

'I don't know precisely. The King thinks of setting out for home on the tenth or twelfth of July, but nothing is settled yet. Of course, it doesn't leave us much time and, with so much happening, the days are flying past. We're swamped with parties, picnics and entertainments of every kind. Gustavus is revelling in it but it's getting me down a trifle and I can't see why he has to keep on accepting all these invitations to Paris drawing-rooms—'

'When you'd much rather be spending your time at Versailles,' Gilles finished for him. 'Well, my friend, I'll leave you to your dissipations and go and get on moving my things.'

144

Axel gripped his arm with a sudden return of his old affection.

'Don't forget what I said – you are the happiest of men, to be going *there*!'

It was an obsession, of course, and Gilles had no trouble diagnosing, with compassionate understanding, what the poor fellow was suffering from. He must be more in love with the Queen than ever, so that he could not get her out of his head. But in the light of what he had just seen in the theatre, what he had thought innocent, if unfortunate, was taking on a disquieting hue. Fersen in love with the Queen was only a mild, harmless dreamer: with the Queen in love with him, he became a danger to the realm ... and to the King.

The white figures of the guests were drifting about the gardens, wonderfully illuminated with shaded lamps in whose soft glimmering light the men and women seemed to float down the long alleys of the garden like so many sparkling ghosts.

By the cascade were huge, painted transparencies representing rocks, grasses and fantastic flowering bushes while, behind the Temple of Love, a massive bonfire had just been set light to, filling the gardens with a golden glow that banished the night.

A firm hand grasped Gilles' arm and a merry voice said in his ear: 'Well and what are you doing standing here star-gazing instead of making for supper like everyone else? Aren't you hungry?'

Hauled out of his deepening meditation, Gilles de Tournemine uttered an exclamation of pleasure as he recognized the cheerful person of the Vicomte de Noailles, one of his earliest and best-loved comrades-in-arms, and the one who had given his fate the first nudge in the right direction by removing Rochambeau's secretary so that Gilles might take his place.

'No, not really. I'm sorry, Vicomte, I haven't got rid of my whiskers yet. All this is still so new to me. I need time to get used to it.'

'You? You're as much at home here as we are. The place is swarming with friends from America.'

'Not all of them, though. I haven't seen either General La Fayette or Lauzun.'

Noailles made a face and concentrated his attention on the delicate adjustment of his exquisite Malines lace cravat.

'You have, as ever, my dear Gilles, put your finger right on it. Neither of them is here. La Fayette, though still the hero of Paris, spends a little too much time with Monseigneur the Duc d'Orléans to be well received at Versailles, where the Palais-Royal people are unpopular in the extreme. In any case, he has just left for America again. As for Lauzun, he's in disgrace.'

'Surely not? What for?'

'He – er – paid a little too much attention to the Queen. In fact he says he had every encouragement but things went wrong. The King has banished him from Versailles.'

'Paid court to the Queen? Just like any lady-in-waiting?' Gilles said, stunned. 'Has Lauzun gone mad?'

Noailles shrugged. 'Come now, Chevalier, whiskers or no, don't tell me you haven't heard the rumours – there are enough of them – about our lovely sovereign lady's friendships? They've already credited her – you notice I say credited, thus proving how objective I can be – with so many lovers. Coigny, Vaudreuil, Besenval. Lauzun might well have felt encouraged. He has a lot of success with women.'

'I shall never bring myself to look on the Queen as a woman,' Gilles said curtly. 'And I'm surprised—'

'Come off your high horse, you damned Breton, and don't be such a prude! There may well be nothing in it but – well, are you quite blind, or haven't you noticed that our dear, romantic Fersen is the hero of the evening? Come now, will you really not have supper with me?'

'I don't feel like any supper, my friend. The gardens are so beautiful and so novel to me. I want to enjoy them while there's no one about. You'll just have to eat for two.'

'I'll do that, you may be sure. I'm hungry enough to eat a cow, two sheep and half a dozen hens, as well as endless desserts.' And, twirling lightly on his red heels, Noailles departed to join the other guests at supper in the various pavilions set about the gardens.

From a distance, those supper pavilions looked like great white lanterns with, coming from them, the sound of laughter and a gentle buzz of conversation against a soft background of music, but Gilles turned away from them. His real wish was to

146

be alone in the landscaped gardens which, that night, seemed to have come, ready-made, straight from a fairy tale and to belong, for a brief while, to himself alone.

In order to enjoy the silence without even the sound of his own footsteps on the sanded alley, he walked over to the edge of the small lake and stayed for a time leaning against a tree, breathing in the cool night air, with the smell of roses and lime blossom. The sounds of revelry came to him only faintly from a distance. He had broken free, out of time, almost out of his own self, into a moment of pure happiness which helped to drive his former sombre thoughts away.

The sound of light footsteps startled him out of the torpor into which he was sliding and he jerked upright, about to show himself, for the person approaching did not seem to be trying to avoid notice. The steps were swift but purposeful, like those of someone going somewhere in a hurry. But Gilles did not step out, in fact he drew back instead because what he saw just rounding a lighted yew was the white bubble of a woman's dress surmounted by a second snowy bubble which was the huge, bobbing head-dress of a lady all but running along the path, both hands holding up her enormous skirts so that her little silk shod feet twinkled underneath.

Thinking that the lady must be going to meet her lover somewhere in the unlighted portion of the garden, and not wishing to be indiscreet, Gilles drew back as far as possible into the shade of his tree, but even so she passed so close to him that a whiff of cool scent came to his nostrils, along with the soft rustle of silk.

At that precise moment, she happened to pass the dim light of one of the covered lanterns and Gilles, pressed against his tree, needed all his presence of mind not to cry out in surprise and joy, for the face beneath the tall powdered head-dress, adorned with a rope of pearls and a saucy little white ostrich feather, was Judith's.

For all his habit of self-control, it seemed to him that his feet had left the ground and he himself about to fly up into the deep starry sky. Judith here! Judith at the Trianon! Judith whom all the efforts of the Provost of Paris or of the Police Lieutenant's spies had failed to find, was simply inhabiting the royal glades of the Trianon as easily as she had once done her family home

147

of Le Frêne, as if it were the most natural thing in the world, as, given her name and quarterings, it should have been. There was, in fact, no reason why Mademoiselle de Saint-Mélaine should not be received at Court.

But the graceful white figure, unaware of Gilles' amazement, had moved on with the same swiftness and was vanishing now in the darkness of an alley leading away towards the outer edge of the gardens. Gilles' momentary happiness was extinguished like a snuffed candle. Where was she going to so fast?

His first idea of a lovers' tryst came back to his mind, bringing with it the inevitable spasm of jealousy. Quite forgetting, with splendid masculine obliviousness, all the women who, by rousing his blood, had helped him to endure her absence, Gilles' love was once more solely and for ever given to Judith. Immediately, he pulled off his shoes, sacrificing his fine silk stockings for the sake of moving silently and set out in pursuit of the hurrying figure, sparing a passing regret for his moccasins.

They ran thus, one behind the other, for a minute or two and Gilles could not help a twinge of furious admiration for the steadiness of that absurd headgear which stuck valiantly to the speeding girl, losing nothing but a little powder on the way.

One of the park gates came in sight and the girl swerved sideways into a little grove, slowing her pace considerably as she did so. Gilles followed cautiously until the sound of voices close by stopped him dead. It seemed they had arrived.

'You don't appear to have hurried, my dear,' a man's voice was saying on a note of annoyance. 'I was on the point of leaving. It's confounded damp among these trees.'

'Then why did your Highness insist on coming? I could as easily have called on you tomorrow morning.'

'You know quite well you must on no account come there again. My wife is stupid but not as stupid as that, and may I remind you I am not supposed to know you. Also, I wished to assure myself personally that all had gone well tonight. And what else could I do, since the King seems to have some grudge against us and would not have the princes present at tonight's entertainment.'

'The King – or the Queen?'

148

'The latter, I rather incline to think,' the unknown Highness answered lightly. 'I expect she was anxious not to let informed eyes see the favours Monsieur de Fersen enjoys. She is giving this evening's party for him. Poor Gustavus is only an excuse. But enough of that. Have you found proof of what I discovered?'

'Yes, Monseigneur. It cost me some trouble, since neither was I invited. I had to wait until they were all in the theatre to enter the Trianon.'

Gilles, screened by bushes, had been silently putting on his shoes, his mind a prey to every kind of bewilderment regarding the woman he had followed. There was disappointment, too, for although the face was Judith's, he could not recognize the voice. This woman's was high, with a metallic timbre absent from hers. But he soon forgot to analyse the sound in the interest of what was being said. Whoever this woman was, she had led him straight to something which must surely be a plot of some kind, or else why should a royal prince be cooling his heels in a camp coppice in the middle of the night? The next thing was to identify the prince and find out what he was up to.

'Who saw you?'

'Why no one! I was surprised, for tonight anyone may walk in. There was not a living soul. The servants and the ladies were all out looking at the lights or trying to see the play. I never saw a royal palace so ill-guarded. I got into the boudoir with no trouble at all. As you see, I am dressed for the occasion and there is nothing that resembles one woman in white so much as another in the same, and if anyone challenged me, I had my excuse all ready.'

'Excellent. So how do we stand? Do you know if Count Esterhazy has been here?'

'Although he is officially on his honeymoon in Normandy? He came, Monseigneur. In matters of the heart, he is the Queen's confidential messenger, which is a source of all kinds of agreeable honours to him. She will certainly have told him of the Swede's return.'

'But have you seen the Count yourself? Has he been to your house?'

'No. If I had not heard from your Highness that he had arrived – privately, I should not have known. Your Highness should know that Count Esterhazy is not anxious to place our relationship on a regular footing. I am not rich or powerful enough for that. It was my good fortune that I took the Cardinal de Rohan's advice and, on the second of February, on the day of the procession of the Order of the Holy Ghost, I went and threw myself at the Queen's feet as she was coming out of the chapel and begged her charity. My name awakened Esterhazy's interest because one of his best friends in Austria is a Count Ferraris, governor of Brussels, who is himself the son of a Valois de Saint-Rémy who was cousin Germane to my father. So it was thanks to him that the Queen took an interest in my wretched fate and, a few days later, sent for me privately to the Trianon. But that was all he did. I owe it to my own talents that I have been received since then, equally privately, for the Queen finds me both interesting and amusing. I entertain her with the gossip of Paris, and in particular with the Cardinal de Rohan's supposed grand passion for her, in which she simply refuses to believe.'

The Prince, whoever he was, laughed.

'I was forgetting that. How are you getting on with him?'

'As mad as ever! He is quite convinced that I have the means to restore him to favour, when in fact the Queen's face is as firmly set against him as ever. I find it tiresome because I should have liked her to agree to meet him, if only once, for the sake of our business, but it is virtually impossible.'

'There may be a way ... and one which will amuse the Queen and give her the opportunity to divert herself at the expense of her enemy, by one of the pieces of playacting she delights in.'

'A way? If your Highness can find one, I will think you a genius.'

'My dear Countess, you should tell that rascally husband of yours to spend more time in those fine new galleries attached to the Palais-Royal which have done so much to improve the amenities of Paris and to bring down the reputation of my cousin of Orléans, turning him into a shopkeeper, as the King so aptly says. My spies tell me there is a woman to be seen there on occasion, a lightskirt named Nicole Legay, though she calls herself d'Oliva, a pretty creature and much like the Queen ... We may think about that later. Did the key work?'

150

'Perfectly, Monseigneur. The little desk opened without a sound. The letters were there, tied with a ribbon of the Queen's favourite blue. There was one with today's date, from which I gathered that Esterhazy had been. The others, dated from Italy, are addressed to someone called Josephine, a code name of course, and came by way of a person named Fontaine. This Fontaine, I gather, must be away, hence the need to summon Esterhazy to carry the messages between Paris and Versailles.'

'You have been working hard, Countess, and here is something for your trouble. But what did the latest letter say? Did you read it?'

The woman – Gilles knew now that she was not Judith, that she could not be Judith, and for all his disappointment had to acknowledge a certain relief that she was not – the woman gave a vulgar little crow of triumph.

'I did better than that, my Prince – I stole it! Here it is.'

'Are you mad? Suppose anyone saw you? How do you know that there was no one there? At Versailles every wall has eyes and ears. And the Queen herself is bound to look for the letter, question her women about it—'

'About a letter from her lover? Come, come, Monseigneur. I don't see how she could go about it. She will think rather that in the confusion of the evening she must have put it somewhere else. She will look for it, yes, but alone, saying nothing to anyone.'

'Nevertheless, you should not have taken it. You should have – oh, I don't know – copied it!'

'And what would that have proved? When you have read the letter, Monseigneur, you will understand why I had to take it. In your hands, it will be a terrible weapon. Think: the absolute, irrefutable proof of a love affair between the Queen and Count Fersen.'

'I know. But I still do not like it. You do not know my sister-in-law. She is hot-tempered and impulsive and at such times her actions are quite unpredictable. So much so, indeed, that one wonders if she has a brain at all.'

'Listen, Monseigneur,' the woman said in a waspish tone that betrayed her annoyance, 'you must know what you want. Have you promised or not to restore to me all my family's lands, goods, titles and privileges on the day that you become regent?'

'I have given my word. I do not go back on it.'

'Then allow me to work for you in my own way. I know there was a risk in stealing the letter, but of so small account compared to its worth! You want proof that Fersen is the Queen's lover? You have it, and, if we can make good use of the Cardinal de Rohan's passion for her also, you will have no trouble in getting her sent back to Austria – and, by throwing doubt on the legitimacy of their birth, having your nephews debarred from the throne.'

There was a silence, broken at last by a sigh.

'You are right. I apologize and thank you. Indeed, my dear Countess, I shall always be grateful to Madame for mentioning to me that you had been taken ill in her antechamber. You are a woman of great price. But never forget that, until the day of our mutual triumph, we have never met and are unacquainted with one another.'

'Have no fear, your Highness. No one shall ever know. I know my own interest too well.'

Gilles' ears were drumming and a cold sweat was trickling unpleasantly down his spine. These two treacherous villains were plotting against the honour of their King and Queen. Bastardize the children of France! What slime were they made of, this woman who claimed descent from the Valois kings and her accomplice, a prince of the blood who did not scruple to soil his hands with any filth so that he might smear it over the throne?

Rochambeau's words came back to him and there was no doubt at all in his mind as to the identity of the royal conspirator. It was Monsieur, the obese Count of Provence and Louis XVI's evil genius. It could be no one else.

The interview in the coppice was all but over. The woman whom the Prince had called 'Countess' was preparing to leave and enter the carriage which was awaiting her in the Allée des Matelots. The Prince, for his part, had a cabriolet at the Porte de la Ferme to take him back to Paris.

Quivering with impatience, Gilles waited for Judith's double to take herself off for, much as he would have liked to follow her and see where she went, what he was about to do required no witnesses. He had to get back Fersen's letter, even if it was necessary to knock a prince of the blood unconscious to do it. Nor did he even try to pretend to himself that there was not a certain relish in the prospect of manhandling that gentleman a little.

Then, just as he was beginning to think the interview at an end, the Prince said suddenly: 'While I think of it, Countess. It is possible, after all, that you may need to get in touch with me urgently. You never know what might crop up in such a business as ours.'

'I am in perfect agreement with your Highness, but did you not say you would prefer me not to call at your house?'

'Your coming there is out of the question. Should the need arise, write me a note. It doesn't matter what it says, only you will sign it J. de Latour and inscribe a star below the signature. I will then appoint a meeting. You'll not forget? J. de Latour?'

'No fear of that, Monseigneur. It so happens that my husband's sister married a Monsieur de Latour. For me it is an easy name to remember.'

'Excellent. Go, now. We have dawdled long enough under these trees. I feel the chill of the night air.'

This time it was the end. Light feet brushed the fallen leaves. The Countess was coming out and Gilles had just time to flatten himself behind a tree before she was on him, the white silk gown brushing his foot as she passed.

The prince had also left the grove, but his feet moved slowly and heavily and he was making much less speed. As soon as the woman had gone, Gilles sped after him. It remained to see whether he was alone or whether some of his gentlemen were awaiting him farther on.

He was alone. The short, dark figure, almost as broad as it was long, was moving slowly among the trees and one glimpse of it was enough to confirm Gilles' belief, if confirmation were needed, that it was indeed the elder of the King's brothers. It was Monsieur.

He was strolling calmly, dead branches cracking under his feet, and brushing aside the foliage in his way. There was no one else in sight. On the other hand, there were still lights from the farm glimmering through the trees. Gilles knew that he could not afford to wait. It was time for the Falcon to reappear.

He crossed himself swiftly, asking God's forgiveness for what he was about to do, and then sprang, as noiselessly as a cat.

The attack caught the man wholly unaware. As he crashed down onto his well-padded, velvet back Gilles' forearm locked beneath his victim's chin, blocking both respiration and blood-supply before the prince could utter more than a strangled gasp. A few seconds more and he slithered like an unwieldy sandbag to the ground.

When he could feel no more resistance, the Chevalier laid him carefully down on the moss and, going through his pockets, pulled out some papers and stuffed them, unopened, into his own. It was too dark to see what he had got so, rising, he pursued his way towards the Trianon stables. What he had to do now was to get his horse and try to catch the woman up and follow her. If he could find out where she was going, he might be able to take from her the duplicate key she had been using to such effect.

It should be possible. She had no great start on him, for the attack on the prince had been no more than the matter of a few moments. Moreover, there was now no reason why she should be hurrying, that being no easy exercise, even for a young and active woman, when encumbered by a dress with paniers. Finally, there were few men who could claim to run faster than the Falcon.

Fresh wonders of illumination were springing up in the Trianon gardens to delight the guests who, having finished their supper, were now beginning to emerge again. Gilles dashed through them at top speed, causing no small surprise to those few who beheld something like a blue and silver meteor which they could not afterwards identify. A few more minutes and he was leaping onto Merlin's back, flashing past the Swiss Guards at the gate, and disappearing down the tree-lined Allée des Trianons.

He turned into the Allée des Matelots at such speed that he was obliged to rein in sharply, pulling Merlin back on his haunches, to avoid a collision with a hired coach coming into it from the other direction. It clattered to a halt amid a torrent of abuse from the driver. The light of the lantern suspended at the intersection fell on the irate head of a fair young man surmounted by a high-crowned hat in the latest mode, crying out in mincing tones: 'Take care, you fool! You all but had us in the ditch!'

'A thousand apologies, Monsieur! But I am in a great hurry ... on the King's service,' Gilles said quickly.

'Damnation take these Guards. They think they can ride roughshod over everyone! Go on then, friend. And bustle along! At this rate we'll not be in Paris before tomorrow morning.'

Gilles pulled his horse back to let the coach get ahead, then spurred forward to overtake and pass it. When it had first stopped he had called himself every kind of a fool for drawing attention to himself in that way. But it had had its reward for behind the young fop's elegant hat, he had caught sight, inside the carriage during its brief halt, of the pale face of the woman who dared to look like Judith and had gleaned the further precious information that the pair were on their way to Paris. That meant he must get there before them and await them at the entrance to the city, a feat which, given Merlin's fine legs against the much slower ones of the hired coachhorse, should present no difficulty. It would even give him time to change his uniform coat for something less conspicuous which would not attract the notice of the coach's irascible occupant a second time.

However, as with any regiment anywhere, the individual officer might propose but his superiors disposed. As Gilles entered the yard of the house in which he was quartered temporarily, until a suitable lodging could be found for him, his heart sank at the sight of his captain, the Comte de Vassy, just about to mount his horse. At the sight of Gilles, he paused.

'Just at the right moment, Monsieur de Tournemine. I've just heard that Lieutenant de Castellane, who was to have been on guard duty at the palace tonight, is indisposed. An – ah – an old wound is apparently troubling him. You can relieve him.'

'Yes, Sir. May I first go up and give an order to my man and change my boots?'

'You have five minutes.'

Cursing the fate which had made him think of changing his coat, Gilles raced up the stairs to his own lodging where he knew he would find Pongo still up and dressed, for nothing would ever make him retire before his master.

'Saddle a horse,' he said to him in staccato snatches, pulling on his boots. 'Take the Paris road. There's a yellow-bodied chaise, with the number twelve on it. Man and woman inside. I want to know where they're going and, if possible, where the woman lives. Got that?'

Pongo nodded. His long teeth showed in a grin, then he picked up his dark cloak, clapped a hat on his head and, slipping a pair of pistols, with 'which weapon he had rapidly become adept, into his belt, he vanished in the direction of the stairs. Confident that his servant would never lose the trail, Gilles relaxed and consulted his watch. The five minutes, he saw, were not yet up so he pulled out of his pocket the papers he had taken from Monsieur.

Except for Fersen's letter, which he found without difficulty, the others were unimportant: a few lines of amorous verse, another letter, signed Montesquiou and promising delivery of a cask of Armagnac, and a few requests for assistance. But Fersen's letter was worth its weight in gunpowder.

No sooner had Gilles cast his eyes over the lines of his friend's writing than his natural reluctance to pry into another man's secrets was augmented by a sense of deep depression. The folly of such a letter! The folly of these burning words of love addressed to a Queen! There was enough in two brief pages to wreck the King's happiness for ever, shatter his trust in his wife and perhaps cause him to repudiate Marie-Antoinette.

Axel began with passionate thanks to his sovereign for an advance of a hundred thousand livres and a pension of twenty thousand which would enable him to buy himself into the Royal Swedish regiment and 'hold his head up' before his father. Next there were some lines of desperation at the inevitability of his approaching departure for Sweden with Count Haga. He finished by imploring his beloved to permit him to return that night to 'the delicious refuge where the goddess had deigned to come to him before'.

Soberly, Gilles refolded the letter and slid it into his waistcoat pocket, buttoning his uniform coat tightly over it for extra security. Then he struck a light and burned the other papers he

156

had taken from the prince in the fireplace. Then, not pausing even for a much-needed glass of wine, he went down to rejoin his fretting captain in the yard.

'A long five minutes, sir. You are excused since you were not expecting to be on guard duty tonight and you have not been long with the regiment. In future, however, be sure not to take seven minutes when you are granted five.'

There was no answer to that. Gilles mounted his horse and rode back to the palace, there to await, at the entrance to the royal apartments, the return of the King who, unlike the Queen, never slept the night at the Trianon.

It was the first time he had mounted guard at Versailles and although he was familiar with the ways of royal palaces from Spain, he was strangely moved by it, so that he felt no inclination for sleep and made no move towards the small room set aside for the use of the officer on duty.

All night long he passed from one guard post to the next, traversing corridors, galleries and stairways between the various royal apartments. The sound of his footsteps awakened the sleeping echoes that belonged to all the years of the past. In answer to the officer's challenge, there rang out at intervals the old cry which had been heard since the fifteenth century in every royal house in France. 'Hamir!'[3]

On anyone, like Gilles, mounting this night guard for the first time, the effect was profound. It swept away the centuries, leaving only the greatness of this monarchy of France. The night filled with ghosts from far back in time, summoned by the living voices of the men who had succeeded them, swearing in their turn to live and die in their positions of trust.

To him, Gilles de Tournemine, there came in the timeless hours of that night, a sharper awareness of his duty to the King whose liegeman and defender, shield and bulwark, he had voluntarily become. In his bosom was Fersen's letter, and it seemed to him to be growing heavier with every passing minute. Its weight was that of a queen's honour and of a threat hanging over an entire family. In those hours, as he measured the pathetic words of human love against the greatness of a

[3] A contraction of the English 'I am here'. The cry was a survival from the days of the first company of Scottish Archers in the service of King Charles VII.

throne, Gilles found himself hating Marie-Antoinette, a woman before she was a queen, for the overwhelming burden she was unwittingly laying on himself.

He thought for a long time about what he ought to do and when, at seven in the morning, the Scottish Guard was relieved by the Gardes de la Porte, he had made his decision. He must return the letter to Fersen who must be made to face the possible consequences of his actions. He must be made to understand, by whatever means, how base was his conduct towards the one whom he wished above all others to serve and who, by her generosity, had given him the means to do so.

'A hundred thousand livres!' Gilles muttered, anger boiling in him. 'A hundred thousand livres and twenty thousand more in annual pension! And what does Count Fersen offer King Louis in exchange? A life of utter devotion and respectful admiration? No, a pair of horns! And he calls himself a gentleman!' After a night spent going over all this in his head, he was still too angry to feel in the least sleepy when he arrived back at his lodging.

It was with the sense of stepping into a soothing bath that he found Pongo, with a big white apron round his waist and as fresh as if he had not spent half the night on horseback, laying out on a clean tablecloth the breakfast he had had brought in from the nearby inn. There was a *noix de veau* with sorrel sauce, fried artichokes and hot pastry rolls with green walnuts.

Pongo greeted his young master with the beaming smile of one well satisfied with his work. Gilles, however, regarded the table with some severity.

'Why have you not laid a place for yourself? When we are alone, there is no reason why we should not eat together. You are my brother-in-arms, not my servant.'

With the pleasure he always showed when Gilles laid emphasis on their past adventures together, and reminded him of his warrior status, Pongo hastened to lay another place and the two sat down opposite one another.

'Well?' Gilles asked, attacking his veal, while the other filled both glasses generously with ruby liquid. There was no doubt that Pongo had taken a fancy to the wines of France. 'Did you find chaise number twelve?'

158

Pongo nodded. 'Yellow chaise enter Paris, then take big road where wall building. Drive long way to small street off big one.'

'Were you able to discover the name of the street?'

The Indian's smile broadened until it almost split his face in two.

'Pongo know all. Rue Neuve Saint-Gilles in the Marais, number ten,' he said, after consulting a scrap of paper covered with a childish hand which he took from one vast pocket. 'Lady named Countess de la Motte Valois. Live there with husband, old lady cousin and writing man in funny black hat.'

'You mean the young man who was with her in the chaise? He is a writer?'

'Not writer, no. Write letters for lady.'

'Her secretary? That's odd. A woman who can't afford a carriage of her own, yet she keeps a secretary? How did you find out all this?'

'Talk with lamplighter in street. He like white wine. Tavern not far off.'

Gilles laughed and refilled his henchman's glass.

'You bought him drink? Wasn't he afraid of you?'

The Iroquois lifted his eyebrows until they formed two perfect semicircles, echoing the shape of eyes like agate marbles.

'Afraid? Why? Pongo say he serve great lord from Spain, in love with lady. Give money and lamplighter man very happy, tell Pongo name pretty serving maid, Rosalie Brissaut.'

'How do you know she's pretty? Have you seen her?'

'Yes. Come out go to church. Very pretty. Very.' And Pongo's hands sketched in the air the outline of a curvaceous feminine figure, while their owner's eyes rolled ecstatically.

'I see,' Gilles said resignedly. 'Just what you like. Well, my friend, I'll not stop you trying your luck. Far from it. If you can get into the countess's house with the help of the maidservant, you'll be doing me a great service. We'll talk of it again tonight. But now, come and help me wash and change. I have to go to Paris. Have a look round Versailles while I'm away and see if you can find us a suitable lodging, not too expensive. My pay is two thousand livres and I don't intend to touch the

159

Duchess's money more than I can help. Something round about fifty livres a month would suit.'

Not many minutes after that, Gilles was standing, shivering, in a large bathtub, naked as the day he was born, while Pongo, perched on a stool, showered him copiously with ice cold water from the can in his hand.

7

A Busy Morning

Axel de Fersen must have been late to bed, for when Gilles walked into his bedroom at the York Hotel towards noon that day the shutters were still tightly closed and the Count, flat on his back in bed with his arms flung wide, was sleeping the sleep of the blessed.

The room smelled strongly of brandy. An open bottle and some glasses suggested that the Swedes had been thirsty on their return from Versailles, possibly on account of the journey and the early morning chill. Gilles crossed to the window, flung it and the shutters open to let in some fresh air, corked up the bottle, having first poured himself a generous glassful, and then, stepping carefully over the assortment of garments strewn about the handsome red carpet on the floor, gripped his friend's shoulder and began to shake it gently.

'Axel!' he said. 'Wake up, Axel! I want to talk to you.'

Since there was no response to this, he shook more vigorously, and when that proved equally useless, decided on more drastic methods. Stepping behind the tall screen which concealed the wash stand, he picked up the handsome china water jug and, with infinite care, allowed a thin trickle to descend upon the face of the sleeper. This time, the results were instantaneous.

Fersen sprang out of bed, coughing, and cursing, and stood swaying a little on his feet like a man uncertain of his balance, and fixed on his friend an eye whose bleariness gradually gave place to anger.

'What the devil—? That's a fine way to wake a man up!' he

spluttered, his voice thickened with drink and sleep. 'It's a – a confounded—'

'Act of friendship. I must talk to you, Axel, and it's too serious to wait until you choose to open your eyes. In fact, since they don't seem to be quite open yet—' Gilles set down his jug and went out into the passage to call Nicolas Carton who, having been a helpless spectator of his unceremonious entry, was now lingering outside the door. Gilles told him to send up a pot of strong coffee and a substantial breakfast. That done, he shut the door again and filled a basin with water.

'Until the coffee comes, you can put your head in that. It will help to clear your eyes.'

Fersen, skinny legs protruding from his nightshirt, was running his hands through his hair with the agonized expression of a man whose head is not what it ought to be.

'What time is it?' he asked at length, making for the wash stand.

'Noon! Do I take it that you've nothing to do today? I thought your king was the busiest fellow in the world?'

'He is. But last night's affair finished late and it was far from warm on the road home in the small hours, so—'

'You felt the need of a little something to warm you? No harm in that. But now I think it's time you got your wits about you again. Haven't you an assignation for tonight?'

'An assignation—? I may have, yes. Who with?'

'With the Queen.'

As he finished speaking Fersen had plunged his head into the basin, but he brought it out again so suddenly that water splashed everywhere. But when his eyes fastened on his friend's implacable face with a look half-frightened and half-angry, Gilles knew that he was more or less sober and in his right mind.

'Did I hear correctly?' he said slowly. 'Did you dare to say—?'

Gilles picked up a towel and tossed it into Fersen's groping hands.

'You heard quite correctly, Axel. You have an assignation tonight with the Queen of France. And don't try to tell me it's not true because I wouldn't believe you. Or tell me that Count

162

Esterhazy wasn't here yesterday, and that he didn't bring you something. I know he did.'

Determined to find out the truth, by whatever means, Gilles had nevertheless taken the precaution of questioning one of the hotel's pretty chambermaids, the very Louison, in fact, who had such a kindness for Pongo.

Louison's entrance at that moment carrying a tray of coffee and followed by one of the waiters with a much larger tray laden with silver dishes, provided an interruption to the conversation. Fersen took advantage of it to dry himself furiously, pull on his breeches and rip off his wet shirt to replace it with a silk dressing gown in a bold floral pattern. Knotting the girdle round his waist, he snapped at the servants.

'Put it all down and get out. Oh, and try and find my man Sven and tell him to have water hot for my bath but not to come until I ring for him.'

Louison and her companion departed and the Swede proceeded to dispose of three cups of scalding coffee in rapid succession.

Sitting relaxed in an armchair by the open window with the noises of the street and the rhythmic call of a fish-seller offering 'Carp, live carp! Buy my carp all alive-o!' in his ears, Gilles stared critically at the gloss on his boots, his long legs stretched out before him, waiting for his friend to finish his coffee and gather his wits together. Unfortunately, neither seemed to be producing the desired result, for the more he recovered physically the further Fersen seemed to become sunk in gloom. Knowing his proud, headstrong and reserved nature, Gilles began to think it might not be so easy to bring him to hear reason as he had hoped.

Abruptly, the Swede pushed back the table and reopened the conversation.

'Now can you tell me where you picked up this nonsensical story? I'm astonished that you should no sooner have been admitted to the Trianon than you must needs fall in with every contemptible scandal-monger in the place!'

Gilles frowned, disliking his friend's tone and in no mood to pander to it, even making allowances for the bad temper inherent in a night on the brandy and its consequential headache.

'This nonsensical story, as you call it, I overheard last night

163

in a grove of trees at the Trianon where two people unknown to me, a man and a woman, were taking a great deal of interest in your private life, yours and another's. Are you acquainted with a Countess de la Motte Valois?'

'Never set eyes on her – or heard of her, either.'

'Well, she seems to me to be a most enterprising lady with a nice touch with a skeleton key for opening drawers she has no business to be anywhere near. She certainly knows a great deal about you—'

'You are doing no more than prove to me what I said to you before,' Fersen broke in impatiently. 'These are mere taradiddles.'

'And is this a taradiddle?'

The half unfolded letter, sent spinning with a flick of Gilles' fingers, lay quivering on the lid of a pot of cherry jam, as though animated by a life of its own. Fersen snatched it up and glanced at it, his face flushing an ugly red. His eyes, when he raised them to the Chevalier, were blazing with blind rage.

'Where did you steal this?' he said through clenched teeth.

Instantly, Gilles was on his feet, which gave him the advantage of height, for he was taller than the count by nearly half a head.

'If you wish this conversation to go any further,' he said, 'you will be good enough to withdraw that word.' But Axel, carried away by the fury within him, was beyond reasoned thought.

'Why should I withdraw it?' he sneered. 'It won't be the first time you've been known to steal.'

Gilles went white. The curl of his nostril deepened and his blue eyes took on the metallic sheen of a glacier under the moon. What he felt was not anger but a kind of inward chill which at that moment made him dead to all feeling. He knew that something was dying, that this could end their friendship, stupidly, and that he would be sorry later, but for the present he could not bring himself to stop.

'Quite right. I did steal that letter,' he said coolly. 'I stole it from the man who had just been given it by his accomplice, from a Prince, I can't say exactly which, only that he was preparing to make use of it to do irreparable damage to the

164

crown. My object being to restore the letter to its writer, the theft seemed to me justifiable.'

Fersen jerked his shoulder angrily.

'A prince now, is it? An unidentified prince! Extremely plausible! I had thought you more inventive.'

Gilles clenched his fists, forcing himself to stay calm.

'And I thought you more intelligent. That you should refuse to admit your – your intimacy with the Queen, an intimacy which is an insult to royalty and to the man who has heaped benefits on you – and continues to do so, if I am to believe the gift which will buy you into the Royal Swedish – that you should refuse to admit it, I say, is not unnatural. Such things are not lightly to be confessed, even to a friend. But I thought you would have understood my motive in coming here. What I have done, I did for you, out of friendship and gratitude for all I owe you, and also from my duty to the King. So tell me, will you or will you not hear what I have to say, and give up this lunatic assignation?'

'No! A hundred times no! I don't want to hear another word about the matter,' Fersen yelled furiously, roused to sheer blind anger by the truth in what the other man had said. 'I will not listen once more while that sacred name is soiled by your damned bastard's lips!'

Tournemine's fist, like a stone from a catapult, caught the Swede full in the face and dropped him with a single choking cry just as the door opened to admit a figure like a fashion plate.

Dressed with the utmost elegance in a coat of a blue and grey striped superfine, cut in the English style, with grey breeches and striped stockings in the same shade as the coat whose high collar framed an exquisitely tied cravat of white muslin, with immaculate cuffs of pleated lawn and the whole surmounted by an immense black hat, the brim startlingly elevated front and back, fingers delicately clasping the gold-mounted ebony cane with which he had just pushed open the unlatched door, Armand de Gontaut-Biron, Duke of Lauzun, achieved an entry which was in itself a work of art. The dignity of it was, however, somewhat marred by the arrival of Fersen's unconscious body in a huddle at his feet.

Lauzun looked at him for a moment, removed his beautiful silver-buckled shoes from his vicinity and then transferred his

165

attention to Fersen's other visitor who was occupied in straightening a uniform coat somewhat disarranged by the force of the blow.

'I would appear to be interrupting, would I not?' he lisped, with all the affectation of the prevailing mode. 'Delighted to see you again, Tournemine, and in fine new feather, too! Lieutenant in the Guard, no less. And in high favour with the King, I hear – just as I foretold, you will recall. A splendid promotion, though. The start of a distinguished career.'

'News travels fast, it seems,' Gilles remarked. Lauzun's arrival at this delicate juncture was by no means welcome. In spite of this, he bowed with perfect politeness. The other man, meanwhile, had detached a small gold quizzing glass from his heavy white silk waistcoat and held it to his eye as he lowered the upper part of his long person towards the unconscious Axel.

'Mmm! A neat piece of work. Faultlessly executed. The Marquis of Queensberry would be proud of you. I was unaware that you were a practitioner of the noble art, however, correct me if I'm wrong, but has the delightful friendship which so edified the expeditionary army been undergoing some strain?'

'Why should you think that?'

'Damnation! When I find Castor and Pollux at fisticuffs, it makes me wonder . . .'

'You were mistaken,' Gilles said gravely. 'I was merely demonstrating to our friend a move which I found useful on many occasions while we were serving under General Washington. I seem to have hit him a trifle too hard.'

'A trifle? The devil you have! I shan't ask you for lessons, my friend. Now what are you about?' he added, seeing Gilles bend down and, without apparent effort, take hold of Fersen and hoist him on to his bed.

'As you see, I'm making him somewhat more presentable for receiving a visitor of your quality, my dear Duke.'

Lauzun shrugged and strolled across to seat himself in the chair Gilles had vacated. He tapped the end of his cane against his red heels.

'Bah! Monsieur de Fersen's position was all one to me. To be quite open with you, I came here to demand satisfaction and to

166

suggest we took a little stroll together to a certain quiet green and shady spot of my acquaintance.'

Gilles' eyebrows rose. He folded his arms.

'A duel? Just like that? No fuss, no witnesses? It sounds almost clandestine.'

'How else to manage it? There are some matters it would be in poor taste to publicize. Nevertheless, I can hardly pass over the fact that last night, at the Valois club, your friend called me a liar.'

'Hardly, I grant you, but if the insult was public I am in a puzzle to know what makes you wish to settle the matter in private.'

'It is not strictly private now, since you are here, my dear. You shall be our second. Although, I may say, I still insist on secrecy. It is vastly preferable when the lady in question is a person of consequence who should by no means be embroiled in affairs of this kind.'

Gilles was frowning now, a prey to the uncomfortable suspicion that this too concerned the Queen. Hadn't Noailles told him only last night that Lauzun had been banished from Versailles for paying court to Marie-Antoinette and even boasting of the fact? If the rumour of that had come to Fersen's ears, the Swede was bound to have reacted by seeking a quarrel with the man who must have seemed to him an intolerable coxcomb. But if Lauzun who, rightly or wrongly, was regarded as a former lover of the Queen's were to meet Fersen, who might well be her current one, in a duel, it might easily damage the Queen's honour beyond repair. As things stood, such a duel would be a honeyfall for every poisonous pamphleteer in Paris. Unless ... Yes, there was a way, one single way to keep the two from meeting before Fersen left France. It was not infallible, but Gilles had no choice.

'My dear Duke,' he said silkily, 'you will understand, of course, that I could nòt agree to stand witness, the only witness, to a meeting of this kind without knowing the cause of the quarrel. Why did Fersen call you a liar?'

Lauzun laughed, somewhat unpleasantly to Gilles' ear.

'Because, to him, any man is a liar who puts forward a truth which does not suit him.'

On the bed, Fersen stirred and sighed in a way that suggested

167

his return to consciousness was not far off. This did not suit Gilles at all and unhesitatingly he delivered another scientifically placed blow which sent the Swede promptly back to dreamland.

Lauzun watched him with astonishment. 'What was that for?' he asked.

'I'm making sure he stays out of this,' Gilles answered, rubbing his sore knuckles. 'We had just got to "truth which does not suit him". Do you mind telling me the nature of that truth?'

It was Lauzun's turn to frown.

'Surely this is going a little far, Tournemine? It is beginning to sound like an interrogation.'

'It is not, however. Merely that I mean to make you mention a name – a name I know already, of course, but which I should like to have confirmed: the name of the lady in question.'

The Duke gave a shout of laughter, revealing a set of perfect, yet wolfishly sharp teeth.

'Why didn't you say so before, my friend,' he said with a sigh. 'I see no cause to make a secret of a name which anyone at the Valois Club might have heard. I said, in effect, that before she fell into Count Fersen's arms, Marie-Antoinette had fallen into mine. That was the truth which displeased him.'

'It displeases me also. You are, Monsieur le Duc de Lauzun, the most despicable liar on this earth.'

The Duke leapt from his chair as though he had been stung.

'Have you taken leave of your senses? I thought we were friends—'

'Perhaps it's because I am still your friend that we are going to fight one another. A duel between you and Fersen would have catastrophic effects for the person I serve with my life.'

'Oho? So you are another who is enrolled in the regiment of the Queen's lovers? I should have guessed it.'

'No, sir, but I am, as you have so rightly remarked, a lieutenant of the Guard. I serve the King, Monsieur de Lauzun. Your King! The husband of the woman whose reputation you are dragging through the mud. Some of that mud could splash onto the crown. That is why I am going to make certain you are out of harm's way for a while, or so I hope.'

168

Lauzen shrugged and strolled over to the mirror to adjust the perfect folds of his cravat.

'Unless I kill you, which would nip your promising career in the bud, while making no difference at all to the general situation since, as soon as you were dead, I should be delighted to come back and run your pretty Swede through to teach him to call a Baron a liar.'

'That is a risk I have to take. It seems to me worth it. When would it suit you to settle the business?'

'At once, if you see no objection? My carriage is below and can take us to a quiet spot. Unless you are anxious to seek out the seconds you appear to set such store by?'

'By all means, let us go. I was hoping we could get it over as soon and as quietly as possible. If you are willing to take me up in your carriage, I shall be delighted to go with you.'

Finding Sven in the passage as they left the room, Gilles responded to his questioning look with an encouraging smile.

'Your master needs you,' he said in English, since Sven did not understand French. 'Go to him and do what you can for him – but do not be surprised if you should happen to notice some slight discolouration around his left eye.'

Half an hour after that, Lauzun's carriage entered the shade of the Bois de Boulogne. The weather was ideal, sunny but not too hot, and the sky above the leafy treetops was of a blue so deep that the occasional small feathery cloud seemed only there to enhance it.

Lauzun stopped the carriage near the Catelan Cross and told his coachman to wait. The two men had elected to continue on foot as far as the little clearing which, according to the Duke, was ideally suited to the kind of encounter they were contemplating, one which they did not wish to have observed by even the most devoted servant. Since, on the other hand, the carriage was likely to be needed to convey at least one of the combatants who might be in no state to walk, it was as well to have it within reach.

A moment more and they were facing one another across a stretch of short, dry grass, on ground firm enough to offer no treacherous footing. The exquisite striped coat and the uniform blue and silver fell to the ground in the same instant, followed by two hats, and, as though taking part in some

169

well-rehearsed ballet, the two opponents saluted and fell on guard as one.

The initial passes were swift and silent. Lauzun fought a trifle carelessly, like a man a little too sure of his skill, Gilles like a man in a hurry who has other things on his mind. This haste was nearly fatal to him as his adversary's point came within a fraction of his breast.

'Our famous Falcon nearly finished on the spit,' Lauzun taunted him.

'The spit is not yet forged that will roast me – but I don't mind acknowledging my mistakes. More haste, less speed.'

'Bah! It's a fault of youth. It will pass.'

'It's past.'

Forcing himself to remain cool, Gilles set himself to study his adversary's play coldly and soon noticed that it was a little too conventional to be really brilliant. Further, the life he led, the wine and the women, had sapped Lauzun's strength. Gilles made sure of this when he trapped his opponent's blade and, with a strong flick of his wrist, sent it spinning ten paces away.

'The devil!' Lauzun muttered. 'You're more dangerous than you look. Disarm!'

'Pick up your sword, Monsieur. We have not finished yet.'

The fight was resumed, the blades more closely engaged now and the pace hotter. But whereas Lauzun was visibly feeling the strain, Tournemine seemed to grow cooler the longer the duel went on. Before long, he was doing little more than parry, as precisely and methodically as if he were at practice. Lauzun was aware of it.

'In God's name, Sir! What are you playing at? Are you humouring me?'

'Not a whit – as you see!'

A swift disengagement followed by a feint still more swift, and Gilles' blade ripped down the duke's ribs, leaving a trail of blood on the fine lawn of his shirt.

Lauzun staggered, the sword dropped from his hand and he would have fallen if Gilles had not sprung forward and caught him in his arms.

'Have I hurt you badly?'

170

'I don't think so,' Lauzun said, with an attempt at a smile. 'But be a good fellow and get me back to the carriage. I'm not feeling quite the thing ...'

Somewhat to Gilles' alarm, for he had not meant to inflict a serious injury, he proceeded to bear this out by fainting away in his adversary's arms. Gilles lowered him to the ground as gently as he could, intending to see what the damage was and do his best to staunch the wound as he had learnt to do in the army.

It was bleeding profusely. In an effort to stop it, Gilles ripped off the already stained shirt and made it into a large pad, which he held in place with his belt, cursing, meanwhile, the excessive caution which had made Lauzun leave the carriage at a distance, as though the driver could have had the smallest doubt about the purpose of two gentlemen vanishing armed into the trees, at the end of a journey passed in the exchange of unnatural courtesies. They could not, of course, have got the carriage itself through the screen of trees and undergrowth all around, but the coachman might have been of considerable assistance in carrying his master back to it. The only thing to do now was to carry the injured man himself.

Confident of his strength, Gilles was preparing to hoist Lauzun over his shoulder, when a voice spoke from behind him, with a pleasant diffidence.

'It would be better not to move him until we know how badly he is hurt. May I look?'

Brought up on the milk of Breton legend, Gilles had a momentary idea that some spirit of the woods had popped out of the bushes to help him. The man standing there was gnomelike, with his spindly legs and narrow chest surmounted by a huge head in which the features were equally haphazard: a leaden complexion, a squashed nose and slightly crooked mouth, with yellow eyes that had a grey fleck in them which gave them a somewhat alarming expression. Yet, ugly as it was, it was a face full of intelligence and the voice, both deep and musical, was curiously attractive.

'Please do, Sir,' Gilles said readily. 'Are you a doctor?'

'I studied at Edinburgh University.'

'You are a Scotsman?' Gilles said in English. 'Yet you have no trace of accent.'

171

The little man had knelt down and was removing the improvised bandage in order to examine the wound. He looked up with a faint smile which did nothing to enhance his looks.

'I had no idea there were linguists among the gentlemen of the Guard,' he remarked in the same tongue. 'They are not generally noted for scholarship.'

'I lay no claim to be a scholar. I learned English as a child. America did the rest.'

'Ah, you went there to fight for the liberty of a nation and here you are fighting one another. Mankind, after all, is still at the caterpillar stage and will never grow wings. Yet aspirations to fraternity should succeed those towards liberty ...'

But the strange yellow eyes, like those of a cat or a tiger, were not without kindness. While he talked, the physician's hands, which were beautiful and well-kept, had been busy at their work, probing the wound and replacing the bandage, merely substituting the man's own cravat for Gilles' belt, which he returned to its owner.

'It is not serious. A week or two in bed and he'll get over it. The sword merely scraped the ribs, unfortunately.'

'*Unfortunately*! Surely you did not mean that?'

'Oh but I did. I cannot believe the world would not be better off without Monsieur de Lauzun's presence in it.'

'You know who he is?'

'Everyone knows Monsieur de Lauzun,' this odd physician said, with sudden hardness. 'He is riotous and debauched enough! He and his like are the tares that choke and destroy the good wheat of the nation. The people are like a sick giant who would be better able to breathe without them.'

Gilles was startled by the bitter irony with which he spoke. 'You – you hate him?' he said wonderingly.

'I? I hate no one, sir. My calling does not allow it. In proof of which, when you've got this man into his carriage, give him a few drops of this.' He took from his pocket a small bottle filled with a dark-coloured fluid. 'It will make him feel better. Only – if I should ever cease being a physician, then, ah yes – then I think I shall know very well how to hate.'

'Cease being a physician? Is that possible? Is your life not vowed to the service of humanity? You speak of it with such feeling?'

'What makes you think I should cease to care for it? On the contrary, I believe I should be more concerned then even I am at present, only in a different way. You see, Sir, it is not only men's bodies that need caring for. There is the spirit also, and the spirit in these times is deadly sick. Now, if you will give me your assistance, we will carry your victim to his coach and after that I shall return to my work.'

'You are working here, in the woods?'

'I am setting traps to catch the animals I need for my experiments with electricity. Until just recently, you understand, I was a surgeon in the Corps of Guards of the Count d'Artois, but my work did not find favour with the gentlemen of the Académie. I was deprived of my post and my finances have suffered as a result.'

Once Lauzun had been settled in the coach, an operation observed by his coachman with perfect indifference, Gilles made him swallow a few drops from the dark bottle and then made to return it to the doctor. He waved it away.

'No, no. You may well have need of it again. You seem to me very handy with your sword arm.'

'Then at least allow me to reimburse you for it,' Gilles said, putting his hand to his pocket, 'and to thank you for your trouble.'

'By no means. It was nothing. As for thanking me – come and call on me one day. I know no greater pleasure than a good talk, and it is a pleasure I have all too seldom now that I am no longer in practice. I live at number 47 Rue du Vieux-Colombier, in Saint-Germain-des-Prés.'

'Very well, Sir. One of these days I shall be happy to oblige you,' Gilles said, bowing slightly. 'Will you tell me who it is I should ask for?'

The little man seemed all at once several inches taller.

'I am Dr Jean-Paul de Marat, born in Switzerland, the last scion of a noble Spanish line,' he said with what, in a face less remarkable, would have been ludicrous emphasis. 'Very much at your service.'

He returned Gilles' bow and disappeared as neatly as a ferret back into the wood. Gilles watched him vanish among the greenery and then climbed up into the carriage where Lauzun was beginning to come round. But first he spoke to the driver.

'Put me down when we reach the city,' he told him, 'and then take your master back to the Hôtel de Biron, quickly!'

'I can easily set you down at the York Hotel, Sir, since your horse is there.'

'Thanks. But do as I say. Your master needs attention as soon as possible. A hired cab will do my business for me.'

Gilles was able to relax a little while the pleasant view beside the Seine rolled by outside the windows and the wounded man sank, under the influence of the odd little doctor's potion, into a restorative slumber. He was satisfied that he had dealt with the most pressing problem, being assured now that Lauzun could not call Fersen out before the latter left for Sweden. It was equally unlikely that Fersen, even supposing the warning he had received was without effect, would take himself to a lovers' tryst, especially with a Queen, adorned with a black eye and a swollen jaw. So that when the coach stopped for him well beyond the Pont Louis XVI, he realized suddenly that it was close on two o'clock and he was very hungry. He decided to buy himself a good dinner before embarking on the rest of the day's business, which concerned Maria-Cayetana's affairs and his own.

Thanks to Jean de Batz, Gilles was familiar with the best places to eat in Paris. Of them all, he was especially fond of Sieur Hué's, in the Passage des Petits Pères, where in a handsome flower-decked room capable of seating nearly eighty people were to be had the finest crayfish and a matelote of eels which was beyond praise. After a brief visit to the York Hotel to pick up Merlin, he set out again, therefore, to hurry back across the Seine, by the Pont-Neuf this time, in the direction of the Palais-Royal, where the building work for the new galleries set in motion by the Duc d'Orléans was turning the area into a dust bowl in dry weather and a sea of mud when it rained.

Today it was the dust and Gilles' throat felt like sackcloth by the time he reached the narrow alley, packed with private coaches, hired vehicles, horses and sedan chairs, above which hung the Sieur Hué's fine painted and gilded signboard. The smells that filled the air promised fare so succulent it would have roused the dead.

There were a great many people in the freshly-painted

interior of the famous restaurant: handsomely dressed men belonging to the best society, magistrates, financiers and army officers, many of them accompanied by pretty women whose slightly over-elaborate style of dress provided the clue to their profession. Here and there, there was even a woman on her own, evidently on the look-out for an escort. Ladies of fashion were not present in any numbers, although there were always one or two who were sufficiently unconventional to find it amusing to rub shoulders with their less respectable sisters.

Sieur Hué himself, flitting about the room like an overworked bumble bee in a rustle of puce-coloured taffeta, conducted the newcomer to the far end of the room, apologizing profusely all the way, for being compelled to ask him to share a table. The occupant of the small table spread with white linen and adorned with a bowl of marguerites, proved to be a well-built young man in the blue and red of an officer in the Swiss Guards, a uniform not so far different from Gilles' own, except that the trimmings were of gold instead of silver. He was engaged in eating his way steadily through a bush of crayfish large enough to cover a regiment.

Hué, bowing low before this valued customer, expressed himself deferentially: 'I ventured to think that perhaps you two gentlemen, being both of the Royal Household, would not object to dining together. I dislike having to ask it of you, but the room is unusually full and those tables still unoccupied are already reserved. I make my apologies but—'

'No need to. I shall be honoured.'

The diner lifted a hazel eye from the pile of debris on his plate, cast it over his proposed companion and uttered these welcoming words in a voice whose accent derived from the northernmost cantons of Switzerland. Thereupon he laid down his napkin, unfolded a body as tall as Gilles', but twice as wide, clicked his heels and added in a deep, almost cavernous voice: 'Baron Ulrich Ernst August Friedrich von Winkleried zu Winkleried. Be seated, I beg.'

Gilles, having introduced himself in his turn, took the seat facing the Swiss and, while he returned to the detailed exploration of his crayfish, embarked on a study of the bill of fare, written in exquisite copperplate on hot-pressed paper embossed with gold.

175

'Have the crayfish,' Winkleried advised him pleasantly. 'They're delicious.'

Gilles thanked him with a smile and did, as well as a matelote of eels and a Chablis to go with them. His neighbour took the opportunity to order more crayfish for himself, having made havoc of his first helping but finding his appetite unsatisfied. In the meanwhile, the restaurant had filled up until there was not a single vacant seat in the room. The air was filled with the fragrant scent of food and with the hum of conversation and Sieur Hué was able to count, to his satisfaction, a great many Parisian notables among those present in his dining room. There was the Marquis Ducret, brother of the celebrated Madame de Genlis, governor to the Duc de Chartres' children, the Duc d'Aiguillon, the appallingly loud Marquis de Mirabeau, Brissot, commissioner to the chancellery of Orléans, the barrister Pétion de Villeneuve, Barère de Vieuzac, the orator of Toulouse, Councillor d'Eprémil, Dr Charles, the well-known physician whose lectures on electricity at the Louvre had attracted the whole of society, and even the famous Robert brothers, builders of hot air balloons, whose workshop in the Place des Victoires was close at hand.

Gilles had no need to eavesdrop to be aware that everyone was in fact talking about the latest of these gigantic balloons which were thrilling Parisians with their exploits. It had been named Caroline and its great blue and gold silken dome was already to be seen looming over the neighbouring houses as it was prepared for the day, the third of July, when it was to have the signal honour of carrying up into the air the Duke of Chartres, own cousin to the King, as well as the Robert brothers. Some said that Duke Philippe was headed for a triumph which would wipe out the disgrace of Ushant, while others, Dr Charles chief among them, were sure that the machine and its latest modifications were less than reliable and that the Duke was simply risking his life.

The hubbub ceased suddenly and then was resumed, louder than before, in tribute to the couple who had just entered. They were a spectacular pair. The gentleman was very tall and elegantly dressed, despite a tendency to fat, in a coat of grey and yellow in the latest fashion from London, with striking blue eyes and a face that would have been handsome but for the

176

skin disorder which left it red and pimpled. The lady, who was small and dark with a warm amber-coloured skin and slanting eyes, with an exceedingly pretty figure, was clearly of the first consequence. In her white muslin dress and big straw hat caught up at the brim with a bunch of white flowers, she might have come straight from being painted by Mr Gainsborough or Mr Lawrence, only the sardonic curl to her sweet lips belied the initially virginal impression. This was a woman who might have the look of a young girl but was not one by any means.

She was, in fact, as much the courted darling of the gilded youth of Paris as she was out of favour at Court where she was scarcely received any more. Baroness Aglae d'Hunolstein was certainly one of the prettiest women in France but she was also one of the most talked about. Not even the high standing of her father, the Marquis de Barbantane, French ambassador to the Grand Duke of Tuscany, and her mother who was governess to the Princess Louise Bathilde of Orléans, could rescue her reputation any longer and when Madame de Barbantane had proposed her daughter's name as lady-in-waiting on the occasion of her pupil's becoming Duchess of Bourbon she had been politely refused.

Not that this had in any way troubled the lovely Aglae. The post of lady-in-waiting was much too much like hard work and she was enjoying her independence. Beneath that delicate skin there burned in her blood all the warmth of her native Provence and she had long lost count of her lovers. La Fayette was only one who had long loved her and at last found a hero's blissful reward in her arms.

Yet he was not the king of this company. That title went to the man who was escorting her today, and had received so warm a welcome from Sieur Hué's customers: Duke Philippe de Chartres.

People were springing up everywhere to offer their seats but the Duke's eyes had already scanned the company and come to rest on the two officers who, absorbed in their crayfish, had not noticed his entrance.

When he spoke, it was to them that he addressed himself.

'Let no one disturb themselves,' he drawled, in the way he affected when in a sarcastic humour. 'God forbid that I should drive away any of my friends when I see some of my cousin

Louis's good servants who will, I am sure, be only too glad to serve a prince of the blood in this way. Ho there, gentlemen of the King's Household, do you hear me? It is to you I am speaking.'

The two looked up at that. Once again, Winkleried abandoned his shellfish and Gilles swung round in his chair.

'Are you speaking to us, sir?' he inquired.

'Monseigneur!' someone hissed close by. 'It is the Duc de Chartres!'

'Oh – er – thank you.' With that he got to his feet courteously and bowed. 'Forgive me, your Highness. I had not the pleasure of your Highness' acquaintance.'

'So I see,' Philippe retorted with heavy irony. 'Well, now that you do know me, kindly vacate your table. We are very hungry.'

The contemptuous tone was more offensive than a direct insult would have been. The Breton's eyes took in the room full of grinning faces. It was clear the Duke was among friends who would be only too delighted at this public humiliation of two of the King's men. On all their faces was the same look of gloating anticipation he remembered seeing round the arena of the Plaza Mayor in Madrid. Gilles, however, had no intention of playing the part of the bull. These princely conspirators and troublemakers were beginning to annoy him. So he answered pleasantly:

'I am sure you are. Perhaps your Highness will tell me if you own this restaurant?'

'Of course not. Do you take me for a shopkeeper?'

'Then perhaps Monseigneur will be good enough to permit us to finish our meal. It does not do to let crayfish get cold and it so happens that we too are hungry. I am sure your Highness will find a dozen tables better situated than this. It would look too shameful for you to occupy such a back seat as we have here.'

He bowed again and was preparing to resume both his place and his meal as the ripple of indignation ran round the room. In an instant, every diner was on his feet, roaring abuse, and fists were being shaken at the man who had dared to speak thus to the Duke. There was even a sword out here and there and the

178

unfortunate Hué was trotting back and forth in horror, striving without success to restore calm.

The Duc de Chartres, for his part, had turned puce in the face and started forward uncontrollably, raising his fists. Whereupon Gilles drew his sword and offered the hilt coldly to the prince, thus effectively forcing him to keep his distance.

'I am a gentleman, Monseigneur. Here is my sword. Kill me, but do not strike me, or I should be obliged to return the blow, were I to be torn between four horses in the Place de Grève for it afterwards.'

'Sir, Sir, I implore you! Monseigneur, for God's sake—'

It was Madame d'Hunolstein, darting swiftly in between the two men. She was no longer smiling and the alarm on her lovely face was plain to see.

'You do not know what you are doing, either of you! Monseigneur, you are too quick-tempered, too hasty in seeking a quarrel with those whose only crime is to serve those you have no love for. As for you, Sir. I do not know who you are, but you should know that more respect is due to a prince of the blood!'

'A man gets the respect he deserves,' Winkleried was heard to mutter at Gilles' back. He, too, had his hand on his sword, ready to lend assistance to his fellow-diner.

At the sound of the woman's voice, the room had fallen silent, every person present waiting to hear the Duke's reply. But it was the Breton who spoke first. Looking at the self-appointed peacemaker, he smiled suddenly and sheathed his sword. Then he bowed.

'I surrender, Madame. I could not forgive myself if I brought tears to those lovely eyes. The table is yours, naturally. Had the circumstances been otherwise, we should have been only too happy to have offered it to you.'

'*Natürlich*,' the voice of the Swiss echoed him.

The Duke's temper, too, had cooled. His face was returning gradually to a more natural colour and his short-sighted blue eyes fastened on the gold eagle pinned to his erstwhile adversary's breast.

'No need to disturb you, gentlemen. We are not staying. You, Sir, have fought in America, I see?'

'Yes, Monseigneur.'

'On that score – and on that score alone, I am prepared to overlook this. Your names, gentlemen?'

Tournemine presented his companion and himself, wondering as he did so what use the Duke would make of the information and whether there might not be a *lettre de cachet* in the air. The Prince, however, merely nodded, not unamiably, and gave them the ghost of a smile.

'Very well. I thank you. Come, my dear,' he went on, slipping the baroness's arm through his, 'you will have to make do with the ordinary at the Palais Royal. We'll come here and sup tonight and I invite those of my friends here present to be my guests.'

These last words served to silence the protests which were arising on all sides and bring the smile back to the face of Sieur Hué, who had been contemplating ruin. He bent himself double bowing the prince and his companion to their carriage.

The incident was over. Across the table, Gilles proffered his hand to Winkleried who shook it with enthusiasm.

'Thank you. Shall we be friends?'

'I think so. I like you.'

'And I you. What shall we do now?'

'Now,' said the Swiss, with a broad smile that displayed a set of teeth as large and white as the keys of a harpsichord, 'Now we shall finish our dinner. I am still a little hungry.'

'So am I, too. Ho there, Maître Hué, let's have your matelote!'

But it was not fated that the King's Guards should ever reach the end of that succulent repast. They were just lifting their glasses to drink to their new friendship when, above the renewed hum of polite conversation, a remark reached them which had them on their feet in a moment.

'Because a man has fought in America, it does not give him the right to do as he likes! The Duke was wrong there. He should have let us chastise the fat swine's minions for him! It's intolerable that a prince of the blood should be forced, in his own country, to—'

But before the disgruntled individual could finish whatever unpleasant remarks he had to make, Gilles had detected his whereabouts and was on him. A powerful hand seized hold of his cravat and hauled him bodily out of his chair which fell with a clatter.

'Well, well! So it's Monsieur d'Antraigues, is it?' Gilles said, recognizing the features, vinously flushed, that choked in his grasp. 'If you're not exercising your filthy tongue on queens, you are insulting kings, it seems! I thought my friend the Baron de Batz, who gave you a handsome thrashing one night outside the Comédie Italienne, had recommended you to watch your language?'

'Let me go!' the other man gasped. 'You're choking me!'

'Am I so? If that's the only way to silence you, I think I had better finish the job.'

The three men who had been sharing the Count's table attempted to intervene but Winkleried, arriving in support, used his apparently limitless strength to such effect that two found themselves sitting on the floor over by the fireplace gasping for breath, while the third dangled puppet-like from his huge arm.

'Carry on, Chevalier,' he said cheerfully. 'Would you like a little more room?'

'No need, my dear Baron. This gentleman and I are going to settle this business outside. We've made enough disturbance in here. Besides, the gutter is the very place for our friend's style of wit.' And, half-carrying and half-thrusting d'Antraigues before him, Gilles left the restaurant amid a deathly silence, followed by Winkleried, still keeping his own hold on his prisoner.

'Come along, my little man,' he was saying kindly. 'We shall go and second these two gentlemen.'

After them, every soul in the restaurant made, crowding, for the door and windows to watch what happened.

Once out in the street, the Chevalier dropped d'Antraigues so abruptly that he stumbled and fell against the wheel of a carriage, and drew his sword.

'Now, sir! *En garde!* I know you can handle a weapon, but I, too, have an ambition to teach you a lesson you will not forget.'

Choking with rage, the Count tried to get to his feet but failed and fell back heavily, groaning.

'Damned scoundrel! I can't! I think you've broken my leg!'

'Have I? Let's see.'

'Don't scratch me! I forbid you to touch me! Help! Where are my servants – anyone! But not you!'

'Let me see.' It was the Swiss, now bending over the fallen man. 'We know all about fractures in our mountains.' His big hand explored the damaged limb with astonishing delicacy. 'Yes,' he diagnosed. 'There's no doubt, it's broken. He must have a doctor.'

Gilles sheathed his sword. 'In that case,' he said, 'I consider myself satisfied. He has had his lesson.'

'You may, Sir, but I do not! I shall find you again! I swear I shall find you!'

'I have no objection. You will not have far to look. I am a second lieutenant in the Scottish Guard. We are generally to be found at Versailles, if anyone cares to take the trouble. Until our next meeting, then, Sir. And take my friend Batz's advice: keep your tongue between your teeth! Or it may get you into more trouble.'

With that, Gilles took no more notice of his mortified opponent, still hurling a torrent of imprecations at him, more imaginative than decent, but fishing a gold coin out of his pocket tossed it to Hué, who had come hurrying out with several waiters at his back to pick up the injured man.

'Here you are, my friend. I'm not fated to eat your matelote today, but I'll be back. Are you coming, Baron? Suppose we go and finish our meal in some quiet place where we can find a good dinner and fellow diners whose only interest is in what is on their plates.'

'Gladly. There's a countryman of mine, not far from the Tuileries, where one can get good food. And eat it in comfort.'

And so, arm in arm, the two new friends strolled off to find the second and third courses of their dinner.

8

... And an Equally Busy Evening

The house of Messrs Boehmer and Bassange, the Queen's jewellers, was at number 2, Rue de Vendôme, hard by the Temple and not far from a *jeu de paume* belonging to the Comte d'Artois. It looked a little like a substantial town house, a little like a warehouse and a great deal like a fortress. The buildings were ranged around a large courtyard in which the carriages of the house's wealthy customers could turn with ease, but the doors, iron-studded in the manner of a prison, would have stood up to an assault by battering ram and the bars guarding the windows were thick enough to defy the biggest file. But, in deference to Madame Boehmer's rustic fancy, a charming honeysuckle scrambled over the walls, filling the place with its sweet scent on summer nights.

It was to this shrine that Tournemine and his new friend Ulrich-August, now satisfactorily fed at last, came at about five o'clock that afternoon. The Swiss had insisted on lending the Breton, still a newcomer to Paris, his company and support, having connections of his own with the elder of the two partners. Charles Auguste Boehmer was of German origin and had once been jeweller to the King of Poland, in whose service the late Baron, Winkleried's father, had spent some years of his life. It was, in fact, his influence which obtained for the Duchess of Alba's representative the reception due to a visitor of consequence.

The clerk who popped up behind the grille told them, to begin with, that the gentlemen were in conference with a distinguished client and had left instructions that they would see no more that day.

The young man was obviously not a Frenchman but he was new to Winkleried. Taking a chance, he barked at him in German, two vigorous, idiomatic sentences which promptly elicited a low bow and sent the youth scurrying away 'to see'.

In a moment, he was back and drawing the bolts of the entrance doors to let the two horsemen into the yard where stood an elegant equipage drawn by a pair of high-bred horses, the sight of which brought a frown to the Chevalier's brow. The body of the chaise was painted a discreet dark green, but there discretion ended. The Spanish coat-of-arms emblazoned on the panel told their own story. The distinguished client in question was, in all likelihood, the Chevalier d'Ocariz, if not the ambassador in person.

'If the gentlemen will follow me,' the clerk said, after a groom had taken their horses, 'Monsieur Boehmer is desolated to be obliged to keep them waiting, only until he has finished with his present customer.'

'Hope it won't be too long,' Winkleried said gruffly. 'I have to get back to Versailles.'

As it turned out, however, they did not have to wait at all. The two young men were following the clerk up the handsome stone staircase when the jewellers began to descend, one on either side of a man whom Gilles had no difficulty in recognizing as the Spanish consul.

The three going up stood to one side to allow those coming down to pass and as they did so Boehmer lifted his hand in a friendly gesture towards the Swiss officer.

'I will be with you in a moment, Monsieur le Baron.'

'When you're ready, friend Boehmer. When you're ready,' Ulrich-August responded, while Gilles, his eyes on nothing in particular, tried not to look at the Spaniard.

'You know the man?' the Swiss whispered, as the two of them resumed their ascent.

'Who? The foreigner? No, but from the arms on the coach and the colour of his complexion, I should suppose him to be Spanish. Why do you ask?'

'Because of the way he looked at you.'

'Oh. Perhaps we met at the Court of King Charles III, only I may not recall,' Gilles said disingenuously.

They were ushered into a handsome salon, furnished in excellent taste but where the principal decoration consisted of a number of glass cases containing various pieces of jewellery and goldsmith's work, rather heavy but beautiful, which Ulrich began to study with the eye of an expert.

'You are a connoisseur of jewellery, Baron?' Gilles asked, watching with amusement as the other took a small glass from his pocket and screwed it into his right eye.

'I am a connoisseur of everything good and beautiful, wines, women, horses.... As to jewels, it is true, I have a little knowledge. The Baroness, *meine Mutter*, had many most beautiful.'

The next moment, Boehmer, rust-coloured velvet suit stretched across a respectable stomach and hair of the same shade, burst into the room and hurried over to Winkleried with hands outstretched.

'Monsieur le Baron! What a pleasure to see you again! It feels like a hundred years! Do, please, be seated. I hope you have not called before? We have been away on business, my partner and I. And what can I do for you?'

'For me, nothing,' the Swiss said equably. 'But for my friend, a great deal. He wants to buy your damned necklace.'

'My necklace? What necklace? Not – not the—?'

'Yes, yes, *the* ...'

'Not, of course, for myself, Sir, as you will have guessed,' Gilles broke in, somewhat put out by the jeweller's startled expression. 'I am merely the envoy of a lady, one of the greatest and wealthiest of these times, her grace the Duchess of Alba, to be precise. As this letter will explain,' he added coolly, taking from his pocket some of the papers which the steward Diego had given him. 'Sufficient funds to cover the transaction have, I may say, already been deposited with the bankers Lecoulteux and will be transferred to you as soon as matters are satisfactorily settled between us. Please, read the letter.'

Boehmer put on his spectacles and perused the letter Gilles had handed to him without undue haste. Then he removed the spectacles and mopped his forehead, which showed beads of sweat. After that, he heaved a deep sigh and returned the letter to the younger man.

'I see. I see. Unfortunately, to my immense sorrow, I must assure you, I am compelled to say I cannot oblige you. The necklace is no longer for sale.'

'What's this? No longer for sale? I thought it was virtually unsaleable?'

Boehmer's face was a picture of contrition.

'But it is sold – or all but. I have given my word and I—'

'Excuse me, Sir,' Gilles interrupted him, 'but was the gentleman who left just now the one to whom you gave your word?'

'Well – yes. That was the gentleman. He was here on behalf of a princess who—'

'The Princess of Asturia. I know. And you have pledged your word? Irrevocably?'

'Not perhaps irrevocably. You will understand that I could not let such a piece leave France without first obtaining the permission of her Majesty the Queen, for whom it was at first destined, and giving her a last opportunity to acquire it for herself. My partner and I are proposing to travel to Versailles tomorrow for that purpose.'

Gilles allowed a silence to develop, during which Boehmer might contemplate the seal and coat-of-arms of the great house of Alba. He seemed unable to take his eyes away from it and Gilles thought he read in them a shadow of regret.

'The price of the necklace was sixteen hundred thousand livres, was it not?' he inquired gently.

'Sixteen hundred thousand livres, yes . . .'

'And that is what the Spanish envoy has offered you?'

The jeweller flushed suddenly and Gilles knew he had touched a sensitive spot.

'Er – yes, that is—'

'That is, not entirely? It was suggested to you, was it not, that in view of the difficulties you were experiencing in finding a purchaser for the necklace, the size of the sum involved and the honour of the necklace becoming a part of the crown jewels . . . ? You were perhaps asked, also, to accept some – accommodation in the matter of payment?'

186

'It is not unusual.'

'Come, come. Not, surely, when one is about to become Queen of Spain and has all the gold of America at one's back? If the Queen had not handsomely refused the gift, the King would have paid you on the nail. And I, Sir, can tell you this, in the name of my principal, the Duchess, should you give us preference in this, not only will you have the money on the day the transaction is completed, but we will better the offer by fifty thousand livres.'

Boehmer was perspiring freely now. He pulled out his handkerchief and began patting his brow, cheeks and neck with vigour.

'You are a devil, Monsieur! I have told you – I have given my word—'

'Not irrevocably. You said that also. Could you not inform the – the gentleman that the Queen desires a little more time to think before making her decision?'

'It is not easy, not easy at all. Sooner or later, the Spanish envoy will know—'

'Nothing. Or, if we go the right way about it, nothing he will be able to utter, at least. Which reminds me, could you not let me see this wonderful thing? It would give you a little time to think, and perhaps to consult your partner . . .'

'An excellent idea!' Winkleried exclaimed. 'Do show it to him, my dear Boehmer!'

'Why – on the instant. I have only to fetch Bassange. We both have a key to the chest it is kept in.'

Boehmer returned after a brief absence accompanied by a dark man, younger than himself, of no great stature but well-made, and with a pleasant face. This was his partner, Paul Bassange. Bassange was carrying an immensely large, hinged casket of red leather with gilding. Attached to it was a label as big as a handkerchief on which the price was inscribed in big black characters.

Boehmer's young partner bowed to Winkleried, smiling, and the 1 turned to Gilles. This time his look held both surprise and wonder.

'You are the gentleman who wishes to purchase our necklace?'

'Yes, on behalf of the Duchess of Alba. Open the case.'

187

Bassange placed the box on the table where a ray of sunshine fell on it, turned the keys in the lock and raised the lid.

'There,' he said.

The two young men could not help a gasp of admiration. As the lid was opened, the box filled with flashing light. A river of fire sparkled against a bed of black velvet, light gleaming from every facet and shooting blinding arrows every colour of the rainbow to all four corners of the room.

'Six hundred and forty-seven diamonds,' Boehmer said.

'Two thousand eight hundred carats,' Bassange echoed.

Winkleried touched the row of seventeen stones, as big as hazelnuts, that formed the first row of the necklace, with a delicate finger.

'Magnificent,' he breathed, his voice suddenly hoarse. 'Truly wonderful! I hope the Princess of Asturia is beautiful, or it would be a pity—'

'She is far from beautiful,' Gilles muttered. He had just been picturing Cayetana's passionate face rising from these fabulous jewels. They would envelope her shoulders like a glittering cloak and flash like lightning down her breasts. 'Her grace of Alba, on the other hand, is one of the most ravishing women I know.'

'The one it would suit best is Marie-Antoinette,' Boehmer cried, with a kind of fury. 'It was made for a fair woman! It would have given us the greatest joy if she would have had it and if it were not that we are obliged to recoup the money, we would never allow it to leave France. But we have our creditors to think of, and the greater part of all we possess is tied up in this necklace.'

'Then have at least the satisfaction of knowing that it adorns one of the prettiest necks in Europe. Go to Versailles tomorrow, gentlemen, but say nothing more to your prospective purchaser until you have spoken to me again. Can you promise me that, at least?'

The two jewellers looked at one another. It was Bassange who answered.

'If we see you again very soon, yes. But what have you in mind?'

'To go and see the Queen myself, and ask her to tell you, if she still declines it, that she would rather the necklace went to the Duchess of Alba than to a cousin for whom, I think, she feels no overwhelming affection. Unless, of course,' he added, with deceptive smoothness, 'you prefer to make your decision this evening? In that event, you will find me at the York Hotel in the Rue du Colombier until tomorrow morning.'

The clerk who had admitted the two young men reappeared, evidently in a state of extreme agitation.

'Well? What is it, Werner?' Boehmer asked testily. 'Have you been letting someone else in? I thought I heard the door.'

'It's – this time it is a Prince, Sir. Monseigneur the Comte de Provence!'

'What? Good God, gentlemen! I shall have to chase you away. I cannot keep a prince of the blood waiting, even for a moment.'

Gilles picked up his hat from the chair where he had left it.

'Do not concern yourself, Monsieur Boehmer. We are going. We have said all we have to say for today. Only think over what I have said.'

He was in a hurry to leave now, hoping to get a glimpse of the man he believed he had knocked down the night before. But, with the sound of footsteps already on the stairs, Bassange blocked their way to the door.

'Not that way, if you please. Or you will come face to face with the prince. You would prefer not to be seen, I imagine?'

'I would prefer not, although the Prince does not know my face.'

'But he might ask tiresome questions. He is a man much moved by curiosity. Come this way.'

He opened a small door concealed in the woodwork behind a glass panel, revealing a dark, narrow passage into which he ushered them, while Boehmer went to meet the illustrious visitor.

'You are about to be shown the secrets of the house,' he said with a smile, 'but from now on you are a very important client. Follow this passage. At the end, you will find a little stair which emerges behind a hanging and will bring you almost out into the yard. Forgive me for leaving you to find your own way.'

'But we'll be left in the dark,' Winkleried protested.

'Not at all. Only let me shut the door. Good day to you, gentlemen.'

As soon as the door closed, Gilles saw that it was no darker than before, for the mirrored panel worked only one way.

'Aha! I understand,' Ulrich murmured. 'Come, let us be gone.'

'One moment. Only a moment.'

Through the glass, Gilles could see the two jewellers come back into the room, ushering in two men, one of whom bore a distinct likeness to the King.

The profile was the same and so was the high, intelligent forehead but the Comte de Provence was noticeably shorter than his brother and also a great deal fatter. For all that he was only twenty-seven years old, the body encased in a coat of taffeta of the same blue as his eyes and artfully embroidered with exotic flowers with silver stamens, was so grossly overweight, thanks to his inordinate love of food and drink, that his little short, fat legs seemed scarcely able to bear him.

'Well?' Ulrich hissed. 'Are you coming?'

'One more second, please!' Gilles answered, his eyes glued to the mirror.

The sight of this smiling, ruddy-complexioned gentleman, gazing pleasantly and contentedly about him, had struck him with sudden doubts. Could this really be the same man he had left unconscious in a grove at the Trianon the night before? He had thought that his victim was taller, and not quite so stout ... But then the prince began speaking and Gilles' doubts fled. This was certainly the man.'

'Gentlemen,' Provence was saying, 'I have come, like the idle Parisian I am, to gaze upon your treasures. I have heard such wonders of your famous necklace that I find myself longing to see it also. Show it to me.'

'Nothing simpler, Monseigneur. We have just this moment taken it from the chest where it is kept in order to examine one of the clasps, which seemed to us to have some flaw in the enamel. Your Royal Highness may have your wish this instant. Here it is.'

Much as he longed to stay and hear what the prince had to say, Gilles turned away with resignation, rather than give Winkleried the impression that he was stopping to spy.

On tiptoe, making as little noise as possible, the two young men made their way down the carpeted passage and down a little staircase cut in the thickness of the wall. The lifting of a curtain brought them, as promised, into a little dark hallway which led them, by way of a heavily bolted door, directly into the courtyard.

'Correct me if I'm wrong,' Winkleried said heaving himself on to the raw-boned Mecklenburger which seemed to carry his considerable weight with such ease, 'but I gained the impression you did not care overmuch for the Comte de Provence?'

'What could make you think a thing like that?'

'The look on your face when you were watching him just now – and also the great liking I have conceived for you. Monsieur Mesmer, the man with the bathtub ...'

'Bathtub?'

'Yes, bathtub. He has a big tub he sits people round to cure them. Have you never heard of Dr Mesmer?'

'Never – or not that I recall.'

'I will explain. He is a great man. Well, Monsieur Mesmer claims that when you have a liking for a person, you feel all that they do.'

'But where does the Comte de Provence fit into all this?'

'It's very simple. I cannot stand the sight of him. He is false and dissembling. That is how I knew so readily that you dislike him.'

Gilles laughed. 'Winkleried, my dear fellow, I have a feeling we are going to be the greatest friends! Already I owe you a great deal.'

'Not at all. Are you coming back to Versailles with me?'

'Not tonight. I have another errand in Paris, and not far from here.'

'Then I will leave you. Where are you lodging at Versailles?'

Gilles explained that he was temporarily living at the Guards' billet but had left his servant with instructions to find him a lodging suitable both to his standing and to a modest purse.

'I think I have what you need. There is a pretty house opposite me which has rooms to let. I'll see to it, if you like?'

191

'Gladly. We shall be neighbours. And that makes one more obligation.'

The Baron took a card from his pocket and scribbled a few lines on it. Gilles read: Pavillon Marjon, Rue de Noailles au Petit-Montreuil. Winkleried's accent might not be good, but his written French was impeccable.

'I shall expect to be asked to dinner,' was all he said, smiling.

'A bargain. I promise you crayfish.'

They parted on that, shaking hands in the English fashion, one to turn back towards the Boulevard St Martin, the other to continue down the Rue de Vendôme into the Rue St Louis until he came to the Rue Neuve St Gilles in the Marais, where dwelled that Countess de la Motte Valois who had the impudence to look like Judith.

It was a narrow, ill-paved street but quiet and very nearly empty. On the corner stood a statue of St Gilles, which the young man took as a happy augury. The street itself was not long, consisting only of three or four private houses, sealed in behind tall carriage doors, the rear walls of the Convent of the Minimes, with one low doorway in it, and a cobbler's shop. It ran into the tree-lined boulevard along what had been the old fortifications of Louis XIII.

Gilles walked Merlin down the length of the little thoroughfare, taking his time to get a good look at number ten, which proved to be a tall, narrow house, handsome enough in its way but more bourgeois than aristocratic. The long windows showed a glimpse of blue silk curtains and the mirrored image of a crystal chandelier.

Horse and rider had just passed the house when a hired chaise drove up in the other direction, coming from the boulevard, and stopped outside number ten. Gilles had only to turn a little in the saddle, with the air of any idle passer-by, to perceive first a charming foot, elegantly shod in silk of a fashionable shade of puce, then an ankle in a clocked stocking followed by the hem of a gown of Parma violet, and finally the whole woman appeared, young, dark and elegant and crowned with an extravagant hat beneath which the watcher had no difficulty at all in recognizing the features of the pseudo-Judith.

By daylight, and wearing her own hair, the resemblance was

less striking. Gilles was aware of some satisfaction, it pleased him to know that his beloved's charms were not of a kind that could be readily reproduced. Judith's glorious red hair gave her a brilliance this woman lacked. Moreover, the Countess seemed to have blue eyes, whereas Mademoiselle de Saint-Mélaine's were black and sparkling like diamonds. And then—

While he was meditating on these differences, the Countess had paid off the driver and was about to enter the house but, catching sight of the handsome horseman riding slowly and apparently regretfully away, she bestowed on him, as if it were the most natural thing in the world, a smile so provocative that it could not be other than an invitation.

It crossed Gilles' mind, then, to wonder how much real title she had to the name of Valois. She certainly had some strange ways for a lady of quality. He was tempted for a moment to accost her but it seemed wiser not to make contact too quickly, so he merely raised his hat, bowed, smiled and went on his way, leaving the lady to enter her house.

Gilles did not go far. Shortly before the boulevard, the Rue St Gilles developed a U-shaped side street, also running into the boulevard, and Gilles turned into this, found a gateway to tie his horse in and remained there watching, determined to see as much as he could of the comings and goings of those frequenting the house.

For quite a long time nothing happened, or nothing in particular. A boy came out to buy some mustard. He came hopping down the street, cocked an impudent eye at Gilles and called out cheekily in passing: 'No good hanging about round here, soldier! Ain't no girls for the like of you!'

'But plenty of boys poking their noses into other people's business. Be off with you, or you'll get my boot to help you!'

'All right, keep your hair on! Only joking, I'm sure! Have a nice time!'

Next Gilles saw an elderly woman with a veil over her head and a prayer book under her arm creeping along to evening service. She glanced at him covertly and went on her way. He was just beginning to think that he was wasting his time as well as risking drawing attention to himself when, as he was on the point of abandoning his vigil and remounting, a rumble of

193

carriage wheels along the boulevard slowed down to turn into the Rue St Gilles and came to a halt outside number ten.

This time, the vehicle was an elegant town chaise, black-bodied and with no other ornament on the panel than a simple rose. The slim, high wheels were lacquered red and the cloth on the box was a handsome black velvet with red quilling and gold acorns, altogether a most lordly equipage. The man who got out was aged about forty and of middle height and his olive skin, thick neck, snub nose with its flaring nostrils and pro-tuberant black eyes, of an unusual depth and penetration, would have made him a striking figure in any company. Warm though it was, he was almost completely enveloped in a large black cloak and a large tricorn, decorated with an odd-looking red plume, was pulled down low over his eyes.

As he stepped down, he swung the cloak over his arm in order to give his hand to a lady, gowned in white, who sprang impulsively from the carriage, rejecting the proffered assist-ance with a laugh.

'I'm not old enough yet to need help, my friend. Keep that for the dowagers.'

At the sound of her voice, Gilles started and bit back a cry. Falling between the full white muslin fichu that covered the girl's firm breasts – for she was no more than a girl – and the wide hat of natural straw with a trimming of green leaves, he could see a cascade of fiery curls framing dark, brilliant eyes, a pert, enchanting profile and a dazzling smile. This time he could not be mistaken. It was Judith, Judith herself, in the flesh, skipping lightly, in the company of an unknown man, into the house of a woman deep in intrigue.

Heaven lay before him. His heart beating a military tattoo against his ribs, Gilles felt himself invaded by a blissful sense of peace, close kin to the feeling he had had in the Trianon gardens but purer and brighter for being clothed in the brilliance of certainty. The moment after he had to hold himself back with a terrible effort, to restrain the impulse to dash forward. If he had not mastered himself in time, he would have been battering at the house doors, seeking the woman who, before all else in the world, he loved, who had been, was and would ever be the ultimate wellspring of all his life's work, its object and, if God willed, its reward. A goal still far ahead, maybe, and a prize never to be fully granted, for Judith was of those women who are only to be won at the price of continual conquest, whose affections and admiration must be constantly earned, for the one would never go without the other.

It would have given Gilles great pleasure to have kicked in the door of that house and snatched Mademoiselle de Saint-Mélaine from under the noses of a company he knew well enough could do her no good, but if he wished to try and find out anything about what was going on behind that quiet, apparently respectable façade, he had to contain his youthful rashness.

Making up his mind to remain at his post, even at the cost of a second sleepless night, and then to follow the elegant black and red chaise wherever it might go, to hell if necessary, Gilles folded his arms and resumed his watch, finding his task immeasurably lightened by his momentary glimpse of the girl and by the dazzle of her beauty which was not only undiminished, but even enhanced by the fine clothes of a kind unknown to that wild creature of the Breton heathland. Only who the devil, he asked himself, was the stout gentleman with the proprietorial air whom she had addressed, with such careless intimacy, as her friend?

It was long past sunset. Darkness was falling, deepening the shadows of the street hemmed in by its tall houses. Standing motionless in his corner, fixed in the absolute stillness he had learned from the Indians and which he knew how to impose on Merlin also, Gilles was all but invisible. He witnessed the arrival of the lamplighter Pongo had found so informative that morning. A few moments later, two lanterns sprang into light, suspended on wires across the street, one illuminating the blue-painted letter box near the junction with the boulevard, the other at the far end of the street, above the little statue of St Gilles. The area in between the two remained in partial shadow.

The lamplighter paused for a moment beside the chaise, helping the coachman, who had got down from the box, to light his own carriage lamps, then he moved on again, coughing, and his dragging footsteps passed on their rounds, leaving the street deserted once again.

Time passed, how long was difficult to tell. There were some signs of life. The sound of voices behind windows open to catch the cool of the evening and the scent of the lime trees whose tops rose rustling above the convent wall. Lights sprang up, too, here and there, but the front of number ten, when Gilles went to look at it in the hope of seeing something, remained dark and silent. The only living being was the coachman dozing on his box, his back hunched with the resignation of his kind, inured to long waiting.

At last, as the clock in the Bastille was striking half past ten, the silent house awoke. So did the coachman. A servant appeared with a lantern that spilled yellow light on the cobbles, the carriage and four people whom Gilles had no difficulty in recognizing as Judith, the man who had been with her, the Countess and the red-headed exquisite who served her as secretary and general factotum.

The farewells were not protracted. Bows were exchanged but the onlooker could not catch a word that was said. Then the girl and her escort climbed back into the chaise, the front door was shut and all was dark again. By the time the chaise moved off, the street was almost completely in darkness. But Gilles was already in the saddle.

He waited, unmoving, while the carriage went on down the street and turned into the Rue St Louis towards the Palais Royal and only then started after it, relying on the noise made by the iron-shod wheels on the cobblestones to cover the sound of Merlin's hooves.

The night was pitch dark, with the stifling heat that foretold a storm, but by keeping his eyes on the lamps he had no trouble in following the carriage through the maze of Parisian streets without coming too close to it.

It was quite a long way. They went along the Rue St Antoine and then by the Rue de la Tissanderie, the Rue de la Coutellerie and the Rue de la Boucherie as far as the Grand Châtelet, then, over the Pont de la Change, along the Rue de la Barillerie and across the Pont St Michel to bring them into the Rue de la Harpe, and all the way up that as far as the Place St Michel. There, emerging from the trees of its large gardens, were the dome, the high slate roofs and Italian walls encased in scaffolding of the Luxembourg Palace, the Parisian home of Monsieur. The chaise turned sharply and made towards the brilliantly-lighted façade of the Théâtre Française, where a performance was clearly in progress, but passed it without stopping, to turn almost at once into an impressive arched gateway surmounted by a dome and guarded by men in the red, gold and silver uniform with the striped gold and silver cross belt of Monsieur's own Guard.

It paused for a moment in the gateway, presumably to satisfy the sentries, then disappeared from view into the interior of the west entrance court. Gilles rode back a little way, hitched Merlin to a bronze ring in the wall and then walked forward again to where one of the sentries was standing. At the approach of an officer, the man came to attention and saluted. He was opening his mouth to speak the appropriate formula when Gilles stopped him.

'It's all right, my man. I don't want to come in. I would merely like some information.'

'Yes, sir.'

'Not so loud, for God's sake. I'm not here to ask for state secrets but all the same, I don't want the whole world to know my business! Tell me, do you know the lady in the black and red chaise who just entered?'

The sentry's face split into a wide grin and he winked knowingly. He knew where he was if there was a lady in the case and had no need to wonder why a lieutenant in his Majesty's Guard should stoop to chat to a common soldier.

'Course I knows her! Lives in the palace, don't she – and there's not a prettier lady in there. I'm not surprised you're interested, lieutenant.'

'Well, who is she?'

'One of the two ladies what reads to Madame. She's been with the princess about two years now.'

'Her name?'

'Mademoiselle de Latour, Julie de Latour. Pretty as a picture, ain't she? But not easy to approach, mind you. If you've a fancy to try your luck in that direction, Sir, you'd best be on your guard. She has a quick hand, a quicker tongue and no known lovers!'

The rough voice of the young soldier was to Gilles like the most celestial music. 'But,' he persisted, 'there was a man with her in the coach. Do you know who he is?'

'Not rightly. Only been here two or three times. Came this time to see Monseigneur and came out with the young lady in one of the carriages belonging to the house. Foreigner, I'd guess, not from Paris any rate. Got a funny name.'

'So he does not live in the palace?'

'Lord, no! Daresay he won't stay much longer, now that he's brought pretty Ju – that is, Mademoiselle de Latour, back home. He left his horse.'

'Thanks, friend. You've been a great help.'

A coin changed hands and the sentry's grin broadened still wider.

'If that's how it is, Sir, come again and welcome. Anything you want to know about the whole household ... My name's Gaubert, Gaubert La Pervenche.'

'Very well, La Pervenche. I'll not forget.'

He returned the young soldier's salute and stepped out from the shadow of the massive gate.

He was on the point of going to fetch his horse, when he changed his mind. He could not leave the place where Judith was living without even speaking to her and at least trying to penetrate to some extent the mystery which surrounded her. It was something to have discovered that she was reader to the Countess of Provence, but why under a false name? From fear of her brothers, perhaps? She would not know of Tudal's death and must be thinking of them still in the plural. But what could two such country bumpkins do to hurt a member of such a princely household? For better concealment, perhaps, and perhaps, too, as a shield against her own terrifying memories, since she had thought good to change her christian name also. Julie de Latour? Why that name?

Abruptly, there came back to his mind the last words that he had overheard between the Comtess de la Motte and Monsieur. 'Should the need arise, write me a note. It doesn't matter what it says, only you will sign it J. de Latour ... You'll not forget? J. de Latour.'

The connection was obvious. The prince had mentioned to his accomplice the very name by which Judith was known in his house. But then, what was the girl doing visiting a woman whom, in the ordinary way, she had no call to know? Was the man with her simply there to introduce them?'

198

Unable to answer any of these questions to his satisfaction, Gilles turned back to the sentry.

'Who is on duty here at night?'

'Lieutenant the Comte de Thézan, sir.'

'Fetch him for me.'

This should have been the signal for La Pervenche to hurry off at once. Instead, to Gilles' surprise, he stood his ground.

'Well? What are you waiting for?'

'I'm sorry, sir, but if I were you, I'd let it rest.'

'Why, may I ask?'

'Because it won't do any good. If it's Mademoiselle de Latour you want to see, neither Monsieur de Thézan nor even the Captain, the Comte d'Auger, could help you. The rules about Madame's ladies are very strict. The Princess is so straight-laced that if Mademoiselle were caught talking to a gentleman at night, she'd be dismissed at once.'

'But she just came home with a man?'

'That's difficult. If he was a member of her family, Madame might have given permission, only, take my word for it, he must have shown a clean bill of health.'

'But – suppose I had a message to deliver? Suppose I were her brother?'

'As far as Madame's ladies are concerned, in her view there's no message that can't wait until the morning. As for trying to pass yourself off as her brother, I'd not try that, if I were you.'

'Oh, indeed? What makes you say that?'

'You'd not ask that, Sir, if you'd ever set eyes on Madame de Montesquiou, who supervises Madame's household. There's not a man here wouldn't rather face an English bullet than her stony eye. If you insist on trying to see Mademoiselle, you're bound to come up against her – and if you come out of that alive, you'll still have nightmares for half a year.'

Gilles laughed. 'Very well. I'll give up for tonight. But I'll be back tomorrow.'

'It'll be daylight tomorrow. You'll stand a much better chance.'

'God grant you're right! Thanks for the advice, anyway.'

He walked away, unhitched Merlin and mounted, but then stayed motionless in the saddle. What he wanted to know now was who was this man who stood so high in favour that he was permitted to take Judith out wherever he liked. It might be interesting to know where this night owl had his roost.

This time, he did not have long to wait. Hoofs rang under the archway and a rider came in sight, muffled in a black cloak with a black hat with a cockade which was only too familiar.

'That's my man,' Gilles muttered through his teeth. 'Now let's see where he goes.'

He hoped with all his heart that his quarry lived, if not in the immediate vicinity, at least not too far off, for he was beginning to feel weighed down with weariness. Used as he was to hard living, he felt that life in civilization, and Paris especially, was more tiring than days spent on horseback in the open air or the life of a soldier in the field. But then he saw the broad ribbon of the Seine gleaming ahead and knew that there was to be no bed for him just yet.

Even so, although he could not have explained why, an impulse stronger than his own will, his curiosity or his longing for sleep, drove him on in the wake of this man. He felt a need that was almost physical to discover more about him, to get closer to this, he instinctively felt, mysterious being who drew him as a magnet draws iron filings.

Once across the Seine, the stranger took more or less the same route as before, although he moved considerably faster, and brought his pursuer at last to the Rue St Louis. It was very late by now, but the two riders, one a cautious distance behind the other, had met no officers of the watch. Even the post at the Grand Châtelet was peacefully silent, as if everyone there were asleep. The weather might have had something to do with it. The storm, although it had not yet burst, was still hovering round the outskirts of Paris with a rumble of thunder and brief flashes of lightning. No one wanted to be outdoors in such threatening weather, not even malefactors.

Then, without warning, the attack came. The rider in front had slowed down as he came to a prosperous-looking house when five or six men burst out of the shadow of the carriage doors and fell upon him. One sprang to the horse's head while the others made a grab for the man himself and hauled him bodily out of the saddle. Gilles' keen eyes saw the whole thing by the light of a lantern hanging nearby. As Merlin shot forward and came to a plunging halt, Gilles had his sword out and felt it bite home twice in human flesh while a third man was sent sprawling by the horse's hooves to lie in a crumpled heap beside the house wall. The stranger, moving with unexpected agility, for a man of his girth, had managed to get to his feet and draw his own sword. But it was two to one. Springing to the ground, Gilles ran forward and engaged one of the rogues and as he did so realized that he, like all the other footpads, was masked.

'Are you hurt, sir?' he asked as he fought.

'No, a little bruised, but –' Whatever else he might have said was lost in the din as a tremendous clap of thunder reverberated along the street. And in that moment, the storm burst. The sluices of heaven were opened and a veritable cataract descended on the earth, making the dust dance as it transformed it first into mud and then into a rushing stream. Gilles' adversary, wounded in the shoulder, decided that discretion was the better part and fled, nor did Gilles pursue him. At that, the stranger's opponent, seeing the last of his comrades deserting him, sprang out of range also and set off after him without more ado. Gilles wiped his sword and thrust it back into its sheath.

'There is no doubt, Sir, that I owe you my life,' the stranger said, speaking in excellent French but with a pronounced Italian accent. 'You have rendered me the greatest service one man may do another. But why were you following me?'

The merciful darkness hid Gilles' blushes.

'How did you know I was following you? I kept a fair distance behind.'

'I do not need to see to be aware, or to hear either. But this is no weather for a christian to be out in. Will you do me the honour of taking a glass with the man you have rescued? My house is here.' He indicated the tall carriage door in which his enemies had been lurking. 'We can at least continue our conversation in the dry.'

'Gladly, sir. I will accept the shelter even more gladly than the glass, and for my horse more thankfully than for myself.'

'Come inside, then.'

The stranger rang the bell whose chain hung down beside the gate and almost at once the heavy doorway swung on its hinges, revealing a fair-sized courtyard lit dimly by a pair of lanterns, one on either side of a flight of steps leading to a door. Standing under an umbrella as large as a small tent was the porter, a huge fellow whom the stranger addressed in a language wholly strange to Gilles. The man nodded and taking the horses by the bridles led them off towards the far end of the courtyard while the stranger guided Gilles through the front door, across a dusty hall and into a large, comfortable library panelled in light oak. In spite of the warmth of the evening before the storm broke, a fire of aromatic branches burned in the grey marble hearth, giving out more fragrance than heat and this, with the long curtains made of grey and tan striped silk, gave to the room for all its size an agreeable feeling of comfort and intimacy.

The stranger stripped off his mud-caked cloak and sodden hat and tossed them into a corner, so that his visitor was able to see a man of no great height but solidly built and well-proportioned, with a slight tendency to corpulence elegantly counteracted by the artistry of the skilful tailor who had cut the admirably fitting coat of dark red silk he wore with black silk breeches and stockings. A high, intelligent forehead did away with the slight impression of coarseness which might have been left by the other features of the face which Gilles had seen outside the house of the Comtesse La Motte. Shapely lips opened on white teeth and the eyes, which were black and very bright, held an almost unforgettable fascination.

'Come up to the fire, Sir, and be seated,' he said, indicating an ample tapestry-covered armchair. 'Make yourself at home, more at home even than I am, since the house belongs to a friend of mine, Count Ossolinski, who is kind enough to offer me his hospitality when I come to Paris.' He smiled, a curiously charming smile, and went on: 'I see that you belong to the King's Household and are one of those who have distinguished themselves during the glorious American Revolution. You hail from the provinces, I think ... a Breton almost certainly, and you have not been long in Paris. You are a bachelor ... in love and very tired! So please, be seated, but do me one more favour and tell me your name. I can divine many things but I cannot tell a man's name.'

'You are very right, Sir. I ought to have introduced myself

before I entered your house. My name is Gilles, Chevalier de Tournemine de la Hunaudaye. And you?'

'I might answer you: I am He who is. But I fear that might be a little hard for you to assimilate. So I will merely tell you the name by which I am known in this base world. I am called Cagliostro, Count Alexandre Cagliostro.'

9

The Strange Count Cagliostro

The name had an outlandish sound which suited the man but which meant nothing at all to the Chevalier. But the man himself, despite a certain grandiloquence, was likeable and even attractive. So that Gilles accepted, without further ado, the armchair he was offered. He sank into it with an involuntary sigh of relief for which he apologized at once.

'As you so rightly guessed, Count, I am very tired. As soon as the storm has passed over a little, I shall ask you to excuse me. Otherwise I might rudely fall asleep before your eyes, I'm afraid.'

'You mean to return to Versailles tonight?'

'No. I was meaning to put up at the York Hotel where I am known, but since I've not bespoken a room I may have to make do with a stable. Not that that matters.'

'You may depart when you wish, only not before you have shared with me this pâté and the bottle of champagne. There is no better combination for a tired body and mind. What is more, you have not yet answered my question.'

As he spoke, he was drawing a small table up to the fire. It was spread for two and he served them both liberally from a quail pâté, its gilded crust shining with health, and filled two tall glasses with sparkling, pale golden wine, thus affording his guest an opportunity to note that the Italian had beautiful hands, excellently well-kept and adorned with what, for a man, was perhaps an excessive quantity of diamonds and rubies.

'No,' Gilles said, 'I haven't.' He accepted the glass being

held out to him. 'You noticed that I was following you and you asked the reason. Only, since then, you have answered the question for yourself, since you have guessed – God knows how – that I am in love. I am, with the young lady in whose company you spent this evening. Now will you tell me how, never having met me before, you could know all this about me?'

Cagliostro laughed. 'There's very little to it. Your face and even more your voice told me you were from Brittany. You are unusually tall, it is true, but your features are the old Celtic in its purest form. Furthermore, although you have no accent, there is the almost imperceptible stress you lay on your consonants which told me, while I was hesitating between Normandy and Brittany. That you have fought in America was not difficult to tell, for it is written on your chest. You have not been long in Paris because you are not yet familiar with the ways of society. Or else you would know that her love of nature and dislike of ostentation have led the Comtesse de Provence to adorn her private carriages – those she uses when visiting for charity, for instance – not with her coat-of-arms but with a simple rose. You are a bachelor because a man of your age, if he is married, is not to be found roaming the streets at night. Finally, you are in love. Well, you could only have been following the young lady I was with tonight. I noticed you as we were going along this very street and not for a moment did it occur to me that I could be your object. You see, I am very little known in Paris as yet and come here only rarely on business. I live in Bordeaux, having moved there last autumn from my estate near Naples.'

'Yet you are sufficiently well known for men to lie in wait for you outside your house and attack you.'

'As I say, you are not yet familiar with Paris. The owner of this house, Count Ossolinski, is a Polish nobleman and extremely rich, nor am I precisely a pauper. They were after my purse, my jewels.' Here he stretched out his beautiful ringed hands complacently. 'Now, tell me how I may serve you, for I am most anxious to repay the debt I owe you.'

'If those men wanted no more than your purse, Count, then the debt is slight and I will hold you quit of it if you will only tell me the nature of your relations with Mademoiselle de – de Latour.'

'Fatherly, I assure you. She is the niece of a most agreeable woman whose acquaintance I made some three years ago, when I was here to tend Marshal de Soubise. I had the happiness of relieving her of some painful ailments, and now I always visit them whenever I am in Paris. Tonight, we called on some mutual friends. That is the whole of the mystery. But do have some more pâté. It is delicious. And a little more wine? Wine that makes glad the heart.'

'So you are a physician?'

'I have told you. I am He who is. I might have said also, He who knows. Yes, my young friend, I am a physician and, without flattering myself, perhaps the best of all because I tend the soul as well as the body. Some of my patients cannot do without me and on this account I am obliged to travel a great deal.'

Instinct told Gilles that the man had not told him the whole truth. There was something wrong, something that did not fit, but he could not think precisely what it was. Perhaps it was that the explanation was too glib, too simple, and nothing involving Monsieur and the strange countess could be so simple. He tried to probe further without appearing to do so.

'Have you a patient at the Luxembourg Palace? The Countess, perhaps? Or Monseigneur himself?'

'Monseigneur has, in fact, been good enough to command my humble services from time to time, when his ailments have troubled him badly, although with the utmost discretion, even, I might say, secrecy, in order not to offend those generally responsible for his health.'

'His ailments? The Prince is not yet thirty—'

'Age has nothing to do with it. He eats and drinks a deal too much. Think of it, his Highness consumes about ten bottles of wine a day. Moreover, although he loves horses and has some of the finest thoroughbreds in Europe in his stables, the prince takes no exercise, unlike the King who eats almost as much but drinks much less and is saved by his daily hunting. With Monsieur, you see, the consequences to his health are many. He suffers from attacks of gout, from varicose veins, from painful liver colic and from erysipelas. It happens that I have certain elixirs which can be of great use to him. It's the only remedy he will seek. When I start talking about diets, he won't listen.'

'I see. And – is the Prince unwell at this moment?'

'Not in the best of health, certainly. Today, I found him suffering from a bad liver attack, which I was happily able to relieve.'

Now Gilles knew that Cagliostro was lying to him and that his relations with the Prince concealed something other than the purely medical, for the man who had called on Boehmer earlier might have been too fat and had too high a colour but he gave no sign of suffering from his liver, or anywhere else.

'So that is the whole of the mystery,' the physician sighed, leaning forward to catch the firelight reflected in his champagne glass. 'But I bless your feeling for the charming Mademoiselle de Latour, since it is to that I owe your fortunate intervention just now. Only, as you have not been in Paris very long, when did you meet her? She goes out very little.'

Gilles' mind was wandering around the enigma of this curious man. He had ceased to be on his guard and answered idly: 'Oh, it was a long time ago. I first met Judith—'

He realized his mistake when his host's voice swelled suddenly.

'Judith? Surely Mademoiselle de Latour's name is Julie?'

The brilliant eyes were fixed commandingly on the Chevalier's suddenly flushed countenance. Gilles smiled, and made a clumsy attempt to retrieve his mistake.

'Did I say Judith? A slip of the tongue.'

'No. Your tongue made no mistake. You said Judith knowing quite well what you did because you have indeed known her for a long time. A very long time. I would say you probably know much more about her than I do.'

His pleasant, kindly tone had changed. It had become faintly charged with menace and Gilles had a sudden feeling that beneath the charming, smiling surface of the man there was concealed something infinitely more formidable. At the same time the fear came to him that his imprudence might have stirred some peril for the one he loved. Cagliostro's gaze upon him was becoming unbearable.

The ringing of the doorbell on the far side of the courtyard freed him from it and spared him the necessity of a reply. The doctor shivered and turned away, frowning.

'Who could be coming here at this hour?' he muttered through his teeth.

The giant porter came in almost at once and murmured something in his master's ear. Cagliostro shrugged and hurrying to Gilles, grasped his arm and drew him to the far end of the room where was a small doorway, snatching up a branch of candles as he went.

'Quickly! Go in there and do not show yourself. An unexpected visitor. I'll not be long.'

'I don't wish to be in your way,' Gilles protested. 'I ought to be going anyway. Tell your servant to bring my horse and I'll leave you.'

'No, no! We have not finished our talk. You are a much more interesting young man than I knew.'

'But really, Sir—'

His protests were in vain. With a hand that seemed suddenly made of iron, Cagliostro thrust his visitor into a small anteroom, set down the candle on a table covered with a black velvet cloth and was gone, shutting the door carefully behind him. So carefully, in fact, that Gilles thought he heard a key turn in the lock. Outraged, he flung himself at it but it held firm and, on reflection, he mastered the impulse to break free by any means. It might be more interesting to try and find out the identity of this unexpected visitor.

A close examination of the door revealed a long crack in the wood, narrow, to be sure, but wide enough, if he glued his eye to it, to enable him to see a large enough area of the library to distinguish both the doctor and the man who had just entered.

He was a man of about fifty, with a handsome face and an impressive bearing, dressed in black silk relieved by jabot and cuffs of fine white lace. Fine silver grey hair, cropped short, curled round a skullcap such as priests wore, only this one was purple and Gilles was too well versed in church hierarchy not to be aware that here was a Prince of the Church. Cagliostro, too, was bowing very low.

'So,' said the newcomer in a soft, well-modulated voice, 'my secretary, Ramon de Carbonnières, was not mistaken when he saw you coming from the house of the charming Countess this evening. You are indeed in Paris, my dear sorcerer – and not in my house. Do you know, I could take offence at that?'

'Your Eminence would be making a mistake. When I called at your house I was told that you were on your estate at Coupvray.'

'A great impediment! A matter of a few leagues! Could you not have come to me there, or sent to inform me? Besides, why not have sent word of your coming? You know how I need you. For months now I have been begging you to come and settle in Paris and you have persisted in remaining in Bordeaux among the lawyers! What is a Chevalier de Rolland, or even a Marquis de Canolle, when a Rohan has need of you? What are they to you that you must dance attendance on them so?'

Gilles, in his closet, could not help the thought that the cardinal, who could be none other than the Grand Almoner of France, Prince Louis de Rohan, Cardinal Archbishop of Strasbourg, was enacting something very like a jealous scene with the Italian, and his curiosity increased. What kind of doctor was this whom a prince of the blood summoned secretly to attend him and a Rohan pleaded with like a discarded mistress? This man who claimed to be Judith's friend? His astonishment increased still further as he heard Cagliostro's resonant voice speak again, for now it was with the sternness, wholly incomprehensible, of a master towards his pupil.

'My work among the jurats of that city is not yet finished and your Eminence knows very well that I shall return to you as soon as that is possible. May I now ask how you knew that I was here in this house?'

The cardinal seated himself in the chair that Gilles had occupied and sighed wearily.

'Ramon, who professes a great admiration for you, wheedled the address out of the Countess. Surely you cannot be angry with the sweet lady,' he added quickly, seeing Cagliostro frown. 'When she heard that I had just arrived in Paris, she must have thought I would be profoundly glad to see you, even for a moment. She can never resist the pleasure of giving happiness to those she loves. But tell me, my dear sorcerer, I did not know you were on such terms with the great men of Poland. This house belongs to Count Ossolinski, does it not?'

209

'Your Eminence moves in diplomatic circles. You must know that I am on terms with most of the Courts of Europe,' the physician answered, more sternly still. 'For your information, I might add that you would be surprised to know how many princes, in Asia and in Africa, and how many distinguished men in America are happy to be numbered among my friends – or under an obligation to me.'

'Forgive me. Good God, I must have come at a horribly inconvenient time!'

The Prince's eyes were resting on the little table with the two glasses, still half full, and the remains of the pâté on the plates.

'Your Eminence's visits are never inconvenient,' Cagliostro said coolly. 'They are always a delight to me and to my friends.'

'Friends whom I put to flight, eh? Then I must offer twofold apologies, dear. Threefold, in fact, if the friend was a woman?' He dropped his voice a little on the last word.

Cagliostro bowed but said nothing and Gilles heard no more after that as both men spoke almost in whispers, but he saw the cardinal leave the room soon afterwards with a warm handshake and every sign of the warmest regard.

Not wishing to be caught eavesdropping, Gilles moved away from the door then and sat in one of the armed chairs which, except for the table on which the candles stood, were the only furnishings of the room. He had not looked much at this before and now its appearance surprised him.

It was not a cheerful place. The black-draped walls were hung with strange figures cut out of brass, all of which seemed to gravitate about a pair of crossed swords. Black, too, was the velvet which covered chairs and table but, now that he came to look more closely at it, Gilles saw that the latter was covered with a peculiar assortment of objects, arranged in a symmetrical pattern. There was a rose, a cross, a triangle and a miniature skull, all very delicately carved in silver. In the centre was a mirror which gave back the light of the candles placed before it, doubling their effect.

Unthinkingly, the young man slumped back in his chair, his eyes fixed on the candle flame which all at once seemed to be shining brighter, with short, regular flashes due to the fact that the mirror had begun, without explanation, to revolve.

Cagliostro was presumably escorting his visitor down to his coach. The silence was deep, a muffling of all sound. It was having an insidious effect on Gilles' exacerbated nerves, he found it intensely soothing. His eyes remained fixed on the source of light but his eyelids, heavy with fatigue, began to droop increasingly.

Realizing all at once that he was on the point of falling asleep, he tried to shake himself awake again, but the more he struggled the more the heaviness seemed to increase while the temptation to yield to sleep was becoming irresistible. It was as though a pair of hands were pressing down, gently but strongly, on his shoulders, keeping him in the chair so that he felt less and less inclined to get up.

Somewhere in the unplumbed depths of his subconscious mind he seemed to hear a voice murmuring, gently commanding, a voice that was telling him to sleep, sleep, sleep ... The mirror was still revolving slowly and Gilles could no longer take his eyes from its fascinating movement. He neither heard nor saw the Italian's slow approach from behind, moving gradually nearer to the chair, his hands stretched out as though performing some incantation. The world dissolved and Gilles slid steeply into the soft chasm of a sleep that was filled with dreams.

Scenes and sensations rose unsought from the depths of memory. He revisited all the people he had been in the course of his short life. Once again, he was Gilles Geolo, the barefoot peasant boy of Kervignac heath, Marie-Jeanne's unloved bastard, the carefree, rebellious pupil of St Yves College at Vannes, the dazzled, resentful lover of the proud Judith de Saint-Mélaine, the destined priest fleeing his seminary and stealing a horse to do so. And after that there was Rochambeau's secretary, the eager young soldier of the Royal Deux-Ponts, La Fayette's and then George Washington's aide-de-camp, the skilled woodsman, Tim Thocker's comrade, the prisoner of the Iroquois and passionate love of the Indian princess Sitapanocki, the warrior of Yorktown, acknowledged on the brink of the grave by the father who had sired him and finally the officer of the Queen's Dragoons, the desperate avenger of Judith, whose brothers had condemned her to a hideous death.

There were more recent memories also. Smiling faces spangled the close weave of memory, women's faces, Maria-Luisa, Cayetana, the mysterious Countess with her strange resemblance to Judith, and the Queen also. Men's faces were there, too. The Comte de Provence emerging from the dark trees at the Trianon, Fersen with a black eye and now, latest of all, the strange Italian doctor . . .

But as the transparent mists of the dream swirled on, remembering became painful and unpleasant, as though the sleeper were overwhelmed with a new kind of fatigue, as if the gates of memory were striving vainly to clang shut.

Then at last it all dissolved in a maelstrom of flashing lights and coloured streaks descending into incalculable gulfs filled with the blackness of time, while from the depths a voice rose up, menacing and absurd, a voice that cried out: 'The Sceptre has struck at the Temple but the Temple shall strike at the Sceptre in its turn and it shall fall in mud and blood! Woe to the Lilies of France and to those that serve them! Woe to the Lilies of France and those that serve them! Woe to the Lilies . . .'

Then there was nothing, nothing but deep black waters on whose bosom, warm and silky, Gilles floated in blessed deliverance.

A ray of morning sun, filtering through the gap between the thick striped silk curtains, came to rest on the Chevalier's eyelids and they opened, blinking. He rubbed his eyes and yawned, tried to raise himself on one elbow and found himself at full length on the floor, swearing copiously, having rolled off the narrow sofa on which he had previously been lying.

He got up quickly and stretched, then looked about him and saw that he was back in the library to which the Italian doctor had brought him the night before. But there remained no trace of the supper they had eaten, or of any human presence. Except for Gilles' own boots set neatly by a chair and his coat spread over it, the room was perfectly tidy. It was also perfectly silent.

Gilles walked over and drew back the curtains, letting the sunlight flood in. He saw that the windows looked on to a small, neglected garden where the briars, to which the original

212

roses had reverted, rioted among the weeds as gracefully as brambles, ending at an ivy-covered wall beyond which tall trees could be seen.

The sound of a door opening made him turn and he saw a fat woman in cap and apron come in, armed with a broom, a duster and a shovel. At the sight of him she uttered a shrill scream and dropped all these implements on the floor.

'Saints alive! What are you doing here? Who are you?'

'Who am I? I don't see what business that is of yours, my good woman. Will you tell Count Cagliostro that I should be glad to take leave of him – and that I could do with a cup of coffee.'

'Tell who?'

'Why, your master! Count Cagliostro.'

'Who is he?'

Except in matters of duty, or when lying in ambush, patience was not Gilles' greatest virtue. For the sake of his dignity, he first pulled on his boots, then, having donned his coat and adjusted his wig, he stood over the servant who had snatched up her broom again, perhaps with the idea of using it against the intruder.

'Suppose we try to understand one another. This house belongs to Count Ossolinski?'

'Yes. Though it might as well belong to a ghost for all the times he comes here.'

'I dare say, but you are surely aware that Count Ossolinski has placed his house at the disposal of his friend Count Cagliostro, whenever that gentleman is in Paris?'

'But I tell you again, Sir, I've never heard of the gentleman. Who is he?'

'But you must have done! I was with the Count here last night. He even gave me supper! Go and fetch the porter.'

'What porter? The house has been empty for months.'

'Well then, who are you?'

'Me? I'm the Widow Radinois. I live in the Rue St Anastase, just round the corner. My late husband, Gratien Radinois, was paid by Monsieur the Count to come in and open the windows every week and tidy up a bit and since the money's gone on coming since he died, I've been doing it instead. But I swear to you on my husband's memory that I've never heard of this

213

Count of yours. No, my goodness, nor of any porter, neither.'

'Try to remember. A big fellow, a foreigner. He would be Polish, I should think.'

'Never seen or heard of him,' the Widow Radinois said firmly. 'When Monsieur the Count comes to Paris, he brings all his servants with him, and that he hasn't done for a good five years. Not that I've anything against it if he wants to let his friends use his house. He must have given this Count of yours a key – well, stands to reason! He couldn't have walked in through the walls. All I say is, he might have let me know. It would have been the proper thing to do. And now what, Sir?'

'Now nothing. Or rather, you get on with your housework as if nothing had happened. I am going to see if I can find my host of yesterday evening. Before that, however . . .'

As he spoke, Gilles was moving towards the far end of the library where he opened the little door leading into the closet hung with black. He drew back with an exclamation of surprise then, for there was no trace now of hangings, velvet-covered chairs, table or silver ornaments. All he saw was a little bare-walled closet with nothing in it but a pile of books lying on the ground and a pair of library steps. Of the disturbing decor of the previous night, there was nothing left at all.

Before he could ponder much on this new mystery, the voice of the Widow Radinois recalled him.

'Excuse me, Sir, but would this be for you?'

'Where did you find this?' Gilles asked, taking the letter she was holding out to him.

'Over there, on the mantelshelf. There's some writing on it only, to be quite honest, I never learned to read. My husband, he could now. Education, that's what he had. The curé at the church of St Louis of the Jesuits used to say even that if he'd wanted to he—'

But Gilles had no interest in the late Radinois' intellectual gifts. The letter was indeed for him, for his name was inscribed in large vigorous characters on the outside, and it was as brief as it was disquieting.

'Do not try to contact Mademoiselle de Saint-Mélaine for the present. You would merely be endangering her life to no purpose.'

Gilles stared at it in bewilderment and then, with an angry

movement, rammed it into his pocket, picked up his hat and clapped it on his head and then made for the door.

'Well now, Sir.' The widow was watching him, her hands on her ample hips and an ingratiating smile on her face. 'If it should so happen as you've a fancy to sleep here another time, just you let me know. I'll make a bed up for you. It'd be better than the sofa, and I always did have a soft spot for a handsome soldier. My house is in the Rue St Anastase, number two.'

But Gilles had no desire at all to enter the house again, least of all with the blessing of the Widow Radinois. He thanked her, however, touched his hat and left to go in search of the stables, hoping to God that Merlin had not been spirited away along with the Italian doctor, the Polish porter and the dream-phantoms of that small black room.

He need not have feared. The Irish horse was still there, standing comfortably in the one clean, well-furnished stall in the huge stables, his saddle and bridle hanging on the wall. He whinnied with delight at the sight of his master and turned his intelligent head for the caress he knew was coming.

'Well you may be a clever old fellow for a horse,' Gilles told him through his teeth as he began to saddle him, 'but you didn't spread straw and fill your manger all by yourself, or unsaddle and rub yourself down, either. And since I don't imagine it was your guardian angel, someone must have done it. Or perhaps I did it myself, walking in my sleep, and I've been having visions into the bargain! My God,' he went on as he tightened the girth, 'if you could talk, you might at least tell me I'm going mad! But then, there was that letter ... That damned magician knows a lot more about Judith than he's willing to admit. Or else how should he have known her real name?'

He paused suddenly, struck by an idea. There was one person who could assure him that all this had not been a dream and that was the illustrious visitor he had glimpsed through the crack in the door. A Rohan, a Prince and a Breton did not lie, much less a cardinal. Of course there might be some difficulties in the way of a plain officer of the Guard's putting questions to the Grand Almoner of France about his secret friendships and nocturnal visitings.

'Yet he might give me the address of this magician of his

215

without offence,' Gilles said to himself. 'At any rate, he won't excommunicate me for asking. At least, we'll see.'

Leading Merlin, he made his way out into the yard. The woman was there before him.

'Ah, so you've a horse that slept here, too? Well, an officer without a horse—'

'Is only half an officer! Your servant, Madame Radinois.' He gave her his most charming smile and a bow which made her blush to the roots of her hair and sink into a flustered curtsy.

'There, but you're a sweet lad,' she exclaimed. 'Come back whenever you like. Just you wait a moment and I'll open the gate for you. Only get up on that great horse of yours so as I can see you.'

To please the good woman, Gilles indulged in a little showing off, leaping into the saddle and making Merlin curvet and sidle to the enthusiastic applause of his audience and then with a final bow walked him proudly through the gate that she was holding open for him. He was just in time to see coming out of a nearby house a magnificent high-crowned hat which had something familiar about it, at the same time he noted with satisfaction that the previous night's corpses had been removed.

He was about to ride off towards the Bastille, then reined in his horse to make sure. Yes, it was undoubtedly the Countess de la Motte's elegant secretary. He had a cane under his arm and was standing drawing on a pair of butter yellow gloves in the relaxed attitude of a man leaving his house after a sound night's sleep and pausing on the threshold to breathe in the morning air before going about his business.

He caught sight of Tournemine at the precise instant that Tournemine caught sight of him. Seeing him riding through the gate of Count Ossolonski's house seemed to startle him a good deal. The expression on his fair, clean-shaven face went from surprise to unconcealed shock. He finished pulling on his gloves in a hurried fashion and brandishing his cane in a manner vaguely threatening, set off striding jerkily in the direction of the Rue St Gilles.

Gilles found his behaviour perplexing. The secretary did not and could not know him. Their brief encounter leaving the Trianon the other evening could not have left any indelible impression since he was not at that time aware that Gilles was intending to follow his mistress. Then why the devil did he look like that when he saw him coming out of this house? Unless it was simply because it was this house. If so, was it merely because he knew it to be unoccupied, or because he was only too well aware of what had taken place outside its doors last night?

As he guided Merlin at a brisk trot through the early morning traffic in the Rue St Louis, where the cries of the street vendors seemed to answer those of the knife grinder who had set up his pitch on the corner of the Rue St Anastase, Gilles caught himself thinking that there was something very strange about this whole small community that thronged the environs of the Temple. His mind checked suddenly at the word Temple as it came into his head. The gigantic voice which, in his dream, had uttered that terrible curse against the Lilies of France was suddenly booming in his ear again, adding to the feeling of unease that had assailed him when he caught sight of the secretary. What was the meaning of that dire threat to a realm, thrusting its way into the humdrum life of a baseborn soldier of fortune whose humble fate seemed in no way destined to be mingled with the exalted doom of kings?

To that question there was no answer, and in the bright morning sun that gilded all Paris, the night's shadows lost their power. At that moment, too, Gilles had no wish to think about anything but himself and his love. His first desire was to find Judith, even if she preferred now to call herself Julie, even, perhaps most of all, if she was mixed up in strange and perilous doings. He knew that he had enough love and determination in him to pull her out of the plot, about whose darker by-ways he was learning more each day. Let that plot be discovered and, as usual, it would not be the principal culprit who would suffer, but those who had worked for him and who had not the good fortune to be born on the steps of a throne.

It was a simple matter to ask someone to point out the Hôtel de Rohan-Strasbourg, where the cardinal lived. But that morning, Gilles' luck was out. When he reached the Rue des Francs-Bourgeois, it was to discover that His Eminence had left Paris at daybreak, leaving no word where he was going. It could be to his estate at Coupvray, it could be to his see of

Strasbourg. It was impossible to extract the least indication from the porter who persisted in refusing all attempts at bribery.

Angry and disappointed, Gilles could only search in some other direction, but the devil alone knew where, he thought. Should he go to Bordeaux? This Cagliostro seemed too cunning for that.

Yet after all, as long as he knew where to find Judith, what need had he to chase after the magician? It was true that behind the dark walls of the old Medici palace she was almost as inaccessible, almost as distant as if she were dwelling on another planet. That she would be in danger if he tried to remove her from it, Gilles was prepared to believe, although his love rebelled against the thought.

He was beginning to realize that a life spent in the orbit of the great ones of this world was more often productive of pain and grief than a life spent in obscurity, especially for the pure in heart, and at that moment he longed passionately to return with Judith to the obscurity which, as a youth, he had so yearned to break free of.

He had dreamed once of carrying Judith off to the wild shores of America to make a new life there and found, with her, a new dynasty of gerfalcons. Now it was to the vale of Hunaudaye, to the shelter of those ancient towers, mantled in the surrounding forest, that he longed to take her, far from the rumour of courts and far from the ambitions of men – far from his own ambitions also, for one day of happiness with Judith seemed to him now infinitely more precious than a whole year spent amid the gilded splendours of Versailles.

But the time for dreams was not yet. Realizing that he was very hungry and anxious to get a shave, Gilles made for the York Hotel where he could be sure that Nicolas Carton would attend to all his needs.

By way of the Place de Grève he came to the Pont Neuf where the booths always delighted an adolescent love of fairs in him.

It was the only bridge which was not lined with the double row of houses, which made all the others into ordinary streets. The Pont Neuf was more like a garden, with the displays of florists and fruit sellers overflowing onto the carriageway. But

218

there were other things, too, on these open air stalls: there were sellers of ribbons and laces, second-hand clothes and makers and menders of shoes. Cooks stirred dubious messes in huge cauldrons, boot blacks and dog trimmers plied their trade and there were charlatans who would pull your teeth to music or sell you potions to cure everything from old age to corns. It was an astonishing daily carnival.

This morning Paris seemed to be in high good humour. The previous night's storm had washed it clean, and the news brought down from Montereau by the barges overnight was good. It said that the harvest was going to be excellent and that there would be bread and to spare for all, at not too high a price.

As the young man guided his horse through the picturesque confusion, smiling as a market woman called a cheeky greeting or a girl gave him a sly wink, his eye was caught by the red cockade in the hat of a tall fellow in the white coat with red facings of the Soissonnais regiment. The man was a recruiting sergeant and evidently hard at work, for his left hand was resting on the shoulder of a lad of about sixteen or seventeen while his right was carelessly tossing what seemed to be a well-filled leather purse.

The deep, carrying voice could be heard some way off, but no one was paying much attention to what the sergeant was saying. He and his like were no rarity on the bridge and almost any Parisian who kept his ears open could have quoted you his panegyric on the glory and pleasure of the King's service, the handsome uniform and its effect on the girls, the fine food to be had in the army and the exceptionally generous pay. But the lad for whose benefit the sergeant was detailing all these things seemed in no hurry to be convinced. He was shaking his head, smiling awkwardly and making timid attempts to shake off the heavy hand clamped on his shoulder. Gilles heard him stammer out:

'I'd like it fine, sergeant, but indeed I cannot. I have to take care of my sister. I am the only person she has in the world and she is lame, as you see.'

Clinging to the boy's arm there was a girl, fourteen or fifteen years old, who was following the exchange between the man and the youth with anguished eyes. She had a sweet, pretty face, although very white, and one shoulder higher than the other, as well as a visible limp.

'You'll be able to take care of her much better when you can send her part of your wages. She could stay at home, she might even have a servant to look after her. You just don't know how much you could earn with us. What's your trade?'

'Trade? I haven't one. I earn my bread, and hers, by running errands.'

'And you live well on that? Thunder and lightning, lad, the kit a soldier carries in the field isn't half the weight of a load of wood or a bag of sand! You can think yourself lucky you met me. Look here, we'll go and have a drink on it. I'm paying. And you can put your name to a bit of paper—'

The little girl was crying now and pulling her brother's arm.

'Don't listen to him, Gildas! He wants to take you away from me! Come away! Oh please, come away!'

'You don't know what you're talking of, little girl. It's for his own good, I'm telling you, and for yours. Now you just let him alone. You'll thank me for it later.'

He gave the girl a push to thrust her off and she tripped and fell with a cry against the kerb. At the same time he beckoned to two of his men who had been standing watching at a little distance. The youth made to go to his sister but the sergeant had him firmly by the arm.

'That's enough! Hold still now!'

'That's enough indeed! Let go of that man!' Gilles spoke curtly, at the same time edging Merlin's broad chest in between the sergeant and his men.

The recruiting sergeant grinned up at him.

'That's all right, Sir. The lad asks nothing better than to serve his King. It's just a matter of coming to an agreement.'

'It's not true!' the boy cried out, his courage clearly returning in the face of this unlooked-for support. 'I've been telling him for the past hour that I don't want to enlist, because of my sister. Oh, please, Sir, please tell him to leave me alone—'

'That is what I am doing. All right, sergeant, you know quite well the King has said this practice of enforced enlistment must cease.'

'He never said it to me,' the man retorted in an ugly voice.

'Nor to my colonel, neither. We're short of recruits and if I come back with no one, I'm the one who'll be in trouble.'

'The day's not over yet. Here, take this and drink my health in the nearest tavern while you think it over!' A coin spun from his fingers into those of the abruptly mollified sergeant.

'Easy to see they've no trouble getting recruits in the Guard,' he said with a shrug. 'Well, we'll do what we can to plug the gap before tonight. Thanks, all the same, lieutenant. Only, if you wouldn't mind in future taking your constitutional somewhere else? You're queering my pitch.'

'Don't worry. I'm not staying.'

He dismounted then as the boy was helping his sister to her feet and wiping away her tears.

'Your name is Gildas? You are from Brittany?' he asked, using the Breton tongue. The boy's grey eyes widened in amazement and the girl's tears ceased abruptly.

'From Landévennec, Sir, if you please.'

'Then what are you doing in Paris? Wouldn't you be better off at home? You're a fisherman, I suppose?'

The boy looked away and reddened under his tan.

'I was a fisherman. I was employed by the monks at the abbey, but I had my own boat. And then I fell on hard times. I had to come away, because of Gaïd, my sister, mostly. She can't do without me. But for you, I don't know what would have become of her.'

The girl had recovered and was clutching her brother's arm with such desperate strength that the knuckles of her hands were white. Her great grey eyes, so amazingly like her brother's, stared up at the officer with mingled fear and admiration. Gilles smiled at her reassuringly.

'Running errands is hard work. Where do you live, both of you?'

An expression of real terror came into the girl's face and she tightened her hold on her brother.

'Don't tell him, Gildas, don't tell! Oh, come away!'

The boy stroked her hand gently, as he might have done to soothe a frightened animal.

'It's all right, Gaïd, he helped us. He was kind. But for him—'

'I know. Only don't tell him—'

221

Just then, a beggar who had been standing a little way off, watching them, came swinging over on two greasy crutches.

'You kids better be off. If the sergeant comes back, you'll be for it. Let them go, Sir. Else they'll be back for the boy the moment you've turned your back.'

'You're right. I'm off. God be with you, Gildas. And, believe me, you should go home. Here, you'll always be like a gull with a broken wing.'

He had one foot in the stirrup and the beggar was already turning away, thrusting the young Bretons before him, when all at once Gaïd let go of her brother and came back to the Chevalier. She was almost running in spite of her bad leg and she was nearly under the horse's hooves as she seized Gilles' hand and kissed it, then made off again as fast as she had come. Her brother had stopped and was waiting for her a little way off. Gilles saw then that his feet in his clogs were bare and that he had a rag tied round one ankle which had slipped a little, showing the half-healed scar around it. Young as he was, the boy had known fetters, and not so long ago. He might well be on the run and that would explain his sister's terror at the thought of telling one of the King's soldiers where they lived. If that were so, then it was better not to try and find out any more but to let his young fellow-countrymen make their own way as best they could. Even so, he felt a twinge of regret, for he would have liked to be able to do more for the pair of children who, though born under the same skies as himself, had clearly been so much less fortunate.

But when he got to the Rue du Colombier the two were quickly forgotten, not in the luxury of a hot bath, a substantial breakfast and some of Nicolas Carton's delicious coffee, but by virtue of a letter which the proprietor handed to him. It had been delivered first thing that morning and was from Boehmer. Its contents did not give him unalloyed pleasure.

What the Queen's jeweller had to convey to him, in the most roundabout way, was that he and his partner could no longer consider selling the necklace out of the kingdom.

'We have learned from the highest authority that her Majesty the Queen might well be distressed to learn that such an exceptional piece of jewellery had been sold to anyone. It appears that her Majesty is still very desirous of possessing the necklace, although she is no longer in a position to ask the King for it, and would be grateful if, before concluding the sale elsewhere, we were to allow her more time for reflection and to consider whether she herself might not be able to raise the required sum.

'Since, however conveyed, the wishes of her gracious Majesty are law to us, her humble servants, we have consequently assured the person of whom we speak of our willing cooperation. We have bowed to this necessity with some regret, perhaps, but you, Sir, will readily comprehend our position, the more readily, I am sure, when I tell you that, in consideration of this, we have been promised, when the time comes, the reversion of the title, at present belonging to Monsieur Aubert, of Jewellers to the Crown of France.

'We are sending by the same messenger a letter to the Spanish Consul General informing him that it is no longer in our power to honour our bargain with him.

'We have agreed to wait until the end of the year and if, at the end of that time, her Majesty should definitely decline to purchase the necklace, we shall be very happy to resume negotiations with you where we left off, trusting in the meanwhile that her grace the Duchess of Alba will bear with us ...'

Any fool, thought Gilles, could have guessed who was the 'highest authority' on whose word Boehmer had rejected, temporarily, to be sure, but nevertheless rejected, so tempting an offer as Cayetana's. Especially as his backers, such as the financier Baudard of St James, who had enabled him to create the necklace, were beginning to look seriously for a return on their money. What was less easily understood was why Monsieur, who was said to dislike his sister-in-law at least as much as his brother, was suddenly so anxious to spare her the misery of knowing that another woman was going to be able to wear a necklace too dear for her. However, it was scarcely possible to go and discuss this finer point of princely psychology with Boehmer and Bassange and so Gilles put the matter aside for later consideration.

He tucked the letter carefully into the inside pocket of his coat, promising to send an answer when he had written to the Duchess of Alba and paid a visit to her banker, Lecoulteux, to let him know how matters stood. After all, Cayetana might well wait six months for the realization of her ruinous ambition, for her envoy did not see how the Queen, who was said to be already heavily in debt and was in the habit of losing heavily at cards, could ever manage to raise sixteen hundred thousand livres.

Before leaving the hotel, Gilles inquired after Fersen, hoping to find him more inclined to listen to the stern voice of common sense and to bury the hatchet, but he was disappointed. The Swede had gone out an hour before with Monsieur de Stedingk.

It was now high time the Chevalier returned to Versailles, but once out in the street he turned Merlin's head almost automatically in the opposite direction. It was too strong for him. He could not leave Paris without going back for one last look at what might be happening in the vicinity of the Luxembourg Palace. The longing gnawed at him to see Judith, if only for a moment, if only through a window.

He had been forbidden to seek out Mademoiselle de Saint-Mélaine but, after all, no one had said anything about Mademoiselle de Latour.

The look of the area had changed with the daylight. The theatre looked lightless and dead, but the workmen had returned to their scaffolding and were singing under the blue sky where, high above, the swallows swooped and dived. At every open window servants could be seen, armed with dusters, some of them a great deal more interested in what was going on in the street than in their work. Others, with big baskets on either arm, were going to the market at St Germain, or coming back, laden with carrots, turnips, leeks, cabbages, salad vegetables and big downy peaches. A good many glanced up at the horse and rider and some even turned round. Gilles wished he could have stopped without drawing attention to himself.

Luck was with him in the end. When he reached the little Rue des Fossoyeurs, he found a large crowd of people gathered in front of a respectable-looking house whose closed shutters and funeral hatchments showed that there had been a death in the building. No one took any notice of the young officer who hitched his horse to a ring outside a nearby house and mingled briefly with the crowd. He stayed long enough to learn that the deceased was a well known sculptor named François Vernet and then faded discreetly away and was next seen strolling back towards the Petit Luxembourg.

He had no particular plan in mind. All he wanted was a closer look, in daylight, at the house where Judith was living. If he was lucky, he might see her come out, to go to mass, perhaps, at St Sulpice or at the nearby convent.

He waited for an hour or more but she did not appear. The Count of Provence's house was oddly still and silent. Nothing moved except the sentries keeping their rigid guard on the gates and every window on the street side was closed.

All at once, Gilles saw an elderly woman, dressed like an upper servant of a great house in a black silk dress with a bunch of keys suspended at her wrist. A smart bonnet with black ribbons was set on her neat grey hair and she had a prayer book under her arm.

She seemed to be in a hurry, but when she crossed the Rue de Vaugirard and came straight towards him, Gilles hesitated no longer. He bowed politely, hat in hand.

'Forgive me for stopping you, Madame, for I can see you are in a hurry, but you behold me in a great fix and I think you are the one person who can help me.'

A bright, inquisitive eye and a mischievous smile looked up at him from beneath the lace bonnet.

'I'd never have believed it was in my power to assist the King's army in any way,' she said.

'I don't know about the army, but I am sure you can assist me. You are, I think, a member of Madame's household?'

'A fine guess! You saw me come out.'

'Bear with me, please, and do not make things more difficult for me. I wish to have news of someone who lives in that house – someone very dear to me.'

'If you say so, Sir. This *someone* is, I presume, a young lady, and pretty. We have not so many of those. Will you tell me her name?'

'Mademoiselle de Latour.'

'Ah!'

It was so brief that Gilles was alarmed.

'You do know her?'

'I know her.'

225

'I asked you – that is, how is she?'

'She is very well.'

'Madame, madame,' the young man said desperately. 'You are tormenting me for your own amusement. What I long for above all is to hear that from her own lips. Could you not lead me to her? My intentions, I assure you, are perfectly honourable. My name is Gilles de Tournemine and I am a cousin of hers.'

This time the woman laughed.

'That is what every lover in the world always says when he wishes to come near the object of his passion! I do not doubt, Sir, that you are a man of honour. I can see it in your eyes. But I doubt very much whether you are a cousin of Mademoiselle Julie's. In any case, I cannot take you to her.'

'Why not?'

'Because it is impossible.'

'But why?'

'It is quite simple. Mademoiselle de Latour is not here any more. She left the palace early this morning with a relative of hers, who ought therefore by the same token to be one of yours also, surely?' She threw him a mocking smile. 'Have you connections in Italy? No, it is clear from your face that you have not. Well, I cannot tell you more than I know myself. An Italian nobleman called for her with a message from her aunt who required her attendance urgently. Good heavens, young man! Don't look like that! No harm has come to Julie, I can assure you.' For Gilles' face had become tight with anger. That damned Cagliostro, he was thinking, had played with him like a child! It was he, it must have been, who had come for her that morning, to keep Gilles from finding her. And where had he taken her? Almost without thinking, he asked: 'Do you know where she has gone?'

'To her aunt's house, I imagine. No, I am not making fun of you. I see that you are troubled and I wish I could help you. You are not acquainted with the aunt?'

'No. But perhaps you, Madame, know her name – and where she lives?'

The lady with the black ribbons did not answer. She seemed thoughtful. Torn, perhaps, between the liking she clearly felt for the young man and something less easily definable but which might have been fear, she was biting her lip and twisting her mittened hands together. The liking won.

'She is the Baroness de St Ange,' she said abruptly. 'Julie calls her aunt but she is not really, only a distant cousin of her mother's.'

'Where does she live?'

'At Argenteuil. But do not go there, for you will not find her. She left a week ago for her estates in Savoy. As it happens, you see, young man, I have known Madame de St Ange for a long time. I met her first in Turin where her late husband was in the service of Duke Victor Emmanuel III, the father of Madame and of the Comtesse d'Artois. In fact, it was through me that her niece entered this household.'

'So – she has gone to Savoy?'

'Perhaps. I do not know. It is possible – but I do not think so. And do not ask me why,' she added, with a touch of irritation, 'for I shall not tell you. Only I can see that you are ready to leap on to a horse and gallop off there, hell for leather. Believe me, you would draw a blank, just as at Argenteuil.'

'I see ...'

Gilles shook his head, overwhelmed with misery. The fragile thread he had found with such trouble had just snapped in his hands. Where was he to search now, where could he go? To what confounded secret hideout had that damned doctor taken her, and why? Had she gone with him to Bordeaux? Must he go there? What were the names of the men who were his patrons in that city, whom he had mentioned last night, to the cardinal? Muddled with grief, his memory was failing ...

Gilles sighed, stepped back and bowed.

'Your pardon, Madame, for importuning you like this. And thank you for speaking to me.'

'You have not been importunate,' she said, very kindly, 'and I wish I could help you. You told me your name was Tournemine, I think?'

'Yes.'

'Well, when Mademoiselle de Latour returns – or when we hear from her, I will write you a little note and send it to the Guard. I am Madame Patri, Madame's principal tirewoman. Now, run along and let me go to my funeral, or else it will all be over but for the candlesmoke.'

227

She moved away, lightly and gracefully in spite of her age, her skirts rustling softly, pursued by warm words of thanks from the young man. He saw her melt into the back of the crowd which was moving slowly in the direction of the church of St Sulpice. The bell had been ringing there for some moments. Soon the street was empty except for Merlin, tied to his ring.

Gilles walked back to him, weighed down with gloom. His heart misgave him, despite Madame Patri's promise. Something told him that it would be a long time before Judith returned to the Luxembourg, if she ever did. She was involved in some dark doings, and how could he know exactly what part she was playing in them, in the hands of that man. Gilles perfectly understood now that someone had wanted to kill him.

And he, who had never before regretted helping his fellow man, was beginning to be sorry, with all his heart, that he had saved Cagliostro from his attackers the night before.

There was nothing he could do now but go back to Versailles and take up the monotonous thread of his life, while still hoping for a miracle.

10

The Woman in the Blue Veil

Baron Ulrich-August von Winkleried zu Winkleried was not a man who lavished his affections idly, nor did he waste friendship. But when he took a liking to someone, he would go to any lengths to serve, help or even make life easier for him.

He had promised his new friend Tournemine to find him a suitable lodging at Versailles and two days after their first meeting the young officer moved into the first floor of a pretty cottage set in a shady garden in the rue de Noailles, almost opposite the house where the Swiss had his own rooms. It was a delightful situation. The garden, not unpleasingly neglected, contained, as well as two chestnut trees, three limes and a clump of lilacs, a whole mass of half wild flowers, most of them coming up out of habit, with no one but one old, rheumaticky gardener to attend to them.

Gilles loved the garden at first sight. It reminded him a little of his mother's at Kervignac. It was the perfect refuge for a grieving heart and here at least he could be sure of finding peace and tranquillity.

The house's owner, Mademoiselle Marguerite Marjon, was a kindly spinster lady, of the same generation as the late King Louis XV and still cherished a tenderness for the Bien-Aimé whose charm had eclipsed that of every other man for her all through her life.

She welcomed her new lodger with courtesy and conducted him over the four bright, newly painted rooms set aside for him. The furniture was old and plain and comfortable and of good quality, although the general effect would have suggested that it was intended for a lady rather than a young army officer, if it had not been for a lingering odour of tobacco.

'I will not pretend that I would have preferred someone of my own age and of similar tastes to myself,' his landlady sighed, 'but although I have had all the rooms repainted, it has been impossible to get rid of the smell. And so, although the rent is, I think, very reasonable, I have not been able to find a single lady willing to endure it.'

'But surely I heard that your previous tenant was a lady? Surely she did not smoke?'

'Oh, but she did! Mademoiselle d'Eon, you know, was not like other ladies. She was quite charming, with delightful manners and always in the best of taste. She belonged to a very noble family in Burgundy and her clothes, so very beautiful they were and made by the Queen's own dressmaker, Mademoiselle Bertin, but she was . . . strange. For one thing, her voice was rather deep for a woman, and then she never had any callers, except, right at the end, a Russian lady, so very pretty. They were always together and she went with her to England.'

'There's nothing very strange in that.'

'Perhaps not, but there were other things. She would sit all day long in the salon, which she had made into a library, scribbling away and smoking a long pipe. It seems it was a habit she had picked up on her travels.'

'Well, among the American Indians I've frequently seen women smoking pipes. They believe tobacco is a medicine and I must confess that I am fond of it. So the smell will not bother me. Is that all?'

It was, although Mademoiselle Marjon clearly had a fund of stories in reserve about her former lodger. They quickly reached an agreement on the rent, which was extremely reasonable, and that same evening Pongo, assisted by Winkleried's valet, Niklaus, transferred his own and his master's clothes, their weapons and the medicine bag which he had brought with him from Virginia, to their new home. The Breton and the Swiss then departed together to seal, over a good supper, a friendship which was to survive the years untarnished.

Madame Patri's promised letter came a few days later. It

230

contained only a few lines, signed with the letter P, but what it had to say was unexpected.

'Mademoiselle de Latour has written to express her wish to quit Madame's service in order to enter a convent. That is all I know. P.'

His mind a confusion of anger, relief and alarm, Gilles tried to ascertain which of the three was uppermost and finally decided that relief predominated. It was annoying that Cagliostro should have chosen a convent for Judith but, on the other hand, she would surely be safer there than anywhere from any repercussions of the plot in which she had become unwittingly involved. It remained to discover which convent out of the many that proliferated throughout the kingdom. It remained, also, to find out whether she had entered it willingly, and for how long. A convent was a highly convenient place for getting rid of someone who had become inconvenient.

Finally, it remained to be seen if it were true, or if the Italian magician were not simply using it as an excuse to carry off and keep for himself a charming girl to whom he had seemed much attached ... When he reached this stage in his cogitations, Gilles felt his blood boiling. The thought of his lovely nymph of the estuary in the Italian's diamond-encrusted hands, a helpless victim of his whims, a prey to his caresses, made him see red.

'I have to find this convent. I must know where it is!'

'It won't be easy,' Winkleried said, for he was now fully conversant with his friend's troubles. 'There must be hundreds of them in France. How can you find out?'

'By looking. Even if I have to visit all of them, one by one, I'll find her. But I think there are some places more likely than others.'

'Brittany, for instance?'

'I don't think she'd be willing to go back there. All the same, so as to leave nothing to chance, I'm going to write to the rector of Hennebont, the Abbé de Talhouet, who is my godfather, and ask him to make inquiries. It won't be difficult for him and if Judith has gone back there, he will know. No, I was thinking rather of the Bordeaux region, which is where that damned Italian lives. Supposing it's true and there is a convent at all.'

'Why should she have written to say so if it was a lie?'

231

'Why not? A person will write anything under duress and Cagliostro might want to cover his tracks.'

Determined to try everything and leave no stone unturned in trying to find the girl, it was only then that he remembered, with some remorse, that he had not called on his friends Antoinette and Teresia Cabarrus since their arrival in Paris. With their connections in the south-west, they could be a great help to him, and he was sure they would not refuse to give him what assistance they could. Antoinette, beneath her affected airs, was a good-hearted woman, while Teresia's heart was never deaf to any appeal. When she knew that he was unhappy, she would take his hand and make him sit beside her and say in her cooing little voice: 'Come here, Señor Gilles, and tell all your troubles to your friend, Teresia.'

In fact, matters turned out rather differently.

Gilles arrived at their house to find both ladies, a good deal to his surprise, so carried away with worldly pleasure that mother and daughter had nothing to choose between them for frivolity.

A ravishing Teresia, who seemed to have grown up remarkably in the space of a few days, reproached him with fashionable languor for 'abandoning' her so shamefully, and then gave him her little hand to kiss with all the airs of a duchess. After that she told him that she could not spare him much time because, being engaged at a ball that night at the house of the Comte de Laborde, she had an urgent appointment with her dressmaker, Madame Eloffe, but she made him promise to be present at the ball her mother meant to give for her very soon. 'And do not think to serve me the same trick as you did at the Pradera of St Isidore! I have promised all my friends to show them the famous Gerfalcon, who was the lover of an Indian princess, and I do not wish to be made to look foolish.' Then, hardly pausing for breath, she vanished in a cloud of muslin and pale pink ribbons.

As for Antoinette, he found her queening it over a salon full of chattering females. She handed him a cup of tea and talked all the time about the trials and inconveniences of the house they were in, which she now considered shabby.

'We cannot stay here. Teresia has set her heart on my giving a ball and that cannot be done in this house. People would think we were dancing in the pantry! So I have written to my husband, telling him to leave his business and come and see what straits we are in, I and the children, and rescue us from this hovel!'

That was that. Rather than make a nuisance of himself, Gilles took his leave, pitying François Cabarrus with all his heart and leaving Antoinette to her 'hovel' which, that afternoon, presented the appearance of a pale panelled salon, filled with flowers and elegantly dressed callers, and opening onto a shady garden, with a pleasant aroma of tea and cakes in the air. He went back to Versailles seething with anger.

How, he wondered, could he have been fool enough to expect any help from a pair of silly geese with nothing in their heads but how to achieve a footing in society and not an idea more serious than the measure of a quadrille or the height of a coiffure. One thing was certain, ball or no ball, he was never going to set foot in the house again. It had irritated him beyond bearing to find himself cast in the role of a curiosity to be gaped at and, in particular, as a kind of Don Juan among the Iroquois to give a cheap thrill to a bevy of idle young ladies of fashion. His days as a drawing room beau were long past and done with.

Fortunately, now that the warm weather was beginning, the pace of social life was slackening. The water level in the Seine fell, bringing disease, and soon there were many houses in the fashionable Faubourg Saint-Germain and in the vicinity of the Place Royal where the shutters were up and the noble owners departed to seek a purer, healthier air on their country estates. Meanwhile the Queen had retired to her beloved Trianon along with a handful of her particular friends and was playing at shepherdesses on her toy farm among a flock of beribboned sheep.

For the Guards, however, there was no retreat for the summer, since the King never left Versailles, and Gilles' efforts to obtain leave in order to pursue his researches in the Bordeaux region were unsuccessful. Count Vassy, his commanding officer, made it quite clear that he would do himself no good by asking to be released after so short a time of service. He was therefore obliged to remain, tied hand and foot to his duty, which in no way improved his temper during the days that followed.

233

He had revisited the house in the rue St Gilles on the off-chance of finding out something and determined, this time, to get inside the house where he had seen Judith and to confront the thief of the Queen's letter. But the house was blank and shuttered, the Countess away and, as he learned from the shoemaker farther down the street, 'gone off with all her servants to the country'.

Among his fellow Scots Guards, Gilles had, however, made friends with standard-bearer, Paul de Neyrac, who hailed from Guyenne and had been fortunate enough to gain leave to visit his father in Bordeaux. Gilles had told him no more of his story than seemed good for him but the young man was a friendly, romantic soul with a head stuffed full of tales of chivalry, and sympathized intensely with his friend's misfortunes. He promised to do everything in his power to help him find the girl he loved.

One evening early in August the two young men had supper together at the inn called 'The Just' in Versailles, named after King Louis XIII whose head appeared on its signboard. Neyrac was to catch the coach for Bordeaux in the morning and was sleeping at the inn and Gilles had insisted on treating him to a meal.

The heat, all day long, had been very nearly unendurable, but at nightfall a light breeze had sprung up, bringing a blessed coolness to the air. After leaving the inn, Gilles decided to walk home in order to enjoy it. He had found of late that strolling gently round the empty streets, breathing in the scent of freshly watered gardens and listening to the murmur of fountains soothed his black mood. He did not even have the urge to get drunk which often affected him when his cup of boredom and impatience was running over.

The thing that would have been best of all for his temper was a good fight but, although he had more than once, on his nocturnal walks, had the fanciful idea that someone was following him, he had never been able to prove it. It must, he decided, be no more than fancy since he could not imagine why anyone should be interested in his actions.

He had gone only a few steps from the porch of 'The Just' when he saw two women coming towards him, both heavily veiled in spite of the warmth of the evening. He stepped aside to let them pass but immediately one of them faded from sight into the shadow of a doorway while the other put a hand on his arm to stop him and requested him, in an unsteady voice, to go with her.

Gilles' new found distrust of all women, with the possible exception of Mademoiselle Marjon, caused him to mutter ungraciously: 'I'm sorry, Madame, but I am in a hurry. I have no time—'

'A man of your age, appearance and name has always time for a woman – for a woman generally thought to be pretty,' the stranger said, more confidently.

'That depends.'

'You are not very gallant, Monsieur de Tournemine. I fear I have been misinformed about you.'

'By whom? And how do you know my name?'

This time the woman in the midnight veil laughed a little.

'You are both inquisitive and ungracious. So you refuse to come with me? It is not far, only to the Rue de l'Orangerie. Say that I am afraid to walk the streets alone at night.'

'It seemed to me that there was another with you. What have you done with your companion?'

'My companion has reached her destination. I live farther on.'

Short of behaving in a thoroughly churlish fashion, there was no possibility of refusal. Moreover, Gilles' curiosity was aroused. Who could this woman be? She knew his name but there was nothing about her person or her voice which struck a chord in his memory. One thing was certain, she was not one of the women of ill fame who haunted the vicinity of the inns and barracks of Versailles. Her clothes were elegant, her carriage distinguished and her voice was that of a woman of quality. Her face, of course, was quite invisible beneath the heavy dark veil that covered her whole head.

Gilles bowed politely and offered his arm. The lady laid her fingers on it lightly and they began to walk together in the direction of the château. At first they proceeded in silence under a sky spangled with stars. From the woman's clothes came a pleasant scent of roses.

'Now that I have agreed to go with you, why do you not take off your veil? It must be uncomfortably hot.'

235

'It is not yet time. And I have never been troubled by the heat.'

She proceeded to reinforce this impression by moving closer to him, until she was all but hanging on his arm in a most inviting manner.

Gilles was seized with annoyance. 'What is the meaning of this?' he asked abruptly. 'What do you want of me?'

'To share the enjoyment of this lovely night, and to please you, if I can.'

'I am not worth your trouble. Besides, I am not easily pleased these days.'

'You are very young to be so jaded. Do you not care for women?'

'There is one woman I love, and she is worth more than all the rest. She is all I want or desire.'

'She is fortunate. But you must never turn your back on what is offered. I have not yet given up hope of pleasing you. Now, here we are.'

She stopped outside a modest house, not at all in keeping with the elegance of her dress and manners. Gilles stepped back.

'Then my mission is complete. You are at home and it only remains for me to bid you a good night, Madame.'

'This is not my home and you shall not leave me so soon. Have you no wish to see my face?'

'Should I know you?'

'Perhaps – if you give me your word of honour never to speak of this affair, supposing my face is known to you.'

'Is it, then, an affair?'

'It could be. I like you, and you may like me. Don't you believe in chance encounters? If so, you are the only man in the army!'

'I have not said so. But you do not seem to me to be one of those women who trade in such encounters.'

'Who mentioned trade? Let us call it a hobby, rather. Will you come?'

She rapped on the door, a series of quick taps, and it was opened almost immediately by a maidservant with a candle who preceded them in silence up the uncarpeted wooden stairs, which creaked at every step. The walls were decorated with the usual engravings of the King and Queen and could have done with a coat of paint.

The silent servant opened the door to a whitewashed room whose chief and almost its only article of furniture was a large bed with curtains of flowered chintz, and stood aside for them to enter. The bed was already turned down, showing clean sheets. On the bedside table stood a candlestick with three lighted candles and next to it a small tray bearing a bottle in a cooler and two glasses, as though they were expected.

The Chevalier's eyes surveyed the room coolly, taking in all these details, and then returned to his companion. She seemed to have brought something of the night into the room with her, for her gown and enveloping veils were the selfsame colour as the darkness outside, while the eyes that sparkled amid the delicate stuffs could have done duty for the stars. But Gilles made no attempt to see her face. Instead he walked over to the window and, lifting the curtain, gazed briefly out into the empty street below.

'Do you come often to this place?' he asked carelessly.

'If it flatters your vanity, no, not very often. Well, Chevalier, are you going to turn your back on me? Don't you want to see my face, or are you afraid?'

'By no means.'

He swung round then and saw that she had thrown back her veil. Gilles gazed at her for a moment without speaking. The woman who stood there was a stranger to him but there was no doubt of her quality. In some ways she even reminded him of Cayetana. She was young, twenty-five or -six perhaps, and had black eyes, a dazzling complexion and a strange beauty that could have left none but a blind man indifferent. But the Duchess of Alba did not possess that saucy, typically French little nose, those mocking lips or that wicked glint in her eyes. Or that thick, pale gold hair.

For the rest, the lady in the blue veil had a slender waist but a generous bosom, largely unconcealed by the low, square-necked dress she wore.

She was growing restive under the young man's silent scrutiny.

'Well? What do you think of your conquest? Does it live up to expectation?'

'You are extremely beautiful, Madame. Perhaps that is why I can hardly believe my luck. I do not deserve such a conquest.'

'You don't believe it?'

'Frankly, no.'

'Then try me. I brought you here for that – and I do not care to have my offers refused.'

'Very well. In that case —'

Deciding to take her at her word, he walked back to her and began, very coolly, to undress her with the cold competence of a lady's maid, an exercise in which the time he had spent in the disguise of a Spanish duenna stood him in good stead. The gown slipped to the floor, followed by a mass of dainty snow-white petticoats, the undergarments of a lady of exalted station, or of a very high-class courtesan: petticoats, lace-trimmed drawers and stays whose white satin prettily disguised their savagery. The woman suffered it unflinchingly. It was not until he reached her shift that he allowed his hands to wander over the soft flesh of shoulders and rigidly pointed breasts. Then, at his touch, the woman moaned softly, her eyes closed and her whole body trembled.

The shift dropped, revealing a nakedness so alluring that Gilles felt his own body responding to it, involving him in the equivocal game of this unknown beauty who had come to him from heaven, or from hell. He wanted her, suddenly, with a violent passion he saw no reason to deny. A hobby, had she said? What could be pleasanter, or more refreshing as a way of passing the time when one's mind was in a turmoil, one's nerves jangled and oneself oppressed by the enervating heat of summer, than making love? It might, in fact, prove almost as beneficial as a battle or a duel. He buried his face in the scented mass of her hair which she had shaken free in a single movement, and his lips explored the long line of her neck while at the same time his hands closed on her breasts. A slow shudder ran through her, then she twisted like an eel.

'Wait,' she gasped. 'Wait a moment!'

Slipping from his arms, she turned and, standing very close to him, began with trembling fingers to undress him in her turn.

'You see, I can do this very well also,' she said with a

mischievous laugh that did not ring quite true and was belied by the lack of laughter in her eyes.

She was every bit as nimble as the young man had been. When he had nothing on, she came into his arms as naturally as if they had known each other for months and then the cool white sheets received them but brought no cooling to the fire that consumed them from the moment their lips touched.

They made love in silence. It was not until the first storm had abated that Gilles asked: 'What is your name?'

'Anne. Call me Anne.'

'I like that. It's a name that belongs to my own country. But Anne what? Anne *de* something, surely, for I would guess that you are noble?'

She laughed. 'You can tell from the way I make love?'

'Far from it. You make love like a courtesan, and better! It's your body, your hands, your voice and the way you speak.'

'I shall take that as a compliment, I think. But for you, I am Anne *de* nothing! Just Anne, if you like. All you need to know at this moment is that you want me as much as I want you,' she whispered, her lips seeking his.

He felt desire rise in him again but when he tried to take her she pushed him away.

'No, not yet! Let's drink first. I'm dying of thirst and the wine should be beautifully cool.'

'What is it?'

'Vouvray. You like it?'

'I like everything good – and beautiful,' he said, making another grab for her, but she eluded him and wriggled off the bed, then walked round to the table and poured the golden wine. She filled the two glasses of red Venice crystal and, sitting on the bed beside him, handed one to Gilles.

'Drink it all. It's a wonderful wine for love.'

'I don't need that, but I am thirsty.' He drank it to the last drop and added: 'It is delicious, certainly. It has an extraordinary bouquet.'

'Some more?'

'Why not?'

She moved away from him while he finished drinking and went to stand before a circular glass that hung on the far wall, studying her face with a comical seriousness.

'What are you doing now? Come back here!'

'In a moment. There is something hurting at the corner of my lip. I must have scratched it.'

'Does it matter? It doesn't make you any less beautiful.'

He set down the empty glass and as he did so noticed that hers was still untouched.

'You haven't drunk your wine. I thought you were dying of thirst.'

She stretched like a cat in the yellow candlelight. Her elongated shadow reached up to the ceiling.

'Well, I found that after all I wasn't.'

'And what does that mean?'

'That I am a slave to my whims and may often change my mind from one moment to the next. That is something you will find out, for I like you even more than I thought I should and I hope to keep you for my lover for a long time.'

'Come back to me, then.'

'In a little while. There is no hurry.'

'As to that, we shall see.'

He made to get up also, to go to her, but no sooner had he put his foot to the ground than the walls of the room began to spin and he felt slightly sick. His sight was blurred. His arms beat the air, he tried to speak and failed, then fell, like a stone, at the feet of the fair Anne.

He had lost consciousness, stark naked, on the bare floor of a hired room. He came to stretched out comfortably, fully dressed, on the embroidered coverlet of a magnificent bed. Furthermore, it was broad daylight, a fact borne witness to by the bars of brightness filtering through the heavy painted and gilded wooden shutters that covered the tall windows.

The room in which he was lying was at once splendid and somewhat decayed. The pillared bed, dating from the days of Louis XIII, was hung with deep blue velvet trimmed with silver and contrasting pleasantly with the grey damask of the walls. But the damask showed the stains of damp and age. A handsome solid silver table bore a looking glass of the same metal, crystal candlesticks with hanging lustres and a huge array of pots, jars and bottles. A dainty dressing robe was thrown over an upright armchair whose worn velvet was split in places and that, combined with the dressing table and the luxuriant mass of fresh flowers filling a tall Chinese vase, declared that the room was used by a woman, although not very often, judging from the dust which overlay most of its contents.

His head aching, Gilles got up from the bed where he had been laid but was obliged to catch hold of one of the posts to keep himself from falling. The drug that had been used to put him to sleep must have been an extremely powerful one, for he had still not shaken off its effects.

He caught sight of an open door leading, apparently, into a small powder closet and made his way unsteadily towards it. The sight of a large water jug and basin and a heap of towels heartened him. He filled the basin and after swiftly stripping off the coat of snuff-coloured cloth he was wearing, plunged his whole head deliciously into the cold water, blessing his preference for wearing his own hair unpowdered and relying on a wig when in uniform.

Having splashed his head in the basin for a while, he dried it vigorously with a towel and then felt a blessed clarity return-ing to his brain. His shirt was soaking wet but the closed room was as hot as an oven and it would soon dry.

To put the finishing touch to his recovery, he drank off three glasses of water in quick succession and then, with a sigh of relief, set about examining his prison, for it was difficult to think of this room as anything else. He had guessed already that the door was locked but he checked to make sure and then tested the shutters which proved to be padlocked, like the windows. Then, having tried to get a glimpse of the outside world through the chink which was letting in the sunlight, he went back and climbed the steps up to the bed and sat down on the end of it.

Where was he? What house was this, wrapped in the silence of the tomb? Where was the sunny landscape he had glimpsed outside, without being able to make out more details than a gleam of water, sun-browned grass and the green of woods? And more than all, who was the ravishing woman who had given herself to him with such unfeigned ardour?

The sound of a key scraping in the lock made him look up. He watched, frowning, as the lady of the blue veil made an entrance no less spectacular than the sunrise by reason of the canary yellow muslin dress she wore and the huge matching hat extravagantly burdened with poppies of various shades, golden ears of corn and immense yellow satin ribbon bows which sat by some miracle of balance on her high-piled hair, its colour now, by the magic of the latest fashionable powder, transformed into an unbelievable dove grey.

'Oh, you are awake!' she exclaimed, switching on a dazzling smile. 'I thought you would be sleeping for a good two hours yet. But you are young and active.'

As she spoke she was setting down the heavy tray she carried, carefully, on a stool. She had borne it as easily as if it too had been laden with flowers and not with solidly fashioned and antique silverware. Then she flitted over to the young man and gazed at him in consternation.

'Good God! You are soaking wet! What have you been doing?'

'Washing. And now, suppose you explain?'

She bent to kiss him but he held her off gently.

'No, please. The time for that is past. Where are we? What am I doing here? Why have you played this grotesque trick on me, and, lastly, who are you?'

The innocent distress depicted on the lovely face was a work of art but Gilles had had his fill of playacting since the previous night.

'Come,' he said impatiently, 'I'm waiting.'

'So stern you are! Such a way to speak to me! Last night you spoke my name so sweetly.'

'Yes, your name. Suppose we begin with that. A lie, no doubt, like all the rest.'

'No, no! My name is really Anne.'

'That is no longer enough. And the rest?'

The big Boule clock on the mantelshelf struck two and she started.

'Oh heavens! So soon! Listen, I have no time to explain now. Only believe that it was not playacting – not really, and much less than you imagine. I do like you and I do not like to see the things I take a fancy to broken before I have a chance to enjoy them. And if I had not acted as I did, you would be dead at this moment!'

242

'Rubbish. Think of something else.'

'I swear by my father's memory that it is the truth! You are in danger, in very grave danger for you have given great offence to a very exalted person, and one whose power is great – who can do anything to you and who does not know the meaning of forgiveness.'

'Who is this person? You will have to tell me that, at least, if you want me to believe you. His name and the way in which I have offended him.'

She sighed but when she spoke it was with extreme deliberation. 'It is,' she said, 'someone who does not care to be attacked at night in gardens and robbed of his letters.'

'I don't understand a word of what you are talking about, Madame.'

'Indeed?'

'Indeed! Will you be good enough to explain who it is I am supposed to have attacked, where, when, and what I took from him?'

She gave a cross little laugh and lifted one shoulder pettishly.

'Such a waste of time! But very well. Since you insist on playing it this way, I will answer your four questions in as many words. Monsieur, the Trianon, the twenty-first of June, a letter. Will that do?'

'A most mysterious incantation!'

'The truth, rather! During the entertainment given for Count Haga, you attacked the Comte de Provence in the Trianon gardens and took from him a letter—'

'Is that all? It's a fine tale but, even supposing it were true, how did you come by it? I have not the honour of Monsieur's acquaintance.'

'I think he knows you very well. And if you will not believe me unless you know how he found out, I will tell you. Monsieur is greatly interested in the affair between the Queen and Count Fersen. Suppose the silly creature should be engaged in foisting a bastard on France? What then? A pretty scandal!'

'Very pretty,' Gilles said expressionlessly. 'And so?'

'So it follows from there. Monsieur's interest led him to set a watch on the Swede. You cannot think how easy it is, with a little money, or a threat, to enlist the aid of a servant, even in the best hotels, such as the York, for instance. Do you believe me now? Oh yes, I feel sure you do.'

Gilles said nothing. He was seeing himself in Fersen's room, just about to return his letter to the Queen. And he was seeing, too, the chambermaid and the waiter coming in with the breakfast trays. Which one had talked? Which one was in Monsieur's pay? The waiter, the girl, or both?

Anne let him think for a moment and then went on very softly: 'As for you, they were waiting for you, last night, outside your house, men with orders to see that you did not escape. I can swear to this on my mother's memory. And I did not wish that to happen.'

'Very kind of you,' the young man said. He sighed. 'But this is madness. Or else – I suppose the next thing is that you will tell me you love me? Is that it? You have never set eyes on me before, you don't know me from Adam, but you are consumed with an undying passion for me and made up your mind all at once to save me—'

'That is more or less the case,' she answered him calmly. Then her eyes clouded and she came to him and stood on tiptoe to reach his lips, but Gilles folded his arms and turned his back, closing his ears to her sigh.

'You fool! You are better known than you think, my fine bird of prey. We know all about your adventures in America and I am not the only woman in Paris who longs to lie with the man of whom the Queen speaks playfully as "My Lord Gerfalcon". I was hoping you would teach me how the Indian ladies make love. There has been talk of a redskin princess ...'

He hunched his shoulders angrily, furious to find that his romance with the Indian princess was now being whispered everywhere, causing an excited flutter among the sensation hungry ladies of fashion. But he refused to rise to the bait.

'I thought you were in haste?' he said, his eyes on the clock.

'You are right! My God, you are right! Listen, you must not leave this room on any account. Indeed, you cannot. I have to go now but I will return tonight and then I promise I will tell you more.'

'And do you mean to keep me long in this airless cage?'

She smiled, a teasing smile that lit up her dark eyes and made her moist lips gleam.

'As long as you are in danger – and as long as I want you. But don't worry. You will not stay long in this house. I have only brought you here as an emergency measure. In a few days I shall take you to another place, a place of my own, very quiet and retired. There we shall be able to compare our various talents and I do not despair of driving from your mind the memory of your beautiful savage, for you must know there is gipsy blood in my veins. It is not generally known, it is a family secret, but you shall find out tonight what it means. I have brought you some food. Eat and rest and build up your strength for tonight. You will need it!'

She vanished, leaving behind her a scent of roses and a somewhat baffled Gilles. The woman was mad, of course, stark raving mad! The kind of exquisitely perverted libertine bred by this century of so-called elegance and taste! But who was she? A powerful woman, certainly, to dare to thwart the Comte de Provence as she was doing. Only where there was power, there was danger also and Gilles had no desire, even for the sake of finding out more, to remain any longer in hers.

'If she wants to discover how the Indians make love,' he thought, 'I'll send Pongo to her.'

At the recollection of the Indian, he felt a pang of concern. What had the lunatic woman said? That there were men lying in wait for him outside his lodging, his lodging where Pongo was all alone? And that they were not to let him, Tournemine, escape? He knew Pongo's stoical courage. He would certainly have tried to defend his master's home, if only for the sake of poor Mademoiselle Marjon, who would be terrified, but what could he do alone against a gang of determined men who might have chosen to revenge the master's absence on the man?

Fear gripped him, and by its intensity Gilles could measure his affection for his servant. Without further delay he set about trying to find the means by which to regain his freedom. He had to know what had taken place in the rue de Noailles on the previous night.

He began by pressing his ear to the door to see if he could hear any sounds from the rest of the house. But once the rumble of wheels from the carriage bearing his fair gaoler away had faded to silence there was nothing more. All around him was a silence so dense as to be almost palpable. Yet, there must

245

be someone, or else who had prepared the food on the tray which, it occurred to him, he was stupidly allowing to grow cold? The aristocratic Anne had surely not turned cook for his sake?

In order to think a little and to recoup his strength, he carried the tray over to the bed and fell to his breakfast. His hostess had provided excellently: there was braised chicken, a ragoût of mushrooms, some brie and a dish of cakes, the whole washed down by a bottle of Chambertin, a very respectable meal.

When he had eaten, Gilles' first action was to bestow a close examination on the shutters that covered the long windows. They were solidly made of wood and the padlocks on the fastenings were also depressingly stout. It would have needed pincers to undo them.

Deciding it was hopeless in that direction, he next turned his attention to the door. That, too, was stout and possessed a handsome gilded bronze lock which seemed just as effective as the padlocks. But if it were possible to unscrew it from the door jamb, then there would be nothing to prevent him getting out. The difficulty lay in finding a suitable tool for going to work on the screws.

Methodically, Gilles set about searching the room. The breakfast tray yielded only a dainty silver knife, much too fragile for any such undertaking, and his sword had, of course, been taken from him. The poker, being a good old-fashioned wrought iron implement, might have served as a lever but it was not what was needed for unscrewing a lock. Gilles relieved his feelings at this point by kicking the door hard for a while, but although it creaked it did not give way and the only effect of his efforts was to set a dog barking somewhere below. This was soon followed by a man's voice shouting, which told Gilles that the building was not as empty as it seemed.

He was beginning to despair of ever finding the tool he wanted when his eye fell on the dressing table. There he discovered a tray containing a collection of the little implements women used for their nails, such as scissors, little sticks for pushing back the cuticles and, in particular, some tiny metal files with a blade slim enough to fit the head of a screw.

It was a long, agonizing job. Never having been obliged to

246

turn his hand to a joiner's trade, Gilles was totally ignorant of everything to do with locks.

'If I'd known,' he muttered to himself aloud, 'I'd have asked the King for lessons!'

He broke one of the files but that did not matter much since there were two more and even the broken pieces could still serve. One screw came out, then a second, and after that a third. Then at last the final screw lay in his hand. Carefully, he drew the lock towards him. But his cry of joy turned at once to one of fury for still the door refused to open. Something was holding it on the outside.

Raging, he fetched a candle and studied the crack. It showed a bar of metal across it, a bolt of some sort, presumably. The next thing was to find out how it worked.

Gilles picked up the last of his files, which was also the longest, poked it cautiously through the crack just underneath the bar and lifted. It was not easy because he had very little purchase, but the bar shifted slightly. It must be one of those hinged fastenings which you had to lift to free the catch. Once, twice ... still the bar, thin as it was, resisted. The sweat pouring down his face and his forehead pressed hard against the door, Gilles swore in a steady stream. It provided some relief to his feelings and gave him the strength to try again.

At last there was a tiny click and the door swung gently open, easily, without the smallest sound, as though of its own accord. The way to freedom lay open.

Joyfully, Gilles went and washed his hands and bathed his perspiring face and then, after draining the last glass from his bottle of Chambertin, he prepared to leave his prison.

The first thing he noticed was that his room lay at the end of a long gallery which was quite empty except for a number of upholstered benches placed in the big window bays which overlooked a wide wooded landscape which surrounded a formal garden ornamented with statues. The second was that it was getting dark. The sun had set and although there was still a tinge of rose in the sky, the countryside was taking on the blue tones of evening.

On tiptoe in his short cuffed boots, Gilles made his way along the gallery, which seemed to be on the second floor of the house. At the far end, he met with another check, a second door, even more substantial than the one to his room, barred his way. This time he did not waste time trying to open it. Darkness was falling and time was running out, for Anne might return at any moment. That left the windows as the only way.

The first one opened easily enough but when he leaned out Gilles saw that he was not much better off. Not only was he on the second floor of a large, lofty house but there was also a basement level sunk into a moat which looked no less discouraging for being dry. Yet he had to get down there somehow.

Studying the position carefully, it occurred to him that for a fit and agile young man, which he was, there might just be a way. The window immediately below his possessed a balcony. If he could manage to drop onto that, he would be at least one stage nearer the ground.

Going back to the room he had just left, he swung with all his weight on the long velvet curtains at the windows and succeeded in pulling down two of them. Hauling them after him to the gallery window, he took the first one and lowered it very carefully down onto the balcony. The second, he tore a short way down the middle and tied the two ends round the centre post of the window frame. Then, praying that it would not disintegrate with age, he straddled the window sill and took a firm grip on the dusty fabric. It held firm as he descended, hand over hand, down the improvised rope to land neatly on the balcony below. A similar operation brought him to the level of the ground floor, only this time his feet found no resting place, for he was still a long way from the bottom of the moat, which was entirely flagged with stone. If he fell awkwardly, he stood a good chance of breaking a limb.

However, he had no choice. Trusting in his woodsman's skills which had given him long practice in the art of dropping safely from a height, he lowered himself to the very foot of his curtain, so as to make the most of his height, let go and landed unharmed on his feet. But now that he was at the bottom of the moat, he had not come to the end of his troubles. His next task was to climb up the other side, which was like climbing a wall topped by an overhang. And this time he had only the strength of his own wrists to help him.

By good luck, the twilight was lingering and promised a clear night and the Falcon's eyes were well used to piercing shadows. Searching for the best possible handholds, he followed the ditch along until he came to a place where a pair of stout piles, supporting a bridge, might offer some additional grip. The wall was built of large blocks and the interstices should offer a sufficient purchase for a man used to rock-climbing.

Making the best use of every available crack, Gilles reached the top of the wall without undue difficulty and an acrobatic twist got him past the overhang. He found himself, sweating a good deal, standing on the edge of the moat looking over a magnificent view of large stretches of water set in wide expanses of velvety turf with, in the background, the tall trees of a large forest.

The château itself, he saw when he turned round to look, was an imposing affair of brick and white stone, dating from the time of Henri IV. Its various wings, pierced by pedimented lights, were surmounted by steeply pitched roofs of thin slates which gleamed softly in the faint starlight. No lights appeared at any of the windows and Gilles wondered where the dog and the man whose voice he had heard could have gone to. Perhaps they were somewhere in the extensive outbuildings which lay to the right of the main house, concealed behind a screen of trees.

Directly in front of him, he could make out a pair of pavilions, dimly lit by lantern light, connected by some iron-work which looked, in the near darkness, more or less unclimbable. This was continued on either side by a high wall.

There must be a village somewhere, Gilles told himself, but where? In which direction? And what village? Where was he in relation to Paris or Versailles?

He had no idea how far he had been brought while under the influence of the drug, or in what direction. The sky, which he had learned to read from the fishermen as a child, was no help to him now.

He decided at random to follow the line of the trees that marched alongside the canals, interspersed with white statuary. They formed a sort of broad avenue vanishing into the distance and in order to make better speed Gilles started running from one statue to the next. The stone ladies would be a great help if he should accidentally meet someone. His feet made no sound on the deep turf and gradually he slowed his pace, lulled by the silent beauty of the shadowy gardens with the peace of the evening lying over them. The moon had risen above the woods and its unreal light bathed the still waters of the canals and turned their white margins to strips of silver.

Suddenly Gilles' ear caught a faint splash and his eyes made out a ripple in the mirrorlike surface nearest to him. Someone was swimming slowly, with long lazy strokes, someone who was taking advantage of the night to seek in the water a little coolness after the stifling heat of the day.

His thoughts on the gardener, the man with the dog perhaps, Gilles withdrew into the shelter of a stone plinth on top of which a large goddess was making unconvincing attempts to conceal her exuberant charms beneath a scrap of drapery. Something caught his foot and he nearly fell then, looking down, he saw that he had walked into a pile of clothes which, by their volume, could only belong to a woman. Unthinkingly, he picked up a white muslin gown from which came a sweet, fresh scent, reminiscent of lilacs in the spring and lily of the valley and wild herbs, which caught at his nostrils with a sudden breath of nostalgia.

He was lost in the depths of bitter-sweet memory. The woman bathing there, in the calm waters of the pool, could not guess that she had reopened an old wound, never completely healed, the scar left in the flesh and the heart of Gilles Goëlo by the red-haired siren of a Breton estuary whose slim, bewitching body he had once briefly clasped in his arms.

Fascinated, Gilles could not take his eyes from the vague figure cleaving the water. Never had he felt so strongly the tearing hunger of separation, the sense of frustration, like the amputation of a limb, which left the body tormented, gasping for air or for the memory of a departed joy.

Then, with a light splash, the bather suddenly tired of swimming and, making for the side of the pool, pulled herself out onto the rim and got to her feet, her back to the eager watcher, oblivious of his presence as his eyes devoured her, gracefully wringing the water from her long hair and

250

tossing it over her shoulder, where it reached almost to her hips.

Her figure was beautifully long and slender. In the cold light of the moon, delicately moulding the curve of her shoulder, she looked like a goddess in silver. The slim, flexible column of her neck supported a little head which Gilles glimpsed only in profile and was unable to understand why his heart had suddenly begun to beat so fast.

She stood for a moment, letting the moonbeams wash over her body, as she might have done in the sun. Then she turned slowly, almost regretfully, and began to move towards him with a light, dancing step and Gilles saw her face. All the stars in the sky seemed to explode simultaneously in his chest as he realized that the miracle had happened, that time had stood still and that it was all going to begin again.

Slowly, as though afraid that with every step he took the dream might vanish, he moved out from the shelter of his plinth, out from the tall shadows of the trees and into the light. Unconsciously, he was holding out his hands.

'Judith,' he murmured, so softly that it seemed that he alone could hear it. 'My siren ... my sea goddess ... Judith, my dream and my despair ...'

For a second he was afraid the vision was about to vanish. At the sight of him, she had paused for an instant, her arms held across her body in the instinctive gesture of all women everywhere, but it was only for an instant. Then her arms dropped and her face lit up with an almost unearthly joy, and as naturally as a lost child runs to its mother Judith sped towards Gilles, her feet hardly more than skimming the grass.

She reached him and her hands touched his shoulders, the arms he did not yet dare to fold around her and his head, as if she could not believe that it was true. Her little hands were cold and trembling.

'You! It is truly you,' she breathed. 'I called you and called you and you did not come. I thought I should never see you again.'

He tried to speak but no sound came from his throat. The warmth of her body, so close that her light breasts brushed his chest, set him aflame but his muscles suddenly refused to obey

251

him and his brain, with the impact of overwhelming joy, was struggling to express itself coherently. Then, with a tiny sigh of annoyance, she reached up on tiptoe and threw her arms tightly round Gilles' neck.

'Kiss me,' she commanded. Then her cool lips touched his and clung in a kiss whose fervour broke through his strange paralysis.

Restraint fled to the winds and his passion unleashed at last, he clasped her to him fiercely, lifting her bodily from the ground the better to hold her and for the joy of feeling her weight and knowing that she was indeed real.

They rolled together on the grass, as though now that they had come together nothing could part them, as though they would never be divided again. They whispered tender, absurd, crazy things to one another, and always returning to the one small phrase common to all parted lovers through the ages, the words that came to Adam in the magic moment when one flesh became two: 'I love you.'

Time, place, everything except the joy they shared was forgotten until, as they kissed, and the heady perfume of her body went to his head, Gilles would have made her wholly his. Judith's body went rigid and she pulled away so violently that it was like the sudden waking from a dream.

'No!'

She wriggled out of the arms that would have restrained her and, running to her clothes, began, hastily and clumsily, to put them on, while Gilles, hurt, frustrated and uncomprehending, watched her, the climax of his burning symphony disintegrating in a crashing discord. All he could manage to say was: 'Why?'

She stared at him through the shining fall of her hair, still frantically throwing up fragile ramparts of muslin and ribbon around her beauty.

'Because—'

And then, as though she sensed that the time-honoured word of feminine excuse was not enough, she added half-unwillingly: 'Because I can't. I must not.'

'Must not? But this is insane! Unless, oh God, you are not—?'

He could not finish, but at the grief and terror in his voice

252

Judith sprang forward with a cry and hurled herself into his arms.

'No! No! Not married, not betrothed, nor promised to anyone at all, not even to God! Only, I must remain a virgin – at least for the present. I have promised. I love you, but I must not!'

'But this is absurd! I love you. I want to be with you always. I will marry you tomorrow – today! I can, you know. Tomorrow I'll ask leave of the King, of Marshal de Castries, my commanding officer, and you shall be my wife.'

He watched with pride and happiness as her eyes rounded with awe.

'The King? Marshal de Castries? But what has happened to you?'

'I am an officer of the Scots Guard, my lady. I know I have a name to offer you, a name to match your own, which I received from my father, Pierre de Tournemine, as he lay dying on the battlefield at Yorktown. You gave me three years, do you remember, to deserve you? It took me only half that time, but when I went back to find you, you were gone.'

She hugged him tighter and burrowed her damp head into his shoulder.

'Tell me,' she whispered. 'I have had no word of you since I left my convent at Hennebont.'

Reassured by this tenderness and trust, he did his best to describe for her all that had happened to him since the evening he had left her at the door of the convent of Our Lady of Joy, beside the Blavet, where she meant to spend the three years' wait she had imposed on them both, while he went to seek fame and fortune across the seas.

Gilles could still not really understand how Judith could be here, in his arms, pressed against his heart, while he was expecting to search every convent in Brittany and Guyenne to find her, but his Breton soul, brought up on legends, had always been receptive to the magical and miraculous and his faith in the ability of God to achieve all things, even the impossible, was unshakeable. But most of all, he did not want to spoil the fragile beauty of this long-awaited moment with questions. The explanations could come later.

· · ·

Gilles' own account of his adventures was not without its difficulties. There were times when he came to things he preferred to skip. He could not, for example, tell her about Sitapanoki, or the various other ladies who had helped a vigorous youth to endure the pains of separation.

Finally, as he came to touch on the dramatic events at Trécesson, he paused. Did his beloved know that he had killed her elder brother and that the younger had barely escaped his vengeance? How was he to tell her, without reawakening hideous memories of that forest grave, what he had learned on that fearful night in the inn at Ploërmel? But then, half-unconsciously, she made it easy for him by asking shyly:

'Did Monsieur de Talhouet get my letter to you?'

'Yes, and I have carried it with me always, along with my memory of you,' he assured her, his lips brushing the beautiful coppery red silk of her hair.

'So you didn't try to find me because you thought I had been given to another?'

'I never stopped looking for you and I found your trail at last, like that of a frightened doe, beside a pool in the forest of Paimpont. Unhappily, I lost it again almost at once. But I found the tracks of your brothers. Tudal died by my hand.'

She shivered so violently that he held her closer, thinking she was about to become hysterical. Then he saw her dark eyes shining in the moonlight.

'You – you killed Tudal?' she whispered incredulously.

'I hanged him from the king beam of his own house, and that was better than he deserved. He merited the wheel!'

'And Morvan?'

He made a little helpless gesture. 'Gone! He was not at Le Frêne when I found Tudal there and I heard later that he had fled. If not, he would have suffered the same fate. But I do not despair. I know that I shall find him one day.'

She was trembling like an autumn leaf and her frightened voice was no louder than a breath as she asked: 'To have taken such a revenge, did you learn what had happened – did you find out everything?'

'Everything. Don't talk about it any more.'

He could feel the ghastly memories flooding back and to

254

stop them he bent his head and sealed her quivering lips with a kiss of infinite tenderness.

'There is nothing more you need to tell me,' he said, 'except what you have been doing since then.'

It troubled him a little that he felt her stiffen then, and drew away a little. It was as if she were closing up suddenly.

'There's not much to tell,' she said, with a little mirthless laugh. 'Nothing very heroic happened to me. I knew that my mother had a distant cousin in Paris, of whose existence my brothers were unaware, I think. I went to her and I told her everything. She took me in and hid me for a while, until I could find a post where I should be safe.'

'It was she who found you the position as reader to the Countess of Provence?'

'Y-yes, only—'

'And so of course it was she who introduced you to the wonderful Italian physician, Count Cagliostro?'

Judith wrenched herself suddenly out of his arms and stood before him like the old Judith of long ago, suspicious, hot-tempered and belligerent.

'How do you know that?'

'It doesn't matter how I know. Is it true?'

'Yes, it's true. She found me the safety of a royal household and the kindness of Madame who likes me and is good to me.'

'Under a false name!'

'Of course under a false name! How could I risk calling myself Judith de Saint-Mélaine, when my brothers might find me and take me back? Thanks to Aunt Félicité, I stopped being afraid.'

'And thanks to Cagliostro, what?'

'An end to my terrors, the chance to live a normal life again! He cured me. Do you know what the nights were like for me in those weeks after – after Trécesson? I couldn't sleep, I daren't let myself go to sleep for fear of the nightmare, always the same hideous nightmare! I couldn't bear to be in the dark. I was ill, delirious, half mad. Then when Aunt Félicité was at her wits' end, she sent for the count. He had cured her once, of a decline, and she had remained in correspondence with him because she revered him as a good man and a friend. He came, a very long way, and he gave me back at last peace, health and something

255

very close to happiness. He is a wonderful man – far more than a mere man, indeed!'

'Yes, well. What a testimonial! Let's call him a god and say no more about it.'

'But I want to say more,' Judith cried, with sudden anger. 'Why should I be cold and ungrateful to a man who has restored my reason?'

Slowly, a bitter jealousy was taking possession of Gilles' heart and mind. He had so looked forward to finding his beloved again and to being for her a refuge, bulwark and protector, a confidant, friend and lover all in one, and now he found that another man had forestalled him and was already nearly all of those things to her, and that other man also possessed the power of healing. Since she refused to take him as a lover, that did not leave him much else.

And so he in turn could not repress the cold, angry words which came to him because it is the nature of humankind to return blow for blow and injury for injury.

'Physicians seem to loom large in your life. The unfortunate you married, whom your brothers killed on your wedding day, was also a physician, I believe?'

He knew that he had hurt her by the sudden tightening of her features and was sorry at once but he could not take back the words.

'Poor Job Kernoa,' she said softly. 'He was kind and gentle. He found me half dead and cared for me and asked nothing in return. I think he loved me.'

'And you, did you love him?'

'I was fond of him. He was so kind, so thoughtful . . . it was not easy to make him declare his love.'

'It seems to me that it was not a case of his marrying you but of you marrying him. Why did you have to marry him? Hadn't you promised me to wait three years?'

'Wait? Who for? I thought you would never come back and I was afraid, do you understand? Afraid of my brothers! Do you know what fear is?'

'Yes, I know what it is. Oh, Judith, Judith! Here we are quarrelling stupidly when I ought to be telling you how much I love you! Why are we standing here, when I ought to be taking you away? Do you know, I thought you were shut up in a convent? I learned that you had written to Madame asking to leave her service to become a nun!'

'You know that, too? You are the devil! Who could have told you?'

'I am not at liberty to tell you, only that I know. Why did you write that?'

'Because I was advised to. The Count thought I should go as far away as possible from Madame – and Monsieur. He said I was not safe there any more. A convent was the simplest explanation, and would cause the least comment.'

'And I could have been setting fire to every religious house in France and Navarre to find you! When you were here all the time! In any case, where are we? What house is this?'

For a moment surprise drove the anger from her face as suddenly as the wind drops at the onset of rain.

'You don't know? Then how did you come here?'

'I was given some kind of drug. I was unconscious.'

'Who brought you?'

'A woman. I don't know who she is. All I know is that her name is Anne.'

'Really? And what is she like, this Anne?'

The sudden hardening of her voice struck Gilles as strange but he gave her a brief, accurate description of his gaoler, glossing over the lady's more obvious charms.

'I see.'

The chill in her tone was not reassuring. Then, without warning, she exploded, not loudly, but her voice cut like a lash.

'What kind of liar have you become, Gilles Goëlo? You claim to be a member of the King's Household, you frequent the Court and yet you dare to tell me that you do know the Comtesse de Balbi, Monsieur's all-powerful mistress? And that you do not know the houses of the princes of the blood? Perhaps you do not know Versailles, either?'

'Well, this is not Versailles, is it?'

'No. It is Grosbois! Only I, although I may not know much about the Court and hardly ever set foot in Versailles, it just so happens that I do know Anne de Balbi very well indeed, and I know she deceives the Prince with any man who takes her fancy and if she goes to the trouble of drugging some fool and bringing him to an empty house it's not for the pleasure of

257

teaching him to knit! What have you been doing here together?'

'Nothing! Nothing at all,' Gilles said, somewhat taken aback by the youthful fury with flashing eyes who seemed about to fly at him with all her claws.

'You're lying! Can you swear you've never slept with her? Dare you swear it? On your father's memory?'

'No, I will not swear. But, God Almighty!' Gilles cried, his own temper running loose, 'I'm a man and there are things a man needs which a child like you can't possibly know! I'd never have touched another woman if you—'

'How dare you speak to me like that! Keep that for your mistresses!' she raged at him, like the child he had called her.

'I have no mistress! She was no more to me than a chance encounter, that is all. For God's sake, if I'd been in love with her, do you think she'd have had to drug me to make me go with her? Judith, you must believe me. I love, have loved and will love no one but you.'

But she was not listening to him. She was standing a little way off, biting her nails and seeming to search her memory for some recollection.

'Judith,' he said reproachfully, 'you are not even listening to what I say.'

'Tournemine ... Tournemine ...' she murmured, looking up at the sky. 'That reminds me of something. Where have I heard of a Tournemine?'

'Why – but at home, in Brittany! It's one of the oldest names there, and the most—'

She brought her eyes back to him and the look in them was as soft as granite.

'I know all about the noble families of Brittany. I studied them long before you did. I know the Tournemines, their arms, titles, lands, blazons and even their legends. I know—'
She stopped suddenly, as though enlightenment had struck all at once. When she continued, it was with a gentleness both unexpected and alarming.

'Tell me, weren't you the man who was with La Fayette, the one the Indians gave the name of a bird? Yes, that's it! The Tournemine who revived the name of the famous gerfalcon, surely that was you?'

258

'Well, of course it was me, but—'

'Oh! How dare you so much as speak to me! You would have ravished me, I swear, if I'd not fought you off! You filthy rake! Libertine! Go back to your female savages, to your harlots and your high-flyers! You are dead to me!'

With that she turned on her heel and gathering up her froth of virginal petticoats ran off among the trees to where the walls of some low building showed dimly through the night.

Feeling both angry and troubled, for he remembered what Madame de Balbi, since that was her name, had told him of the tales concerning his romance with the fair Indian which were going the rounds of the salons, Gilles set off in pursuit. He caught her easily and grasping her firmly by both arms succeeded in holding her still despite her efforts to break free.

'Are you going to stop talking nonsense? I don't know what kind of gossip you've been listening to in your confounded salons, but I have a good idea. People in this country seem to have nothing better to do than go about casting slurs on one another's behaviour, and the less they know about the truth the better! You want the truth? Well, will you listen to it?'

'I challenge you to tell me!'

'Very well. Since that is what you want. It's quite true, I did have a mistress, the wife of a great chief of the Iroquois. She was very, very beautiful and I thought for a time that I might be in love with her, because I loved her body.'

'Be quiet! I forbid you to say another word!'

'Too late. I thought you were brave? You wanted the truth and believe me you're going to hear it, all of it. This woman was my mistress and she was not the only one because I am a man made of flesh and blood and because a man's body needs a woman to keep it sane. I have made love to other women, women of humble birth and from among the highest in the land. They were all of them delightful and some were more than beautiful. But in my heart I never managed to forget you. Do you understand? I left all these women to look for you, to find you and to make you mine because, from amongst all the millions of women in this world, there is, after all, only one for me, the loveliest, most adorable, the only one who has the power to make me suffer and to drag me through hell. You are

259

that woman, you . . . my love, my terrible, wonderful love, my beloved . . . Now stop fighting me, fighting us! Haven't we been unhappy enough?'

Little by little his arms had closed, imprisoning her. He could feel Judith's heart beating wildly against his as she yielded to him, her body limp and her strength gone. He bent his head and as, with passion, he sought her mouth, he knew that her cheeks were wet with tears.

The kiss endured for a long time and was filled, for him, with an immense tenderness, with his need to hold her always like this, fragile and vulnerable, within the shelter of his strong arms and his love. In another moment he would lift her off her feet and carry her far away from this empty château, this refuge which the disturbing Cagliostro had found for her, deep in its park, and where he was keeping her in fear of God knew what obscure menace, carry her away to his own small lodging in the rue de Noailles where Mademoiselle Marjon would know how to take care of her. And after that they would go away together, as far as possible to a place where they could build their happiness on a firm foundation, as they could not do on the shifting sands of a royal Court.

Seeing again his old dream of a white house on the prairie in Virginia, he loosened his hold a little so as to lift her slender, girlish form in his arms but as he did so she thrust him off with a blow so fierce that he fell back before it. It knocked him off his balance and he found himself sitting on the grass and Judith running once more towards the building whose lighted window gleamed at the far end of a ride.

Gilles sprang up cursing and raced after her but she could run as swiftly as a hunted deer and he had ricked his ankle as he fell. He reached the house just in time to have the door slammed in his face.

He was about to fling himself on it, battering at it in his rage, when he heard a woman's voice, speaking softly and affectionately. 'I was just coming to look for you, child. I was worried. You ought not to linger in the park so late when there is no one at the château. But you have been crying?'

'It's nothing. I fell and hurt myself. Don't be anxious, my dear. I won't go in the park again – ever. I think I caught sight of a prowler. You should tell Pierre to go the rounds.'

'A good idea. I'll do it straight away.'

It would be dangerous to stay longer. Not far from the little house, Gilles saw the boundary wall in the moonlight and sprinted towards it without further delay, promising himself to return on the morrow. There was a good chance of finding a road running outside the wall.

Once he had reached the top, he saw that the road was quite a broad one and there were lights gleaming some distance along it. The village, probably. He had sprung down and was beginning to walk towards them when the sound of a coach coming swiftly urged him to remain out of sight. He crouched down among the long grass in the ditch.

The next moment, an elegant travelling chaise passed close by him, making briskly for the main gates to the château, the lanterns of which were just within sight. This was surely Madame de Balbi returning according to her promise and the thought of her disappointment, her anger even, when she found that he had flown, made him smile a little. But that was one more reason not to linger.

In a few minutes he had reached the lights he had seen shining and found that they belonged to the posting inn in the village of Boissy St Léger. The hire of a horse was easily accomplished and then, following the directions given him by one of the postilions, he was up in the saddle and riding hell for leather for Versailles.

By the time he reached it, the early summer daylight was beginning to touch the gold on the vanes and railings of the palace. In a little, the sun would be up and spreading its light over the sleeping gardens where gardeners were already at work raking down alleys and clearing the canals between the fountains.

The streets were quiet and empty and in spite of all the emotions of the previous hours Gilles felt amazingly alert. The ride in the cool breeze of the early morning had whipped up his blood and lessened the impact of Judith's slap. He could smile at it now, seeing it as no more than a last desperate defence, the reaction of a young girl to her own weakness. She had been punishing him because she had not been able to prevent herself responding, with all her being, to that last kiss of his. What was more, tonight he would go back to Grosbois again, with Winkleried and their servants. The four of them should surely be able to seize her and carry her off to Versailles.

By tomorrow, he told himself hopefully, I shall be able to go to the Queen and ask her to give Judith her protection, and then in a week we shall be married!

These agreeable reflections lasted him for the rest of the way but when he came to the Rue de Noailles it was to find his arrival the cause of something like a miniature revolution. His landlady, Mademoiselle Marjon, who, her head surmounted by a voluminous cap, was just on the point of shutting the front door behind her on her way to early mass, saw him dismount and promptly casting keys and prayer book from her screamed aloud: 'My God! Here he comes!'

Her cry brought Pongo scrambling down from the tree where he had been sitting, musket in hand, and Niklaus, Winkleried's valet, surging out of the bushes armed with a pair of pistols. Practically simultaneously, one of Gilles' bed-room windows was thrust open and Winkleried's hairy head appeared. He, too, had a sword in one hand and a pistol in the other.

'Well, well!' he called down. 'Here's a relief! I was beginning to give you up for dead. Where have you been?'

'In heaven and hell, both at once! But heaven had the best of it, I promise you!'

Minutes later, they were all gathered in Gilles' sitting-room round a large pot of coffee, fragrant as only Niklaus could make it, and Mademoiselle Marjon, her devotions and her principles both for once forgotten, was telling Gilles all that had happened two nights before. There was not, in the event, a great deal to tell. At dead of night, a number of masked men had invaded the garden and locked her in her house, threaten-ing to burn it down around her if she stirred.

'Did you have any idea who they might be?'

'No. All I noticed was that their leader had black eyes that gleamed through the slits in his mask and that his bearing in general was that of a gentleman. He was tall with a rather metallic voice – oh, and a slight accent that could have been from the south. But I had no time to see more.'

'I am sorry. You must have been horribly frightened.'

But she only laughed at that and there was a belligerent light in the eyes that twinkled under her lace cap.

'You need not be. I wasn't frightened for a moment. I don't dislike the smell of powder, you know – or of tobacco either, if the truth be told,' she added, holding out her cup to Niklaus to be refilled. 'I let them shut me up in my own part of the house without a word, but then I ran up the inside staircase to warn Monsieur Pongo. I must say, his reaction to the news was interesting.'

'Good God, what did he do?'

'Took all his clothes off. In no time at all, I found myself looking at a real Indian chief – except for the feathers, of course.'

'Clothes not good for crawling through bushes with no noise,' the culprit explained. 'Pongo go out by kitchen window, very easy, creep into bushes and get out of garden. No one hear or see.'

'He ought never to dress like other people,' Ulrich Auguste said with a laugh. 'His birthday suit suits him far better! When I saw him coming, I was only sorry he had left off the paint and feathers. And that my landlady doesn't live on the premises. It would have killed her.'

'Of course, he went straight across to warn you?'

'*Natürlich!* I had just come in. I got my sword and Niklaus a kitchen knife and a pistol.'

'And after that,' Mademoiselle Marjon said, by no means willing to abandon the star role, 'the baron and his man went next door to Lolandre, the innkeeper, where some of the gentlemen from the Swiss Guard were supping.'

'With Pongo still naked? You must have been popular.'

'I had lent him a pair of breeches,' Winkleried said virtuously.

'They all came back here in a body,' the landlady finished up, 'and cleared the garden in a moment. The bullies all ran away in confusion, taking their shame and one or two of their wounded who couldn't walk.'

Ulrich Auguste then thanked his friends and the old lady entertained them all to a glass or two of quince ratafia and anisette. When they had gone and Tournemine had still not come home, Winkleried and Mademoiselle Marjon, with

Pongo and Niklaus, had held a council of war, the outcome of which was a decision to mount guard between them until he reappeared. But the night had gone by and still brought no sign of Gilles.

At first his friends had not been unduly anxious. The fact that they had succeeded in springing the trap was reassuring. But when the whole day passed with no news, anxiety returned with the onset of darkness. From Winkleried's hasty inquiries, it emerged that Tournemine had vanished into thin air after he left 'The Just'. With the exception of Mademoiselle Marjon, who went to bed, the friends determined to keep up their vigil. But this time nothing happened to disturb the tranquillity of the neighbourhood.

Touched by these proofs of friendship, even from an elderly spinster he had known for only a few weeks, Gilles did his best to reassure them, explaining in a few words that the whole thing was merely the outcome of an affair of the heart and the men lying in wait for him had been paid, and most probably led, by a jealous husband. In this, however, he was not entirely successful.

'My goodness,' Mademoiselle Marjon said scathingly. 'Twenty men for one pair of horns? Your jealous husband must surely be a duke at the least! I make you my compliments.'

She then took herself off downstairs, declaring that to be on the safe side she was going out to buy the biggest dog she could lay hands on.

Left alone with Winkleried, Gilles shut the doors carefully and told the truth of his adventures in every detail.

'The fact seems to be that the night before last, the Comte de Provence tried, if not to murder me, at least to have me kidnapped,' he concluded.

'My money is on murder. What would you expect him to do with you? You're going to have to take care because when he sees he's failed, he's going to turn nasty.'

'I hope he won't have time,' Gilles said smiling. 'If all goes as I hope, in a few days I'll be married and asking for leave to take my wife to Brittany.'

Their conference was interrupted at that moment by the entrance of a young soldier bringing a letter which had arrived at the Guards headquarters for the Chevalier de Tournemine.

The letter, judging from its brief wording and the ornate capital C which did duty as a signature, was from Cagliostro.

'You did very wrong not to follow my advice, Chevalier. It is useless to return to the place you know of for by the time you read this letter the person you are concerned with will have left. I am taking her to a place of safety. Rest still and let time and men do their work in peace.'

Watched interestedly by Ulrich Auguste, Gilles screwed up the letter in his fist and cast it into a corner of the room. Then, filled with rage and desolation at the knowledge that his beloved had eluded him once again, he sank into a chair, his elbows on his knees and his head resting on his hands.

'Gone! She is gone! That cursed Italian has taken her from me again! That devil with whom she is so infatuated! But I shall find them yet and then that charlatan will have me to reckon with!'

Winkleried, meanwhile, had moved coolly to pick up the ball of paper, smoothed it out on a corner of the table and was quietly acquainting himself with its contents.

'I'd like to meet this Cagliostro,' he said breathily. 'If only to find out whether a magician is immune to shot and steel.'

'Your bullets would be turned back on you and your sword would break. That man is the devil! But devil or not, one of these days I'll have to kill him,' Gilles swore fiercely.

11

Queen's Play

On Wednesday the eleventh of August, the King commanded an evening's gaming.

By seven o'clock, the series of six rooms which made up the Grand Appartement were a blaze of light, even though it was not yet dark outside, the coloured marbles, gilded bronze, porphyry, gold brocade and tapestries shimmering in the glare of hundreds of scented candles burning in the great solid silver candelabra and the rock crystal chandeliers. The plethora of lights made the heat worse than ever and the windows were wide open to the straight paths and flat turf of the north parterre. Gradually, the Court was filling up the fabulous setting prepared for it two centuries earlier and now bathed in the glory of a sunset glow.

For once, too, the whole Court was assembling, including the Queen and her exclusive coterie from the Trianon, who had taken particular care to be present since this evening's gaming was the outcome of an uncharacteristic burst of ill humour on the part of the usually good-tempered King Louis. But that afternoon the King had been the victim of a practical joke in questionable taste, a pastime to which his wife's irresponsible friends were somewhat too addicted. He had retired after dinner for a gentle nap on a seat in the Trianon and had found, on awaking, the hunting manual he had been reading replaced by a volume of Aretine decorated with engravings so obscene that, given the King's horror of debauchery, they had produced an outburst of royal rage. He had been overheard saying roundly to the Queen that since her guests were incapable of a

266

proper respect for the King, she would have to excuse him if he returned to his own house. 'Your brother, the Emperor Joseph was right,' he went on, 'when he said that you know no better than to surround yourself with oafs and libertines. The only amiable and respectable person here is your farm-manager, Valy. I will thank you to see that my book is returned. It is clean and I am fond of it.'

Whereupon, casting the offending volume into a corner, Louis had marched off back to Versailles refusing to listen to another word.

The effects of this were likely to be felt in the evening's atmosphere. The royal family and the high officers of the Household gathered round the tables which had been set up in the handsome Salon de Mercure, now unhappily bereft of the fabulous solid silver furnishings formerly ordered for it by Louis XIV, and in the hushed voices proper to a church prepared to devote themselves to the sober joys of a game of lotto.

Lotto was the one game the King really enjoyed. He hated faro, of which the Queen was so fond that she would spend whole nights at it, resulting in such perilous inroads into her finances that the King had banned the disreputable game. So Marie-Antoinette, who in her turn found lotto heartily boring, was putting a good face on it. Not that this was difficult for her for she was a natural hostess and possessed the art of smiling graciously on everyone, while at the same time casting the occasional anxious glance at her husband's stormy face.

'Look out for squalls,' Winkleried whispered from his post beside the doors leading to the Grand Appartement as Gilles passed by.

But the Chevalier, standing at the King's command behind the royal chair, paid very little attention, being content to enjoy the sunshine of this unlooked-for favour, expressed publicly before the whole Court.

From this privileged position, he watched the arrival of the uncomfortable threesome who were having such an effect on his life. It was the first time he had seen them together: Monsieur, fatter than ever in a fabulous dress which seemed intended to rival the sun; Madame, ugly and moustached, her only beauty in her regal bearing and immense dark eyes, unfortunately somewhat devoid of expression; and finally, glittering

267

in a carapace of sapphires and yards of pale blue satin, the exquisite Comtesse de Balbi, in whom Gilles had no trouble recognizing his mistress of a night and gaoler of a day.

The prince and the countess seemed to be in high good humour. Their laughter and joking was in pleasant contrast to the general atmosphere of constraint and brought about a slight degree of relaxation. It also drew comment from the King.

'You seem very cheerful tonight, brother?' he remarked with a slight narrowing of his short-sighted eyes.

'I am always cheerful, Sire, when I have the pleasure of an evening spent in your company and the Queen's, who appears to me to be looking more dazzling than usual tonight.'

'Very polite, as well,' the King muttered. 'He's hiding something.'

Gentle Madame Elisabeth, seated next to the King, tapped his hand lightly with her fan.

'Why shouldn't it be true? *I* am always the happier for being with you.'

'You, sister, are an angel. Besides, you love me. I cannot say as much for everyone,' he added with a black look at the Comte de Vaudreuil, a coarse-natured Creole of a consumptive habit but not unattractive, whom he suspected of being the author of the afternoon's ill-timed pleasantry.

Vaudreuil, sitting beside the Queen, studying her cards, appeared not to notice. He was one of her closest friends.

'Enough. Let us play,' the King said impatiently as the Comte d'Artois made a tempestuous entrance, nose in the air and dressed all in white from head to foot. 'And let people who cannot manage to arrive in time at least try to do so unnoticed.'

Disregarding this brotherly ill-humour, Artois moved to kiss his sister-in-law's hand and compliment her on the elegance of her blue dress, delicately striped with silver, the latest work of art to emerge, only that morning, from the workrooms of the Queen's 'Minister of Fashion', the influential Rose Bertin.

'Sit down by me, brother, and pick up your cards, or else we shall all be scolded,' the Queen said, laughing.

Play began, to a background of music by Glück played in the adjoining room by the violins of the Chambre du Roi. Tournemine tried not to stare too fixedly at the Comte de

268

Provence who was seated directly facing him, opposite the King. But he was obliged to realize that the Prince's gaze, from under his heavy lids, was bent frequently and studiously on him. Also, since Madame de Balbi was standing just behind Provence, he was able to avoid the one only at the cost of encountering the other, with its mixture of impudence and mockery.

It was becoming uncomfortably hot. The heavy perfumes worn by men and women added immensely to the stifling atmosphere.

'I'm thirsty,' Louis announced suddenly. He was in the process of being fleeced by his brother and it was doing no good to his temper.

The Duc de Coigny, First Gentleman of the Bedchamber, sprang forward bearing a tray with a glass of champagne and offered it to his sovereign, but the King waved it away without a glance.

'No, no! That won't do me any good. Monsieur de Tournemine,' he went on, half turning to the young officer, 'get me a glass of Vichy water.'

'Water! For you, brother?' Provence exclaimed in amazement.

'Yes, by heaven! My physician, Lasson, insists I drink a great deal of it. He claims it can cure me of the sleepiness which affects me after meals, and makes me feel so unwell. You are surprised, I dare say, but as a good brother surely you will encourage me in this. My health is a matter of concern to you, is it not?'

'I hope you do not doubt that?'

'By no means. Forty-nine! Ah, mine this time, I think! Is your luck changing, brother? A little Vichy water, perhaps . . .'

During this exchange between the King and Monsieur, Gilles had departed hastily to the Salon de l'Abondance, where the refreshments were usually served. Quick as he was, however, he was not in time to escape Anne de Balbi.

'Since it is your night for running errands, Chevalier, will you bring me a sorbet?'

'In a moment, Madame. When the King is served.'

'As gallant as ever, I perceive. I have to talk to you, my friend. I think you owe me some explanation . . .'

'I was not aware of it, Madame. The King is waiting.'

'Devil take the King!' The words were a hiss through clenched teeth. 'I want to see you, do you hear? Tonight! I will wait for you until dawn – at the place you know of.'

He turned his back without answering and, going to the sideboard, was given the water the King had asked for and made his way back with it. But she was waiting for him in the doorway of the Salon de Vénus and, warned by the quick, nervous flutter of her fan, he dared not push past her.

'Will you come?' she whispered.

'I don't care for your Vouvray.'

'There will be none. But I advise you to come. I have managed to ensure that there will be no further – visits to your garden at night. Surely that deserves some thanks? So, you'll come?'

'In that case, perhaps.'

He gave her a courteous bow and moved past to offer the King the glass he had asked for.

When ten o'clock struck on Morand's fine clock with the automata which was the room's chief ornament, the King swept the pile of gold in front of him into his pocket and moved to offer his hand to the Queen, while the other players rose hastily.

'Let us go and sup,' Louis said. His good humour, never long absent, seemed to have returned. 'Are you coming, Madame?' But the Queen, instead of taking the hand held out to her, sank into a curtsy.

'No, Sire, with your permission. It is intolerably hot and I am not feeling hungry. I would rather go out onto the terrace with my ladies and get some fresh air.'

She enveloped her husband in the miraculous charm of her lovely smile and he, as always, yielded to it.

'Very well, run along. But do not linger too long in the garden. The nights can turn unexpectedly chilly after midnight and you might catch cold. As for ourselves, gentlemen, whose nature is somewhat less ethereal, let us go sup!'

The procession of the two sovereigns, flanked by their bodyguard, divided into two and while the Queen, leaning on the arm of her bosom friend the Duchesse de Polignac, returned to her own apartment to change her clothes, the King made for the dining-room next door to his library for what was one of the most important events in his life, his supper. Before he took his seat, however, he stepped aside into the library, making a sign to Tournemine to follow.

'Come, Monsieur. I have a word to say to you.'

So, while the Court commented on this fresh mark of favour, Gilles stood in an attitude of respectful attention before his sovereign in the centre of the vast white room.

Louis did not speak at once. Then he said: 'You once told me, Chevalier, here in this very room, that there were no limits to what I could ask of your loyalty.'

'None, Sire! I could know no greater happiness than to lay down my life for your Majesty – as your Majesty knows.'

'It won't come to that tonight. I wish to ask a service of you, of a very private nature. Do not misunderstand me, I am not asking you to spy for me, but I should like you to go out to the terrace and observe the Queen discreetly. No! Once again, let there be no misunderstanding,' he added quickly. 'I do not suspect her Majesty of any misconduct. Only, I wish to be assured that she will not allow her friends to mislead her into returning to the Trianon tonight, to play at faro in the privacy of her own house. Away from my eyes. She – she finds it difficult to resist her friends, you know.'

'And if her Majesty should in fact return to the Trianon?'

'You will come and inform me. You have my permission to ask that I be woken. If not, if the Queen retires to her chamber after her stroll, well, then, my friend, you may do as everyone else does and seek your own bed, and nothing more need be said of the matter. Understood?'

'Understood, Sire. I shall obey your Majesty to the letter.'

'I thank you. Go, then, Sir.'

The King re-entered the dining-room and Gilles left by the other door and made his way through the Cabinet Doré to the staircase leading down to the north parterre and the terrace.

He had some trouble finding the Queen at first, because the place was crowded. On summer evenings, when the town in its damp hollow was stifling, the public, as long as it was respectably dressed, was permitted to come and take the air on the terrace, rubbing shoulders with the inhabitants of the château, the Court and even the royal family itself in the most demo-

271

cratic way in the world. People would stroll up and down listening to the music of the Swiss and French Guards, who played alternately. Sometimes, on Sundays and public holidays, they could also watch the fountains playing.

On this particular evening, it was the turn of the French Guards to provide the music and the infectious strains of *Malbrouk s'en va-t'en guerre* floated pleasantly above the talk and laughter of the crowd in its light-coloured clothes, echoing in a more genuine and spontaneous fashion the royal occasion which had just come to an end in the palace above.

Failing to perceive Marie-Antoinette, Gilles addressed one of the pages who were wandering about between the groups, always on the look-out for mischief, for this evening promenade of the population of Versailles was a happy hunting ground for them.

The young imp he spoke to might have had some thoughts of sending the officer on a wild goose chase to the Orangery or to some distant coppice but Tournemine's size and the look in his eye boded no good to the perpetrator of such jokes, so he answered politely enough and pointed towards the steps leading to the Latona parterre.

'Her Majesty is over there with her ladies and gentlemen. You'll find her on a seat by the Lizard pool.'

He was right, the Queen was there. Dressed now in a simple white gown of spotted lawn, with one of the charmingly airy hats known as a 'Thérèse', a muslin wrap thrown over her shoulders and a huge fan in one hand, she was sitting on a bench amid a semi-circle of ladies and gentlemen, the oldest but not the least loquacious of whom was the Colonel of the Swiss Guards, the Baron de Besenval, the life and soul of the little group.

One of the Queen's ladies, Mademoiselle Dorvat, was sitting next to her, and on the other side was the exquisite and idle Duchesse de Polignac whose blue eyes seemed always lost in a misty dream. Marie-Antoinette was holding her hand affectionately. Standing a little in front of them was a plain young woman, but whose plainness had something high-strung and wholly elegant about it. She and Besenval were engaged in some sort of dialogue which was evidently very funny, for the whole company was laughing heartily. This was the Comtesse

272

Diane de Polignac, the duchess's sister-in-law and the possessor of what was certainly the most biting tongue in the whole Court.

Not daring to approach any nearer, Gilles took up a position behind one of the clipped yews lining the semi-circular alley that sloped gently down towards the pools, at a point just above the bench where the Queen was seated.

The crowd strolling about the terrace and parterre gradually thinned. By about midnight there was hardly anyone left and the musicians were embarking on their last piece when Tournemine, who was beginning to be tired of waiting, started suddenly. Out of the darkness of the more distant reaches of the gardens, a man had appeared, a man whom Gilles recognized to his astonishment as the red-haired dandy who acted as secretary to Madame de la Motte.

The newcomer made straight for the merry group below which parted to admit him and bowed deeply to the Queen. He said something to her but not loudly enough for Gilles to hear. Marie-Antoinette rose at once.

'Come along all of you,' she cried happily. 'I think we are about to see some fun!'

There was one defection. Madame de Polignac was evidently tired and begged leave to retire. She curtseyed and went away on her husband's arm. Marie-Antoinette laid her arm in Mademoiselle Dorvat's and the whole party moved off in the wake of the secretary towards the dark area beyond. Gilles followed unhesitatingly, walking on the grass to muffle the sound of his footsteps. The Queen was not apparently going to the Trianon. But in that case, where was she going, and in the company of a man so closely linked to a woman of dubious reputation?

The little group of people walked as far as the Allée de L'Automne, past the Ballroom Copse and entered Louis XIV's old maze, now redesigned and replanted with a collection of rare trees and rechristened the Bosquet de Vénus.

It was cool and dark here, under the retaining wall of the massive Stair of a Hundred Steps, and well screened from prying eyes by the trellised hedges lining the circular paths.

Gilles was easily able to keep the light dresses of the Queen and her ladies in sight in the dim light. Once in the Bosquet, it was child's play to move up close in the shelter of the hedge.

The group had come to a halt in a space between two thin walls of foliage, heavy with the scent of acacias and liriodendrons. There was not a sound to be heard. The Queen and her friends were watching something in absolute silence. Suddenly, the figure of a woman appeared and curtseyed.

'Well, Countess,' the Queen whispered. 'Is all ready?'

'Quite ready, Madame,' replied the new arrival, who was none other than Madame de la Motte. 'If your Majesty will only take a look through the leaves, you will be able to see the woman. Someone will bring him in a moment.'

'Is she very like me?'

'Your Majesty shall judge.'

Feeling that some interesting scene was about to be played out in the middle of the Bosquet, Gilles decided that it would be as well if he, too, were able to get a glimpse of the actors.

He moved along the path until he was far enough away not to be seen by the Queen's party and then slipped through one of the gaps in the green wall between one circle and the next. Then he crept close up to the hedge in question and peered cautiously through the branches.

What he saw astonished him beyond belief.

Standing in the centre of the open space beyond was a woman. She held a rose in her hand and she was tall, slim and dressed all in white. Just then a sliver of a moon moved out from behind a cloud and threw a faint light on her, enough for keen eyes to see that she looked very like the Queen and her dress was exactly similar.

The woman seemed to be nervous. From where he was hidden Gilles could hear her breathing. She was finding it hard to stand still and now and then moved a few steps to and fro in a nervous fashion. All at once the Countess reappeared, not easily recognizable because she had donned a black domino and accompanied by a man also dressed in black, in a kind of long coat buttoned to the neck, his features hidden by a wide-brimmed hat.

Madame de la Motte made a gesture towards the supposed Queen. The man drew back as if a bullet had struck him and laid his hand on his breast. Then he swept off his hat and bowed so deeply that his knee all but touched the ground. After that

274

he came forward, as though in a trance, until he reached the white figure and there his strength seemed to give way and he dropped heavily to his knees and prostrated himself as if to a goddess. Gilles heard his sobbing murmur: 'Oh, my lady, my lady! Has your Majesty forgiven me at last?'

The man was the same Gilles had seen through a crack in the door in the house used by Cagliostro. The man so prostrating himself before a woman was a priest. More, he was the Grand Almoner of France, Cardinal Louis de Rohan.

Gilles watched with stupefaction as he embraced the feet of the illusory Queen and pressed his lips to them, while she let fall the rose she held in her hand.

'You know,' she whispered softly, 'what this signifies.'

The next moment the voice of the foppish secretary was heard saying: 'Beware! Madame and the Comtesse d'Artois are coming this way!'

Madame de la Motte rushed forward, pulled the cardinal to his feet and practically dragged him with her to the other end of the grove, giving him barely time to snatch up the rose and press it to his lips. At the same time the secretary, accompanied by another man whom Gilles had not seen before, went to the pretended Queen and, throwing a cloak over her shoulders, hurried her off in the opposite direction.

Silence fell once more on the Bosquet as the sound of their hastening footsteps died away. Only then did a light, silvery laugh break out, followed by another and another.

'I feel we ought to applaud,' said a man's voice. 'The Countess is to be congratulated. She has a perfect touch as a producer of comedies! You should appoint her to your theatre at the Trianon, Madame.'

'She might do wonders there.' This time the voice was Marie-Antoinette's. 'At all events, it is a long time since I was so entertained. Poor man, wasn't he ridiculous? Did you see him fall on his face? I thought for a moment he was going to cry.'

'But who was the woman?' asked another voice. 'It may have been the clothes, but in this dim light, with only the fitful moonlight to see by, she looked to me most convincing.'

'That is why I say the cardinal is a fool and a wretch,' the Queen said, with a touch of anger. 'Do you know who it was this Prince of the Church, this Grand Almoner of France,

275

sometime ambassador to the Empress my mother in Vienna, mistook for me? Do you know? A woman of the streets! A creature out of the gutter, a girl called Oliva who makes a living from her charms at the Palais Royal! It is true and beyond everything. I would have given my finest diamonds to have had the King and the whole Court see him crawling at the feet of a harlot!'

A woman's voice, gentle and compassionate, made itself heard.

'Oh Madame! How your Majesty hates him! To me he did not seem so much ridiculous as pitiable, and unhappy! Remember he is desperately in love, in love with someone who detests him, and he thought he had reached the end of a nightmare.'

'Detests him? Loathes him, you should say! Come, child, you are wasting your pity. You saw a man in love where I saw only one who is bold, impudent and ambitious. Do you know that man's dream? It is to be first minister of France and he hopes to achieve it by seducing me, France's Queen!'

'He is a Rohan,' the man's voice which had spoken first said daringly. 'Do you forget the motto of that house, Madame? "Not King, not Prince, but Rohan"! It may not seem so impossible to him. The Rohans are older than the Hapsburgs.'

'Monsieur de Vaudreuil,' the Queen said, quivering with anger, 'I would ask you, if you wish to remain one of my friends, not to indulge in such pleasantries again. Let us go in. I am beginning to feel the cold.'

They were coming back. Gilles had just time to whisk himself into another path and step behind the trunk of a tulip tree, holding his breath. The soft whisper of silk gowns rustled past him, and a waft of scent reached his nostrils. Then the footsteps receded.

There was nothing more for Gilles to do but imitate them. But instead of going straight back to the château, it occurred to him to take a look at the scene of the strange comedy he had just witnessed. Marie-Antoinette's love of all things theatrical was well known, as was the basic vulgarity which led her to find funny things that should have shocked her as a Queen, if not as a woman. Was it not she who had persuaded King Louis to revoke his ban and permit the public showing of Pierre Caron de Beaumarchais' scandalous play, *The Marriage of Figaro*? Which, indeed, her friend Vaudreuil had not scrupled to put on in private although it was a most dangerous piece of political polemicism against the monarchy. So there was nothing unduly surprising in this. But it was none the less to be deplored and one could only pray that if the rats of the Temple were allowed to continue nibbling at the feet of the throne, the irresponsibility of it would not result in some huge tragedy.

As he strolled over the grass thinking these thoughts, Gilles caught sight of something white lying there. He picked it up and saw that it was a folded scrap of paper dropped, probably, by one of the two people who had stood there. He put it in his pocket. Then, since the place had nothing more to tell him, he, too, made his way back to the palace where the lights were going out now, one by one, in the various apartments.

When he reached the Cour de Marbre, he looked up at the King's darkened windows, a prey to a last, momentary doubt. On his way back through the gardens he had pondered very carefully on what he should do and had decided, finally, to keep his own counsel. Louis had said: 'If the Queen goes to the Trianon . . .' But the Queen, whose own rooms were now the only ones still ablaze with light, had not gone to the Trianon. She was back in her own apartments. So there was nothing for Gilles to do but mind his own business. He could not see himself describing to the King the curious spectacle he had just witnessed.

On the other hand, it did seem urgent to talk to the Queen herself. It was high time Marie-Antoinette was enlightened about the woman she was allowing, so unfortunately, to arrange these nightly distractions for her, especially since, despite his warning, Axel de Fersen seemed to have said nothing before his departure.

A strong Swiss voice roused him from his meditations. Coming out of the Grand Vestibule at the head of a company of his fellow-countrymen in red and gold, their faces framed in goffered ruffs and halbards gleaming like a phalanx of avenging angels, was Ulrich-August.

'Going to bed? You're in luck! I'm dead tired but I'm here for a good few hours yet.'

'Winkleried, my friend, you eat too much. It's a full stomach that makes you so sleepy. But if it's any comfort to you, I'm not going to bed. I've someone to see first.'

He had in fact only just remembered his assignation with Anne de Balbi in the Rue de l'Orangerie, which, in view of its penitential nature, it might not be politic to miss. If she had really persuaded Provence to leave him alone, she deserved something of him, since, once made a corpse of, he would lose all hope of ever finding Judith again except in the next world.

But when he followed the unsmiling maidservant into the room he remembered, he was given no time to so much as open his mouth to speak before a warm fragrant bundle of light muslins and eager flesh landed in his arms and a pair of burning lips were murmuring against his: 'You came! I knew you would! I love you! I'm going to love you so that you will never, ever want to leave me again! Quickly! Come, quickly!'

It occurred to Gilles then that what he had told Ulrich-August was a lie. He was going to bed. But not alone and that, he supposed, made all the difference, since in this bed there would be little chance of sleep. In any case, however he spent the night, what mattered was not to find himself transported magically to some strange house. And so, to prevent his partner feeling the need to ply him with perilous drinks, Gilles entered enthusiastically into the proceedings.

By the time he left her, at dawn, Madame de Balbi was exhausted, with blue shadows round her heavy eyes, yet even then she would not easily let him go and only did so at last in return for his sworn promise to return that evening.

'I'll send for you. I don't want to come here again. I want you in my own house – in my own bed! I have a charming bed in a pretty little cottage by the woods at Satory, you'll see!'

'And what will his Royal Highness do meanwhile? They say Monsieur cannot live without you.'

'It's true. But I deserve a holiday now and then. You can't imagine what it's like making love with an elephant! I shall say I am ill.'

'You don't look ill.'

The first ray of sunlight, filtering into the moist dimness of the room, was shining on her rosy lips and drawing a gleam from eyes deep in blissful weariness. She was bursting with health and vitality. She pouted her lips for one last kiss.

'When I say I am ill, I should like to see who would dare to contradict me. Not even Zaza!'

'Zaza?'

'Louis-Xavier! I call him Zaza. He indulges all my whims and he will just have to indulge this one, too. Until this evening, then?'

Once outside, Gilles thought that before seeking an audience with the Queen it might be as well to get in two or three hours' sleep and change his clothes. Fortunately, it was not far to the Rue de Noailles and within fifteen minutes he was stretched out on his bed fast asleep, not having troubled even to remove his boots.

Early in the afternoon, neat in his dress uniform, with not a hair out of place and shining like a new penny, the Chevalier de Tournemine was seated astride Merlin, as perfectly groomed as himself, and riding up to the gates of the Trianon to beg the Queen to grant him the favour of an audience.

A groom led his horse away to the stables and the usher who had carried the request returned after a little while accompanied by one of the Queen's favourite ladies, young Madame de Campan, the wife of her librarian. She was a rather heavy-featured blonde, not particularly pretty but with a pleasant face. At least, in general, for at the moment her expression was not encouraging.

'Is her Majesty expecting you, Monsieur?'

'No, Madame, and I assure you I am only too aware of my presumption. But if you would be good enough to beg her Majesty to believe that only a matter of the utmost urgency would have led me to this.'

'Too urgent to wait until tomorrow morning? The Queen, as you know, is happy to grant audiences after mass at the château, but she dislikes above all things to be pursued here and we do our best to preserve the little privacy which is available to a queen. If you would perhaps tell me what it is about?'

'I regret, Madame, that that is not possible. I must speak to her Majesty alone. If you would be good enough to give her this. I will wait here.'

Foreseeing difficulties, he had taken the precaution of

folding the note he had found in the Bosquet de Vénus in a clean sheet of paper and sealing it with his own seal. The paper itself was a pretty sheet of gilt-edged vellum headed with a gilt fleur de lys upon which, in a flowing hand, were inscribed a few brief lines urging the recipient to be patient in the hope of one day achieving 'by perfect obedience the supreme rewards which fall to the lot of noble minds'. It was signed simply with an M and an A.

Madame de Campan took the note and scurried away up the elegant staircase of pale stone at the foot of which she had been speaking to the younger man. She was not away long. After a few moments, she reappeared and, from a point halfway up, commanded him curtly to follow her.

She led him through the antechamber furnished with seats upholstered in red velvet and two large porcelain stoves in the Austrian style, in white and gold, and then into a pleasant dining-room with some fine paintings in it. Here, Madame de Campan turned to the visitor. He saw that she was looking worried.

'I fear this visit is not to the Queen's liking. She looked most displeased. I beg you to do nothing to upset her.'

'Like yourself, Madame, I am her Majesty's loyal servant and, like yourself, I desire nothing but her happiness,' Gilles said, a trifle huffily. The woman was a perfect watchdog and he sensed that she would have been only too happy to throw him out of the window, on a charge of disturbing the Queen's peace. 'Is her Majesty expecting me or not?'

'I will take you to her,' the woman said with a sigh, and she led the way to a pair of double doors. 'She is playing billiards with the Comtesse d'Ossun, but I will announce you.'

Marie-Antoinette was in the small, pretty apartment which was known as the 'Florist's Room' from the fact that it gave on to a flower-filled parterre. It was here that she had her billiard table. When Gilles was shown in, she was playing with her mistress of the robes and was just engaged in bringing off what, from her set lips and the frown between her eyes, was evidently a shot of some unusual difficulty.

'You asked to see me, Sir,' she said coldly, without taking her eyes from the end of her ivory and gold cue. 'Here I am. Speak! What have you to say?'

280

The young man's bow was perfection, a tribute not only to the Queen but also to the woman, charmingly attired in white cambric gown with a fichu of soft pink muslin.

'I thank your Majesty for condescending to see me – but I did ask for an audience in private.'

Marie-Antoinette tossed the long cue on to the red cloth table and straightened with an angry jerk. She looked at the young officer severely.

'I have always had a kindness for you, Monsieur de Tournemine, but as an officer of the Guard, you should know that I endeavour not to let matters of state intrude into my beloved Trianon. They are troublesome and bring an air of gloom.'

'This is not a matter of state, Madame, but one which nearly concerns your Majesty. That is why I have presumed to come here.'

'Indeed? Then what is this paper you have sent me? Where did you get it?'

Gilles glanced at the good-looking young woman, dressed in precisely similar fashion to the Queen, who had withdrawn discreetly and was examining a large vase of roses at the other end of the room. Then he answered in an undertone: 'From the Bosquet de Vénus, your Majesty. A little after midnight last night.'

'Ah.'

There was a moment's silence in which Gilles marvelled at the Queen's self-command. If the words had startled her, she scarcely showed it: a faint surprise, an almost imperceptible frown in the rather prominent blue eyes, but that was all. Then, with a charming smile, she turned to Madame d'Ossun.

'Leave us, if you will, my dear Geneviève. I believe I shall have to see this young man alone after all. Take the small carriage and have them drive you to the Hameau. I will join you there presently.'

She waited until the lady-in-waiting's white dress had disappeared through the door and then turned back to her visitor, all trace of a smile wiped from her face.

'Very well. Speak now, Monsieur. We are alone and none can overhear us. What do you know of the Bosquet de Vénus and, more important, what were you doing there? I believe you said you found the note yourself?'

281

'I found it. As to what I was doing there, Madame, I was merely enjoying a stroll.' Gilles brought out the words with a confidence which he was far from feeling, but nothing would have made him admit to the fact that he had been sent by the King, and risk causing unpleasant friction between the royal couple. So he went on: 'It is cool and quiet there these hot nights, and soothing to one whose heart is troubled. It is a pleasant place to dream in.'

'Is it so? I did not know the gentlemen of the Guards were so poetically inclined. However, let that be. Tell me, then, Sir. What is it you have to say to me?'

Beneath the piled-up mass of her pale hair, Marie-Antoinette's brow was stormy and the Hapsburg lip much in evidence. Staking everything, Gilles knelt, straight-backed, before her.

'Let the Queen pardon my boldness and see me only as her most humble, loyal and devoted servant. I have sworn my life to the service and the happiness of my King and Queen and have come here with no other purpose in mind.'

'I have never doubted it, Sir,' the Queen said testily but with the faintest softening of her tone. 'What then?'

'What I have to say to your Majesty is this. Madame de la Motte Valois is an adventuress, unworthy of the name which fate has bestowed on her, a creature unfit to set foot in the palace kitchens, let alone the apartments of a Queen. You must be rid of her, Madame, as soon as maybe, for she is capable, I believe, of doing your Majesty great harm.'

'Harm to me? That poor creature who endures her poverty so bravely? A poverty all the more appalling in view of the illustrious name of which you speak so slightingly. I confess I should like to help her, but what has the poor woman done to you, that you should judge her so harshly?'

'To me, nothing. But to your Majesty, a great deal. I swear to your Majesty on my honour that Madame de la Motte's devotion is given far less to your Majesty than to another member of the royal family. May I ask your Majesty one question?'

'Ask it.'

'Before he left for Sweden, did Count Fersen say anything to your Majesty regarding Madame de la Motte?'

282

'Count— No. Nothing.'

The Queen put both hands to her head, as though she felt suddenly dizzy. Her voice changed.

'Axel! My God – of course! You are a friend of his.'

She swayed, turned and sank abruptly into a low armchair which creaked under her weight. Gilles saw to his horror that her face was perfectly white and her delicate nostrils pinched. He sprang to his feet.

'Your Majesty is unwell?'

'Yes – no! It is nothing. If you please, Chevalier, summon Madame de Misery – or Madame de Campan – anyone ...'

The librarian's wife was not far off and the Queen's chief tirewoman with her. They came hurrying at the young man's call and ran to their mistress, little Madame de Campan casting a dagger look at Gilles as she passed.

'I told you not to upset the Queen, Sir!'

Marie-Antoinette managed a wan smile.

'Do – do not be cross with the young man, my good Campan. But rather take me to my chamber, for I am feeling a trifle unwell.... Wait here, Chevalier. I will send for—' She broke off with a little cry and, half-carried by her women, left the room precipitately, leaving Gilles somewhat bewildered. Was the Queen really ill, or had she merely availed herself of a simple method of breaking off a disagreeable interview? No doubt in a moment one of her women, the disapproving Madame de Campan at a guess, would come and bring him her Majesty's regrets at being obliged to postpone the continuance of their conversation to some later date, so much later, probably, that it would never happen.

He soon had cause to swallow these uncharitable thoughts, however, for when Madame de Campan reappeared it was not to dismiss him but, on the contrary, to ask him to follow her into the Queen's own chamber, where she was lying on a day bed, wrapped in shawls.

She was looking somewhat less pale but the faint sour smell which lingered in the air, despite the open windows and a lavish recourse to the scent spray, testified that her Majesty had been sick.

'Is your Majesty feeling better?' Gilles asked in a hushed voice, alarmed by the Queen's shadowed eyes.

Marie-Antoinette's smile held a trace of mischief.

'I must ask your pardon for my regrettable lapse of manners, Chevalier. It means that you will be among the first people in France to learn that before many months are out your Queen will give birth to a prince – or a princess.'

Gilles bowed with great respect but did not speak for a moment. This was important news but he could not stop himself wondering if it were really as good as it seemed. Supposing by some misfortune the child had been conceived while Fersen was at Court ... But he could hardly ask the Queen to tell him the date. Nor could he continue to stand silent for much longer. He had, after all, just received a signal mark of royal favour.

'I am greatly honoured, Madame,' he managed to say. 'I am happy to be among the first of your subjects to wish your Majesty safely delivered. I thank your Majesty.'

Marie-Antoinette laughed openly now, having no idea of the unsuitable thoughts passing through her visitor's mind.

'Well done. You will make an admirable ambassador once you have acquired a few more wrinkles to your brow. But we have not finished our conversation. Sit here.' She indicated a small chair placed close by her sofa. 'You may leave me now, Madame de Misery,' she added to the woman who was ranging the jars on her dressing table. 'I am feeling quite well now.'

After the woman had gone, she went on: 'As I recall, you were saying, when I was so unhappily taken ill, that Count Fersen might have spoken to me about Madame de la Motte?'

'Yes, Madame. And I am sorry he should not have done so for it was on a matter of some seriousness. A theft, in point of fact.

'A theft committed in this very room on the night of the entertainment given by your Majesties in honour of King Gustav of Sweden. From, I should imagine, that desk,' he added, turning slightly to indicate the small, delicately made bureau he had noticed on entering the room.

'But that is impossible! It is always kept locked and I carry the key with me.'

'I am sure that is so but I suggest your Majesty asks Madame de la Motte for the key which she has had made from a wax impression. Such things are not difficult to do.'

Then, as Marie-Antoinette remained speechless, he embarked on a detailed account of all that had taken place in the Trianon gardens on the night in question.

As the tale progressed, he could see the Queen's brow darkening and her lovely hands clenching but the expression of anger and disgust that appeared on her face told him that she no longer doubted that what he said was true.

'This stolen letter,' she said at last, in an altered voice. 'Did you read it?'

Gilles hesitated briefly, moved by her distress. Here, he thought, was a young and beautiful woman to whom life had given every gift. He was tempted to lie to her. But he knew that he could not, for the smallest falsehood would cast doubt on everything.

'Yes, Madame,' he said gently, 'or how should I have known to whom it belonged? But I have already forgotten its contents and I can at least assure your Majesty that the Comte de Provence had no time to so much as glance at it.'

A smile fleetingly curved the Queen's blanched lips.

'So you dared to attack Monsieur, and knock him down? Do you know that for that crime against a royal person you could be torn between four horses in the Place de Grève?'

'I am a member of your Majesties' Guard, not of Monsieur's, and it is my duty to attack anyone, king or pope even, who threatens your Majesties' safety. But you may have me arrested, if you please ...'

'On the Comte de Provence's account? You must be joking, my friend! There is much good in your American way, Sir Falcon, and the Queen is your debtor. What I cannot understand is why Count Fersen said nothing of this to me. It is true I saw little of him before he left and then only in the presence of Count Haga, but he might have written to me. What did he say when you gave him the letter?'

The young man's tanned face flushed dark red. It was not going to be easy to tell the Queen that he had given her favourite a black eye.

'I fear your Majesty will not be pleased with the rest of my story,' he said awkwardly. 'You may find it more in your heart

285

to forgive me for attacking Monsieur than for knocking Fersen unconscious.'

'What's this? Unconscious, do you say?'

'Yes, Madame. Unfortunately I was unable to offer him my apologies since I found myself, immediately afterwards, under the painful necessity of putting a sword through Monsieur de Lauzun.'

'Oh, as to that I acquit you – What did you say? Put a sword through Lauzun? So you are responsible for the wound which has been keeping him within doors?'

'Yes, Madame. And, with respect to your Majesty, I cannot say that I am sorry.'

The Queen gave a weary little shrug.

'Neither am I, Sir. I have been hearing a good deal about Monsieur de Lauzun's blustering. There is no worse enemy, you know, than a friend who believes he has a grievance. I have heard of scurrilous verses . . . It is intolerable. But to return to yourself. What passed between you and Count Fersen?'

Mention of Count Fersen seemed to be the only subject which could rouse Marie-Antoinette from her troubles. Gilles did as he was told, briefly, and this time had the satisfaction of making the Queen laugh.

'So that was why he was so shy of appearing in public those last days? A black eye! Good heavens! Is he so vain? But I am afraid, then, that the two of you have fallen out?'

'Quite seriously, I fear, Madame. I am sorry for it, for I owe him a great deal.'

'I will arrange matters. His anger was uncalled for. What is more, it seems to me that if you owe a great deal to Count Fersen, you have repaid him. It is the Queen, now, who stands in your debt.'

'The Queen owes me nothing. I am her servant and her smile is my reward.'

She inclined her head gracefully.

'You must not become a courtier, Sir Falcon, or I shall not like you as well. Only continue to serve the King as you have done, for it is to the King, is it not, that the chief of your devotion is given? It is right that it should be so.'

'I belong to the King, yes, but also to the Queen. How should it be for me to place one before the other?'

'Perhaps because the King has no secrets – and the Queen has. A secret which you now share,' she added, blushing faintly.

The arrogant young face before her broke into a smile.

'I should be a poor thing, Madame, if I were to become privy to any woman's secrets, Queen or no, and not contrive to forget them on the instant. The heart's secrets belong to God and the Queen is sacred.'

She put out her hand in a charmingly spontaneous gesture.

'You are a very nice young man, Chevalier, and I like you very much.' Then, as he knelt to kiss the royal hand, she added: 'Which reminds me, how do matters stand regarding your family castle? You have never spoken to me about it since.'

'There was little point in doing so. Matters stand still where they were, Madame. But your Majesty must not be disturbed. One of these days, I hope to be able to get together the sum demanded by the present owner.'

'On a Guard's pay? I know it is the best in the army, but even so—'

'With the help of a friend of mine, Baron de Batz, who is at present in Spain. He is expert in matters of finance, of which I know nothing, and we have a fifty–fifty arrangement together. May I ask your Majesty's permission to withdraw?'

Gilles was growing uncomfortable, disliking this talk of money coming so soon on top of their other conversation. The Queen sensed it.

'Go, then, Sir,' she said quietly. 'The Queen is your debtor but the woman would be your friend.' Raising her voice then, she called: 'Madame de Campan!'

Madame de Campan appeared so promptly that Gilles thought, amused, that she must have been hovering just outside the door, ready to intervene at once should the importunate officer dare to disturb her mistress again. She dropped a little curtsey.

'Majesty?'

'Take a good look at this young man, Campan, and look at him kindly. His name is the Chevalier de Tournemine and he is to be permitted in future to approach me at all times. See that his name is known at the door. And I have an order for you, also. When Madame de la Motte comes here again, today or

287

tomorrow, you are to say nothing but bring her to me. And on all future occasions you are to see to it that she is never permitted to enter these grounds again. Is that clear?'

Madame de Campan's face lit up and she even allowed some of the smile to rest on Gilles.

'Quite clear, I am glad to say.'

Which gladness said a good deal, Gilles thought, about the fair countess's popularity in that quarter, at any rate. Madame de Campan's satisfaction even led her to accompany Gilles all the way downstairs and out to where his horse was waiting, perhaps to make amends for her previous brusqueness. She waited while he mounted.

'I hope you will come back often, Chevalier, if it is always to bring us such good news. We shall be most happy to welcome you.'

'I shall do my best, Madame.'

Then, certain of having shielded the Queen for the present from her brother-in-law's malice, he rode off, feeling well content.

PART THREE

Storm over Versailles

1784–5

12

The House of Monsieur Beausire

The note, written on rose-coloured paper and coquettishly folded, was charming. It looked childishly innocent. Its contents, however, offered food for thought.

'If you would like to have news of a young lady with red hair, ask your friend M. Lecoulteux de la Noraye to take you to one of the gaming parties which are held several times a week at number ten in the Rue Neuve St Gilles in the Marais ...'

There was no signature, except for a crude drawing of a four-leaved clover, the symbol of luck. The writing, although elegant enough, was quite unfamiliar.

'Who could have sent it to me?' Gilles wondered. He rose to his feet, meaning to go downstairs and ask Mademoiselle Marjon who had brought it.

He handed it to Winkleried who was sitting with half-closed eyes, smoking, with his feet on the fender and an expression of catlike content on his face, the large pipe which, for him, was the only real aid to digestion.

'Here,' Gilles said. 'Tell me when I get back what you make of it.'

From his landlady, he learned nothing of any interest. The note had been brought by a messenger, any one of a hundred, who had said nothing of where it came from. That was all he could discover.

When he got back to his sitting-room, it was to find that Ulrich-August had opened his eyes and abandoned his relaxed attitude. He was turning the note over and over between his fingers.

'Well?' he said, looking up at his friend.

'Nothing. A messenger. What do you think?'

'That it was written by a woman. The colour, the handwriting ... but which woman?'

'That is the question,' Gilles said, stopping to put another log on the fire. 'Number ten, the Rue Neuve St Gilles is Madame de la Motte's house. The last time I passed it, ten days ago, the house was shut up and empty. When I questioned the neighbours, they said that the La Mottes, husband and wife, had gone off to Bar-sur-Aube to visit relations, taking the whole household with them.'

Nearly four months had passed since Gilles' audience with the Queen at the Trianon. Four desperate months in the course of which he had felt himself going steadily mad with the strain of boredom and ignorance. But for Winkleried's bracing friendship, he might have sailed back to America. The Swiss, for whom patience was the supreme virtue, did his best to soothe his friend's exacerbated nerves. He had listened to so many descriptions of Judith that he would have recognized her in the street without a shadow of hesitation. But he was also well aware that her character was not an easy one and the philosophical discourses to which he treated his friend at regular intervals generally concluded with some lapidary statement of this kind: 'Women like that make excellent wives but there are times when they can make life very unpleasant for you. For my part, I am in no hurry to marry my Ursula. There may come a day when you will look back on the days of your untrammelled bachelorhood and be sorry.'

'I'd give a good deal just now to be sure of that,' Gilles would sigh, and then the two friends would sink back, each with his pipe, into a thoughtful silence.

Gilles' thoughts were not usually of a very cheerful kind. He saw the sky darkening all around him. Judith had vanished without trace, as if a giant hand had suddenly swept her out of existence. As for his reluctant affair with Madame de Balbi, Gilles was beginning to find that increasingly onerous. He had never been in love with her and desire, lacking the impetus of passion, was waning rapidly.

She was too intelligent not to know it and, more and more, their meetings were degenerating into unpleasant scenes, violent on her part and irritable on his, as he tried to break off a tie which she was fiercely determined not to release him from.

'I know you don't love me,' she would say. 'I don't care about that. All I want is to keep you for as long as I like. Take care! If you should think of trying to leave me before I am ready to let you go, beware, not for yourself but perhaps for those whom you hold dear.'

And so, for fear that Judith, about whom he knew nothing but she might well know something, should not have to suffer from her resentment, Gilles stayed.

The atmosphere in Paris was no better. Those who served the crown were compelled to realize that the Queen's popularity was waning with terrifying speed, while she herself seemed not in the least aware of it.

The news of her latest pregnancy was received, thanks to the numerous pamphleteers in the pay of Monsieur or the Orléans, with a flood of abusive libels and verses. One of the least scurrilous of those being currently sung in the streets to a popular dance tune suggested that the babe was probably a gift from another planet. And the name of Fersen, who had, of course, been in Paris at the time of the child's conception, was beginning to be heard on the lips of those ill-disposed towards the Queen. It was even said that the Comte de Provence meant to raise the matter of the legitimacy of his brother's children in a secret letter to the Parliament. It was said – but what was there that was not said? And during those melancholy weeks the flat of the Falcon's sword had administered chastisement more than once to some pamphleteer whose identity he had managed to discover. In this he was frequently assisted by Ulrich-August, who had taken hugely to this form of sport.

'The hunting season has begun!' he would roar, descending joyously on some unfortunate scribbler and finishing by up-ending the contents of his own inkpot over the man's head. But what was harder to counteract was the widespread campaign of denigration which was developing against Marie-Antoinette and for which she, unfortunately, provided all too much material.

In the cafés and the clubs and under the new arcades of the Palais Royal, where the building works were still drawing curious eyes, there was angry discussion of the news from

Versailles. To begin with there was the matter of the Château of St Cloud. In order to complete those very building works, the Duke of Orléans was considering selling his finest château and Marie-Antoinette was urging the King to buy it for her for the sum of six million.

The Trianon is not enough for her now, she must have St Cloud as well, grumbled the indignant public. She will ruin us!.

Infinitely more serious was the affair at the mouth of the River Scheldt, which blew up in October between the Queen's brother, the Emperor Joseph II, and the Netherlands, when the latter opened fire on an Austrian brig which was attempting to force an entry to the river. This led to instant preparations for war and while the Emperor was raising an army of eighty thousand men, France, in the role of protector of the Netherlands, was sending two regiments, under the Prince of Condé, to Flanders and the Rhine. At which point Marie-Antoinette, forgetting that she was Queen of France and worked on by her brother from Vienna, through the Austrian ambassador, Mercy-Argenteau, persuaded Louis XVI to a shameful change of heart, insisting that he withdrew his troops and make the Netherlands apologize to Austria and even pay money in reparation.

On guard outside the royal apartments a few days previously Gilles had missed nothing of the Queen's rage and the violent scene to which she had treated the Comte de Vergennes, who was naturally strongly opposed to a policy of such servility towards Austria, even going so far as to demand his resignation which, happily, King Louis had refused to accept.

Not one word of all that he had heard, or of the distress it had caused him, had passed Gilles' lips, it went without saying, but Versailles was a sieve, open to all winds that blew, and the news of that scene was common knowledge in Paris by the same evening. It was then the cry had gone up from one crowded café, a stigma which was to cling to the Queen like a shirt of Nessus from then until the hour of her death: 'Down with the Austrian!'

This time, Tournemine was obliged to keep his sword sheathed. How could he take arms against an entire nation, especially when the nation was in the right? But the instinct

294

which had come to him from the Breton soil where he was born, told him that a storm was brewing and that the good but, alas, too timid Louis XVI would have need of a stout rampart of unquestioningly loyal and devoted men to stand by him and fight for his throne.

Both Gilles and Ulrich-August, knowing as they did the king's real goodness, generosity, piety and cultivated mind, were burning to defend him at this moment, even at need against a wife who was capable of using his love for her, which she did not return, to serve the interests of Austria.

'Perhaps we just have a liking for lost causes,' Gilles said. 'I don't like sounding like a prophet of doom but I fear the Queen's folly may bring the King down. Yet she knows how his enemies, Provence and Orléans, are on the watch for the least false step on her part, to exaggerate and use it as a weapon against her! And she will go on adding to her mistakes. Yet she is not a fool—'

'No,' Winkleried cut in. 'She has wit and charm and a radiant beauty, but she is not really intelligent or she would not stay shut up in Versailles while winter ravages the country and causes untold misery. She will be the only Queen of France never to have set foot outside Paris and Versailles.'

For in the early days of December, winter had descended on Paris like a curse, a winter that promised to be as hard and killing as the one before. Thick snow, driven by an icy wind, lay over everything and remained, with no sign of melting, 'waiting for the next fall', as the peasants said. The old and sick died in their fireless attics, even the birds died in the gutters and on the frozen ground which yielded no food for any beast. Wolves had even been seen in the woods at Marly. The King, who was giving generously and incessantly, went hunting and killed two, with the skill which never failed to astonish his courtiers. Where did a man so short-sighted he could not recognize a friend at ten yards' distance get his amazingly sure eye?

'He's a born huntsman,' Gilles said. 'He smells the game and hardly needs to see it.'

He had risen, the pink note still in his hand, and went over to the window to re-read it, as if the daylight would reveal some hidden sign.

'What are you going to do about it?' Ulrich-August asked, emptying his pipe by tapping it on the mantelshelf, preparatory to filling it again.

'Go, of course. I don't know who sent me this note but if there is the smallest chance of finding Judith, I wouldn't neglect it for the world.'

'And if it's a trap?'

'A trap? Good God, who'd set it? And what for? There's no reason why the Queen should have told La Motte that I was the cause why she was no longer received. For months now I've been biting my nails, waiting for a sign, a word. I'd follow any trail, to hell if need be! No, the thing that puzzles me is the reference to Lecoulteux. He's hardly a friend. Not much more than an acquaintance, in fact. A former acquaintance, more like, because we haven't met since I called on him after the Duchess's letter.'

In fact, contrary to Gilles' expectations, Cayetana had taken Boehmer's request for more time as a personal affront. Her envoy had received a perfectly pleasantly worded but peremptory letter from her, enjoining him to break off all negotiations with the jewellers absolutely from that moment.

'I have a great admiration for Queen Marie-Antoinette,' she wrote, 'but there is no reason why I should wait humbly on her whim. You, my dear Chevalier, have made on my behalf a more than generous offer. Since the Paris jewellers have failed to close with it immediately, I shall let them keep their necklace, with the less regret now that I know it will not be attempting to adorn a certain graceless head already quite sufficiently unsuited to a crown ...'

It seemed, in effect, that the jewellers of the Rue de Vendôme had lost both their Spanish clients at a stroke. The Chevalier d'Ocariz had returned to Madrid to face the displeasure of his master, since it now appeared that Maria Luisa had not thought it worth her while to enlist the approval of her father-in-law before despatching the Spanish consul in quest of Boehmer's diamonds. Charles III, however, considered, with some justification perhaps, that the future queen had quite enough diamonds as it was and that the royal treasury was in no case to bear such an extravagance.

Had her rival's enforced economy been the signal for the

duchess's, or was it her mania for new building works which had made her think that the money for the necklace could be better spent on yet another palace? The letter did not say but, in between the careless lines, Gilles thought he sensed a kind of relief. But then, with a woman so capricious, who could boast of ever following her mind? She had wanted the necklace, now she had ceased to want it. What could be more simple?

Boehmer and Bassange, on the other hand, were reduced to something near despair by the withdrawal of both their Spanish customers. If the Queen decided not to buy the necklace, they faced financial ruin. Now the time asked for by the Comte de Provence was running out and no sign had been received from Versailles, so that the partners were coming to the point of offering a thousand écus to anyone who could find them a purchaser for their too expensive artefact.

As far as Lecoulteux was concerned, matters had been very simple. The banker had merely informed the Cadiz house that the transaction would not now be taking place and offered Gilles, on behalf of the duchess, a compensatory sum which he had refused.

'I have been put to no trouble other than that of making your acquaintance and that of the Queen's jewellers,' the young man had told the banker. 'That is not really enough to call for compensation.'

Lecoulteux de la Noraye had burst out laughing.

'As a man of the world, Chevalier, I agree, but not as a man of business. Fine gestures rarely lead to a fortune. But setting that aside, I shall always be pleased to see you.'

Gilles had just decided to take him at his word and ask him, the next day, to introduce him to the La Motte house, when Javotte, Mademoiselle Marjon's servant, appeared with another note.

There was nothing feminine about this one. It looked much more like an official document than a *billet doux*. It was signed, as if by coincidence, Lecoulteux de La Noraye.

'It occurs to me, Chevalier, that chance may offer you the financial advantage you refuse to take from a lady. Give me the pleasure of introducing you to it in the room of a charming lady where cheating is unknown and the company of the best. If the idea appeals to you, come to my house at about seven o'clock tomorrow evening and we will go together to the Rue Neuve St Gilles in the Marais ...'

'Well, what do you say to that?' Gilles exclaimed, when he had read the letter aloud. 'I think we should be wrong to be suspicious after this. Lecoulteux is an upright man, and a wealthy one, and has no particular connection with Monsieur.'

'I agree. In fact if my colonel weren't giving a dinner for his officers tomorrow night to which I'm bound to go, I'd even come with you. The pink note may have come from a pretty lady—'

'It may have! At all events, I shall see. And, if it's interesting, I'll take you along next time.'

The next day, just as seven o'clock was striking from the church of the Capucines, Gilles entered the Place Louis-le-Grand where a huge bronze equestrian statue of Louis XIV was caracoling under a deep layer of snow, and knocked on the door of number nineteen, from which house various members of the vast Lecoulteux family conducted their banking operations. It was also the Paris residence of the two bankers, Lecoulteux de la Noraye and his cousin Lecoulteux de Cantelou.

Gilles received his usual welcome and his horse was taken round to the banker's stables while he himself joined Lecoulteux in the latter's carriage.

'I admire you for going about on horseback in this weather,' the banker said, arranging a thick fox fur rug over his silk clad legs. 'I should be afraid of freezing to death.'

'We military men are tough,' Gilles said, laughing. 'Now tell me, my dear Sir, whose house is this you are taking me to in the Rue Neuve St Gilles?'

'Aha! You are intrigued. It belongs to a charming friend of mine, the Comtesse de la Motte Valois. She keeps a most agreeable salon, especially now that the Queen's kindness has relieved a genuine descendant of the kings of France of her disgraceful poverty.'

'She was poor?'

'Horribly. She and her sister were taken in as children by the admirable Marquise de Boulainvilliers, the Provost of Paris' late wife, who took their education in hand and married Jeanne to the Comte de la Motte, a delightful and high-spirited cavalryman, but without a feather to fly with. They had some trouble making both ends meet in their early days, but such charming young people! They were befriended by Cardinal Louis de Rohan first and he gave them some assistance. I, too, have done what I could but of course without her Majesty's great kindness and protection they would not be where they are today.'

'Oh, so things are better with them now?'

'Very much, especially of late. The husband is in the Guard of the Comte d'Artois, and Jeanne's brother—'

'Jeanne?'

'The Countess. You really do not know her at all, I see?'

'Not at all,' Gilles said truthfully. 'I have heard of the Countess but I have never spoken to her.'

'That is odd, because it was she who suggested to me that she would like to see you at her house. Of course, it is true that you are one of our magnificent American heroes and you, in particular, are surrounded by an aura of legend that excites all our romantically-minded ladies. Madame de la Motte must have heard of you and wished all the more ardently to lure you to her house because you are said to be hard to get.'

'But how did she know of our acquaintance?'

'I think I must plead guilty there. I am a frequent visitor and I daresay I may have mentioned that I knew you. You do not mind, I hope?'

'Not in the least. It is always a pleasure to meet charming people.'

'And a very lovely woman! She is, you will see, irresistible. Such grace and charm! Her sister lives with her but she is much less lovely. It's a very good family, of course. Jeanne's brother is a chevalier of St Louis and in the navy. He commands a frigate—'

Jean-Jacques Lecoulteux was an extremely nice man but a fearful chatterbox, not a particularly good fault in a banker. Once launched, there was no stopping him and Gilles let him run on in praise of the St Rémy de Valois and the La Mottes while he sank into his own thoughts. It was odd, none the less, he reflected, that this woman should no sooner be back in Paris, for she had certainly returned not many days before, than she should be expressing a wish to meet him. She was

299

almost certainly the person who had written the pink note, although he had wondered for a moment whether it could have come from Cagliostro.

But then the woman knew Judith, might even be her friend, and apart from the Italian, there was no one but she and Madame de Balbi who could have news of her. What mattered was to find Judith without troubling too much about the means by which news reached him.

Bowing over the little ringed hand she offered him, on the threshold of an elegant salon hung with figured silk on a blue ground, Gilles surprised himself with the thought that Lecoulteux's praise of her beauty was to a great extent justified.

In the golden light of innumerable pink candles, the resemblance to Judith was less obvious. She was older, for one thing, and the lines of her face were softer than the girl's. Nor had she Mademoiselle de Saint-Mélaine's imperious little carriage of her head, or the almost transparent brilliance of her complexion, or the diamond sparkle of her black eyes. Madame de la Motte's eyes were blue, filled with a real flirtatiousness and a feigned innocence that he found unendearing. But he had no fault to find with the lovely bosom, revealed rather than concealed by the foam of black lace low on her shoulders and the handsome gold and topaz necklace which matched her earrings and the bracelets gleaming on her arms.

'I am grateful to Monsieur Lecoulteux de la Noraye for persuading you to come to us, Sir. It is not a privilege you are disposed to grant to everyone, I hear.'

'You are too kind, Madame, in treating a visit from a mere Guards officer as a privilege. You had only to ask. Who could refuse anything to so lovely a lady?'

'As to that, we shall see. Come and be introduced.'

She laid one slender hand on his arm and drew him farther into the lighted rooms filled with silk- and velvet-clad figures, the great majority of them men. There, in the big square mirror above the flaming hearth, Gilles saw his own blue and silver reflection coming to meet him, a smiling woman in black and gold on his arm whose white-powdered head seemed disposed at any moment to rest on his shoulder. The tense expression on his own tanned face, made all the grimmer by his white wig, took him aback. He forced himself to smile so that none of those present should guess at the vague unease, or rather the instinctive mistrust which had taken possession of him the moment Jeanne had placed her hand on his sleeve.

He was introduced to the Countess's sister, 'Mademoiselle de St Rémy de Valois', a plump, somewhat faded blonde with none of her sister's piquant charm, but who seemed nevertheless to have succeeded in attaching to herself a good-looking young man with a pair of enigmatic green eyes, dressed in a rather shabby uniform. This, Gilles was told, was 'our dear Marie-Anne's accepted lover, a nice young man from Provence. His name is the Vicomte Paul de Barras.'

About a dozen people were gathered round the tables set out in the main room. At one large one, a taciturn banker was dealing out cards and counters for faro, while at a number of smaller ones those who preferred were sitting down to whist or Pope Joan. But apart from the countess and her sister, the only woman present was a withered elderly spinster with a roving eye and an amazing cap with flame-coloured ribbons who introduced herself as 'Mademoiselle Colson, the countess's reader – when she has time to read, and a distant cousin.'

The men belonged to the worlds of high administration and finance. In addition to the husband, who was good-looking in a foppish way, talked a good deal about himself, smiled too much and was, Gilles decided, fundamentally antipathetic, they included the Intendant of Champagne Rouillé d'Orfeuil, the Comte de Saisseval, a compulsive gambler, the Receiver General Dorcy, and a high court judge, the Abbé de Calbris. There was one soldier, but one of consequence, the Comte d'Estaing. Gilles stared at him in amazement, wondering what the hero of Grenada, a general abruptly transformed into an admiral by royal decree, could be doing in this company. There was evidently a premium on warriors from the American war in the Rue Neuve St Gilles.

Jeanne's voice, more softly cooing than ever, roused him from his brief reverie.

'And here is one of our dearest friends, the Chevalier Reteau de Vilette, a most talented writer and a charming poet.'

Gilles found himself bowing politely to the foppish secretary, more foppish than ever tonight in an astonishing bright blue coat with gold buttons. At close quarters, however, he was able to see that the man's build was almost equal to his own and that the dainty poet had hands like a navvy.

'There's one they could do with in the galleys,' he caught himself thinking.

The last person Gilles met in this odd collection was a monk, as incongruous a figure in this polite gaming den as a virgin in a house of ill fame. But Father Loth, Superior of the Minimes in the Place Royal, seemed surprisingly at ease among the players and described himself as 'a friend of the family and confessor to the Countess Jeanne'.

'Are your sins so grave, Countess, that you need to have your confessor constantly at hand?' Gilles whispered in his hostess's pretty ear.

She laughed and cast down her eyes.

'Are we not all of us sinners, Chevalier?' she sighed. 'We live in such difficult times that a great many of the things we do every day must be offensive to Our Lord.'

'Such as gaming, for instance?'

'How could I imagine that gaming offended God when the greatest of his servants do not disdain it? Look there!'

As she spoke, she released his arm at last, a good deal to Gilles' relief, oddly enough. Perhaps it was the way in which she had trumpeted his name to every corner of the room, as though making sure that no one present should forget it, that he had not cared for. She was making, he saw, for the doorway, framed in which now stood the impressive figure of the Cardinal de Rohan.

The handsome prelate was dressed as he had been for his visit to Cagliostro, but his face which had been strained and tense on that occasion, was now illumined by a smile which enveloped the young woman before him in a look of extraordinary delight and affection.

'My dear Countess! You are back again at last! We have missed you extremely!'

As the young woman bent to kiss the cardinal's ring, Gilles, who had joined Lecoulteux near the fireplace, could not help overhearing what the Abbé de Calbris, standing with his back to him, was murmuring to his neighbour.

'He may have missed her, but I'll warrant his purse hasn't.

Our lovely Jeanne is costing him a fortune. She's had this house completely done up in the last four months!'

'And you think it's the cardinal who—'

'Of course. Jeanne is his mistress. The whole world knows it.'

'They say, though, that the Queen has been exceedingly generous.'

'The Queen? She never has enough money. Besides, the Polignacs wouldn't see this sort of money going to any but themselves and their friends.'

Now that the principal guest had arrived, accompanied by a friend, the Baron de Planta, and a young secretary, introduced as Ramon de Carbonnières, the serious business of the evening could begin. It did not escape Gilles that the fair Jeanne had not considered it worthwhile to present him to the cardinal. She had, he thought, been in something of a hurry to settle His Eminence to a foursome of whist with Admiral D'Estaing, Baron de Planta and the Abbé de Calbris, allowing him almost no time to talk to any of the other persons in the room.

Gilles himself was preparing to join Lecoulteux at the faro table when the alarmingly dressed Mademoiselle Colson spoke to him.

'You are a young man, Chevalier, and your eyes are good. I wonder, will you help me?'

'Gladly, mademoiselle. I am yours to command.'

'Oh, thank you. Then will you see if you can see my spectacles anywhere? I am always losing them and I cannot see a thing without them. So, as to playing, you see . . .'

She followed him as he toured the room, peering on top of tables, underneath sideboards. on the mantelshelf. Suddenly, as they had their heads together over the shelves of a small bookcase, he heard her mutter quickly: 'Find some excuse to leave and go away from here at once! Something unpleasant will happen if you stay.'

There was no alteration to the smile on Gilles' face as he whispered back: 'What do you mean?'

'I do not know. I heard only a few words. But what I do know is that there are those here who mean you no good.'

Already, she was moving away and in her hands,

half-hidden by her black mittens, he could see the spectacles they had ostensibly been searching for.

'There, what an angel you are!' she exclaimed aloud. 'Now go along and play and pardon me for holding you up.'

Gilles hesitated for an instant. So Winkleried had been right first of all. The pink note was a trap, laid, it seemed, by the Countess. She must have learned by some means or other, that he was her enemy and had determined to be revenged.

What the kindly little lady with the eager, inquisitive face and bright brown eyes had told him was clearly good advice, but he disliked the idea of running away, and especially from a woman. Moreover it was possible, even now, that he might learn something about Judith. Finally, he had his sword and knew how to use it and in the last resort was determined to sell his life dearly.

The room was filling up. More people were arriving. It would have been the simplest thing in the world to slip out without being seen but that he was reluctant to look a fool in front of Lecoulteux. So Gilles smiled reassuringly at Mademoiselle Colson, who was peering at him anxiously over her fan, and strolling over to the table where the banker had kept a place for him, he took a louis from his pocket and placed it on the table and tried to take an interest in the game, but without much success. Gaming, to Gilles, was no more than a pastime while for most of the others, Lecoulteux in particular, it was a passion which brought a flush to their cheeks and a gleam into their eyes.

Gilles had the usual beginner's luck and before long the little heap of coins in front of him was beginning to increase.

'I told you chance would smile on you,' his companion remarked.

'Nobody more surprised than I am.'

'Then you ought to stop now,' advised his left-hand neighbour. It was the young Vicomte de Barras who was paying such marked attention to the apathetic Mademoiselle de St Rémy de Valois. He was evidently better endowed with quarterings than with actual cash and it was almost certainly the smart new appearance of the house which attracted him, but his curious combination of shyness and arrogance was not without its charm.

'Stop? Why?'

'Because chance is more capricious even than a pretty woman. This is the first time you have played, I think?'

'Is it so obvious?'

'No, not really, but everyone's luck is good the first time. You can see from mine, that we have been acquainted for too long,' he added with a grin that suddenly restored to its real age, which was twenty-nine, a face that for all its handsome features and fair curling hair was already marked by loose living. His slender hand brushed the cloth in front of him, obstinately bare of coins.

'If you are leaving, I will come with you,' he said again, but with a sigh which spoke volumes for his reluctance to do so.

Gilles divided his own pile into two.

'I'll share with you,' he said on a sudden impulse.

Barras' green eyes widened. 'Are you crazy? You've never let me! I may be a Captain Sharp—'

'Nonsense! Anyway, I'll run the risk. You know, I can't really bring myself to believe that all this is truly mine. And besides that, well, you bear a name I learned to respect in America, at Newport.'

'But I wasn't there!' the other said, a mixture of defiance and regret in his voice.

'I knew an Admiral de Barras though, at Newport.'

'My uncle. The family hero. I, on the other hand, am the black sheep. While he was winning fame in America, I was getting eaten by mosquitoes in Pondicherry, and not exactly finding the treasure of Golconda for my pains.'

'You are a comrade-in-arms, at all events. So take it! You can pay me back one day when your luck is in.'

The young Provençal's chilly, sardonic face softened into something that was almost warmth.

'I can only think you must be a saint,' he said. 'But I'll thank you and try to pay you back for it somehow.'

The eagerness with which he fell to play once more spoke for his delight. Miraculously, his luck changed and after an hour he was able to pay Gilles back the sum he had borrowed.

'You're better than a damned mascot, my friend,' he said, offering his hand. 'I'll not soon forget this.'

'No one here would ever wish to forget Monsieur de

Tournemine.' The Countess's voice spoke pleasantly from behind them. 'Rather it is he, I think, who in the excitement of play is forgetting his hostess, one who has not so far had a chance to exchange more than a few words with the Falcon and is dying to remedy that.'

Gilles was on his feet in a moment.

'No, really, Countess! You can't carry him off like this,' Barras protested. 'This is too bad! Just when his luck is in!'

The Countess's fan tapped him lightly on the cheek.

'You are impertinent, Vicomte, and if you wish to become my brother I would advise you to go to work a different way. For all you know, I may have much better luck to offer him.'

The Vicomte shrugged. 'It all depends, my dear, on the kind of offer you have in mind,' he said audaciously. 'No one denies a lovely woman has treasures compared to which the bank's riches are but dust. Ah well, good luck, Chevalier, and come back to us soon.'

'Let us leave the rude fellow, Chevalier, and go and drink a glass of *Giroflée du Daphiné* together, or perhaps a cup of coffee. There is nothing like sharing one's bread and salt for making friends.'

They moved off together towards the dining room where refreshments had been laid out on a large oval table adorned with a pyramid of fruit and a pair of fine crystal and silver ewers. Gilles accepted a cup of coffee and waited for Jeanne to begin the conversation. But she seemed in no hurry and had not in fact uttered a single word since they quitted the table, merely smiling graciously and waving her black lace fan with slow, rhythmic movements as they strolled through the two rooms.

She, too, was drinking coffee and her blue eyes watched him attentively over the gilded rim of her cup, but still she did not speak. The yellow candlelight accentuated the green in her eyes and made her look more than ever like a pretty cat playing delicately with a mouse.

'Very well, Countess,' Gilles said at last, smiling easily, 'what do you want to talk to me about?'

'About you – and me. Why do you dislike me when you do not know me?' she asked point blank. 'Is it because of my resemblance, my very strong resemblance, to the one you love?'

'Who told you I disliked you, Madame?'

'No one. It is – an impression I have.'

'A mistaken impression. How could I dislike you when we have not spoken before tonight?'

'We have not spoken before, but we have seen one another. One evening, in this very street, do you recall? You seemed to be waiting for something and I thought, in my innocence, that it was for me, that you were – attracted to me. Whereas in reality it was someone else you were waiting for, someone who came here later, with whom you are in love. You do love her, don't you, that Julie de Latour?'

'If I had met you first, I might have loved you,' Gilles said, surprised by the unexpected note of sadness in her voice.

She shrugged her white shoulders. 'No, you would not. I am not the sort of woman who can be loved by a man of honour, am I?'

'Madame, your husband—'

The cup she was holding rattled suddenly and she set it down. Unshed tears were standing, bright, in her eyes.

'Don't talk of him,' she said in a bitter undertone. 'He is the evil genius of the girl I was then, and perhaps may be still, but what else could I expect? Have you ever known abject poverty, Chevalier?'

'Not abject, no, Madame. But I have been very poor.'

'It is not the same. When you are hungry, cold, when it is snowing as it is tonight and you have no recourse against it, and you are only a little girl, that is not the kind of thing you ever forget. To stop that nightmare recurring you would do any-thing.'

Startled by her unhappiness and a prey to the pity which any form of suffering always aroused in him, he reached out and gently took the hand which Jeanne was clenching on the fragile sticks of her fan.

'You are a long way from poverty now. You will never see it again. You have friends who are rich and powerful—'

'What are rich, powerful friends compared to true love?' she gasped, almost furiously. 'You have a love like that, guard it, guard it with your life! Now go, Chevalier, go at once. Do not stay another moment in this house. My husband – he hates you. He fears you, I do not know why.'

'Your husband? What have I done to him?'

'Nothing, I daresay. But with him that is enough.'

She seemed all at once so feverishly anxious that he smiled reassuringly. Was this the danger Mademoiselle Colson had spoken of? If so, it was not so great after all, although La Motte might well take on the appearance of a bogyman to an elderly spinster.

'I am going,' he said, 'and thank you. But wasn't there something you wished to tell me, or was the pink note merely a trap?'

'The note – oh my God, yes! I nearly forgot! No, it was not simply a trap. They have succeeded in getting Julie out of the hands of that monster Cagliostro, that accursed magician who was using her for his devilish experiments, only—'

'*They*? Who are *they*?'

'That I cannot tell you, but she is obliged to remain in hiding, for the devil is powerful and cunning. He seems to have eyes everywhere.'

'Tell me where she is, only that and I will go.'

She cast a glance around her as though fearing to be over-heard, then spread her fan and waved it gently, while the smile returned to her lips.

'Number fifteen, Rue de Cléry, in the house of a man named Beausire, a police officer. But for the love of God let no one know that you know. They are watching us.' Aloud, she went on: 'I am so sorry you have to leave us, Chevalier, but you will come again, won't you?'

She gave him her hand and he took it and kissed it.

'Without fail, Countess. I shall be delighted to come whenever you are pleased to ask me.'

He turned back into the other room. The play was at its height but he could hardly leave without a word to Lecoulteux. He went up quietly behind him.

'Must you go so soon?' the banker said. 'It's a shame, just as things are getting exciting.'

'I have to get back. I'm on duty at the palace early in the morning.'

'Then at least take my coach back to the Place Louis-Le-Grand and tell the man to return for me later. The weather is diabolical.'

Gilles thanked him, bade a general farewell to the company

and returned the hearty handshake he received from Barras, accompanied by a strong, southern: 'Until our next meeting, then!'

On his way to the door, he had to pass quite close to Cardinal Rohan who, apparently tiring of the game, had risen and was strolling with his hostess towards the haven of a window embrasure. Gilles bowed and, without meaning to, caught something that Jeanne, now all smiles once more, was saying to her clerical admirer.

'I assure you, Eminence, my woman's curiosity couldn't resist it. I have been to look at Messrs Boehmer and Bassange's famous necklace. What a miracle! And such a pity our Queen was not able to have it.'

In another minute, Gilles was leaning back in the banker's warm, scented carriage being driven to the Rue de Cléry, without the faintest suspicion that in another vehicle only a little way ahead was the elegant Reteau de Vilette, into whose ear Jeanne had whispered a few words while the Chevalier was saying his farewells at the card table.

He no longer knew quite what to think of Jeanne. Was she really, as she had given him to understand, a victim rather than the shameless adventuress she had appeared to him in the gardens of the Trianon and of Versailles? If that were so, she must possess the most astonishing powers of self-control to have played her part to such perfection. But then perhaps poverty, that ruthless underminer of human dignity, was capable of leading astray a weak creature who, if born to comfort and security, would never have erred? The real guilt in this far-reaching plot, some fragments of which he had begun to glimpse, was not with the woman he had seen tonight, her eyes brimming with tears, not even if she were a willing tool, the real guilt lay with the man who was so coldly manipulating her, the greedy, ambitious and unscrupulous Prince, the cool, calculating brain who sat in his palace and wove, like some patient spider, the deadly web in which he hoped to entangle his own brother, unaware that the crown he meant to win from it would be soiled in the process. If, through her help, Judith were restored to him, then, Gilles thought, he might try to help Jeanne to escape from what for her must, after all, be a kind of nightmare.

When he reached the Rue de Cléry, it was not difficult to identify the house of the man Beausire. It was a tall, narrow building in an old-fashioned, unpretentious style, sandwiched in between a grand town house dating from the previous century but newly renovated and the shuttered premises of a cloth merchant. Having found the place, Gilles sent the carriage back for Lecoulteux, trusting that when his business there was over he would be able to find a vehicle for hire at the stand not far from the Porte St Denis, in the nearby boulevard.

The street in which Corneille had lived almost up to the time of his death had once been a place of ill-repute but it had changed a great deal since the Marquise de Pompadour had done it the honour of being born there. The majority of the houses were, if not luxurious, at least perfectly respectable. Many of them had gardens and the lanterns strung across the flagway, making big, shifting patches of pale light on the snow, were all of them working, which could not be said of every street.

Once the coach had vanished round the corner into the boulevard, there was not a sound to be heard. It was after ten o'clock and most of the inhabitants must be asleep but, in the house in which Gilles was interested, a little light filtered underneath a shutter on the top floor, while from the larger one next door there came the muffled music of a harp.

Gilles walked up to the door of number fifteen and raised the bronze knocker. Then he let it fall again, softly, taking care it did not make a sound. He had just noticed that the door itself was ajar. Beyond it lay a dark passage leading into a courtyard which would have been invisible but for the layer of snow that lay there.

He got out flint and steel and struck a brief glimmer of light. It showed one door in the wall of the passage but it was made of crude boards roughly knocked together and led, presumably, only to a cellar or wood store. Gilles walked past it into the courtyard.

Here, on the far side, there was a doorway reached by a pair of worn steps, hollow with use, and a ruddy glow of light from the fanlight above it. Opposite, forming the front of the building, a stairway opening gaped, but Gilles made naturally for the light. The people who lived there appeared to be still up and

310

should at least be able to tell him where to find the man Beausire.

He knocked gently and then more loudly, but there was no answer. Yet there must be someone there, or else why the light? Gilles knocked again, resting his left hand on the handle which turned under it. The door opened with only the faintest squeak and he found himself in a small entrance hall, meagrely furnished with two caned chairs and a chest on which was a brass candlestick with a lighted candle in it.

He walked inside, his footsteps loud on the red-tiled floor, hoping that someone would come, but nothing happened.

The passage ended in a closed door and there was another opposite the chest with a line of light visible below it. On this, Gilles rapped.

'Come in,' a voice called faintly.

The door opened into a fair-sized room evidently used for both sitting and eating. The furniture amounted to no more than a table, a few chairs with worn fabric seats, a sideboard, three armchairs covered in strident chintz, a small chest of drawers and a clock. A woman was sitting in one of the armchairs, her back turned to the door and her feet resting on the fender before the flaming hearth.

'Madame,' Gilles began, 'I apologize for this intrusion, especially at this late hour, but I am looking for the house of Monsieur Beausire.'

The woman got up slowly, supporting herself with both hands on the arms of her chair, as though she found it difficult to move. She was tall and fair and when she turned to face him, Gilles bit back an exclamation of surprise, for this was the woman he had seen in the Bosquet de Vénus, the woman who bore such an extraordinary resemblance to the Queen. She was, he also saw, scantily clothed in a transparent muslin wrapper which gaped open in the front.

'This is the house, Monsieur. May I ask your business?'

She spoke almost inaudibly and was plainly in a state of terror. But before Gilles could begin to ask himself the reason, a curtain apparently masking the entrance to some other room was lifted and two men appeared. Both wore black masks and had swords in their hands. At the same time, three more emerged from what was presumably the kitchen.

311

Gilles stood for a moment rooted to the spot. The woman, however, uttered a feeble cry and flung herself forward, as though to shield him with her body, with an unconvincing display of anguish.

'Fly! Fly if you love me!' she gasped in a stifled moan.

Gilles thrust her off so roughly that she fell back into a chair which collapsed with her. He drew his sword and held it, point downwards, before him.

'What is the meaning of this?' he demanded coldly.

One of the two who had appeared first advanced on him in a parody of wrathful indignation.

'Vile seducer! That is for you to tell us. I have suspected something of this sort all along but now I have you red-handed, my turtle doves! You gentlemen will bear me witness that I have just caught my wife, half-naked, entertaining her lover.'

There was a murmur of agreement. Gilles laughed.

'I suppose you are this fellow Beausire? Well, my lad, I can't compliment you on your acting. As for this woman, I've no idea who she is. She's handsome enough, I grant, but what am I supposed to do with her?'

'You hear!' the other man roared. 'You hear! I not only catch him with my wife in his arms—'

He broke off, springing backwards with a yell of pain. Gilles' sword arm had flashed out and severed the strings of his mask. It dropped to the floor, revealing a face which might have been handsome but for a certain coarseness, exaggerated by all the signs of habitual drunkenness. Blood was dripping from a long cut in one cheek.

'If I'm to be accused of making a cuckold of you, my fine fellow, I may as well know what you look like! Besides, you're making a deal too much noise.' He let his eyes rove over the masked group before him. 'Well? Are you sticking to this nonsensical story? You're all here to avenge this paltry fellow's honour, are you? Myself, I don't believe a word of it, but let's have some show of spirit, devil take you! You're five to one – you might at least give up the sordid pretence!'

'Look again,' said the man who had come in with Beausire. 'There are eight of us – and more out in the passage.'

More men were crowding in from the kitchen and Gilles

knew that he had small chance now of ever leaving the house alive, especially now that he could identify the man who had just spoken.

'Oh, so it's you, is it, Monsieur d'Antraigues? You might have spared yourself the mask. I know you well enough. So you're not satisfied with insulting the Crown. You must needs turn murderer too? Well you might have found some better pretext than a trumped up liaison with a creature of low birth married to a rogue!'

'I do not care to leave my debts unpaid. And who said anything about murder? You have a sword. Defend yourself!'

'That is just what I mean to do. But perhaps you will tell me first who it is dislikes me enough to go to all this trouble? You can't all be working for our dear Countess Jeanne? Especially not you, a d'Antraigues?'

'And why not?' put in another voice, which Gilles had no trouble recognizing. 'Why should a d'Antraigues not serve a Valois?'

'Well well! So you are here, too, Monsieur Jack-of-all-trades Secretary? The trap was well laid, indeed. Make my compliments to your mistress. To think I believed for a moment that she meant to have me cut down in her own house! How foolish of me. But you must admit, she is a splendid actress! And now, my fine gentlemen, what shall we do? Must I ask you to make way for me?'

The light, bantering tone finally got the better of d'Antraigues' temper.

'Have at him, men! For the honour of the Duc de Chartres! Remember the money he promised you!'

'The Duc de Chartres!' Gilles echoed, genuinely taken aback. 'And what the devil has he to do with this? Ah well, since we're fallen among madmen, let's act accordingly. Have at you, gentlemen!'

He set his blade whirling in a flashing circle which made the first of his attackers fall back hastily. Grabbing a chair with his free hand, he tossed it at one who subsided, struck on the head. After that, moving backwards to the wall beside the door, he got a grip on one of the carved angles of the sideboard and with a terrific wrench hurled it to the ground. It fell with a crash of breaking china and provided him with an effective bulwark on his right.

'My sideboard! My china!' Beausire yelped in such grotesque anguish that Gilles laughed aloud.

'Send the bill to the Duke of Chartres, since it seems to be his party!'

Then, taking no further notice of the man, he set about carving his way to the door, using the sideboard as a shield. But there were three men in front, each one intent on spitting him like a wild boar in its lair. A swift lunge pierced the throat of one, followed by a quick withdrawal and a second lunge to reach the chest of another, and then an unexpected leap for the doorway brought his foot in contact with his third adversary's groin. The man doubled up with a howl of agony.

He was out in the passage then, but his satisfaction was short-lived for another six or seven barred the way out to the court.

'Oh Lord,' Gilles found himself praying, 'now is the time to ask forgiveness for my sins because if I leave it any longer I'm going to be too late!'

He got his back up against the wall so that at least he would die with his face to his enemies. One blade drove into his shoulder and he got a cut on the thigh from another but he managed to account for four of his assailants. In another moment it would all be over. Already, he could feel the warm blood pulsing inside his shirt.

Then suddenly a shout rang out: 'Blessed St Anne! 'Tis he! This way, Sir! I am with you!'

Stupefied, Gilles saw that one of the masked men in the passage had turned on his companions, had struck one in the back and leaped to join him.

'What the devil's got into you?' one of the others was snarling.

'I was paid to slay a villain, not a man of worth, and one I call friend! Come, Sir, you are hurt but between the two of us, we may do it yet.'

With that he launched himself like a tiger against his former friends, giving Gilles the relief he needed to reach the court-yard.

'But who are you?' the Chevalier gasped. 'And why did you decide to help me?'

'Remember the Pont Neuf? You saved me from the recruiting sergeant. I am Gildas, the Breton.' With that he snatched off his mask and flung it to the ground.

The fight continued in the courtyard, swirling round the two who now fought back to back, guarding each other's rear. With a cut in his right arm, Gilles was fighting left-handed now. He knew that he had been hit twice more, though he did not know how badly, but he knew that he was weakening. Loss of blood, probably . . . It seemed as though d'Antraigues had brought an army against him. The mass of swords before him was so thick that it was like a nest of angry vipers into which he must keep driving his own sword tirelessly to clear a way. Gildas, too, was fighting like a lion. Gilles caught himself wondering where the devil the boy had learned to use a sword. He'd almost certainly spent time in the galleys. The snow around them was red with blood and strewn with bodies.

'Try to get to the street,' Gilles panted. 'We may get help there.'

Together they broke and ran for the passage.

'Look out!' It was d'Antraigues shouting. 'They're getting clear!'

'Coward! Fight yourself, damn you, instead of getting others to do your dirty work!' Gilles turned, roaring, raging mad, to face three oncoming swords and cover Gildas whose footsteps he could hear clattering down the passage. He lunged again and heard a yell of pain, echoed by another of pure terror.

'This man is the devil himself!'

'As you say!' Gilles gasped and ran him through the chest. The falling body blocked the passage briefly, giving him a moment's respite. He hurried down the passage as fast as his failing legs would allow, but as he came level with the wooden door he had noticed before it opened and a man rose up behind it, a dagger in his hand. An arm rose and fell, striking at Gilles' back. He cried out hoarsely and staggered but did not fall. His legs, buckling under him, continued to move of their own accord until he stumbled out into the street and into the arms of

Gildas, who was on his way back after dealing with the fellow who had been left there on guard.

Gilles' eyes were glazing. As through a mist, he saw the Breton's anxious face and tried to smile.

'I ... I have it!' he breathed. 'Farewell. . . . my friend.'

Then, slipping from the other's exhausted grasp, he sprawled face downwards in the snow, just as d'Antraigues and the remainder of his men poured from the deadly trap they had set for the Falcon.

'Help!' Gildas shouted at the top of his voice. 'Help! Murder!'

A sword caught him on the shoulder. He, too, was wounded in several places, but none deadly. But he knew that he could not hold out alone against the mob of his enemies, for depleted as they were their fury was all the greater. And so, before the whole pack could fall on him, Gildas slid to the ground with a well-simulated gurgle, covering, as he did so, as much of the Chevalier's prostrate body as he could and praying desperately that their attackers would not stay to make quite sure of them.

'Dead, both of them,' said a voice. 'Let's go!'

'Better make sure.' That was d'Antraigues' chilly tones. 'Run them through again.'

But Gildas' shouts had woken the street and already windows were being flung open. Shutters banged and heads appeared. People were calling for the watch.

'No time now,' said the leader of the band. 'We'll have the watch from the Porte St Denis down on us any moment.'

They fled like a flock of sinister crows down the whitened street, dragging their wounded with them, shunning the boulevards and lighted places. With a feeling of indescribable relief, Gildas realized that he was saved. He struggled up painfully, hoping that the weight of his body had not extinguished any spark of life remaining in the tall figure he had tried to protect. He wanted to weep but could not. He tried to pray, but no words would come. Kneeling there in the snow, he was unaware of the cold or of his own wounds, and so exhausted that his limbs refused to obey him. He could not even call out.

There was a voice calling, though. 'Hold on,' it cried. 'I'm with you!'

316

In the same instant, a horseman came swiftly up the short slope from the boulevard and flung himself to the ground beside the kneeling boy.

'Sweet God in heaven!' he said grimly, as he saw the body in its ripped and bloodsoaked uniform lying in the snow. 'I'm too late. Is he dead?'

'I don't know, Monsieur. I don't like to move him.'

'Quite right. We must have help.'

With that, the Vicomte Paul de Barras strode to the door of the big house next door and rang a loud peal on the bell. The strains of music could still be heard from within. At the same time, he shouted in a voice so stentorian that within seconds it had brought half a dozen worthy citizens out into the snow in their nightcaps, coats and blankets thrown over their nightshirts, giving rise to a great deal of horrified outcry but no very practical assistance. Barras learned only that a gang of men had tried to murder the gentleman and the lad kneeling by him and had then run away.

'Confound it,' Barras was muttering to himself, 'I knew there was something wrong when Lecoulteux's coachman said he'd brought him to the Rue de Cléry, to the house of that rogue Beausire. If only – Ah, here you are at last!'

The front door had been opened at length and from it poured a crowd of men and women whose appearance, for the time and season, was odd in the extreme. Underneath the sumptuous fur coats draped about their shoulders, every one of them was dressed in a toga or a Grecian tunic of the finest Lyon silk. For the house belonged to the celebrated painter, Lebrun, and his no less famous young wife, Madame Vigée-Lebrun, painter of Marie-Antoinette and of all the loveliest ladies of her Court. The couple were in fact, that night, engaged in holding one of their well-publicized Antique Soirées, at which the guests endeavoured to forget the civilized graces of the eighteenth century and live instead in the days of Periclean Athens.

'I don't know what you're playing at,' Barras snapped, glaring at them with a sort of outrage, 'but you'd be better occupied taking note of what's going on on your doorstep. There is an officer of the King's being murdered here.'

Lebrun rounded on the flock of servants now hurrying forward with lights. 'You there! Not so much light and a little

317

more help, if you please. Bring a stretcher, and blankets! Carry these wounded men into the house. And the rest of you can go home,' he added in a lordly fashion to the neighbours who did not need telling twice, being only too anxious to return to the warmth of their own homes.

With infinite care, Gilles' bleeding body was lifted onto a stretcher and carried into the bright, flower-filled entrance hall. Gildas, who seemed half-dazed, was helped in after him. Barras directed operations with as much authority as if he had been in his own house.

'Someone send for a surgeon,' he commanded.

'I am one,' volunteered a fair young man whose fresh, open countenance, improbably surmounted by a wreath of roses, had that moment emerged from within the drawing-room, followed by an even younger lady whose disordered headgear provided a sufficient indication of the kind of converse which had been occupying them until that moment.

'Then you can get to work,' Barras said peremptorily.

The young man pulled off his rose wreath and pushed his way firmly through the crowd of Athenians gathered round the stretcher, beside which Madame Vigée-Lebrun was on her knees, wiping the snow and dirt from Gilles' pallid face with a delicate handkerchief.

'Oh, but he is so handsome!' a woman sighed.

'What a shame,' said another. 'So young! But is he really dead?'

'How do you expect me to find out,' the young physician said irritably, 'if you don't let me get near him.'

'Good God! Why, I know him!' the cry came from an exquisite creature whose draperies of heavy silk, clasped with a brooch of emeralds, did full justice to her lovely figure.

Aglae d'Hunolstein made swiftly for Gildas, who had been led meanwhile into a sort of dining-room, in which the usual table had been replaced by a number of couches arranged like the spokes of a wheel, and made to sit by the fire. A servant was helping him off with his torn and sodden black outer garment and Lebrun was pouring him a glass of wine.

'What happened?' the young woman asked in so peremptory a tone that it penetrated Gildas' stupefied mind. 'Who did this?'

The Breton looked up at her, a glimmer of life returning to his eyes.

'They said – they said it was the Duc de Chartres.'

Aglae cried out indignantly. 'But this is dreadful! Who could say such things? The Duke would never order such a murder, least of all of an officer of the King's! He is not mad!'

'I am of the same opinion, Madame,' Barras said, overhearing. 'I know the Duke. He is proud, violent and hot-tempered, but he is a true gentleman. If this young man had offended him, he might have sought satisfaction with the sword, but he would never have set ruffians to foully murder him. It were as well he should be warned of this. Oh, but I'll get to the bottom of it!'

A murmur of relief came from the hall. The young doctor appeared saying: 'He is not dead yet. But it is touch and go. I shall need a bedchamber and a proper bed for him if I am to examine him properly.'

The pretty face of the Queen's portrait painter went perfectly white.

'Here? Corvisart, are you mad? Until this affair is sorted out it could get us into trouble both with Versailles and the Palais-Royal. Is there nowhere else he could be taken? To, I don't know, to some friend's house, perhaps?'

'To mine,' Madame d'Hunolstein said crisply. 'There could be no better way of showing that Duke Philippe was in no way concerned in this attack. Can he be moved, Sir?'

Nicolas Corvisart shrugged. 'He'll have to be. In any event, he could die as easily while being carried upstairs.'

'Then let my carriage and servants be sent for at once.' She turned to the painters, husband and wife. 'I imagine it will not compromise you overmuch to provide blankets, furs and hot bricks to prevent him taking cold? You shall come also,' she added to Gildas, and then to the young physician: 'and you, too, Sir, I hope?'

'Only give me time to put on some more suitable garments, even for a disciple of Aesculapius. Where are you taking him, Madame?'

'I am living at present in the cottage called the Hermitage, attached to the Château de Bagnolet, which is the property of Monseigneur the Duc d'Orléans. If we go by the boulevards it won't take long.'

Minutes later, cocooned like a silkworm, Gilles was lying on the cream velvet cushions of a handsome carriage furnished with every attention necessary to the comfort of a delicate woman. Madame d'Hunolstein took her place, supporting the wounded man's head on her lap. Corvisart and Gildas, his wounds bandaged and himself wrapped in a borrowed fur-lined overcoat, occupied the forward seat and Barras mounted his horse once more.

'Hurry, Florentin!' the baroness besought her driver. 'Only try to avoid jolting him all you can.'

The coachman touched up the horses, shod for icy weather, with a light hand and the carriage slid rather than rolled forward along the boulevard where the braziers belonging to the various posts of the watch glowed intermittently. The front door of the Lebruns' house closed again and, next door, the man named Beausire set about ridding his rooms and courtyard of the litter of corpses, aided by the only one of his accomplices who had not deserted him. He had no wish to hang for the sake of a few pieces of gold. Happily for his peace of mind, it snowed again heavily during the night, covering over the bloodstains and other traces of the fight.

13

Aglae

The room looked like a field dressing station. Nicolas Corvisart was finishing bandaging Gilles' wounds and everywhere
was a litter of fresh lint, bloodied cloths and the remains of the
clothes which had been cut from his body. A chambermaid was
on her knees gathering the debris into a basket. The body,
stretched on a table for ease of working, had the beauty of an
antique marble and the tragic stillness of a cathedral monu-
ment. At either end of the table stood a servant in blue livery
holding up a branch of candles for the surgeon who was hard at
work, shirt-sleeves rolled up over muscular forearms. Seated
not far off, in a welter of white lace, Aglae d'Hunolstein, her
own face almost as pale as his, was gazing wide-eyed at the
shuttered features, now marked by an alarming bluish tinge.
The only sounds were the injured man's difficult breathing, the
occasional clatter of the surgeon's implements and, now and
then, the crack of a log in the fire.

'Will you be able to save him?' the woman asked softly at
last.

'Honestly, I don't know. He is in a bad way. If it were only
the four sword-cuts, I'd be sure of it, but the knife wound in
the back is far more serious, for the lung is touched. There is
mounting fever ...'

As he spoke, he was tapping lightly with two fingers on the
exposed chest, as though listening for some echo from within.

'What are you doing?' Aglae asked.

'I'm using a new method of examination invented by a
Viennese physician named Auenbrugger. My teacher, Desbois

de Rochefort, believes it to be an infinitely more precise means of investigation than palpation, in pulmonary infections in particular. It enables us to estimate the damage much more accurately. Have you succeeded in persuading the other victim to go to bed and take the soporific I prepared for him?'

'Unfortunately no. He insisted on going away at all costs. He spoke of an invalid sister who would be wild with anxiety if he were not there in the morning and when I offered to send for her, he smiled in a most peculiar fashion and said if my people were to go to the place where he lives they would probably not come back alive. "The quarries of Montmartre are no place to walk by night, my lady," he said, and then added that he must go himself.'

'To Montmartre, in this snow? On foot and injured? It's madness! He'll be dead before he gets there.'

'Perhaps not. I gave him some warm clothes and a little money to get his sister away from that dreadful place. He is waiting for you downstairs now. My coachman will drop him at the Barrière des Martyrs after he has taken you home. And he has promised me to return.'

'Not on your life! We'll set him down before me. I want to be sure of his condition, or else I'm taking him to the Quarries myself.'

As he spoke, the young doctor was laying down his last implement. He walked over and washed his hands in the bowl of hot water a maidservant had ready for him, then came back and watched while two stalwart footmen lifted his patient and carried him carefully to the well-warmed bed. There his back was propped up on a pile of pillows to prevent him coughing up more blood, as he had done on his arrival at the Hermitage. Corvisart stood looking down at him for a moment, a frown on his face.

'You are anxious?' Madame d'Hunolstein asked.

'Yes, I don't deny it. I don't like his breathing and the fever is mounting too quickly. The time he spent in the snow after he was wounded could prove fatal. It might lead to pleurisy and I'm not sure I wouldn't rather have him cough up the blood than see it remain in the pulmonary cavity. At any rate I'll be paying a call on Baune, the chemist, first thing in the morning and I'll be back here with some drugs that may help. And, if I may, I'd like to bring Philippe Pelletan with me. He's the best surgeon we have and it may be advisable to perform a thoracentesis – that is, drawing off the fluid by means of a trocar – unless, of course, you'd prefer to have him in the hands of your own physician?'

'I haven't one. I enjoy excellent health, in general, and since the death of Tronchin, my admirable physician, I have not cared to entrust myself to his successor.'

'Very well. May I then advise you also to take some rest? A servant may easily keep an eye on the patient.'

'I would rather watch myself. In any case, I am not sleepy.'

Corvisart rolled down his sleeves, put on his coat and looked curiously at the young woman before him.

'Why are you doing this? You tell me you hardly know the fellow. You met him once in a restaurant, I think you said. And yet you are turning your whole household upside down for him. Is it merely to protect the reputation of the Orléans?'

Aglae jerked her lovely shoulders with a carelessness belied by the melancholy in her eyes.

'How should I know? Perhaps because there are times when I tire of a life devoted entirely to pleasure. It is so futile and, at times, lonely. My husband spends all his time on his estates in Lorraine, my sons are at school. While as to the thoughts of love which are no doubt in your mind, I may as well tell you my relations with the Duc de Chartres are more those of a valued friend than a sultan's concubine. So why should I not devote a little of my time to helping my fellow beings?'

The physician subdued a twitching lip as he reflected how readily a clever woman could arrive at such accommodations with her conscience. He also took care not to point out that the action would no doubt have been harder, though perhaps more meritorious, had the fellow being in question not been young and handsome. The fine figure of a man at present reposing beneath the bed's sky blue canopy would have been enough to rouse the sympathetic interest of any woman worthy of the name, regardless of age or social position. The only thing still in doubt was whether he would quit that bed for that of the lovely Aglae, or for the four boards of a coffin. Not only had

323

he so far not recovered consciousness but there were signs of an increasing feverishness which could soon lead to delirium.

      ·   ·   ·

When the injured man emerged from his coma later that night, no one was aware of it, least of all himself. He was in a raging fever that dried his lips and lit a scorching fire in his chest. Memories of the gory scene in the Rue de Cléry rose to the surface of his mind in incoherent fragments, mingled with more distant images of war and death. At other times he fell whirling into fiery chasms where boulders of intolerable weight came down on him to crush him and the screams of demon hordes rang in his ears. Hell itself seemed gaping before the tortured spirit, its ties with the body now stretched so painfully thin.

Caught in an endless series of terrifying nightmares, Gilles was still aware of the pain in his lacerated body. Every breath he took was a choking agony and the fire that was burning in him would not go out.

For days and nights, his whole being a prey to the violence of delirium, he battled unconsciously with death. The cries, supplications and entreaties wrenched from him by his fever terrified all those who came near him and blanched the face of the woman sitting motionless at his bedside. Sometimes, at grips with the phantoms in his mind, the wounded man would shriek out curses, challenges and accusations of so strange a nature that Aglae would rise anxiously and go to doors and windows, securing them so that the servants at least should not hear.

There were times, too, when the ragged voice would speak imploringly to one who was not there, a phantom whose name was Judith, addressing her in accents of such passionate, such heartrending love that the face of the silent watcher by the bed was wet with tears and her hand bruised from the clasp of those burning fingers. And other times, when she pressed both hands to her ears to shut out the sounds.

Then Pongo, who never left his master's chamber night or day, would come and take her gently by the arm and lead her into the adjoining salon and make her sit down in a chair.

'Bad sounds,' he would say. 'Dangerous. Caused by bad spirit. Woman lack strength to endure ...'

Winkleried and the Indian had arrived tempestuously some twelve hours after the event. Paul Barras had knocked up Lecoulteux at daybreak to get the injured man's address and had galloped all the way to Versailles to alert the young Breton's family, supposing him to have any. What he had found there was something quite as strong: in Mademoiselle Marjon, who burst into tears and rushed straight to the nearest church, not pausing even to put on her hat; in Pongo, who said nothing at all, only his face had turned grey; and lastly, in Winkleried, so distraught that he all but strangled the messenger in his eagerness to get at the truth.

With Barras to guide them, the two men had reached the Hermitage in time to meet the Duc de Chartres, then staying at the Château de Bagnolet and informed by Aglae, just coming out.

'I can only advise you to do as I am doing, gentlemen, and wait,' the Duke said, recognizing the Swiss at a glance. 'The doctors are with your friend now.' Then turning to Barras who, as a frequenter of the Palais-Royal, was an old acquaintance: 'I trust, Vicomte, that you will have assured these gentlemen that I had no hand in the base attempt on your friend's life? I am even now on my way to call on the Lieutenant of Police, Lenoir, to demand a full inquiry into this appalling business. I shall not rest until the perpetrators are under lock and key.'

'Monseigneur,' Ulrich-August said quickly, 'I think I speak for my friend Tournemine in begging your Highness to do no such thing. Indeed, it would be an unfair burden to lay on Monsieur Lenoir, who could never bring the crime home to its real culprit.'

'What's this? Are you saying—'

'That the real culprit is beyond the reach of the law?' Barras said, his eyes on the Baron's embarrassed face. 'For my part, I'm very willing to believe it.'

Phillipe of Orléans looked at all three men in turn and nodded.

'I see. Well, for the moment we'll confine ourselves to the tools, this Beausire for example. You've nothing against that, Barras?'

The Provençal laughed. 'Nothing at all. But I fear your

Highness will draw a blank there also. I know the fellow. He'll have made off while the going's good.'

The Prince sighed. 'Ah well, we shall just have to hope the victim survives and is able to enlighten us. It seems he recognized the leader of the men who attacked him, or so the young man who helped to save him claims, although he made nothing of the name he heard spoken.'

They were interrupted then by the arrival of Jean-Nicolas Corvisart and Philippe Pelletan, emerging from the sickroom. Madame d'Hunolstein was with them and all three looked so grave that each of those present felt a shock of fear.

'Well?' the Duke asked.

'We can only wait, Monseigneur,' Pelletan said. 'We shall do our best but the patient's life is in God's hands. His youth and strength are certainly his strongest weapons.'

Pongo, without speaking, walked straight into the bedroom. For a long moment, he stood looking at Gilles and then, before the Baroness's startled eyes, pulled off his wig, revealing his shaven crown and the single lock of black hair upon it. Next he ripped open his shirt and, taking the little leather bag containing his private charms which lay always against his chest, he placed it round the neck of the dying man.

'Me stay here by Lord Falcon,' he told the blinking woman austerely. 'Me with him until Great Spirit say live or die. If die, then Pongo die too.'

Thereupon he sat down cross-legged on the carpet at the foot of the bed, his back as straight as a ramrod and his arms folded on his chest, and embarked on a vigil which he interrupted only at rare intervals to satisfy the demands of a body which was only human or to soothe, by a word or a gesture, the Baroness's fears.

But if the presence of the Iroquois made a strong impression on the servants and surrounded the sickroom with an aura of mystical terror, Aglae herself soon grew accustomed to the sight of that still, bronze figure, erect at the foot of the bed, like some tutelary deity set there to ward off the approach of death. And during the long hours they spent, face to face, without a word being spoken, the woman drew a strange comfort from the long communion, for Pongo could make silence more eloquent than many words.

Winkleried, on the other hand, after that first day had completely vanished, telling Madame d'Hunolstein only that he expected to be absent for some time. He had not been seen since.

One night, when Gilles, in the grip of one of his terrible dreams, was threshing so wildly in his bed that Pongo could no longer hold him, the demons assailing his fevered mind left him suddenly. Their grinning faces gave place to a single, steady, glittering regard, a pair of huge eyes, dark and luminous, which pierced the injured man to his very soul and brought him relief by enabling him all at once to break free. It was as if his spirit suddenly liberated itself from the intolerable burden of the suffering flesh and soared above it, like a bird hovering over the fallen creature on the ground.

At that moment, Gilles saw himself lying there in the tangled bed in the centre of a room that was strange to him. He saw a beautiful dark woman whose face he did not recognize. He saw Pongo standing impassively, arms folded, at the far side of the room and next to him Winkleried, mud-splashed and weary to the point of collapse. And then he saw Judith, kneeling sobbing beside the bed on which his fleshly double lay, her head pressed against the sheet in the same attitude as he had seen her at Hennebont on the night her father died.

There was another man also, and it was he who occupied the centre of the picture. A man of medium height and strongly built, dressed all in black but with beautiful hands covered in rings with which he was making strange movements before the closed eyes of the sick man in the bed, movements that were gentle and yet full of a power that made his rings flash with light. At the same time, he was murmuring strange words in an unknown tongue. The man was Cagliostro.

Gilles identified him without surprise, without anger either, as though his presence at his death bed were the most natural thing in the world. From the heights where his spirit was hovering the moral gangrene of the earth lost all significance and he could sense now that the man's intentions were good.

The doctor's hands completed their weird ballet and he took from his pocket a small brown glass phial. He poured a few drops from it between the patient's parted lips and then, beckoning to Pongo, handed him the phial.

After that there was nothing more. Gilles' wandering spirit re-entered the exhausted shell of his body and sank with it, quiet at last, into a sleep deep as the ocean and dreamless, while the death that was already lurking behind the canopy of the bed rose up and fled away into the darkness that preceded the dawn.

That healing sleep lasted a long time. When, for the first time for weeks, Gilles' eyes opened intelligently on his surroundings, the pain was no more than a slight difficulty in breathing and the fever had sweated itself out to such an extent that his nurses had been obliged to change his sheets constantly.

The room on which his gaze rested was large and light and hung with a blue fabric with a design of scattered flowers, amongst which fanciful shepherdesses frolicked with beribboned sheep. A fire of fragrant pine logs burned in a white marble hearth and the furnishings were white-painted and fashionably modern. Incongruous in the midst of so much femininity, Pongo was sitting cross-legged on the pink and white flowered carpet. He was so still that he looked like a carved image of himself but his eyes were like lighted candles in his hollow face.

'Pongo,' Gilles called, in a thread of a voice that to himself seemed scarcely strong enough to pass his lips.

But the one-time medicine man of the Onondagas had no need to hear. He was on his feet at once.

'Master!' he breathed in a voice of almost incredulous joy. 'Master – you live. You see, hear?'

For the first time in his life, Gilles saw a tear on the Indian's worn, expressionless cheek.

'Yes ... I think so,' he said, with a feeble attempt at a smile. 'But tell me ... where are we?'

'You are in my house.'

Cool as a fresh-gathered lettuce in a leaf green gown, her lovely black hair swept up, shining and unpowdered, under a scrap of green muslin which did duty for a cap, Aglae entered the room, bearing a small silver tray with a steaming cup on it.

Her white teeth gleamed in a smile which illumined her whole face.

'God be thanked!' she said as she set the tray down on the table by the bed. 'I think we shall be able to breathe again. You have returned to us. How do you feel?'

'About as steady as a fistful of sand. But I'll believe I'm myself again when I can make my poor addled brain recall just when and where we two have met before, Madame.'

'A pretty compliment, I must say! Think, then! And let me tell you, you are fortunate to have given us all such a fright, for not many women care to have their first meetings forgotten. But you are to be indulged. Would you like me to help you?'

'No, no ... It's only that my memory is still a trifle fogged. Wait – I think I have it. Yes! Sieur Hué's restaurant! You rescued me from committing an appalling crime against the person of the Duc de Chartres. Unhappily, no one ever told me your name.'

'Well done! As to the rest, I am Aglae de Barbentane, Baroness Hunolstein. This house is called the Hermitage and it lies by the Bagnolet road, just on the edge of the park. I have rented it in order to be near my Orléans friends and also because I can be more informal here than in my house in the Faubourg St Germain. It is surrounded on all sides by the park belonging to the château.

'There, now you know everything you need to know and you can stop talking or you will tire yourself. And drink this.'

Helped by Pongo, she raised the pillows so that her patient could drink the tisane sweetened with honey she had brought him. He swallowed it unprotesting, but made a face.

'Am I to live on herbs? I'd give a month's pay for a good cup of coffee. I'm sure that would make me feel a lot stronger.'

'If the doctor agrees, you shall have your coffee, only for heaven's sake stop talking. Excitement is bad for you. Remember it's only thirty-six hours since you were dying!'

He smiled faintly as the helpful arms lowered him onto his pillows again. Even that simple movement, in which no effort had been required of him, left him exhausted.

'I ... haven't forgotten, I assure you. Only ... there are ... so many things ... I should like to know.'

'You will have plenty of time to ask questions. You are a

329

long way yet from jumping on your horse and cantering away, you know. So, for the present, just lie quietly.'

He drew his hands out from under the clothes and stretched them in front of him. They were so thin that they looked unbelievably long, nothing but bones encased in skin.

'Have I changed so much?'

'You want to see for yourself?'

She fetched a hand mirror from a small table and gave it to him. She did not tell him they had used it more than once to make sure he was still breathing.

What he saw was far from gratifying. Beneath a skin too deeply browned by sun and sea winds ever to lose all its tan, the flesh had melted away leaving nothing but the firm bone structure and a pair of eyes, sunk deep in their sockets, whose colour would have been hard to tell except that, in the general greyness, there showed no trace of blue.

Aglae did not give him long to contemplate this dismal spectacle. She removed the mirror, gently but firmly.

'There. The reason I let you see, my friend, was not from cruelty but to make you understand that if you want to look your handsome self again as quickly as possible, you must be sensible. You shall not have the glass back again, I promise you, until I approve of what you will see. Go to sleep now. You shall have something to eat when the doctor has seen you.'

'Who is the doctor?'

'A very clever and learned young man who works at the Charity Hospital. His name is Doctor Corvisart.'

'Oh.' Gilles was disappointed, for he had expected another name. As he recovered consciousness, he had recalled again the strange dream in which he had seen Cagliostro at his bedside and Judith. Judith on her knees beside him, the tears pouring down her face and her lips pressed to his hand.

But it seemed that that was indeed no more than a dream, engendered by delirium and by his crying need for her. In his present plight he was forced to recognize again, with helpless fury, how deep was his love for her. Judith! She had made his boy's heart beat for the first time as a man's, she, through the innocent spell of her beauty, had first awakened desire in him. No one else could ever take the place that she had made her own and Gilles knew now that, however many other women

330

he held in his arms, he would hold nothing but emptiness, for it had been written in the book of fate from the beginning that he was only half of a whole which, complete, might be called happiness. And the other half was Judith.

Then, because there was nothing else that mattered to him to know, Gilles turned his head to the wall and closed his eyes and tried to sleep, hoping in that way his dream might come back to him.

When Corvisart came to visit his patient a little later in the day, he appeared extremely satisfied as well as more than a little surprised at the remarkable change which had taken place in the course of a few hours. His wounds were healing, the tube which Pelletan had inserted after the operation was no longer draining off any fluid, his breathing was almost normal again and he was going on very well indeed.

'It's quite amazing,' Corvisart admitted honestly. 'I thought the lung would never stop bleeding. The patient seemed to have only a few hours to live and I felt utterly helpless and now, for no reason that I can discover, everything has come right. I'll never forget how surprised I was last night to find him sleeping peacefully, when I had been expecting a very different kind of sleep.' He smiled. 'Which means that today my prescription can be summed up in two words: food and sleep. What we have to do now is to let nature take its course, which in this young man's case, it seems very well able to do.'

Gilles got his coffee and felt stronger for it. The pleasure he took in it was almost childlike. After the hell that he had been through, it was wonderful to feel life flowing back gently, like a spring welling up suddenly and filtering gradually through parched earth.

His thoughts, too, were gaining in clarity and the odd thing was that he found it less easy to keep them from reverting to his dream. They seemed to be clinging to it, in fact, for ever searching out fresh details.

He tried, of course, to find out from Aglae whether anyone or anything had really come to him during the night when he was slipping ineluctably into the arms of death, but she had looked at him almost indignantly.

'Don't you believe in miracles, and in the power of God? And you, a Breton?'

'On the contrary, I have a very firm belief in them. Only, I can't see why God should have taken the trouble to work a miracle for someone as unimportant as I am.'

'Leave it to God to decide which of his creatures are important, and stop asking stupid questions.'

With which forceful words, she swept out of the room, although not without Gilles' noticing that she had not really answered his question.

Quite suddenly, he remembered something and he beckoned Pongo over to the bed.

'Pongo,' he said softly, 'where have you put the little bottle the foreign doctor gave you the other night?'

For all his self-command, the Indian tensed slightly.

'Bottle? Medicine?' he echoed, with an involuntary glance towards the door. But Gilles had guessed now that there was some truth at least in his dream and that some kind of conspiracy of silence had been agreed on, perhaps inspired by his hostess and possibly with the best of intentions for his own good, although he could not see for the life of him what harm such happiness could do him.

Gilles reached out and grasped the Indian's hand.

'Pongo, you are far more my friend than my servant and you have never lied to me. It may be that you have been asked to keep a secret and you never go back on your word. But I need you to help me to know whether I am still in my right mind, or if I am going mad and seeing visions. Will you answer a question or two?'

The Indian hesitated only briefly.

'Pongo promise not tell,' he said with a grin that showed his huge rabbit's teeth. 'Not promise not answer questions. Say!'

'Good. Did you see a man come here, a man in black clothes who was a doctor from a foreign country, and did he have with him a very beautiful young lady with red hair?'

'Yes. Not last night. Night before last. Very near morning. Young lady cry very much. Not wish to go, not wish to leave you. But made to. Man in black say much danger for her if she stay. She do as he say, on condition black man cure you. He swear.'

'I see. And who brought them here?'

'Chief Red Bear,' declared Pongo, for whom the name of

Winkleried was almost as strange and unpronounceable as if it were Chinese. 'He go on horse, same day you hurt. Go long way. Bad weather. Come back that night with man in black and Fire Flower.'

Gilles smiled at the Indian name, thinking how well it suited Judith. So it was Winkleried who had gone to fetch Cagliostro and Judith. But where? And how was he able to find them in so short a time when he, Gilles, had been searching in vain for months?

'Which reminds me, where is he? I haven't seen him since I recovered consciousness.'

'He promise come back quick. But he very tired. Many days no food.'

'Well if that isn't an amazing proof of friendship,' Gilles said weakly, 'I'll be hanged! He must have shrunk by half!'

But when Ulrich-August entered his friend's room there was nothing about him to inspire compassion. Looking more resplendent than ever in his magnificent uniform of red, blue and gold, the cocked hat with its white cockade and gold plume perched dashingly over one ear, he was the picture of health and complacency. He first marched to the foot of the bed and stood looking at his friend with an eye at once suspicious and intent.

'Well?' Gilles said. 'How do I look?'

'Not nearly so dusty! You're not precisely flourishing yet, but you're beginning to look like yourself again. Yes, I am more pleased than I can say.'

With that he moved swiftly round the bed and embraced Gilles with such force that he protested feebly: 'Here, gently! I'm still fragile, you know.'

'I am so sorry—'

'You don't have to be. It's the thought that counts. Ulrich, I – I know how much I owe you. I know what you did for me. The fact that I'm alive at this moment is solely thanks to you.'

'To me? What I did was nothing, only a little riding.'

'Then let's say it's thanks to you and your horse.'

'Horses. I think I rode ten of them into the ground.'

'Ten? Where the devil did you go?'

'Lyon. That's where your Italian magician is living. I had to

333

go there to tell him you needed help and, more to the point, if you were going to die you needed one more look at a certain beautiful young lady who from the colour of her hair could well be my sister. My compliments, by the way. What an exquisite creature! She outshines even Ursula. Only, the tears she shed when I told her of the pitiful case you were in, you can't imagine. Enough to fill the Lake of Zurich! And such screams and entreaties and tantrums and abuse, all because the doctor didn't get himself into the carriage fast enough! She swore to kill herself on your grave if she came too late, or if Cagliostro wasn't able to save you. I think she wept all the way here.'

Gilles' heart glowed. The Swiss had a voice made to be heard amid the din of battle, but his friend listened to it now as if it were the sweetest music. Judith's despair was balm to his soul and sweet promise to his hopes.

'You can't know how happy you've made me, Ulrich. But what I can't understand is how you found them. You didn't know where Cagliostro was at that time any more than I did?'

'No, but when I came to think about it a little, and remembering all you'd told me, I came to the conclusion that there was one person in Paris who must know. And so I simply went and asked him.'

'Who, by God?'

Like an actor making the most of his effect, Winkleried took his time about replying. Then, beaming broadly, he said: 'Cardinal de Rohan.'

'You dared to go and ask Cardinal de Rohan? And he didn't throw you out on your ear? The Grand Almoner of France?'

'What is the Grand Almoner of France when my friend's life is at stake? I'd have asked the Pope if need be. Or the Comte de Provence, which is as good as to say the devil. Besides, I am a protestant. I must say he was very kind, most understandable.'

'Understanding,' Gilles corrected him automatically. 'What did he say?'

'That Cagliostro had left Bordeaux and gone to Lyon, in order to build a lodging of masonry for some Egyptians.'

'A Masonic Lodge, you mean. But why Egyptians?'

'I do not know. In any case, he was in Lyon only for a short visit. The cardinal told me, as if it were great good news, that

334

Cagliostro has at last made up his mind to settle in Paris, and that his secretary, a man called Ramon de Carbonnières, has been given the task of finding a house for him and his family.'

'So he has a family?'

'He has a wife at least, and a very lovely one. She is a great Roman lady, it seems, and her name is Serafina. But don't ask me where all these people are at present because I don't know in the least. Let us talk of other things. Tell me—'

'Just one word more. Pongo told me Judith wanted to stay with me and that she was not permitted to. Do you know why?'

'Not really. She may perhaps be in danger. The doctor said to her: "You know you have nothing to fear while you remain under my protection." Even so, he had to swear by every god in the firmament that you were going to get better before she would agree to go with him. But how do you know all this, may I ask? You were at death's door and Cagliostro insisted on secrecy.'

'I think it's just because I was at death's door that I saw it all, I *saw* it, do you see? As if I were part of the audience in a theatre, I saw everything that took place in this room. I know that standing round my bed were Cagliostro, Judith, you, Pongo and Madame d'Hunolstein, but no one else at all. What do you say to that?'

'That it is most peculiar and also that, since that is how it is, you would do better not to tell your hostess that you know. She is frightened to death of Cagliostro.'

'I'm beginning to think that everyone's afraid of everyone else here. But you're right. I'll say nothing to her.'

There were in fact no more questions he needed to ask. He knew he was not mad, he knew that the Italian doctor was coming to live in Paris and, above all, he knew that Judith loved him with a love equal to his own. He could await his recovery with patience.

As often happens, the long convalescence he had to endure proved to have its own agreeable compensations. The Hermitage was a delightful house and Aglae a charming hostess who did everything she could to amuse and bring back to health an invalid of whom she was clearly growing extremely fond. This

335

fondness was returned. She was a young woman whose attractions did not easily pall.

On Tournemine's side, affection went hand in hand with a lively gratitude, but the strange thing was that, for all the southerner's essentially voluptuous beauty, the feelings she awoke in him were free from all trace of desire. What he felt for her was the warm love of a brother for a beautiful and admired older sister, but nothing more.

Encouraged by her, Gilles' friends formed the habit of meeting almost daily round the bed, and later on the sofa where he lay recovering. Winkleried especially, whenever he was not on duty, would hurry from Versailles, always bringing with him a sane breath of keen outdoor air from his reckless ride. Barras, next, scraping a hand-to-mouth living from the gaming tables, and at a loose end whenever he was not in some hell, would come and warm his feet at the fire and drink endless cups of chocolate, while retailing the latest Paris gossip. Dear Mademoiselle Marjon, too, several times made the trip from the Rue de Noailles to assure her lodger that he was not forgotten by her, and also to bring him an endless stream of rose-scented missives whose provenance Gilles was only too well aware of and which he regularly requested her to take home again without so much as opening them.

'If anyone comes and asks, you had better say you don't know where I am. That way, it will be easier for you if you ever have a chance to return the letters to their owner.'

She submitted gracefully, and with an inward pang that she was not able to preside personally over her lodger's convalescence. But, remembering the attack on her house, she readily admitted that the Hermitage, surrounded as it was by the Orléans estate, was a far safer place than her own little house could ever be.

The Duke of Chartres, who came one morning, accompanied by the policeman Lenoir, said as much in so many words.

'Your attackers used my name, Chevalier,' he told him, 'and so it is a matter for my honour that you should not leave this house until you are quite recovered and capable of resuming your duties with the King once more. This I must insist upon and we will say no more about it, if you please. I cannot think anyone would be fool enough to try to harm a friend of mine on my own land. And now I should like you, if you will, to listen to what Monsieur Lenoir has to say.'

Lenoir had come, it turned out, to take the injured man's evidence. He made no secret of the fact that the inquiry, ordered by the King himself acting on Winkleried's information and urged on by Chartres, was getting nowhere. Beausire had vanished into thin air and his mistress, the woman called Nicole Legay and also known as Oliva, who bore such a striking resemblance to the Queen, had also disappeared. Even the house where they had lived had been subjected to such a thorough cleaning that no one could have guessed at the bloodshed which had taken place there.

It must, indeed, have been arranged from the first with that in mind for, but for the victim's desperate defence and the unexpected help he had received which enabled him to carry the fight out into the street, no one would ever have suspected anything. Gilles would simply have vanished from the face of the earth and no one would ever have found out what had become of him.

However, the young man met Lenoir's questions with a wall of blank refusal. He knew nothing of any of his attackers.

'The boy who helped you, but who has not been seen since, said when you were brought here that you had recognized the leader of the gang, but that he was unable to catch the name you uttered. We have had a search made among the quarries of Montmartre but no one knows what has become of him.'

'In any case, he was mistaken,' Tournemine said, repelled by the role of informer, even against such wretches as Antraigues or Reteau. 'I may have thought I recognized one of them at one time but I am by no means certain, so you will understand that I can scarcely put a name to him.'

'Let us be the judge of that. These people did their best to murder you, Monsieur. There is no code of honour that obliges you to protect murderers.'

'Or to accuse an innocent man without proof. I am sorry, Monsieur Lenoir, but there is nothing more I can tell you.'

Lenoir got up with a sigh. A dedicated policeman, but one in the great tradition of La Reynie, he had a long experience of men and there were few who could boast of concealing their inmost thoughts from that quietly penetrating eye. But exceptions did exist, as he was brought from time to time reluctantly to acknowledge.

'I do not believe you, Monsieur,' he said heavily. 'But it is your life, after all, and I cannot do more. I will bid you a good evening, in the hope that you will think again.'

The Duc de Chartres did not go with him. It seemed that he still had something more to say.

'I admire your discretion, Chevalier,' he said, placing himself with his back to the fire, hands clasped behind his back and his eyes on the younger man. 'However, if I am to believe Madame d'Hunolstein, you were not quite so – close, shall we say, in your delirium. You spoke one name. Several times over, in fact. It was a name very familiar to the Baroness, for it was the name of a friend of hers, and mine also. Was it because I was present that you refused to name the Comte d'Antraigues?'

'No, Monseigneur, it was not. I have the greatest respect for your Highness but you will forgive me, I hope, if I say that I am not afraid of you. I said nothing because, now that I am on the road to recovery, thanks very largely to Madame d'Hunolstein's care of me, there is no reason why I should leave to the police the conduct of my own affairs. I have already crossed swords with Monsieur d'Antraigues before this, to his discomfiture. Next time, I shall kill him, that is all.'

The Prince's high-coloured face broke into a smile, but it did not reach his eyes, which remained cold and watchful.

'Then, are you quite certain it was d'Antraigues? He was out of Paris in December and on the day you were attacked he had already left, three days earlier, to spend Christmas with his family on his estate at Vivarais. There must be some mistake.'

Gilles' answering smile also left his eyes untouched.

'If your Highness says so, then it must be true,' he said tranquilly. 'So you see, Monseigneur, I was quite right to say nothing – since the Count was not here. What I saw or heard must have been a phantom.'

There was a little silence, employed by both men in summing the other up. Philippe de Chartres broke it with a sudden bark of laughter.

'Do as you will, Chevalier! You are certainly no fool! I shall give myself the pleasure of coming to talk with you again

338

during your stay here. I may even bring some friends with me. Your exploits in America have made you highly popular with the ladies. We shall see how you go down with the men. And that reminds me, as I came in here I saw that you have a somewhat unusual servant. An Indian, is he not?'

'Yes, Monseigneur. He is a warrior of the Onondagas, a tribe of the Iroquois. I earned his gratitude by, er, helping him across the Delaware river in spate. In fact, he is a medicine man.'

'Wonderful! You must sell him to me! I shall dress him in his native costume and he will be a great success to greet my guests with.'

'Sell him?' Gilles cried, shocked beyond measure. 'Monseigneur, I could not possibly! One does not sell one's friends, and Pongo is a friend to me – a very dear friend, indeed!'

'Bah! I know what friends are worth. It all depends on the price. And I am ready to pay a fortune for that lad. You see, my dear fellow, it's like this. Our good La Fayette is just returned from what he claims was a triumphal tour with General Washington, and he has brought back a young Indian, splendidly feathered, who acts as his servant and goes with him everywhere. He gets so much attention that it maddens me. But with your man, now, I could get the upper hand of him.'

Gilles laughed. 'You don't mean to tell me, Monseigneur, that the first prince daring enough to venture up into the sky needs an ornamental Redskin to make an impression in a salon? I'm sorry, sir. If Pongo were an ordinary servant, I would give him to you with pleasure, and no question of payment. But he is a trusty friend and a free man. I could not dispose of him in that way. Permit me, if you please, to act as scrupulously towards my own friends as to your Highness's.'

'*Touché!*' Philippe exclaimed at once. 'Young man, I am beginning to like you. We shall meet again.'

Philippe de Chartres was as good as his word. When Gilles, one hand leaning on Pongo's shoulder and the other supported by a stick, was able to leave his chamber for the large circular salon which took up most of the building, he found, assembled for the tea-drinking which the Prince, a passionate anglophile, affected, quite a number of Philippe's particular circle. They included Victor de Broglie, Mathieu de Montmorency, Louis

XV's handsome bastard Louis de Narbonne, the Girardins and various others of his old comrades-in-arms such as the two Lameths. There was also one who was a real friend of his own, the Vicomte de Noailles, who sprang up and embraced him with enthusiasm and thanks to whose presence the tea table began to sound like a veterans' reunion.

'The King's service has nothing to offer except in time of war,' de Noailles declared roundly. 'You're wasting your time at Versailles, my friend. The time for servitude is over. Come with us and watch the day of freedom dawning, the blessed age of liberty. America is showing us the way—'

'Noailles, my friend, in another moment you are going to start preaching republicanism and I am going to say something very rude and we shall be obliged to call one another out. Wait until I'm fully recovered, please. Have you any news of Fersen?'

'None at all. Still in Sweden. You know La Fayette is back? He charged me to bring you his warmest regards and best wishes for your health.'

'Why didn't he come himself? We've shared so many engagements together, I'd have been glad to see him.'

'So would he but he has already gone again, not just from Paris, either. He's off on a new crusade. This time he's out to improve the condition of French Protestants. He says it is disgraceful because, although there is no outright persecution, yet they are dependent on the whims of the King and Queen, of the courts and ministers, and it is true. The days of the dragonnades are over but their marriages are not always legal, their wills not recognized, their children practically illegitimate and even those of gentle birth can be hanged like common criminals. La Fayette says it has gone on long enough.'

Gilles sighed. 'You can see he has been in America,' he said. 'I'd like to help him. You're right when you say Versailles warps people. The splendour of palaces and the glamour of royalty can cover too much that is devious, dirty and self-interested. You can't think how I long, sometimes, to be back in Virginia!'

'Then why don't you? Go back there! I am going one day. Listen,' he lowered his voice. 'I don't know what this business was that nearly cost you your life, but I do know you've been

340

making enemies, or one powerful enemy, at least. The King is weak, he'll not be able to protect you from that enemy indefinitely, and your Guards' coat won't be much of a breastplate. Go back. You're a legend there and you have powerful friends. You could have land, a position and, more to the point, you'd be a free man.'

'I know,' Gilles sighed. 'But there is such a thing as duty. A soldier's duty is to fight for his king, not to look to him for protection. And I am very much afraid that mine is going to need all the soldiers he can muster before long.'

To Aglae's warm salon, filled with the scent of purple lilac from the hothouses of Bagnolet, news came quickly, borne on the last snows of a winter which was dying hard and the first blasts of a reluctant spring. Day by day, the country drowned under torrential rainstorms while at the same time a sudden rise in temperature hastened the melting of the snows, producing tragic floods in many places, increasing the people's wretchedness and leading to fresh moods of anger and hatred.

When it became known in Paris that the Queen had finally succeeded in persuading the King to purchase St Cloud, there was an outburst of anger. The clubs, cafés, masonic lodges and the faubourgs were breathing fire and fury, the pamphleteers let themselves go with greater violence than ever, while with the six million realized from the sale and the remainder from the disposal of his hunting assets to the Comte d'Artois, the Duc d'Orléans set about completing his arcades at the Palais-Royal. The Orléans were lauded to the skies, the Queen's name dragged in the mud and when, on the twenty-seventh of March, a salute of a hundred guns broke over Paris, signifying that Marie-Antoinette had been successfully brought to bed of a boy, there was none of the spontaneous explosion of popular rejoicing which had greeted the birth of the dauphin four years earlier.

Paris, in any case, had other things on its mind. In the hope of currying favour with the Church, the Comte de Provence and the Baron de Breuteuil had obtained a *lettre de cachet* against Beaumarchais and the author of *The Marriage of Figaro* had been given the opportunity to reflect in the Saint-Lazare prison, designated bourn of rogues and vagabonds, on the unwisdom of offending an archbishop of Paris, in this case

Mgr. de Juigné, whom he had been careless enough to lampoon. That he was not flogged, as most new inmates were, was purely his good fortune, as was the fact that he remained there only five days. On his release, he made straight for the Queen's friends for consolation and was promised that his play *The Barber of Seville* would be put on at the Trianon, with the Queen herself playing the part of Rosina, in flagrant disobedience of the King's command.

Paris had also discovered itself a doctor. Count Alexandro Cagliostro had moved into the handsome Hôtel d'Orvilliers in the Rue St Claude in the Marais, rented for him by his protector the Cardinal de Rohan. He was a huge and immediate success, in much the same way as the mysterious Comte de Saint-Germain had been a generation before. He was said to be able to manufacture gold and diamonds, to possess an elixir of eternal youth, to be able to cure any disease, to foretell the future and any number of other things. People thronged to his door.

Gilles, at that time, was living for the day when he would be strong enough to leave the Hermitage and able to visit the man also, although his value to his eyes was simple enough: he knew where Judith was.

Meanwhile, as her guest grew stronger, so Aglae's lovely face grew more and more pensive until, one day in April, as they were walking together in the garden in between showers, she could not help saying with a sigh: 'In a very little while now, you will be quite recovered, my friend. In a little while we shall not see each other any more.'

'Not see each other? But why not? Do you mean to close your doors to me because I am no longer your patient? I should be very sad if you did.'

'Should you? You have a great deal to occupy your heart, without worrying about a friend.'

They had come to a halt beside a clump of newly-opened peonies, as pink as the woman's cheeks. Gilles took her hand and planted a kiss on its palm.

'A friend? You are much more than a friend to me, Aglae.'

'A sister, then? Very well, I shall be your sister, and only too happy if ever a day comes when you have need of her again.'

'Need? What a word!'

342

She smiled a little sadly. 'The future looks very black to me, Gilles my dear. The things I hear on all sides make me shudder. I fear that we are heading for dreadful times, when families will be divided against each other, fathers denying their sons and brothers hating sisters.'

'Who could hate you? You, who are all that is graceful, sweet, charming and generous?'

'I, the mistress of the Duc de Chartres who will soon be Duc d'Orléans, for his father's failing fast. I, who will one day be in a different camp from you, an enemy camp. Philippe is not really bad, but the resentment is growing in his heart. Slowly but surely. One day, it will take over entirely. He might have lived as a happy sheep, but the intrigues of Versailles will make him a ravening wolf. When that happens, yes, you will begin to hate me.'

'Never! Even if Orléans were in a state of open rebellion, you would still be the dearest of women to me.'

'Are you really sure of that?'

'On my honour, and by the affection I have for you.'

She smiled at him, pushing back a lock of hair the wind was blowing across her face.

'God grant I may never have to remind you of that oath, my friend.'

14

Two Women

Two months later, Gilles de Tournemine, once more reunited with Merlin, was sitting in the saddle gazing at the uncommunicative façade of Cagliostro's house.

In the fading twilight, the building in which the magician lived seemed to be waiting for something. It crouched behind its triple bulwark of the trees in the boulevard, a ditch deep enough to look almost like a moat and high walls topped with clusters of iron spikes which hid everything except the upper windows and steep, slate-covered roof, looking like some fat, patient cat, curled up but ready at any moment to reach out a paw and trap any imprudent mouse that came too near. To one side of it a steep alley ran down from the Rue St Claud to the Convent of the Daughters of the Holy Sacrament. It was here that the entrance gates to the house were situated, an entrance which could scarcely have been more forbidding with its massive nail-studded doors and the fierce bronze head of a griffin which served as a knocker.

Yet no dwelling of kings, not dazzling Versailles or delightful Trianon, had ever inspired the Chevalier with such joy as this grim and faintly disturbing house. He was not at all sure what would be the tone of the forthcoming interview between himself and the Italian. Their conversation might be as deadly as an exchange of pistol shots. Certainly it must settle things, one way or another.

The servant who answered his knock was, he saw, the elusive giant from the Hôtel Ossolinski. But if the man recognized Gilles he gave no sign of it.

When Gilles asked to see his master, he merely nodded, beckoned a groom to take charge of his horse and led the visitor across the courtyard to where a portico reminiscent of a Greek temple opened into a large entrance hall, into which curved the bottom flight of a handsome white stone staircase. Seats covered in red velvet had been placed near the foot of the stairs for the convenience of the countless visitors who every day flocked to the miracle worker's house, as eagerly as, not so long before, they had been flocking to Mesmer's magnetic bath. Now the hour was late and Gilles found himself alone as he was waved to a seat. Then the servant vanished into the upper reaches of the house, seeking his master.

The place was perfectly silent. Not a sound was to be heard, not the squeak of a door, not the creak of a floorboard, not the echo of a footfall. It was as if the house was seeking to create an air of mystery, to prepare the minds of those entering from the moment they crossed the threshold. Then, before he had been there more than a few moments, the silence was shattered utterly by the clatter of a carriage entering the courtyard.

Grooms dashed forward. The lackeys clinging to the back of the magnificent vehicle, its purple lacquered surface gleaming with an impressive coat-of-arms, sprang to earth and let down the steps and Cardinal de Rohan, brilliant in his red robes, emerged from within.

The cardinal descended from the coach, trod briskly into the house and made for the staircase, like a man who knew where he was going and had no need to be announced. Gilles saw the red robe sweep up the stairs and vanish. There was the sound of a door opening and closing, an echo of voices and then nothing. The house relapsed into silence again.

The giant servant reappeared, noiselessly as a cat, to inform Gilles, in bad French, that the Count asked if he would be good enough to wait a while and then disappeared again, leaving the young man to his own gloomy reflections. If the cardinal had come to pay a protracted visit, then he was likely to be in for a long wait.

But at the end of half an hour, the cardinal reappeared, alone, which was strange since it was usual for the host to accompany his visitors back to their carriages, and especially so when the visitor was a prince of the Church. Seeing him descending the stairs, Gilles rose and bowed. To his surprise, the cardinal came towards him.

'We have met before, Monsieur de Tournemine,' he said pleasantly, 'but I was not granted the pleasure of an introduction. Charming ladies will have such lapses. You are from Brittany, of course, and you are the man the Indians called the Falcon?'

'That is so, Monseigneur. Your Eminence honours me by your interest.'

'You are Tournemine, sir, and I am Rohan. In Brittany our families are of like antiquity.'

'Although mine is far less distinguished,' Gilles said with the smile that gave his face such charm. The Cardinal was not immune to it.

'That is nothing. Our forbears have often fought side by side. Moreover I had a rather more personal account of you some months ago from a young Swiss gentleman who virtually forced his way into my house, somewhat manhandled my servants and burst into my study in a most spectacular fashion. You have some good friends, Sir.'

'Baron Winkleried is not one for half measures, Eminence. The tempest in his native element. He didn't tell me, of course, that he had accomplished things quite so dramatically. I apologize on his behalf. His excuse must be that he was, I believe, suffering from a considerable degree of anxiety.'

'He needs no excuse. You were dying – a very nasty business, I gather – and the poor fellow had need of the one person who could do anything to save you. I always find myself in complete agreement with anyone who wants the great Cagliostro. And I can see that once again, he wrought miracles. You are alive and, as far as I can see, in perfect health.'

'Perfect health indeed. But, may I inquire, did Winkleried inform your eminence how, and through whom, I received my injuries?'

The cardinal nodded and his blue eyes darkened.

'Yes, he did. I told him I could scarcely credit it. There must be some mistake. The charming Countess is—'

'A dangerous woman, Monseigneur. By the memory of all those earlier Tournemines who often rendered good service to the Rohans, I must beg your Eminence to be on your guard.'

346

'How strange. Do you know, you have just said to me, almost word for word, the same thing as Cagliostro. There is, I admit, a flightiness in her, some contradictions and irresponsibility now and then, but I am sure her heart is good and she has done great things for me which I can never forget. That may sound puzzling to you. But you may understand it better one day soon, when fate has raised me to a position so exalted that nothing can matter to me any more, except perhaps the pleasure of surrounding myself with men such as yourself, Sir, and doing what good I may for them.'

Gilles found himself remembering what he had seen and heard that night in the Bosquet de Vénus, and above all the Queen's voice saying angrily: 'Do you know that man's dream? It is to be first minister . . .' What crazy illusions was that infernal Comtesse de la Motte encouraging this too credulous man to cherish?

'Monseigneur—' he began. But already Rohan was offering him his ring in farewell and Gilles, out of respect for his office, could only bow and kiss it.

'I shall always be glad to see you, Monsieur de Tournemine. Do not forget.'

Gilles would have tried to detain him even then, risking the breach of etiquette it entailed, but that he felt a touch on his sleeve and saw that the servant had returned again unheard and was making signs to him to follow. And by that time the Cardinal was already halfway to his coach.

He mounted in the man's wake to the first floor and through a windowless antechamber lit by a profusion of candles, on one wall of which was a large black marble plaque engraved with some oriental characters and with a kind of prayer the first words of which were: 'Universal Father, Intelligence Supreme . . .'

The servant opened a door and Gilles found himself in the presence of the master of the house.

'Come in, Chevalier,' Cagliostro said. 'I have been waiting for you.'

The room in which he was standing was a large study, austerely furnished in dark oak and filled with a host of strange objects ranging from alchemical retorts to Egyptian statuettes, green with age. Shelves of books climbed the walls. More books, huge folio volumes, were piled on the floor. A desk covered with papers and mineral samples took up only a fraction of a room whose real size was difficult to estimate, since those walls that were not lined with books had been hung with black velvet, behind which, presumably, lay other doors. The air was thick with the smell of burning incense and myrrh, rising in a blue smoke that was coming from a large bronze incense burner mounted on a tripod.

Cagliostro himself was no less impressive than his setting, conceived, as it undoubtedly was, to strike the imagination of the public. His fine limbs were covered by the folds of a long robe or tunic on which the signs of the zodiac were embroidered in red and silver thread. His hair, parted into separate tresses, was gathered into a ribbon on the nape of his neck and his hands were almost invisible beneath a glittering array of rubies and diamonds.

Gilles sat mechanically in the chair indicated for him.

'You say you were waiting for me? How can that be? Your servant did not even ask my name.'

'It was unnecessary. I knew that you were coming as I have known of all your actions for the past months.'

'That would hardly have been difficult, given where I was. You would only have to bribe one of Madame d'Hunolstein's servants.'

'You credit me with very small powers, Sir,' the physician said disdainfully. 'I do not go in for bribing servants. Since you doubt my powers, would you like me to tell you what you have been doing during the last twenty-four hours? It will show you that no paid informer could have told me so much.'

'Fire away!'

'You left the Hermitage, not intending to return, at ten minutes past ten, in a carriage brought for you by your friend Winkleried. You accused him, in fact, of treating you like an old woman, telling him he would have done better to have brought your horse, Merlin. Your farewell to the Baroness brought tears to her eyes. I think, yes, she would have liked to keep you longer, but she will see you again. From there you went straight to Versailles, where your landlady was waiting for you.

'She is a maiden lady of great charm. She feels for you like a mother and she had dressed in her best to welcome you home. A grey silk dress, was it not, with pink ribbons and a pink bonnet? She meant to give you her hand to kiss in the grand manner, but when she saw you she could not help herself but threw her arms round your neck and wept. She had also, I may add, prepared an excellent repast for you. There was, I believe, a shad in butter sauce, some stuffed quails, cardoons with marrow and, to drink, the Burgundy you like so much. But you would not sit down to it at once. You hurried to the stables to see your horse and you held his head in your hands – and you kissed him. Have I said enough, or is there anything else you would like to know?'

'Good God, no! That's enough,' Gilles said hastily. He sounded stunned. 'It's magic – witchcraft!'

'Let us call it clairvoyance, that is a pleasanter word, less perilous also, even though in this enlightened age we no longer burn witches.'

'Excellent. In that case, since you seem to possess the gift of reading people's minds, you must also know what brings me here tonight?'

'Certainly. Although your mind is not altogether clear, even to yourself. You came here torn between a wish to express your gratitude and the desire to fight me because you think I stand in the way of your happiness.'

Cagliostro had seated himself in the large brown leather armchair, shiny with age, at his desk. With his elbows resting on the desk and his chin in his hands, he was gazing at the young man with a look of such brilliance that Gilles felt suddenly ill at ease. To escape its power, he got up and moved away, ostensibly to examine some objects in a glass case.

'Are you not?' he said bitterly.

'Not in the least.'

'Come, Sir! You claim to be able to read what is in men's souls, you must know how much I love Mademoiselle de Saint-Mélaine. You must know that I have sworn my life to her and that there is not one thing I do, outside my service to the King, for which she is not the motive, the inspiration and the goal. Yet, knowing all this, are you trying to make me believe that my love can harm her?'

'I am not trying to make you believe it, because you would

349

never be brought to do so. Yet it is so,' the magus said sadly. 'Because you love very deeply and with great passion, you believe that you can overcome all obstacles, vanquish all the armies of the world in defence of your happiness. Yet you are but a man, a fact which has been tragically proved to you. By my humble intermission, the Creator restored you to life and strength, but not to peace, for your destiny still drives you onward. You are of those who may be marked out for greatness. Unhappily your way lies through too much peril, through too much bloodshed and tragedy, for it to be wise to join a woman to it.'

'What do you know of destiny?' Gilles cried angrily. 'And why should I be the only officer of the King to be denied a home and family? In the name of what are you keeping Judith from me?'

'In the name of her own right to be protected and kept safe. She has no call to meddle with greatness. Have you forgotten the terrible experiences of her own girlhood?'

'I killed one of the two villains who cast her living into a muddy grave. And I will kill the other as soon as I find him.'

'But you will never kill the memory of it. It would have driven any woman mad. Judith has survived, but it has left its mark on her. She needs calm, peace, security, all the things she cannot find. Look at what has happened to her since you saw her again. She is obliged to go into hiding to escape the devious schemes of a Prince whose enemy you are, who knows it and who knows also that he can reach you through her weakness.'

'Do you think I do not know all that? As much as yourself, I want to give her the peace and quiet happiness of a home, and freedom! Give her back to me and I will take her away from here. Ever since I have known her, I have dreamed of taking her to America, where men are beginning to learn how to live in freedom. We'll go and build ourselves a house in Virginia—'

'You, the King's man, the hawk who is his weapon and defence? You, the Falcon, would go and involve yourself in the disputes of those talking fools in Congress, in the squalid conflicts of self-interest which are starting to develop over there? You would beat your sword into a ploughshare?'

'Why not? I was born a peasant. As for the Falcon you have

thrown in my face, let me tell you he is born there and lives there as he will. There is enough space, huge forests and virgin lands, far out of earshot of the noise of Congress. I wear the eagle of Cincinnatus. Like him, I can go back to the soil if, when I come home at night, I find Judith's smile and Judith's arms and Judith's love. When will you get it into your head that I love her?'

'And she? You are sure that she loves you also? You don't know how she feels. Perhaps she does not love you.'

'Yes! Oh yes!'

One of the velvet hangings was brushed aside by the girl's light fingers as she ran from the darkness beyond, straight into Gilles' arms.

'Oh yes, I love you! Don't listen to him! He can't know anything about it! He shut me away, but I saw you come! Oh, you are here, alive – truly alive! You are better, and they were trying to make you believe I do not love you? You are the breath of life to me!'

She had her arms round him and was holding him to her, her whole body shaking. With infinite tenderness, he took the lovely tearstained face between his two hands and set a long kiss on the quivering lips.

'Sweetheart . . . my love, don't cry, don't shake like that . . . It's over now, we're going away.'

'He won't let me! He'll never let me! He says I cannot be yours – or any man's. He says I must remain a virgin so that the Spirit can dwell in me!'

Gilles clasped the fragile white form fiercely in his arms and his eyes on the Italian were like ice.

'Here is a fresh mystery, master magician. Perhaps you will explain it? It seems you arrogate to yourself the right to deny her love, and happiness, even the right to give herself? By what right? Are you God? Or are you, perhaps, in love with her yourself? That's it, isn't it? You don't want me to have her because you want to keep her for yourself?'

'Fool!'

Cagliostro moved slowly to take up a branched candle-stick full of lighted candles and carried it to an alcove in which, Gilles saw suddenly, was standing the table with the black cloth and the silver objects which had disappeared so unaccountably from the Hôtel Ossolinski. Only this time, instead of the revolving mirror, there was a plain crystal ewer filled with water.

'Judith,' Cagliostro called, without raising his voice. 'Come here.'

Gilles felt the girl tremble within the shelter of his arms. 'Leave her alone,' he said furiously. 'I forbid her to move!'

'I mean her no harm. I merely wish you to understand.'

As though commanded by some irresistible force, the young man's arms dropped to his sides, releasing Judith who made no protest. Instead, she turned away from him to face the glittering eyes that summoned her and walked towards them, not with her usual light step, but like one in a trance.

'I am here, master.'

Then she went, without being told, to kneel before the table.

'What new trick is this?' Tournemine snarled. 'What do you want with her? Judith, come back! Don't listen to him!'

'She cannot hear you. Rest easy, I have told you that no harm will come to her from this. But you, you who are so deaf and blind that you reduce the manifestations of the divine power to the miserable bounds of human love, I am going to make you realize your error and your blindness. Out there, in the hall, just now, you met, did you not, the Cardinal de Rohan? He spoke to you?'

'Yes, but—'

'I am going to tell you more. You were about to tell him certain things which he is not capable of hearing because he, like you, is deaf and blind to everything but his own passion. Would you like to know what the cardinal is doing at this precise moment?'

The young man's eyes met the physician's dark, brilliant gaze without flinching.

'Very well.'

Cagliostro nodded and laid his right hand very gently on the girl's head.

'An important person left this house not long ago. A priest, a cardinal. Find him. Is he still in his coach?'

The girl's eyelids blinked rapidly a few times, then her gaze fixed itself upon the water jug within which the light was creating patches of light and darkness. She spoke, her voice sounding strangely distant.

'I see a carriage. It is standing outside the door of a house where there are lights, but it is empty.'

'Where is the cardinal? I told you to find him.'

'He is in a big room, a very beautiful room, richly furnished.'

'Can you describe it?'

'It is like a garden in a dream ... There are painted wooden panels. I can see flowers and trees, oh, and some little black creatures, monkeys, I think.'

'Very good. The cardinal is in his room. What is he doing?'

'He is writing.'

'To whom is he writing?'

'To a woman ... a woman he calls "Master".'

'Do you know who this woman is?'

'That is not hard. She is occupying all his thoughts. It is the Queen.'

'What is he saying to her?'

'Nothing at present. He is not pleased with what he has written. He is screwing up the letter and throwing it away. He is picking up another letter which lies open in front of him. He is reading it. It is a pretty letter. I can see gilt-edged paper and a fleur de lys engraved in the corner.'

'Can you read the letter while he is doing so?'

The clairvoyant's brow furrowed with effort and Gilles wiped the sweat from his own forehead with the back of his hand.

'"From everything I have heard about the remarkable man you speak of, I cannot think him anything but a charlatan. This may be prejudice on my part and I know from experience that one should never judge a person by the reports of others, but I have many reasons for not yielding to your request. I am not superstitious and not readily brought to believe in such things, but since people of that sort frequently perform wonders to amaze and make you accept whatever they tell you, I am in no state to undergo such a test. Moreover it would be very difficult, not to say impossible, to receive him with the secrecy I should wish for and you know how cautious I am obliged to be at present.

' "The countess made me laugh a great deal with her description of the last scene: it sounds quite extraordinary and gives me the liveliest wish to behold the Great Copt. If I am to believe the Countess, however, one must be very innocent in order to behold this great man's mysteries, although to judge from all the mumbo jumbo that surrounds them, I should rather think that he regards you, and the Countess also, as a pair of innocents to be treated as a pair of dupes. Do not be angry at my frankness, I assure you I judge by myself.

' "The Minister[4] leaves me alone as little as he can. I am not yet sure of the reason, but I shall know soon enough. Fortunately I am not dealing with an Egyptian like your Cagliostro who can divine the past and predict the future. He does not possess the secret of making jewels speak, so I may be at peace and not fear any indiscretions on the part of mine.

' "Forgive my levity. I have had so few occasions for mirth in these late times that I am sure you will be pleased to know that you have brought a moment's gaiety." '

Judith stopped speaking. Cagliostro rested his hand on her shoulder.

'Well done. Now rest for a moment. We will begin again in a little while.'

The girl sank down until she was sitting on her heels and then appeared to go to sleep while Cagliostro turned to Gilles who was staring at him with a sort of horror.

'Well?'

'It is terrifying!'

'Not at all. Merely that in a hypnotic trance unsuspected powers can be called forth from the depths of a person's being, on condition that they are wholly pure. Judith is a clairvoyant of the finest quality. I became aware of it when I was trying to snatch her from madness. But this gift, which is a spark of pure divinity, can only exist in the body of a child or of a virgin. That is why I am trying to preserve her from love, and from your own in particular, because she returns your love. Would you like to know more?'

Almost without his being aware of it, Gilles' interest had been awakened. It almost drove the thought of his own love

[4] i.e. the King.

354

from his mind, for the girl's words had opened strange, dark and menacing avenues.

'Yes. That incredible letter— It can't have been written by the Queen!'

'That is what we are about to find out. You must be rested now, my dove. Let us begin again.'

The girl sat up with a graceful movement. Once again her large, luminous eyes gazed into the crystal.

'Let us go back to the letter you have just read. Study it well. Look at the handwriting.'

'I am looking.'

'Can you tell who wrote it? Was it the Queen?'

'No.'

'Was it a woman?'

'A woman brought it but it was not she who wrote it.'

'So it was a man?'

'Yes.'

'Stay with the letter. Can you see the man who wrote it?'

Judith hesitated. She was frowning again.

'I don't know. I can't see him.'

'Can you see the woman who brought the letter?'

'Yes.'

'Look around her.'

There was a moment's silence, then, all at once, with a look of indescribable relief, the girl cried: 'Yes, I see him! He is a young man with a pale face . . . He has red hair. He is dressed in the English style . . . very elegant.'

'Reteau de Vilette,' Gilles said instantly. 'Him again! But what is he doing in this business?'

Cagliostro shrugged. 'He is the Countess's lover and her tool, and the Countess hates you because you denounced her to the Queen, as she also hates me, indeed. It was she who sent men to murder me, the time you came to my assistance.'

'But why? I thought you were friends?'

'We were, for a time, associates. Acting on higher orders. But she soon became afraid of me and determined to destroy me. At present our relations are superficially excellent. We have supper together and flirt a little. She is impressed by my success in Paris, and also by my wealth, and she is trying to attract me. She is attracted by everything that glitters, gold, diamonds, jewels of every kind . . .' He spread his ringed hands before him and they sparkled in the light of the candle flames. An idea came to Gilles suddenly.

'There was one passage in that so-called letter of the Queen's that I did not understand. What was the jewel she referred to? Surely the cardinal has not had the effrontery to offer jewels to the Queen?'

He started suddenly as Judith gave a little moan. Still kneeling bolt upright, her eyes fixed on the glass, the girl was crying softly: 'I'm tired. I'm so very tired!'

Cagliostro went to her at once and lifted her to her feet.

'It was too long! Forgive me, and thank you. Go and sleep now . . . Sleep for a long time to rest after your labours. Serafina!'

As though she had been waiting for the call, a woman entered the room. She was fair and very beautiful, dressed with great elegance in a dress of blue faille the same colour as her eyes. She went quickly to Judith and took her from Cagliostro's arms, while her eyes rested curiously on the Chevalier.

'This is Countess Cagliostro, my wife,' the Italian said. 'She is very fond of Judith and looks after her like an elder sister. You may trust her implicitly,' he added with a smile, 'however suspicious you are of me. Take her away, Serafina, and see that she is put to bed. She is very tired.'

With her head on the Countess's shoulder and the Countess's arm around her, Judith left the room without a word or a look towards Gilles. He watched her go with a mixture of grief and anger.

'You've won, haven't you?' he said bitterly to Cagliostro. 'I was determined not to leave here without her.'

'I will not win for ever,' the Italian said gravely. 'One day, you and she will be united for good. I can promise you that. But the time is not yet come, nor will it for a long while yet. You will need to have great patience, and great love also.'

'Who says I have to believe you?'

'No one. Fate will make it clear to you. Sit down, now, and have a glass of Spanish wine, you will need it to hear what I have to tell you concerning the Queen's jewels, or rather one particular piece of jewellery which you know well.'

Gilles took the seat and the wine which was warm and comforting. Despite the mildness of the spring night, he felt chilled to the marrow. Curiously, now, he was also afraid to ask the question which the thaumaturgist's last words had naturally raised. But he was not the man to let fear get the better of him for long.

He drained the precious gilt-engraved Venetian glass and set it down.

'Which I know well?' he repeated. 'Don't tell me it concerns that confounded diamond necklace?'

'Certainly it does. Did you not hear, in your Hermitage, that Boehmer and Bassange have sold the troublesome thing at last? It had, of course, to be managed with great secrecy.'

'So the Queen's answer, finally, was yes? She has taken up the option which expired in January?'

'So Boehmer believes. In actual fact, the Queen has no idea that she has bought the necklace.'

Gilles frowned. 'You talk in riddles, Sir. How is that possible? How could the Queen have bought a necklace worth sixteen hundred thousand livres and not be aware of it?'

'In the easiest way in the world. Cardinal de Rohan purchased it for her.'

'The Cardinal? So he has seen the Queen and made his peace with her?'

'I am endeavouring to tell you that the Queen knows nothing about it,' Cagliostro said impatiently. 'The Cardinal bought the necklace on the Queen's behalf because he firmly believes that the Queen instructed him to. You see, ever since a certain night in August last year, the cardinal has been perfectly convinced that he stands now on friendly terms, on very friendly terms indeed, with the Queen. Have you forgotten the Bosquet de Vénus, Chevalier? Surely you were present there?'

'If you know that, you must surely be the devil himself! It is true, I was there. But I saw nothing more than a pathetic comedy acted out to amuse the Queen, in which a great deal of amusement was derived from the sight of the Grand Almoner of France on his knees, kissing the feet of a whore!'

'If you want to live a free man and not rot in prison for the remainder of your days, Sir Falcon, I would advise you to forget that the Queen was a spectator on that occasion.

357

However that may be, the Cardinal swallowed the bait, hook, line and sinker. He is convinced that the Queen loves him dearly and that she is only waiting for a suitable moment to declare publicly that, far from still cherishing any grudge against him, she wishes to see him occupying the position of First Minister. He sees himself as a Mazarin or even a Richelieu! Consequently, there is nothing he would not do for one whom he calls his Master, and, of course, for those purporting to come from her.'

'But the Queen loathes him! I heard her say so with my own ears!'

'Try telling that to Rohan. He wouldn't believe you. He is sure that he is loved. He has proof of it, letters ... Nor will it do any good to try and make him understand that the fair Jeanne is a thief and an adventuress. He thinks that, thanks to her, he will soon be a minister of the crown!'

'I know. He said as much to me just now.'

'You see. She can get what she likes out of him. Not long after the affair of the Bosquet, for instance, she told him the Queen needed a hundred and twenty thousand livres to give to a deserving family and was at a loss for the money, whereupon our dupe, notwithstanding financial problems of his own, gave her the hundred and twenty thousand without a blink.'

'The hundred and twenty thousand which formed the basis of the La Mottes' sudden affluence, I take it?'

'Precisely. Our Countess might have been satisfied with that, but appetite grows with feeding. There is, moreover, another figure in the background pulling this pretty puppet's strings, someone who has long known there was advantage to be derived from Marie-Antoinette's pleasure-seeking, her passion for diamonds and from the cardinal's love for his Queen. What that person was hoping for was that Jeanne would succeed in getting the Cardinal restored to favour and that he would then seduce the Queen.'

'Seduce the Queen! Do you know what you're saying?'

'That, Monsieur, is a question you should put to your friend Fersen. Unkind gossip has it that he is the father of the little Duke of Normandy who was born in March. But the Queen continued to hold Rohan in aversion so another, subtler way was found. All Jeanne had to do was tell him how unhappy it had made the Queen not to be able to let the King buy her the necklace – added to the six million for St Cloud, it would have caused a revolution! – and that she would be eternally grateful to anyone who could intercede to keep it for her. Our Cardinal rushed straight off to Boehmer. On the twenty-fourth of January, he bought the necklace in the Queen's name, making a down payment of one hundred thousand livres and arranging for the rest to be paid over in instalments of four hundred thousand every six months. On February the first, the cardinal got possession of the necklace and took it to Madame de la Motte's house in the Place Dauphine at Versailles, where he was to hand it over to a man calling himself a servant of the Queen's. In fact, he was none other than the Unspeakable Reteau in disguise.'

'But the necklace? What became of the necklace?'

'It has ceased to exist. Boehmer and Bassange's masterpiece has presumably been reduced by now to a heap of individual stones which the lucky Jeanne is disposing of in dribs and drabs, here and in England.'

Gilles stood up with such violence that the chair in which he had been sitting fell over with a clatter. There was an icy sweat trickling down his spine and he felt as though a bottomless gulf had just opened at his feet. The look he turned on the Italian was full of anger and disgust.

'What sort of a man are you? You know all this, you know the Queen's name has been taken in vain, that the Grand Almoner of France has been entangled in a mire of trickery, and yet you sit there and do nothing? Why have you not gone straight to the police, to the cardinal, to the Queen herself?'

'And be sent to the Bastille, or perhaps to Charenton? Calm yourself, my friend, and understand that nothing I could do at present would be any use. The damage is done. The necklace is sold and gone. It is too late. There is nothing anyone can do now. Do you think I said nothing to the Cardinal when he first told me about this business? I swear to you, I tried to warn him. He only laughed at me, blinded as he is by dreams of love and office.'

'The cardinal's mad, I don't deny that, but the King is not! He shall hear the truth tomorrow.'

Snatching up his hat from the chair where it lay, the young man was already half out of the room when Cagliostro gripped him with an iron hand.

'What are you going to do? You love the King, I think? Then how are you proposing to tell him, a husband deeply in love with his wife, that his Grand Almoner, believing himself to be as good as her lover, has taken the liberty of buying for her a necklace originally ordered by Louis XV for the woman who was his mistress? Do you really feel brave enough to tell him that to his face? Unless you would prefer to tell him that his brother is a villain who is secretly weaving the darkest plots against his honour and his crown – perhaps even his very life?'

Feeling as though his legs had been cut from under him, Gilles sank down on a bench seat underneath the black marble plaque with Pope's prayer on it.

'No . . . you're quite right. I couldn't do it. Yet he must find out one day.'

'Not necessarily. The Countess and her accomplice have laid their plans well. She thinks that when the time comes to make the first payment, realizing that he has been duped, he will have no alternative but to pay for the necklace quietly, in order to escape becoming a laughing stock. It won't be easy, but if he sells lands, abbeys and whatnot. The Rohans are still very rich, despite the recent bankruptcy of the Prince de Guémémée. They'll hush the matter up.'

'But the Queen? The Queen is bound to know. And then what will she do?'

'If she were told, I don't know exactly how she would react. She is unpredictable, and I cannot divine a person's thoughts in the future. But it is possible that it will all be settled between the Prince and the jewellers. They have just been appointed jewellers to the Crown, in succession to M. Aubert, who died recently. They are at the height of their success and I cannot really see them jeopardizing their new status by letting a fearful scandal break on Versailles. My own view is that things will be kept quiet. Unless—'

'Unless what?'

'You know the Baron de Breteuil?'

'Secretary of State to the King's Household? Of course.'

'He is a deadly enemy of the Cardinal's, who once filched the appointment to the embassy in Vienna from under his nose. He is also friendly with Monsieur. If he gets wind of the matter, he'll do his utmost to drag down a man he hates, even if the mud splashes the very steps of the throne in the process. So now do you understand that the only hope of preventing the slightest stink arising from this affair is to keep quiet? The only hope!'

Gilles got to his feet with an effort, standing a head higher than Cagliostro, whose eyes were boring into his.

'Why did you tell me all this if you were so afraid I would talk?'

'Because I had to give you some proof of confidence in order to make you trust me. And so that you would understand that I mean no harm, either to you or to Judith. This kingdom is doomed, Chevalier de Tournemine. Sooner or later the storm will break over it and sweep it clean. Too many men, like you, have crossed the ocean and learned to speak a new word, the best of all words and yet the most formidable also, for the traps it conceals. That word is Liberty. Turn your back on this decaying old world. Leave it! Cross the seas again. Go to virgin lands where man can live with a pure heart. When you have made up your mind to it, when you are quite ready, then come back and ask me for Mademoiselle de Saint-Mélaine and, I give you my word, I will give her into your arms myself, and gladly.'

'I shall remember that. Good night, Count.'

Standing alone in the antechamber with the light of the candles reflected in the plaque of polished black marble, Cagliostro listened to the young man's footsteps fading quickly down the stairs. He heard his voice ringing in the courtyard and the creak of the stable door as his horse was brought out to him, and then he smiled and walked slowly back into his study.

'He will not go,' he murmured, shrugging a little. 'It would be too simple.'

Gilles, waiting for the groom to lead out Merlin, saw a scrap of paper fluttering at his feet and stooped to pick it up. It was a portrait of Cagliostro, gazing up to heaven with an inspired look on his face and underneath a four-line verse:

'See in this face the friend of all mankind
Who every day new blessings brings to mind,
Long life to some, relief from want to others,
Seeking no gain except to serve his brothers.'

With a jerk of annoyance, Gilles crumpled the paper and threw it on the ground again. But he's a strange fellow, all the same, he thought. Superman or cunning charlatan? That crude advertisement was aimed at the stupidest section of society, and yet the man seemed to possess strange powers which should have enabled him to do without that. And he was privy to the secrets of kings. What was the truth?

Putting off consideration of this until some later time, he sprang lightly into the saddle, quite in his old way, and rode off briskly in the direction of the Barrière de la Conférence and the road to Versailles. He was determined to go back that night. After all he had just heard, he could not bear the thought of shutting himself up in a hotel room. The ride in the fresh air would do him good and help to clear his brain of the stifling fumes which the magician in the Rue Saint-Claud had made him breathe in. What he needed was the cool night air, the glimmer of the Seine and the smell of roses from the gardens along the way. The earth, saturated during the floods, had finally burgeoned into a late but lovely spring.

It was nearly midnight by the time he reached the outskirts of the city, after a ride which, lost in his thoughts, seemed to him to have taken an extraordinarily short time. If Cagliostro could have looked into his mind then, while he trotted through the streets in time to the cheerful clatter of Merlin's hooves, he might have felt some surprise, for the young man's head was filled with nothing but the time when he would go and claim his beloved and how soonest to arrive at that longed-for day.

Once past the Barrière de la Conférence and riding along the river by the village of Passy, Gilles could see the lights from the magnificent Hôtel de Valentinois gleaming through the darkness beyond the Princess de Lamballe's gardens. This was the property of the financier Leray de Chaumont, who with his ships and money had given such powerful aid to the American rebels. There, Gilles knew, still lived the man whose word had stirred a whole generation of young men and sealed the union between the old France and the youthful United States, the man who was now revered on both sides of the Atlantic as a prophet of genius: Benjamin Franklin.

According to Philippe de Chartres, who was on the best of terms with him, Franklin, his task at an end, was preparing to leave France and return to Philadelphia, while a new American ambassador would be arriving in the person of Thomas Jefferson. Why, Gilles asked himself, should he not go with him?

By the time he reached the Rue de Noailles he had still found no very satisfactory answer to this important question, but he was not unduly cast down. The hope of happiness alone was sufficiently intoxicating.

He found Pongo at the foot of the front steps and tossed Merlin's bridle to him.

'Don't tell me you were worrying, you old nursemaid? You know I'm as fit as a fiddle now.'

'Pongo not worry over health. Pongo worry because of woman wait upstairs. Pongo not like.'

'A woman? What's she like?'

'Hard to tell. She wear big blue veil. But all same Pongo not like.'

So Madame de Balbi knew already that he was back? What kind of a watch had been kept on the quiet little house in the Rue de Noailles?

She was there, standing by the fireplace in the salon where, now that the mild weather made a fire unnecessary, Mademoiselle Marjon had filled the grate instead with a blaze of golden broom. She was dressed exactly as she had been on the night of their first meeting, only now the blue veil had been laid aside on a chair and a little ivory fan was moving gently to and fro between her slim fingers.

Its rhythm did not quicken noticeably as Gilles came into the room and bowed to his visitor with deliberate formality. But she was not going to let him keep the conversation on a strictly social footing. She opened her attack without a pause.

'Why did you answer none of my letters?'

'Why should I have answered them?' he asked softly.

'Because it is natural! Didn't you like what I wrote?'

363

'I cannot tell. I never read them.'

'Liar! You are simply trying to be disagreeable. What man could let a woman's letters pile up unread?'

Instead of answering, he went to a small desk half-concealed by the heavy folds of grey silk that curtained his windows and, taking a key from his pocket, opened it and removed a bundle tied with blue ribbon. This he handed to her.

'Count them,' he said briefly. 'They are all there.'

She made no move to take the letters, so that he was obliged to put them on the table. In the silence that followed he could hear the increased rate of her breathing and the little fan, too, was fluttering faster. She had turned her head away, so that he could not see her face.

At last, with a little sigh, she moved away from her corner of the fireplace and came towards him.

'You no longer love me?'

'Did I ever tell you that I loved you? I don't recall it.'

'Very well. Then let us say that your behaviour was such as to foster the illusion. Besides, what a stupidly bourgeois idea to bring love into everything. Was there ever any question of anything between us other than a pleasure we both shared?'

'I should be an ingrate to deny the pleasure I have had in your company.'

'Then why not come back to me?'

Insensibly, she had moved closer, enveloping him in the rose scent she used. Her full, red lips were trembling a little, she was on the point of lifting them to his when, with extreme gentleness, he put her away from him.

'No. Can you not understand that there can be nothing more between us, not even pleasure?'

Her eyes widened in a look of unbelievable innocence.

'But why?'

'Because, my dear, the death warrant of our pleasant little relationship was signed, on my body, by the swords and daggers of a gang of assassins paid by your royal lover. You claimed, as I understood, that you had persuaded him to leave me alone? I can still feel how well you succeeded – when it rains, at least.'

'Well the weather today is perfect! Besides, it was not him! It

364

cannot have been him! The murderers were in the pay of the Duc de Chartres and their leader—'

'I know who was their leader. As the Duc de Chartres does also. It was simply convenient to try and shift the matter on to him in order to avoid trouble with the King. But that tale won't hold water now. The Prince has told me too much.'

'But—'

'You are wasting your breath and your time, Madame. It was certainly on the orders of Monseigneur de Provence that the Comte d'Antraigues was there that night, and to settle a score of his own, for we are old enemies. So you see, it is no longer possible for there to be anything between us.'

A flash of anger showed in the Countess's dark eyes.

'It's her, isn't it? It's that strumpet Hunolstein? She entrapped you with her nursing? I can guess how! I'll wager you found your strength come back to you fast enough there, so hot as she is! There's not a whore in all France goes to it more willingly—'

'You are becoming vulgar,' Gilles' voice was pure ice. 'It is time you left. Allow me to conduct you to your carriage.'

He went to the door and held it open for her.

'Tell me first!' she cried. 'Did you sleep with her?'

'No. If it will relieve your mind at all, Madame d'Hunolstein behaved to me like a devoted and affectionate sister. That devotion and affection I return with interest and I will not permit anyone to insult her in my hearing. Once and for all, are you going, Madame, or do I have to carry you out? And will you please never come to this house again.'

Anne de Balbi picked up her veil and cast it over one arm and stalked to the door. In the doorway, she paused and looked Gilles in the eye.

'Very well. I am going. There is no need for you to see me out, it would be perfectly absurd. One word more. I shall never set foot in this house again, you may be sure of that. But you have not done with me, for all that, my fine friend. We shall meet again.'

He bowed with ironic detachment.

'I shall look forward to it. But not too soon, I hope. I am in no state yet to bear too much excitement. Farewell, Madame.'

When he was alone, he picked up the bundle of letters left

lying on the table and walked with it into the kitchen where Pongo, knowing his master, was busy making coffee, following Niklaus' careful instructions to the letter.

'Here,' Gilles said. 'Put those on the fire. There are some things better not left lying about an honest house.'

15

Arrest the Cardinal!

On Monday, the fifteenth of August 1785, Versailles was preparing for the combined celebrations of the great religious feast of the Assumption, the renewal of Louis XIII's dedication of France to the Virgin Mary and the Queen's name day. Consequently, by nine o'clock in the morning the Grands Appartements and the Galerie des Glaces were filling with a huge, gorgeously dressed crowd drawn from the whole Court, the *corps diplomatique*, the population of Versailles, visitors from Paris and farther afield, and even from abroad. For on that day the Palace doors were open, more widely even than usual, to those who wished to gaze at the magnificent, traditional procession in which, in a little while, the entire royal family would move through the state rooms to go and hear High Mass, traditionally celebrated by the Grand Almoner of France.

Through the windows of the Galerie des Glaces, wide open to the long blue perspective of the Grand Canal, the flower-filled parterres and the dancing magic of the fountains flinging their tall rainbow plumes high in the air to fall back into the deep reflected blue of the sky in the stone basins, the sun streamed in to light up the gilding on wood and bronze, furnishings, candelabra, the shining surfaces of the long mirrors and the richly decorated dresses of the holiday crowd pressing on either side of the clear path, lined by the soldiers of the King's Household. Bodyguards, Swiss Guards, Guards of the Porte or the Prévoté, of all the regiments whose business was the personal protection of the sovereign, were strung out along the way from the doors of the royal apartments to the chapel.

The overall buzz of conversation and the shimmer of waving fans made the palace seem more than ever like a vast aviary, reeking with the perfumed hair powders and toilet waters with which the fashionable crowd had drenched itself.

Standing in the room called the Oeil-de-Boeuf which functioned as the King's antechamber, where the ministers and heads of the most exalted noble families assembled, Gilles, resplendent in uniform, was in command of the guard on the doors of King Louis's apartments, where two men of the Garde de la Porte in blue and red with white and gold checked crossbelts stood rigidly still and silent. Over in one corner, Calonne, the handsome finance minister, was deep in conversation with Vergennes and a little farther off Miromesnil, Keeper of the Seals, was having what appeared to be an unusually vigorous exchange with the Baron de Breteuil.

Quite suddenly, the holiday atmosphere had altered. Gilles was the first of those in the room to sense that something untoward was happening. The Queen, emerging without warning from her own apartment, swept through the Oeil-de-Boeuf without a glance for anyone and disappeared into the King's Chamber at such a speed that the footmen dashing after her had no time even to fling wide the double doors.

A startled murmur ran through the room, for the Queen's face, usually so smiling, wore a strained, tense expression and showed the trace of recent tears. What was more, although her Majesty was dressed with the utmost elegance in a mottled lilac gown of Chinese silk heavily overburdened with lace, it was perfectly obvious that her head was still undressed. Her lovely ash-blonde hair, innocent of powder, lay in soft curls on her shoulders, a negligence which, on such a day, for a Queen who took such pride in her appearance, was the most glaring offence against decorum.

The occupants of the antechamber had barely time to comment on this occurrence before an usher emerged from the King's Chamber, sought out Breteuil and Miromesnil and hurried them in to the King.

Winkleried, whose men were on duty outside the Queen's door and who was at that moment carrying out a brief inspection, took the opportunity to sidle unobtrusively up to his friend.

'I don't know what's going on,' he whispered, 'but there's something dramatic in the air.'

'What do you think it's all about? I can't understand it at all.'

Ulrich-August shrugged his extravagantly gold-braided shoulders.

'Wait and see! The Comtesse de Provence, the Comtesse d'Artois and Mesdames Tantes are kicking their heels in the Queen's Cabinet waiting for her to receive them and she has just come storming out and gone into the King's room. I heard angry shouting and weeping. If it goes on like this the procession to the chapel will never get started on time. The Cardinal will be kept waiting.'

'I doubt it,' Gilles said. 'The King is always very punctual.'

'Well, he's going to be late today. Can you imagine the Queen attending mass with her hair all down her back? Good God! Talking of the Cardinal, here he comes! And one of the King's ushers with him. What can it all mean? Madame Etiquette will never get over it,' he added, with a glance at the austere Duchesse de Noailles, to whom this nickname had been pinned long ago by the Dauphine, and who had been following the Queen's progress through the room through her lorgnette with an outraged expression.

The Cardinal de Rohan had entered the antechamber, decked in his ecclesiastical vestments, the red silk skirts of his robe licking like a tongue of fire at his heels. The jewels in his cross of the Holy Ghost and in the rings that covered his red gloves rivalled the sunbeams in brightness and glittered amid the priceless lace of his rochet. In one hand he carried a large rectangular hat made of red velvet while the other he extended automatically for the devout nobility to kiss. His face was radiant. He had never looked so splendid. He seemed to draw all the light in the room to himself.

He and his escort vanished also into the King's Chamber and the doors closed behind them. Once again there was nothing to do but wait. This time the wait lasted for an hour, by which time the courtiers' curiosity was practically bursting. The famous antechamber which had been the source of nearly every piece of gossip in Versailles ever since it was first built, was seething like water coming to the boil. Eyes moved incessantly from the big ormolu clock on the mantelshelf to the closed doors of the Chamber. Something was going to happen, certainly. Everyone could sense it, but no one could say what.

Then, all at once, Tournemine understood. Emerging from the Queen's rooms and slipping through the ranks of courtiers, his eye had just caught the nervous figures of the royal jewellers, Boehmer and Bassange. With their dark coats and shifty expressions, they looked like rats fleeing from a sinking ship. Boehmer had tears in his eyes and Gilles heard him muttering: 'We are ruined ... ruined ...'

And so the disaster Cagliostro had thought would never happen had happened after all. The Queen, it seemed, had just learned the truth about the necklace. That would explain her agitation and distress but—

Just then the King's door opened wide. Not for the procession but for the Cardinal, alone. A murmur of surprise greeted his appearance. He was whiter than his own lace and his eyes had the blankness of a man who had received a mortal blow. He was followed by the Baron de Breteuil who was, quite clearly, in the grip of a fearful joy which he was striving to suppress.

Once outside the door, he moved up beside the Cardinal and the two walked on together a little way, as though continuing a conversation. Then, as they neared the door into the Galerie des Glaces, Gilles heard the Cardinal murmur: 'Could we not leave it like this? Could you not keep me under guard while we walk together?'

As he spoke, he entered the gallery and began to pass between the packed ranks of courtiers. And it was at that precise moment that Breteuil's eyes met Gilles' and the thing happened.

The Minister for the King's Household raised his voice and addressed the young officer in tones loud enough to roll over the sea of heads, already bending in reverence, as far as the Salon de Guerre.

'I order you in the King's name to arrest the Cardinal de Rohan!'

If the magnificent ceiling had fallen on him, the young man

could not have been more stunned. He stared at Breteuil as if he had taken leave of his senses.

'Do as I bid you!' Breteuil hissed between clenched teeth. 'Secure him and escort him to his apartment.'

At the sound of that shattering command, the Cardinal had stopped dead and was standing, flanked by the crowd on either side on whom a terrified hush had fallen, so still that Gilles caught himself thinking he might have been turned to stone. There was no choice but to obey.

'Guard!' The voice in which he gave the order was so hoarse he scarcely recognized it. 'Fall in around the Cardinal.'

Then the Duc de Villeroi, duty officer of the Bodyguard, arrived, charged by the King with the task of securing the Cardinal's person. He informed the prisoner that it was his duty to escort him to the apartment close by the chapel to which his office entitled him, and take possession of any papers he might find there.

Surrounded by guards, with Villeroi at his side and Tournemine bringing up the rear, the Cardinal Prince de Rohan paced calmly through the beautiful gallery with its brilliant holiday crowds, and on through the Grands Appartements, the salons of War, Apollo, Mercury, Mars, Diana, Venus, Plenty, Hercules ...

Everything in him, his Breton pride and his reverence for the Church alike, rebelling against an arrest which he knew to be undeserved and dictated solely by private spite, the Chevalier de Tournemine followed the tall red and white figure as it passed, like the wraith of a glory that was already dying, through the noble rooms furnished with the treasures of three kings.

As they came to the Salon D'Hercule, the Cardinal paused briefly and appeared to bow his head. Gilles saw that he was scribbling a few words on a scrap of paper concealed inside his hat but, naturally, he said nothing. Villeroi was busy giving the order to his subordinate, the Comte d'Agout, to send for the Cardinal's carriage and prepare to accompany him to Paris, and had noticed nothing. Breteuil, having beheld his triumph with obvious relish, had disappeared after they passed out of the gallery.

The news had spread through the palace like wildfire. By the

371

time he reached the door of his apartment, the Cardinal found his manservant waiting for him in tears. As he fell on his knees to kiss his hand, Rohan bent forward as if to draw him to his feet and as he did so the slip of paper changed hands and he muttered a few words in the servant's ear.

'This to the Abbé Georgel! And hurry!'

The man rose, suddenly dry-eyed, and slipped away before anyone could think of stopping him. The Cardinal, meanwhile, had entered his own room to change his robes for clothes more suitable to his prisoner's condition. As he went, he made a sign to the Chevalier to follow, while Villeroi began collecting up the papers scattered on the desk.

'I am your prisoner, Sir,' he said with dignity, 'and I suppose it is your duty to keep me in sight.'

'Go with the Cardinal,' Villeroi confirmed, hearing him. 'Do not let him out of your sight until you hand him over to the Comte d'Agout.'

Gilles bowed and turned to follow the Cardinal. As soon as the door was shut behind him, the Cardinal spoke.

'You are a Breton, Monsieur de Tournemine and I am Rohan. May I trust to your honour?'

'Yes, your Eminence, in everything that does not conflict with my duty to my King.'

'Naturally. If I had attained to the heights I was led to hope for, you would have been sure of my protection. It was an insane dream, I know that now, and I am forced to abandon it. Even so, will you do one service for an unhappy prisoner of state?'

'With all my heart,' Gilles exclaimed, more eagerly perhaps than he intended. The real nobility with which this man of exalted birth was bearing the disaster which had fallen on his head compelled his admiration.

Swiftly, the Cardinal unfastened his robe and the shirt beneath it and took from round his neck a little bag of red silk on which was embroidered the eight gold mascles, his family's arms. Pulling the fine gold chain on which it was suspended over his head, he put it into the young man's hand.

'In this there is a letter and a portrait. Burn the letter, but keep the portrait. If I ever regain my freedom you may return it to me and it will be a consolation to me. Should I die in prison, keep it as a mark of the friendship I had no time to show you.'

Gilles carried the little bag to his lips and kissed it soberly, an act which brought tears to the Cardinal's eyes, then tucked it away in his waistcoat pocket.

'I will return it to your Eminence one day,' he said stoutly as he helped the Cardinal out of his red silk robes and into a simple black suit. 'There is no reason why the King should make you end your days in prison.'

The Cardinal smiled bitterly as he finished tying his cravat. Then he turned to Gilles.

'Do you know what it is I am accused of, Chevalier?'

'You have incurred the King's displeasure, or the Queen's. Or so I guess?'

'If that were all! I am accused of having stolen a diamond necklace – a necklace the Queen herself charged me to buy for her.'

The words rose to Gilles' lips before he had time to think what he was saying.

'But it was not you who stole it! It was Madame de la Motte!'

The Cardinal stared at him in genuine amazement.

'Do you really believe that? That charming woman, a true friend. . . .'

'Is the greatest cheat! On my honour, I believe every word I say! And Cagliostro even more than me!'

There was silence.

'Cagliostro,' Rohan said, and sighed. 'Why would I not listen to him? So many times he tried to warn me. He, too, plays a strange game, but I believe he means well to me.'

The Duc de Villeroi's entrance into the room put an end to the conversation. Seeing that the prisoner was ready, he made a gesture of approval and bowed.

'With your permission, Monseigneur, we are about to leave.'

'Where are you taking me?'

'To your own house, first of all, the Hôtel de Rohan-Strasbourg, and from there to the Bastille.'

'I see.'

As the Chevalier knelt, he made a rapid sign of the cross in blessing and then left the room which he was never to see again.

Gilles watched the coach as it drove away through the fine sunshine of that Assumption day, surrounded by a company of mounted guards, bearing the Grand Almoner of France away to imprisonment. It was just twelve o'clock.

When he reached home, he asked Pongo to light the fire in his library and then leave him alone. Then he took the red silk bag out of his pocket and opened it. Of the two things it contained, one was a brief letter, written in an awkward, faded hand on aged paper with a faint scent still clinging to it. He put it into the fire without allowing his eyes to rest even on the superscription. The other was a miniature in a gold and sapphire frame. It was, of course, a portrait of the Queen.

But the mischievous smile the painter had caught so well on that small slip of ivory was not the look of the mature woman, angry and vengeful, whom he had seen that day sweep into the King's room. It belonged to a very young girl, a fair-haired, enchanting Marie-Antoinette fifteen years old, the picture of the fresh and youthful Dauphine, at a time when there was not a man in France but was in love with her.

Gilles sat for a long time with it in the palm of his hand, staring vaguely into the leaping flames which had long ago consumed the slender note. He was conscious of a deep compassion for the man who had kept those relics close to his heart for so many years. Who could tell how long Louis de Rohan had loved the woman who had become the wife of his King? Who could say whether his longing to be first minister did not spring from his desperate need to be near her and if it was not, after all, in its way, a kind of love? There was that in the history of Mazarin to inspire a lesser man than Rohan!

At length, Gilles locked the miniature away in a little box in a drawer of his writing table and went to join Ulrich-August, whose rich voice he could hear booming away in the sitting room.

'I'm inviting you to have supper with me at the *Juste*,' the Swiss declared. 'It's not every day a man arrests a prince of the Church in the very middle of Versailles! You have been making history. It needs to be celebrated!'

'Celebrated?' Gilles said, shocked. 'What a thing to say! My poor friend, that public arrest was an appalling thing to

374

happen! Terrible! And it seems that it was the Queen, urged on by Breteuil and her confessor, the Abbé de Vermond, who insisted on the King's doing it. She must be mad not to have thought of the effect it could have on the people and on her own reputation. Can you imagine the row it will cause in Paris? The pamphleteers will have a field day!'

'Then so shall we!' Winkleried retorted, beaming. 'Pamphleteer-baiting is my favourite sport. Just give me a nice little pamphleteer on a spit. He may not be edible, but he's a pretty sight! Now will you come and have some supper?'

Gilles laughed. 'I never said I meant to starve to death,' he said. 'Of course I'm coming. If only to hear what they're saying in the *Juste* tonight. Next to the Oeil-de-Boeuf, it's the biggest hotbed of gossip in Versailles!'

'At last!' Ulrich-August said. 'You see what I'm driving at!'

Actually, the famous dining room was more like a witches' cauldron than an ordinary gossip-shop that night. The appalled silence which had descended on the palace at the moment of the Cardinal's arrest had burst out, as soon as he was gone, into an indescribable babble of comment which only the somewhat belated arrival of the royal procession had temporarily damped. Even then, the Queen's set face and the shocked expressions of her sisters and aunts-in-law had provided additional fuel for speculation. Ten minutes after mass was finished, the rumour of the scandal was all over Versailles and two hours after that it was sweeping through Paris like a flood of foul water, bringing evil-smelling bubbles to the surface.

When the official court newspaper, the *Gazette de France*, came out forty-eight hours later, every copy was seized on eagerly in the hope of further details about what was already becoming known as 'the affair', but such hopes were disappointed. Overtaken by belated good sense, the Court had released nothing more than the barest announcement to the effect that: 'On the 15th, the Feast of the Assumption of the Virgin, their Majesties attended high mass celebrated in the palace chapel by the Bishop of Digne and sung by the King's choir. The plate was taken round by the Comtesse de Sérent. In the afternoon the King, accompanied by the Royal family,

375

went to the chapel to take part in the annual procession for the renewal of the vow made by Louis XIII . . .'

That was all. Regarding the drama in the Galerie des Glaces, not a word. This was a mistake since, with nothing to feed on, imagination ran riot and the most shocking rumours spread abroad, the commonest being that the necklace had been stolen from the Queen's jewellers by the Cardinal de Rohan, who was her lover, acting on her own instructions. It was a story that was to die hard. By giving way to her anger and letting herself be swayed by bad counsellors, the Queen was stirring up an evil in the depths of her kingdom whose virulence she could not yet imagine.

In the meanwhile, Versailles continued to act with incredible shortsightedness. While Marie-Antoinette hastened to her beloved Trianon to wipe the traces of her anger away with a resumption of rehearsals of *The Barber of Seville*, oblivious of the fact that this was scarcely the moment to appear in the role of the delightful Rosina, 'the prettiest little charmer, sweet and tender, fresh and lovely and altogether delectable', the orders for the arrest of the real culprits went out with extraordinary discrimination and lack of urgency. The fact was that the upper echelons of the police were at that time in a state of some confusion, the capable Lenoir having been removed from his post, only four days before the scandal broke at Versailles, on the instigation of the Comte de Provence, and replaced by the weakling Thierry de Crosne. Lenoir had been sent to lavish his dangerous abilities on the Bibliothèque Royale.

Consequently, it was not until three days after the Cardinal's arrest that Jeanne de la Motte was taken at Bar-sur-Aube as she was returning from a party given by the Duc de Penthièvre at Châteauvillain. Even then her husband was left at liberty to collect his jewels together and leave quietly for England. The foppish secretary had disappeared likewise. The Baron de Breteuil seemed, in fact, to be going to a lot of trouble to ensure that the Cardinal should bear the whole blame.

On the evening of August the twenty-third, Gilles and Ulrich-August were seated by the library window which was open to let in the cool air from the garden, engaged in a silent, furious struggle over the chess board, Mademoiselle Marjon

376

was ensconced in her big wicker chair, taking the air under the walnut tree, her cat, Bogonia, on her lap and the enormous sheep-dog, Brutus, lying at her feet, when there was a ring at the doorbell. Berthe, the maidservant, had gone to bed and so it was the old lady herself who answered.

By the light of the candle she had taken up in the hall, she saw a young, tear-stained face framed in the hood of a brown cloak.

'Does the Chevalier de Tournemine live here?' the girl stammered, looking so distraught that Mademoiselle Marjon asked herself seriously whether the poor creature had not escaped from some asylum for lunatics.

'Yes, he does but—'

She drew back hastily to avoid being knocked down as the mad girl, for surely she could be nothing else, sprang past her with an inarticulate cry and rushed inside, calling Gilles' name in frantic tones.

The chessmen went flying as Gilles leaped to his feet, scarcely able to believe his ears.

'Judith!' he cried. 'Good God—!'

In another moment he was hurtling down the stairs, flinging his arms wide open to receive a desperately sobbing Judith who was clinging to him like a woman blinded. He hugged her close.

'My heart! Sweet one! What is it? What have they done to you?'

There was no answer. With a little sigh of relief, the girl had fainted. Swiftly, he picked her up in his arms and carried her upstairs, where he found Winkleried and Pongo hurrying to meet him.

'What's the matter with her?' Winkleried asked. 'She's not hurt?'

'I don't think so. I'll lay her on my bed. Pongo, run and ask Mademoiselle Marjon for some salts, a cordial, anything!'

'Don't trouble,' came that lady's voice from halfway up the stairs. 'I'm coming! I'm bringing everything you need.'

Seconds later, she appeared, clutching an assortment of bottles. Gilles had laid the girl down with infinite care and had taken off the long dark cloak. Underneath it she wore a simple white cambric dress with green spots, with a muslin scarf folded across her breast. The dress was torn in places and bore the marks of dust and dirt. A handkerchief was clasped tightly in one bloodstained hand. The tangled hair, hanging loose about her shoulders, was damp with sweat.

'She looks as though she's been caught up in a riot,' Ulrich-August commented. 'Poor little thing, she looked like a frightened bird when I saw her running across the garden!'

'If you were to move yourselves out of the way,' Mademoiselle Marjon said tartly, 'I might be able to do something for her. You gentlemen have no business unlacing a young lady's stays.'

'That's an idea, though,' Winkleried said thoughtfully. 'I'm awfully good at it.'

'Oh, are you indeed! Well you can just take yourself off outside, Don Juan!' And with that she took the young Swiss firmly by the arm and thrust him out of the door. Then she looked doubtfully at Gilles.

'Is she related to you?'

'I am going to marry her.'

'Congratulations! I'm sure she's very lovely when she's clean. In that case, you may stay.'

She went quickly to work, opening the dress and loosening the whalebone stays which were hindering the girl's breathing, then she bathed her forehead with aromatic vinegar and held a flask of *sal volatile* under her nose. The effects of this were remarkable. Judith sneezed violently and opened huge, terrified eyes which quickly filled with tears. Then, as she saw Gilles holding out his arms to her she gave a desperate sob. 'Oh, you are here, at last! Don't leave me!'

After that she began to cry in good earnest. Gilles sat on the edge of the bed and held her hands, bringing them together within his own and kissing them gently.

'Hush, my darling,' he said, his heart aching at the sight of this dreadful grief. 'You're safe here. No one shall hurt you. They are all friends here, and I shan't leave you again.'

'T-t-truly? You p-promise?'

Her breathing was ragged with shock.

'Here, get her to drink this,' Mademoiselle Marjon said, pouring something from one of her many bottles into a glass. 'It will do her good.'

Gilles held her while she drank, his heart absurdly moved by

378

the sight of her rosy lips sipping the golden liquid. He was almost as much in need of a restorative himself, for his love at that moment was as much as he could bear. When, calmer now, she sank back on the pillows with a sigh, he seated himself beside her again and took her hand, striving not to look at the ravishing disorder of her dress and the fine, almost transparent shift beneath.

'If you are feeling better,' he said quietly, 'can you tell me what happened? Or would you rather sleep a little first?'

She gave him a quavering smile. 'No, I'll tell you. My God, I must look like a mad creature! But it's been such a terrible day! Forgive me, Madame,' she turned to look at Mademoiselle Marjon,' for rushing past you like that. I hardly knew what I was doing any more. I was ... so dreadfully upset!'

'That much was obvious, you poor child,' Mademoiselle Marjon said, smiling warmly at her. 'Nobody blames you. But you must lie still now. You are quite safe here. I am going to leave the two of you together and go downstairs to my own room. Would you like me to prepare a room for her?' she added, speaking to Gilles. 'If so, I can come back for her later.'

But it was Judith who answered. Her dark eyes filled with terror and she clung to the young man in desperate protest. 'No – no! Oh, please! I don't want to go anywhere else! I want to stay with him!'

Gilles bent and kissed her cheek soothingly.

'I'm here. Don't be afraid.' Then he looked at the old lady. 'She can sleep here for tonight, dear Mademoiselle. I'll make do on the sofa in the sitting room.'

'As you wish. Just call me if there is anything you need.'

She tiptoed softly out of the room, leaving the two young people together. Only, once the door was firmly shut behind her, she permitted herself a mischievous little twinkle.

'She's no fool, that little thing,' she chuckled softly. 'At her age I'd have preferred a good-looking young man's bed to an old maid's any day. And, really, I think our young Chevalier might be even more of a charmer than the late King Louis.'

She listened for a moment outside the door before going downstairs, but she heard nothing. This was largely because the two young people were no sooner left alone than they fell passionately into one another's arms.

379

Only when they had kissed for a long time did Judith, securely lodged within the crook of Gilles' arm, finally consent to unburden herself of all that had happened. It did not take long. At seven o'clock that morning, Procurator Chesnon, accompanied by a police inspector named de Brugnières and a posse of armed men, had burst into Cagliostro's house, while Cagliostro and his wife were still in bed. They were both placed under arrest, but whereas the doctor was taken away at once, being given no more than time to dress, Serafina, out of consideration for her sex, was permitted not only to dress and gather together some necessities against her stay in prison, but also to collect her jewels and other valuables in a case to which the procurator, clearly much affected by her beauty, affixed his official seal. After that he made her lock all the doors to her private apartments and keep the key in her pocket, rather than giving it into the keeping of her maid, which had been her first intention. The servants, who had been kept in another part of the house, were ordered to put the shutters up at the windows and leave, while two policemen were left to watch the main door until further notice.

'And so Cagliostro has been arrested,' Gilles said thoughtfully. 'Do you know what the charge is?'

'The procurator said that dreadful La Motte woman who tried to make friends with me had denounced him as an accomplice of the Cardinal's in the theft of the necklace. What a terrible thing to do! The woman must be a perfect devil! Poor Count Alessandro! He is so good, so—'

'But where were you all this time?' Gilles broke in, not particularly relishing this. 'Along with the servants?'

'No. My room was only separated from that used by the Count and Countess by a little dark passage in the thickness of the wall. The only way out was through their bedchamber. The Master liked to keep me always under his care—'

'Under his eye, more like,' Gilles said acidly. 'What was he to you?'

'A father,' Judith said severely. 'He was very fond of me. He feared a great many dangers for me.'

'But the Countess let you out surely, before she locked up?'

Judith shook her head.

'She was always very nice, quite loving to me in fact, in front

380

of him, but I knew that she disliked me really. I expect she was pleased to be able to do me a bad turn. Unless she just forgot all about me. I must say, she had some reason!'

'But, if you overheard it all, why didn't you come out yourself? Why didn't you show yourself? You might have passed yourself off as one of the maids and left quietly along with the servants.'

'No. I couldn't do that. If I let them see me, I was lost.' She pressed herself closer, burying her face in his neck, and he realized suddenly that she was trembling.

'But – why, you're still frightened!' he said, moved. She had started to cry again and he covered the watery little face with kisses. 'You're frightened to death! And more tears! Oh God! What can I do?'

'Nothing, my love, nothing! Only you'll have to know. From the passage leading to my room I could not only hear, I could see as well. I saw the men who were with the Countess and one of them – one of the policemen – I knew, only too well. I nearly fainted for a moment when I saw him.'

'A policeman? How do you come to know such a person? Who was he?'

'It was my brother.'

'Your—'

'Yes. Morvan.'

There was a moment's silence while there rose up before Gilles' mind's eye the brutal figure of the younger Saint-Mélaine. He felt a bitter surge of loathing. So the man he had vowed to find and send to join his brother Tudal in hell, was actually in Paris? He might even have brushed past him in the street, unknowing.

Feeling that Judith was still shaking, he stroked her head gently and said, forcing himself to keep his voice perfectly calm: 'Well, I suppose it could be called good news. If he's in the police, I shan't have much trouble finding him.'

'What are you going to do?'

'Kill him, that's all. You will never be able to rest as long as he's alive and I don't want to see you looking like a hunted deer again. I love you, Judith. You are my whole life and I want to be yours. There is no room between us for a beast like Morvan. Forget him for the present. One day you'll be able to forget

381

him altogether. But now tell me the rest of your story. How did you manage to get out of your mousetrap?'

'Over the roof. There are attics over the Count's room, and one loft you can get to by way of a little stair. I got out that way and along the gutters, like a cat. Only this cat was terrified! I managed somehow to get on to the roof of the house next door. I was lucky, being summer there was a skylight open. I got through it into a garret full of junk and filthy dirty. That was where I hurt my hand on the door latch. But I found the stairs and got out into the street at last. Then I turned my back on the boulevard and ran and ran until I found a coach for hire that would agree to take me to Versailles. And even then he put me down at the entrance to the town because he was in a hurry to get back to Boulogne to his stable. I had to find this wretched Rue de Noailles all by myself and I was so tired and frightened I thought I'd never get here. I was expecting to see Morvan come up behind me any moment . . .'

'You shall never see him again! I'll see to that. But how were you able to pay for the coach? Had you any money?'

For the first time since she had arrived, he saw her dark eyes light up with amusement. She even laughed.

'Oh yes! I'm rich, you must know! Well, quite rich. Look!'

She bent forward and lifted the hem of her dress and the embroidered petticoat beneath it and revealed, sewn into the strong canvas underskirt that gave fullness to her gown, a large pocket of cloth from which she withdrew a large bundle of notes and a small purse of gold which she tossed on to the bed.

'What's all this?'

'What was in Serafina's wallet. Wax seals aren't very strong, you know, however big they are. And that will teach her to forget me, whether she meant to or not! She's lucky I left her her diamonds.'

'And what about your dear Count Alessandro? I thought you were so fond of him? This money belongs to him.'

'He would have been the first to give it to me if he had been there. Gold means nothing to him, you know. He makes it.'

'Makes it!' Gilles echoed, startled.

'Yes. In the cellar. He has all sorts of strange things down there, retorts and furnaces and things. I saw him doing it once.

It was terribly impressive! That's why I didn't mind taking the money. Oh Gilles, I heard you telling Cagliostro you were ready to give up everything for me, Versailles, the King, your career, and take me to America, but when I talked about it to the master, he only smiled and said he was sure you meant it but you hadn't nearly enough money. Now that we have, when shall we go?'

'Very soon. In fact I was hoping we could have sailed with Benjamin Franklin, but when I called at his house he had already left for Brest. It was too late.'

'It doesn't matter now that we've got all this money. We can leave straight away, tomorrow . . . We're going to be able to be happy at last.'

All her liveliness recovered, she slid from his arms and from the bed and, clutching her unfastened dress about her, began pirouetting round the room with the light grace of a dancer before collapsing next to Gilles and laying her red head on his knee, the bright curls reaching to the floor.

'Come on then . . . carry me off to the ends of the earth, my handsome Chevalier! We'll love one another and I'll give you sons as brave as you and daughters as hateful as I am and I'll love you, oh, I'll love you so much! I've so much love to give you! Marry me and let's go!'

Completely overcome, he bent over her so that his lips were pressed to the silky mass of her hair.

'Judith, my love,' he murmured. 'Do you know what you're saying?'

He heard her laughter, close to his face.

'Of course I do! I may be a fool but I know what marriage is. And I want to be your wife.'

'Have you forgotten what Cagliostro said? He said you should not give way to love, that you were a rare being and because of that you should remain—'

She sprang up and faced him with sparkling eyes.

'A virgin? I know. Only I don't want to any more. It is all so stupid, and why should I be deprived of the ordinary joys that any woman can have? Cagliostro is in prison. He may never come out. He doesn't need me and I don't want to be a clairvoyant any more, a hybrid creature, neither one thing nor the other! All I want to be now is a woman, and your wife! I love you, Gilles. I love you with all the madness that is in me and I want to be yours, do you hear me? I want to belong to you and you alone, completely.'

'You want that? You really want it?' he said, his voice already a little unsteady with desire.

'Look and see!'

Parting the hands that held her dress, she gave a deft little wriggle of her shoulders and rose slowly, so that gown and petticoats slid slowly from her breast and body. Like Venus rising from the sea, she stood before his dazzled eyes, amid the pale foam of cambric and lawn. The soft light of the candles gleamed gold on her smooth, firm flesh, moulding it with such delicate light and shade that he could only fall to his knees, as though before a goddess, prostrate with adoration of the heady beauty which was his, and which, fully ripened now, had moved far beyond the fragile little siren of the Blavet.

But the goddess had no mind to be worshipped from a distance. Taking the young man's head between her hands, she gazed into his eyes, her own eyes blazing through the coppery brightness of her hair.

'Love me,' she whispered. 'My body has wanted you so long – ever since that first day! I loathed you but I couldn't help liking you, too. If you had tried to take me then, I think I should have yielded. Although I might have scratched your face for it afterwards.'

He held her between his two hands, her waist so slender that they all but spanned it, while his lips moved slowly over her firm belly and the delicate curve of the perfect small breasts, lingering on the soft pink tips that quivered and hardened under his touch. Judith stood with closed eyes and head flung back, letting him have his way. He could feel her long legs trembling against his body.

Then, suddenly, he rose to his feet and, swinging her into his arms, carried her to the bed, where she lay writhing and holding out her arms.

'Come to me . . .'

'In a moment.'

Thinking he would be undressing, she opened her eyes, wide with curiosity and a kind of odd challenging look. But she saw that he was going round the room, lighting all the candles.

384

That done, he vanished into the sitting room and returned with two great lighted candelabra which he set on either side of the bed, and after that he went back and fetched another pair and placed them, for want of anywhere else, upon the floor.

Judith gazed round her in amazement at the brilliant room, brighter even than Versailles on a gala night.

'What are you doing?' she breathed.

'I want it to be very bright,' he said tenderly. 'I always dreamed of making love to you for the first time in brilliant sunshine so that your beauty should be free of all shadow, and your eyes too, when I made you mine. Tomorrow, I shall make you my wife in the sight of God. Tonight, our first night, I want to be bright and pagan and, because you are my goddess incomparable, I want to build an altar for you.'

While he spoke, he had been swiftly pulling off his clothes. For a moment he stood in the blaze of candlelight beside the bed, lighting the tall, slim body, the brown skin, moulding the play of powerful muscles, marked still with the pale, rose-coloured scars of recent injuries and those, already mellowed, of older wounds. Then, setting one knee on the red silk coverlet, he slid onto the bed beside her and her arms went round his neck as he sought her mouth and, with his free hand, began to wake the music in the exquisite, untried instrument of her body. It was a new, intoxicating joy to feel her vibrating response to his will. He had everything to teach her about love but she had been made for him from all time and he knew that even if in future they might quarrel in their daily lives, as even the closest couples sometimes did, they would only have to come together in bed and their bodies, at least, would also find agreement.

She gave a little cry as he entered her, with all the care and gentleness at his command, and he silenced it with a kiss, then raised himself on his arms and gazed into her wide open eyes. They were brilliant, at once misty and triumphant.

'Did I hurt you?' he asked her gently.

Her smile was radiant. 'I'm so happy ... I love you!'

'My wife! My adored Judith ...'

He lay down again and his arms went round her, holding her fast against him as slowly he began his dance of love, feeling her body so closely attuned to his that there was no room for doubt that she had been destined for him, out of the deeps of time, that she was in truth the other half of a being more perfectly divine than either could be alone, a being whose name was love.

16

Until Death Us Do Part

Three days later, in the lady chapel of the cathedral church of St Louis, Gilles de Tournemine was married to Judith de Saint-Mélaine. The service was very simple. It was eight o'clock in the evening. The darkened church was lighted only by a handful of candles and there were only two witnesses for the young couple: Mademoiselle Marguerite Marjon, very fine in fashionable puce-coloured silk with a matching hat of lace and feathers, and Baron Ulrich-August von Winkleried zu Winkleried in his dress uniform. The congregation, noticeably more modest, consisted of Pongo, Niklaus, Berthe, the old lady's maidservant, the rheumatic gardener who, on the strength of the friendship he had struck up with Pongo, now regarded himself as a member of the family, the cathedral verger, who was there to ensure that the candles were not left burning longer than necessary, and the church's official beggar, putting in overtime that day in honour of the wedding. They had tried to find Barras, but without success. He seemed to have unaccountably disappeared.

The couple themselves could not have been happier or more radiant if their marriage had been taking place in the palace chapel with the whole Court attending. In fact they would not have been as happy, for in the peace of that small lady chapel they had no jealousy or ill will to fear. Only their friends were there.

Judith, wearing a gown of white Indian muslin lightly picked out in silver obtained for her from that admirable Parisian seamstress Madame Eloffe by Mademoiselle Marjon,

387

delightedly assuming the role of the bride's mother, looked angelically lovely, like a vision of spring. She had, somewhat unaccountably, refused to have word sent to her aunt in Paris. She had also refused, with a pretty confusion which had made Mademoiselle Marjon smile, to wear the orange blossom suggested for her bouquet and her headdress. A simple cluster of near-white roses pinned the cloud of white veiling to her auburn head and identical roses were at her breast and in the posy she carried in her hand. She looked so beautiful that Gilles could not take his dazzled eyes away from her.

Their happiness was so patent that the old priest, limping sourly to meet them flanked by a pair of apathetic choirboys, could not help breaking into a smile at the sight of so perfectly matched a pair, while the two urchins stared open-mouthed at the lovely bride and had to be shaken out of their rapture to perform their part in the service.

As in a dream, Gilles took Judith's hand and repeated after the priest, in a voice whose strength and purpose rang like a challenge, the words of the marriage vow.

'I, Gilles, take thee, Judith, to my wedded wife, to have and to hold from this day forward, for better for worse, for richer for poorer, in sickness and in health, to love and to cherish, till death us do part....'

Then it was Judith's turn. Her voice spoke clearly and firmly amid the silence:

'I, Judith, take thee, Gilles, to my wedded husband, to have and to hold from this day forward, for better for worse, for richer for poorer, in sickness and in health, to love, cherish and to obey, till death us do part ...'

The bridegroom slipped a gold ring on to the little hand resting in his and a moment later Judith placed a similar one on his, while the priest pronounced the blessing over their joined hands which united them for life. Then, kneeling side by side on the red velvet cushions, they heard the short mass said. And so at last, after Judith had laid her bride's bouquet at the feet of the Mother of God, they left the church on one another's arms, carrying their glowing happiness out into the Versailles night while their witnesses pressed lavish alms on the delighted beggar. Life, a whole new life of shared love and daily toil awaited them across the Atlantic and they had already made up their minds to sail as soon as possible.

Tenderly, handing her into the carriage, Gilles kissed his new wife's fingers.

'Your servant, Madame de Tournemine.'

She flushed pink with happiness.

'It's true? It's really true? We are married?'

'Couldn't be more so. Hadn't you noticed?'

'Not really. It was like a dream. I felt as if I were sailing about in an immense blue sky.'

He got in beside her. Mademoiselle Marjon and Ulrich-August took their places in the second carriage. Then at last, as the little procession moved off in the direction of the Rue de Noailles where their two witnesses had arranged a supper for them, Gilles was able to put both arms round his wife and kiss her properly.

In the three days that had passed since Judith's arrival, Gilles had turned his life upside down. To start with, he had obtained from the King, who viewed his eagerness with some amusement, indefinite leave and permission to marry without delay.

'I don't want to sell out,' he explained to a somewhat bewildered and distressed Winkleried. 'I have sworn an oath to the King and if, by ill chance, he were ever to need me I should come back at once and take my place at his side.'

'In other words, unless something should happen to the King, we won't see you again?'

'Why shouldn't I come back? And why should you not come to visit me? I know you have your house and lands and are engaged to be married but, believe me, you'd like America. It is so large – you could carve yourself out a domain almost the size of Switzerland if you wanted. Marry Ursula and come!'

'On the contrary, it might be a very excellent excuse not to marry Ursula,' Ulrich-August said, blustering. 'Upon reflection, she's not the world's greatest beauty, after all.' It was evident that Judith's charm and loveliness had been revealing new possibilities to the Baron.

With the help of the palace chaplain and the Bishop of Versailles, Gilles had obtained the proper dispensation for his hasty marriage and now that the knot was tied, nothing remained but

389

to put into execution the plan, so simple and straightforward, that he and Judith had laid down for their future. In two days, they would set out for Brittany. Gilles wanted to see La Hunaudaye and old Gauthier once more. He also wanted to revisit the scenes of his childhood and the banks of the Blavet on whose waters, one evening long ago, Judith had first come to him. He wanted to introduce her to his godfather, the Abbé de Talhouet, and say farewell to him, and also to his old nurse, Rozenn. Perhaps, too, now that he was leaving France for he could not tell how long, he might try and make his peace at last with his mother, now a Benedictine nun at Locmaria. Finding him married and about to start founding a family of his own, even the unyielding Marie-Jeanne might melt and perhaps consent to show, for once, a trace of maternal feeling.

After that, they would travel to Brest and there, with Pongo and Merlin, they would find a ship to take all four of them to the new world. Judith herself had no one she wished to take leave of, except perhaps the grave of her father in the church-yard at Hennebont and the convent where she had spent her shadowed girlhood.

With a good deal of difficulty, she had succeeded in persuad-ing Gilles to leave Morvan to his own fate. This was not from any residue of family feeling, for after the hideous thing that he had done to her Morvan had ceased to be her brother, but because she feared that by venturing into the dim underworld inhabited by the lower ranks of the police Gilles would be risking his life more surely than on any field of battle.

'Besides,' she had told him, choosing a moment when no man in love could refuse the wife of his bosom anything at all, 'looking for him would take time. We should have to stay here and wait. And I am still alive, after all, so let us leave him to the wretched life he has chosen for himself and go away. That will be a far better revenge!'

It was a good argument, and it prevailed. In any case, Gilles' heart was then so full of love that there was no room at all left in it for hate.

The house, when they reached it, was decked with flowers up to the ceiling and ablaze with light, so determined was the dear lady to give them pleasure. Gilles who, with his wife, had a request to make, began by asking her permission to kiss her.

390

Mademoiselle Marjon granted it gladly, blushing like a girl.

'That is first of all to say thank you, dear Mademoiselle Marguerite, thank you with all our hearts. It is also by way of an entreaty.'

'An entreaty? Good heavens, you know that I ask nothing better than to please you. I owe you so much. I was all alone and now, thanks to you, I have a family again. I am only sorry to be losing it so soon.'

'That's just what we wanted to talk to you about, Judith and I,' he said, drawing his new wife close to him. 'We have known you for so short a time, yet you have treated us as if we were your own children. Well, your children don't want to lose you, either. Come with us.'

'Yes,' Judith added her voice to his. 'Come with us.'

'Go with you? Good God, where? To Brittany?'

'No. To America. It's a wonderful, amazing country. I'm sure you'll like it. You'll find ladies you will want to be friends with, the kind of society you have no idea of. And there will be us. Our house will be yours.'

'Me? Go to America? But, my poor child, I don't speak English—'

'Neither does Judith. You can learn together.'

She laughed aloud, but he could see that she was tempted.

'Such madness! You want to take an old maid with you on your great adventure? Two is company, you know, where happiness is concerned.'

'Happiness that confines itself to two is selfish and does not deserve to last. Besides, you will be able to watch our children grow up,' Judith said, so confidently that the tears sprang into Mademoiselle Marjon's eyes. 'Come with us! You will have plenty of time to make your preparations while we are in Brittany and then you can join us at Brest with Berthe, Brutus and Begonia – and even the gardener, because I don't think he'd want to be parted from Pongo!'

'Well, well. I'll think about it, I promise. Now, let us sit down to supper. Oh dear, I really think this is the happiest day of my whole life.'

Ulrich-August, who had insisted on preparing for his friends a magnificent wedding pâté after the fashion of his country,

391

now appeared bearing his masterpiece, a vast white apron pinned over his gold embroidered waistcoat and an expression of unclouded triumph on his face.

The laughter and admiring cries that greeted him died away suddenly as Berthe came hurrying in, saying breathlessly: 'Oh Monsieur le Chevalier, there's a man downstairs who insists on speaking to you at once. He says it's urgent!' Judith moved instinctively closer to her husband.

'A man? What sort of man?' Gilles asked.

'One of the Queen's servants, I think. He has her livery on under his black cloak and there is a Court carriage stopped outside the house.'

'All right. I'm coming.'

The man waiting at the foot of the stairs was indeed dressed in the red and gold livery worn by all the servants at the Trianon. Nor was his face quite unknown to Gilles who thought that he remembered it from his audience there with Marie-Antoinette. At the sight of the Chevalier, he bowed correctly and taking a carefully sealed note out of his cuff, presented it to the young man.

'From the Queen,' he said simply.

Gilles broke the seal quickly and unfolded the letter. It contained less than a dozen words. 'Come. This man will bring you. Only you can save me.'

The tone of the message was so strange that Gilles could not help asking: 'Was it – her Majesty who gave you this note?'

'It was Madame de Campan, Sir, from her Majesty. She was very urgent with me to be quick about it.'

'You have a carriage?'

'It's waiting outside.'

'I'll be with you. Wait for me a moment.'

Stuffing the note into his pocket, he hurried back to his friends. Judith, her eyes already filled with alarm, flung herself into his arms. He kissed her.

'Forgive me! I have to leave you for a moment.'

'Tonight! When you have only just been married!' Mademoiselle Marjon exclaimed, horrified.

'Except for those of you here now, very few people knew that I was getting married today. I don't expect to be long, but I have to go to the Trianon. The Queen has sent for me.'

'The Queen? But why? What does she want with you?' Judith cried, torn between tears and anger.

He stroked her cheek and smiled. 'Nothing very important, probably, but I can hardly fail to go, sweetheart. Winkleried will tell you that once before this I have been unintentionally involved in a private matter of her Majesty's, to do with this dreadful business of the stolen necklace. No doubt this is to do with that again. I have to go.'

'But why you? The Queen has plenty of other people to serve her, surely?'

'Perhaps because she knows that I am both loyal and devoted to herself and to the King. Don't cry, my heart. There's no reason to. I shan't be away for long. Begin supper without me, only don't,' he added gaily, 'eat all the pâté! That would be crueller than I deserve!'

After one last kiss for his wife, he picked up his hat and sword, slapped Ulrich-August, thoughtfully removing his apron, on the back and went downstairs to join the Queen's messenger.

Out in the street a town carriage identical to those that served the Court was waiting with lamps alight, steps down and door hanging open.

The messenger held it wide and Gilles sprang inside.

'One word, one cry, even as much as a whisper, Chevalier, and you are a dead man,' a voice said pleasantly. Then Gilles saw the large pistol aimed at him, held firmly in the hand of a man dressed all in black who occupied the far seat of the carriage.

'What does this mean? Who are you?'

'Sit down and be quiet. You are going to find out.'

Gilles had no alternative but to obey. He seated himself next to the man in black and the weapon moved in a half circle so that it continued to aim at his heart. The liveried messenger climbed in behind him and after that Gilles saw nothing more, for a bandage was placed over his eyes.

The door slammed shut. The carriage moved off, jolting over the cobbled street. Squeezed in between his two captors, Gilles tried to sort out his tumultuous thoughts while preserving an outward calm.

'Where are you taking me?' he asked coolly.

393

'We can't tell you that. Don't worry, though. You'll come to no harm. Our orders are to treat you with the greatest consideration.'

'Consideration! That's rich! But you're hardy rogues, certainly, taking the Queen's name in vain like this! Because I assume the Queen has nothing to do with it?'

'Nothing at all,' the man in black said cheerfully. 'And now, with your permission, I think we'll take a little extra precaution. You'll have to forgive us if the consideration seems to have slipped a bit but they didn't tell us, you see, that you were quite so big, and it's better to be safe than sorry.'

The next moment, with the speed of long practice, Gilles' hands were securely bound and the other man settled back into his seat with a sigh of relief. The drive continued in silence.

To begin with, Gilles had tried to follow their route in his head but he was soon sure that they were driving in circles to cover their tracks, so that when at last the horses picked up speed along a straight road they had changed direction so many times that he was perfectly lost. All he could tell was that they were no longer moving over town cobbles.

At length the coach swung round a bend and lurched up a short slope, throwing the passengers about in a way that suggested an atrociously bad surface, and then came to a halt. The journey, Gilles estimated, had taken about an hour. His captors took his arms and guided him down the steps and then, with great care, across what seemed to be some kind of lawn, for he could feel a grassy slope under his feet. There was a dampness in the night air. There was also a faint noise of running water. A door creaked as one of his captors pushed it open.

'Mind the step,' he said.

Then they were inside a building, a rather old building to judge from the powerful smell of mildew and the cellar-like atmosphere. Gilles had the impression that they were walking along a stone-flagged passage. A door opened, followed by another and finally, after they had descended a flight of slippery steps, a little light filtered under his blindfold. But still it was not removed.

He was led, blind, to what was evidently some kind of bed covered with a fur and made to lie down on it, while someone

394

checked the bandage over his eyes and made sure that his wrists were still firmly tied. But when hands were laid on his legs to tie his ankles also he began to struggle furiously.

'I've had enough of this,' he yelled fiercely. 'Tell me what you want of me and make an end!'

There was no answer. The men finished their work, one of them slipped a pillow under his head and after that they appeared to go away. Gilles heard their footsteps on some uneven surface. For a short while there was silence, through which he eventually became aware of other, lighter footsteps, accompanied by the rustle of a silk gown. A scent of roses invaded his nostrils.

'Well, Chevalier,' said a voice which he had no trouble at all in identifying,' how do you feel? I hope my people have not mishandled you? My orders were to treat you with the greatest respect.'

'So it was you,' Gilles said. His voice held nothing but a controlled exasperation. 'I hope you weren't expecting to frighten me?'

'That was not my object. I merely wished to offer you my congratulations in privacy, and to tell you how much I admire your taste. The child is charming, quite delightful . . . Not very intelligent, perhaps, a little . . . countrified, but charming. It's a shame you are going to have to put off your wedding night. Your young bride, I fear, will find the time hangs heavily on her hands. As for yourself, we'll do our best to ease your impatience.'

'So this is your revenge, is it? This is your idea? To keep me from my wife on our wedding night?' Gilles said contemptuously. 'I cannot congratulate you. I am married, my dear, and there is nothing you can do about that. As for easing my impatience, as you put it. Don't count on it. You don't intend to rape me, I imagine?'

She uttered a soft cooing laugh that grated like iron on the young man's nerves.

'It might be amusing. But you know, if I really wanted to, I'd have no need to resort to rape. I know so well how to arouse you. Tonight, however, I prefer to leave you to your regrets. Good night, my love. Sleep well.'

She must have made a sign to someone else for Gilles felt

395

himself raised by an arm under his shoulders while a glass was pressed to his lips. He clenched his teeth. At that, ungentle fingers pinched his nostrils so that he was obliged to open his mouth for air, whereupon a sugary but not unpleasant tasting drink was tipped down his throat. It was certainly not poisoned, as he had at first suspected. Then he was laid down again.

'It is no use struggling,' Madame de Balbi said with a laugh. 'I don't mean to poison you. For one thing, it's not my style and for another, did I not tell you we would not part finally until I tired of you? And that is not yet. You are going to sleep now. Tomorrow you will have a little more of this delicious drink, and the day after, also. You need not worry. It will do you no harm. Sleep ... only sleep. Poor little Madame de Tournemine! She's going to have to keep her maidenhead a little longer than she thought.'

She moved away, still laughing and he heard her laughter dying away in the farther reaches of the house. For a moment, Gilles was tempted to shout after her that this absurd revenge of hers was pointless, because Judith was his wife in every sense already, but he restrained himself for fear of exposing his little siren to possible further action on the part of this harpy. Besides, he was so sleepy ... so terribly sleepy ...

When he awoke, after how long he could not tell, he only knew that even in the oblivion of sleep the time had seemed interminable, he opened his eyes on the greyness of a cellar or dungeon and it took him some moments to gather his wits together. The effects of the drug he had been made to swallow were slow to wear off and he did not remember all at once. But he had the use of his eyes again.

When his blurred gaze cleared a little, he saw that his wrists and ankles had also been unbound and that he was lying on some sort of mattress covered with sheepskins. Daylight was filtering into his prison through an opening, high up, masked by a trail of vegetation. He was alone.

He sat up and remained sitting on his improvised bed until the dizziness which had affected him cleared away. On the ground was a tray on which was a cold roast chicken, some bread and a bottle of wine.

Hunger assailed him at the sight of the food. He had never felt so empty. Anne was considerate to her prisoners, he thought, as he fell to build up his strength, tearing at the chicken hungrily with both hands. Only when he had eaten did he attempt to stand, testing the muscles of his arms and legs. Then he walked over to the door to assess the chances of escape. To his surprise, he found that it was open.

Gilles wasted no more time. Moving swiftly down a kind of tunnel, he came to a rickety stair, the treads slippery with damp, and going up it found himself in the stone-flagged passage he remembered. The passage ended in a door, open likewise onto sunlit grass. Tendrils of virginia creeper waved gently about the doorway. It was utterly quiet. The house was silent and empty.

As he stepped outside, Gilles closed his eyes for a moment, feeling the warmth of the morning sun on his face. It was like waking after a fearful nightmare.

A whinny close by drew his attention and he saw a horse, ready saddled and tied to a poplar tree a little way off.

The building, he now saw, was a half-ruined mill house. He stared around him. A stream ran tinkling close by, past the skeletal wheel, most of its paddles gone. Gilles walked over and plunged his head into the cool water to clear his brain, then he made quickly for the horse. It whinnied again, as though calling him to hurry. Unfastening its bridle from the tree, he sprang into the saddle and set off at a canter across the sloping field towards the road. Once there, he took the direction which seemed likely to lead to Versailles and increased speed to a gallop. There was now only one clear thought in his mind: to get to Judith.

'You! My God, where have you been?'

Berthe had opened the door to him and Mademoiselle Marjon came running to her sitting room door to meet him. She had him by the shoulders and was staring at him in a kind of terror, as if he had returned from hell. He saw that her eyes were red and her face wan, as though she had been weeping a great deal.

'I don't know myself. I was kidnapped. Let me by. I must

see Judith.' And he made for the stairs, calling at the top of his voice: 'Judith! Judith, my heart, where are you?'

But the person who came to the stairhead was only Pongo and Pongo with the sunken eyes and grey skin of a man who had suffered a long illness. At the tragic look on his face, Gilles was seized with terror. He raced up to the Indian and grasped him by the shoulders and shook him.

'Where is she? Where is my wife?'

'Gone ... yesterday night,' Mademoiselle Marjon's voice said flatly behind him.

'Gone? But where to? How?'

'I don't know. She had seemed calmer. She was asleep. I went out to church while Berthe was getting supper. Pongo was in the stable seeing to the horses. When we came back, the bed was empty and she had gone. Oh Gilles, how could you do this to her?'

'Do what to her? Will you only tell me what I have done? I'm telling you I have been the victim of a foul plot!'

The old lady turned her head away, her eyes filling with fresh tears, and groped for her handkerchief.

'Oh, I don't know precisely ... only to be away for three days like this, with no news at all! Three days! Poor child ... Not even a Queen has the right to do such a thing! It was wicked!'

'The Queen had nothing to do with it. It was a trap. And I fell into it. I have powerful enemies, you should know that.'

She twitched her shoulders, too wretched to look up.

'And friends you cannot refuse also, it seems! Holy Mother of God! Heaven can witness that I have never listened to the gossip there has been about the Queen but—'

'Once and for all,' Gilles shouted furiously, 'I'm trying to tell you the Queen had nothing at all to do with this!'

'And this?'

She took from her bosom a soiled and crumpled scrap of paper and gave it to Gilles.

'Take it. A messenger brought it to your wife the day after you disappeared. Judith had spent the whole night sitting at the window waiting for you. She read the letter and then she uttered a dreadful cry and fainted in Pongo's arms. It may not

398

be easy for you to read. She cried over it so much before I could get it away from her.'

Smoothing the letter out as best he could with hands that trembled, Gilles was able to decipher the few lines written in an obviously female hand.

'Be patient, little lady, for it will be some time before you see your charming husband again. One must needs be very simple, very deaf or very fresh from the country – all of which you are – to be unaware that your handsome Chevalier is the Queen's lover, and Marie-Antoinette never lets go. Be comforted. You are young. Your turn will come. A sincere friend.'

Gilles crushed the poisonous little missive in his fist. He felt as if he were going mad and had to shut his eyes to keep back the tears.

'She read that? She read it? But how could she believe it? She knows I love only her! Oh God! I love her so!'

'She – she find portrait, too. Then . . . she believe.'

And Pongo placed in his master's hands the box in which he had locked the cardinal's miniature. The box was empty.

Gilles fingers hardened on the wood which he had never guessed would one day cause him such agony and he hurled it with all his strength straight through the window. Then, with the crash of breaking glass still in the air, he cast himself down on the bed, which no one had had the heart to make so that it still bore the faint imprint of Judith's slender body. For hours they heard him calling her name, hoarsely, like an animal in pain.

When, towards evening, the garden filled with soldiers, he heard nothing of it. Not until a hand grasped his shoulder did he rouse himself from the abyss of misery into which he had fallen.

Lifting his head, he saw without surprise that there was an officer standing by his head. He recognized him. It was Gaudron de Tilloy, Lieutenant of the Provost's Guard, and he was looking at him with profound compassion. But his voice, when he spoke, was clipped and formal as he uttered the fateful words: 'Chevalier de Tournemine de la Hunaudaye, I arrest you in the name of the Queen.'

Still struggling to find some meaning in the incredible

399

words, Gilles got to his feet, saying dazedly: 'You are arresting me? Me?'

'You have been accused of conspiring with the Cardinal Prince de Rohan to commit theft and to injure the crown. You are to come with me.'

Gilles gazed round the room, scarcely able to see for the tears he had shed. He saw Mademoiselle Marjon, down on her knees on the floor, weeping and praying. He saw Winkleried standing in one corner, clenching his fists. He saw Pongo, stiff as a poker beside the valise he had been hastily filling with necessities, ready to go with his master. He brought his eyes back to the officer, waiting without impatience. He shrugged.

'I am ready, Sir. After all, why not?'

Nothing mattered any more.

Saint-Mandé, 1977.